Cat in a Jeweled Jumpsuit

A MIDNIGHT LOUIE MYSTERY

Carole Nelson Douglas

A Tom Doherty Associates Book
New York

This is a work of fiction. All the characters and events portrayed in this novel are either products of the author's imagination or are used fictitiously.

CAT IN A JEWELED JUMPSUIT

Copyright © 1999 by Carole Nelson Douglas

A Forge Book
Published by Tom Doherty Associates, LLC
175 Fifth Avenue
New York, NY 10010

www.tor.com

Forge® is a registered trademark of Tom Doherty Associates, LLC.

ISBN 0-812-56674-2
Library of Congress Catalog Card Number: 99-38123

First edition: November 1999
First mass market edition: May 2000

Printed in the United States of America

0 9 8 7 6 5 4 3 2 1

Praise for Carole Nelson Douglas

Cat in an Indigo Mood

"Feline P.I. Midnight Louie prowls the alleys of Las Vegas, solving crimes and romancing runaways like a furry Sam Spade. This time out, his quick-thinking daughter, Midnight Louise, lends a paw as the always engaging Louie stalks a serial killer." —*People* magazine

"Midnight Louie is back and he is as good as ever. . . . All mysteries are cleared up and the reader is richer for meeting all of these characters. Most of all Midnight Louie is always a delight. As he teams up with his daughter, Midnight Louise, and a mop of a dog who has a nose that can find any smell, the book just gets more fun." —*Rainbo Reviews*

"The tenth Midnight Louie novel retains all the freshness of the previous books as the characters continue to be interesting and entertaining. . . . A crisp story line, highlighted with new insights into several of the secondary protagonists." —*Midwest Book Review*

"A new Midnight Louie book is pure reading catnip, as Ms. Douglas exquisitely crafts a clever puzzler in style noir with striking characterization and a rare clarity of vision—not only does she set a scene with vivid precision, but she in turn uses it as an incandescent prism through which she superbly illuminates the human experience. And in the irresistibly witty Louie, she creates a legendary sleuth who ranks right up with the greats—Travis McGee in fur!" —*Romantic Times*

Cat on a Hyacinth Hunt

"*Cat on a Hyacinth Hunt* is the ninth entry in the Midnight Louie cat series and surprisingly the book retains the fresh and exciting perspective of its forerunners. The mystery remains first rate while the romantic triangle (or is that rectangle with Louie being the other corner) has become more complex and interesting. The brilliantly talented Carole Nelson Douglas has set in motion story-line twists leading the series in a new direction that is sure to surprise yet please Louie's biggest fans." —*Affaire de Coeur*

By Carole Nelson Douglas from Tom Doherty Associates

MYSTERY

MIDNIGHT LOUIE MYSTERIES:
Catnap
Pussyfoot
Cat on a Blue Monday
Cat in a Crimson Haze
Cat in a Diamond Dazzle
Cat with an Emerald Eye
Cat in a Flamingo Fedora
Cat in a Golden Garland
Cat on a Hyacinth Hunt
Cat in an Indigo Mood
Cat in a Jeweled Jumpsuit
Midnight Louie's Pet Detectives (anthology)

IRENE ADLER ADVENTURES:
Good Night, Mr. Holmes
Good Morning, Irene
Irene at Large
Irene's Last Waltz

Marilyn: Shades of Blonde (anthology)

HISTORICAL ROMANCE
*Amberleigh**
*Lady Rogue**
Fair Wind, Fiery Star

SCIENCE FICTION
*Probe**
*Counterprobe**

FANTASY
TALISWOMAN:
Cup of Clay
Seed upon the Wind

SWORD AND CIRCLET:
Keepers of Edanvant
Heir of Rengarth
Seven of Swords

*also mystery

For the real and original Midnight Louie,
nine lives were not enough.

Contents

Cat in a
Jeweled Jumpsuit

Dead Man Walking

He was born during the Depression in a two-room shack, in Tupelo, Mississippi, a surviving twin and a hillbilly, into a family lineage of poverty, alcoholism, and little more than barely getting by.

He became the world's most well-known, wealthy, and successful entertainer.

An eternal adolescent reared by a passive father and a mother both doting and domineering, he was a lonely mama's boy who believed in work and the golden rule, who dreamed of performing but had been conditioned to expect pampering.

He was the first in his family to graduate from high school, a hyperactive, nervous outsider, a boy whose love of religion and music would lead him to identify with black culture in a segregated South before the sixties' Civil Rights movement.

He was a shrewd, intelligent, magnetic performer, who created his own image as an international singing star and sex symbol by blending two socially segregated traditions of music, black and white, into the worldwide phenomenon of rock 'n' roll.

He was modest, polite, generous, and even tender, a young man who won the eternal loyalty of men and women who knew him, and millions who didn't.

From the outset, his meteoric career defied all odds, and accelerated his utter destruction on all fronts.

From the outset, the seeds of addiction were sown in his dysfunctional upbringing and a borrowed fistful of his mother's diet pills, then a handful of Dexedrine tablets in the Army, then the live performer's night-is-day Draculian lifestyle, and finally pills by the literal gallon from an array of "feel-good" doctors.

In his early twenties, death would separate him from his adored mother Gladys, leaving in her place Colonel Tom Parker, the controlling personal manager and ex-carnival hustler who would indenture his young property into servitude in low-grade films, confine him to songs that enriched the pockets but not the soul, and finally send him sick and sick at heart into years of relentless touring, all to underwrite the Colonel's elephantine ego and eventual million-dollar gambling debts.

His performing career became a manic-depressive's endurance contest as his obsessive personality dove into toys, girls, and pills in the face of boredom and fatigue. The Colonel quashed all attempts by him and others to revitalize his career. After the entertainer's death, estate lawyers would strip Parker of control, but the estate didn't have the deep pockets to reclaim millions from a manager who shamelessly took the lion's share of his financially unsophisticated sole client's enormous income.

Dogged by Parker's soulless management, drugged by the side-effects of fame and prescribed uppers and downers, pursued and isolated by fans, he became an egocentric monster who indulged in spasms of compulsive generosity and grandiose mysticism behind a protective circle of flunkies and thugs, within a rotating harem of dozens of young, pliable women from whom he craved cuddles rather than sex.

By many accounts, he was the most charismatic performer ever to take the stage, a singer whose moves to the music mesmerized his audiences into an orgasmic love feast. By all accounts, during the last two of his forty-two years on earth, he was a dead man walking, self-medicated into a stumbling parody of himself, lost in a self-destructive stupor.

Finally, shortly after three of his once-loyal inner circle published a tell-all book revealing his eccentricities and drug abuse, enter ignominious death. He was found dead in 1977, age forty-two, in his bathroom, autopsied (drug abuse was denied as a cause of death then), and buried in Cadillac state amid a fan outpouring of hysterical grief.

He left everything to his only daughter, but on his father's death two years later, his ex-wife became executor and tried to redeem the careless losses of the past with post-mortem merchandising. Under her management team, the home he'd bought in the first fever of success, Graceland in Memphis, Tennessee, became a mélange of unofficial national monument, tourist Mecca, and shrine that attracted fans from all over the world. Disneyland for a dead rock star.

His fans never deserted him. His genuine talent, charisma, and generosity outweighed his tragic flaws. The contradictions he embodied in larger-than-life fashion are the common mysteries of life, death, and human personality, but to conventional society, he had always been a threat and a joke, from his rural rocker beginnings to his overblown Las Vegas lounge-act end. Big names in music like Bob Dylan and John Lennon had always credited him for the birth of rock 'n' roll even while many black musical artists accused him of co-opting their musical thunder. Now revisionist rock history has enhanced his performing reputation. A video and book industry memorializes him to this day, for good or ill. Supermarket tabloids report people sighting him here and there. His songs have sold millions and millions and continue to sell.

Exit the man who was born to be Fate's most famous dead man walking. Still walking.

Enter the fabulously flawed legend that won't die.

Enter the King.

The King of Rock 'n' Roll

The King was getting a bad feeling, the way his mama used to sometimes.

She'd been right about the Colonel.

Beware the blue-eyed woman.

Huh! She'd been *damn* right about that one.

Look at Cilla, running the whole shootin' match at Graceland now. Who'da thought that pretty little thing would turn out to be tougher than 'em all, in the end? 'Course, he'd raised her up. And if there was a lot he'd sheltered her from *bein'*, there was a lot he didn't shelter her from *seein'*, maybe just to learn what not to do.

Taking Care of Business was an okay motto, but all Cilla had wanted then was TLC. That's what all the King's men and women got: gold bracelets and necklaces reading TCB for the guys, TLC for the girls. He was good at handing out the trinkets. But the fact was he'd never been any damn good at TCB, anyway. He just let his father Vernon run things, or not run things, and let the Colonel take over. Anybody walking in off the street wantin' to do-for him was welcome, then they'd take-from . . . hell, if he'da known, he should have given Cilla the TCB job. Woulda given her something to do at Graceland 'sides bitchin' about his boys . . . and his girls.

'Course she had something to work with when she took over. Bein' dead does a lot to raise certain people's stock. Look at JFK. Or Marilyn. Man, he never met her, and she was a little old for him and a little fat (look who's talkin'). Didja see her in *Let's Make Love*, where they were spoofing his sudden fame in a musical routine? One hot number. Not the delicate, dark-haired type he loved. Still, that woulda been something. But it ain't over till it's over, you know?

Lookin' back does no damn good. The tell-all books and coffee-table picture books and the movies and videotapes and miniseries and the special edition watches and the pink, white, and blue trinkets; they do the talkin' nowadays. TCB.

Only one who hasn't been heard from on the grand glory days and sad last nights of Elvis Aaron Presley is the King his own self. And even that isn't impossible. Heck, all the King's men had mostly used ghost writers to get their side of things down on paper.

And here he *was* one.

The King laughed, staring at the two silent-running TV sets tilted like gaming consoles into the green Naugahyde ceiling above him in the blacked-out bedroom. He shot the remote at them in turn, revving up the sound, speeding through channels, past reruns of old movies featuring dead pals and girl-friends. But some of them were still alive and kicking, his ex-buddies, ex-babes, ex-hangers-on.

Just like him.

The King is dead. Long live the King. *Live and in person!*
News flash: It lives!

Even the word "lives" is just a mixed-up Elvis.

He laughed, and hummed a few bars of "It's Now or Never"

while surfing the babbling channels over and over and over.

The place was dark as a tomb, and freezing cold. He couldn't tell day from night.

He had always liked it that way.

Chapter 1

The King of Rock and Roll 'em!

I am taking my ease in the living room of Miss Temple Barr's flat at the Circle Ritz apartments and condominiums, a snazzy fifties joint built like a four-story black-marble hockey puck. In other words, it is round, and therefore definitely not square.

You could say the same about me.

Miss Temple has shut all the miniblinds to dim the chamber, and is now cursing the darkness because the VCR is not working and she cannot see to correct the problem.

I myself have never troubled to keep up with these new-fangled devices. Remote controls and answering machines are as much as I care to deal with. So although she is invoking my name—along with those of others often employed in such circumstances, such as "for Pete's sake, for the love of Mike" etc.—I know that she expects no more help from my quarter than she does from the ever-absent Pete and Mike.

"Two stars in the building is one too many," she grumbles, punching buttons that punch right back by refusing to stay depressed. "The Mystifying Max's greatest sleight-of-hand trick on or off stage was making this zippety-doo-dah machine work! Where is the man of the house when you really need him?"

I am right here, where I always am—when I am not off on my investigations—ready to absorb all gripes. But operating VCRs is not in my contract, not even when I am the partial reason for the technological trials I see unfolding before me.

"There!" Miss Temple sits back on the parquet floor with a satisfied sigh. "Better watch, Louie. You are up first!"

That is only the natural order of things, so I stretch, yawn, manicure my nails, and scratch behind my ears.

"Do not turn your head away," she beseeches. "Your segment is coming up."

Yes, I see that my rear appendage is lofting to great advantage. . . .

"Louie! You are on!"

I am forced at last to play couch potato and turn to view the television screen. It is rerunning the ending of my least favorite show, *Sabrina*. I have nothing against teenage witches, although I have never consorted with them, but that black, mothball-mouthed feline supporting puppet is one bad actor. I could chew the scenery with far more effectiveness.

In fact, a demonstration of this is coming up, as I come on. Eat your heart out, Salem. And then lend it to me for a snack.

In a moment a perky voice-over chorus pipes into the room: Ooo-la-la. À la Cat!

We see white-gloved hands removing a crystal dish from a cupboard. A silver spoon deposits some wet glop the color of Silly Putty into the dish's pristine center. The entire mess (I am speaking metaphorically here of a product I dearly love, of course) is gently laid on a high-gloss white floor.

"Dinner is served," announces Jeeves Black-sleeves the butler. A pale, patrician pussycat ankles over to inspect the offering and begin eating with dainty abandon. Mon amour, the Divine Yvette, draped in silver foxiness.

The camera pulls back to reveal a Big White Set from the Hollywood musical heyday of the thirties and a flight of stairs to cat heaven, lined by dancing dudes in jelly-bean-colored zoot suits. Down the center aisle, floating like a butterfly, windmilling his limbs like an aerialist, hustles yours truly in full black formal attire, crowned by a flamingo-pink fedora that perches precariously over one ear and eye.

I four-step from left to right in the wide center aisle, gaining momentum as the music swells into a full orchestration. Suddenly, I do a Fred Astaire drag to the left, ratchet up the mandarine-orange leg and torso of a chorus boy, and end up balanced on his shoulder like an epaulette with the black spot.

The guy's grinning face assumes an even more frozen expression as all sixteen of my extended shivs sink through fabric into flesh.

After flourishing my only unclawed member, I leap down to the white stairs again and continue my descent.

While watching my acrobatics, I squint at the small screen, hoping to see the noose of twine that a rival has slipped into my path to trip me up. Alas, apparently the evidence has ended up on the cutting room floor, just like my competition for the job of À La Cat spokesdude, the yellow-bellied Maurice.

"You certainly are quite the high-stepper," my Miss Temple comments. "I wonder what made you improvise a straight-up two-yard dash? That poor dancer looks like he's been spindled, stapled, and mutilated. But he kept a game smile on his face. What a pro!"

Hey! I am the pro here. It is not every day one has to

dodge a bullet, so to speak, on camera without mussing a hair.

And I certainly am slick and sleek as I finish my descent by nosing up to the Divine Yvette and sharing her repast of À La Cat on Baccarat crystal.

"Ooo-la-la. À la Cat! Ooo-la-la. À la Cat!" the offscreen kitty chorus trills while I preen and lick my chops and the Divine Yvette lowers her smoky eyelashes to snick a crumb from my chin.

"What a natural," Miss Temple declares, stealing the words from my mind. She ought to know, being an ace freelance public relations lady, and now manager of my sudden performing career. Considering my real profession is private dick, I am doing all right as a TV star.

She rewinds the bit, so we can play it again, Sam Spade.

We are no less impressed on second sight.

"Well," she says, "if they do not get a good response from that commercial, there is something very wrong with the American viewing public."

This disturbs me. Of course there is something very wrong with the American viewing public! They are only human. I had no idea that my media fate would depend on them. I can only hope that cats everywhere know where the remote control is, and use it.

But Miss Temple is never content to let me rest upon my laurels, as firm and fluffy as they may be.

She is fooling with the VCR again, her curly red head shaking in disgust as it snaps and whirls its defiance at her manipulations. I do think these particular devices have been planted among humans by subversive alien visitors. I have never known a household appliance more capable of driving people to extreme measures.

"I know I got it," Miss Temple is muttering, whether to herself or to me it makes no difference. She is clearly out of control in either case. "I double-checked the time and channel . . . do not tell me—! Ah."

I watch some dopey introductory shots filled with nothing but close-ups of people's faces. They are all grinning like pumpkins, and it is not even Halloween, except for the faces that are grimacing as if they had just eaten fermented Free-to-Be-Feline, my least favorite health food.

Thinking of which, I burp.

Miss Temple is oblivious to my digestive distress, absorbed instead by the whirring sound the tape player makes as it reels and unreels until she has the exact place she wanted.

"Now." She rises, aims the remote at the machine, and zaps it into loud life.

I flatten my ears. These afternoon talk shows are filled with yowling, keening people lined up to engage in hissy fits and claws-out fist-fights, making a spectacle of themselves. If I had a shoe, I would heave it at them. In fact, I watch with interest as Miss Temple comes to curl up beside me on the couch, kicking off her navy-and-burgundy high heels with the leather rosettes on the toes so delectable for chewing.

She settles in, absently patting my head off-center. I hate that!

I observe the scene on the screen: the usual lineup, the usual host pacing like a major cat behind bars, the usual zoo of exotic guests, the usual peanut gallery of a growling and spitting audience. Miss Temple leans forward when our upstairs neighbor, Mr. Matt Devine, walks on, and from then on I do not even get my head patted off-center. Not only is this show interminable—unlike my snappy sixty second commercial debut—but Miss Temple keeps rewinding the tape to run Mr. Matt's segments over again. It is like watching an entire television program with a bad case of the stutters.

I cannot take it, and soon drift off to Lullaby Land, where cat food commercials are the main event, and people are confined to sixty second cameos. In my dreams, the Divine Yvette, shaded-silver queen of the screen, is joined by her glorious shaded-golden sister, the Sublime

Solange. I feel my whiskers twitch with bliss. I am not only skimming down the endless flight of steps to their supple Persian sides, but I manage to give the evil Maurice a karate kick on the way down. He flies into the air and disappears in the dark wings of the stage set.

My triumph is complete . . . until the buzzer rings and hauls us all offstage.

I wake up punch-drunk and blinking, to find Miss Temple on the telephone and the VCR tape on permanent hold. Mr. Matt Devine's earnest face is frozen on the screen, but Miss Temple has finally turned her back on it.

"What?" she is saying. "That cannot be. It is ridiculous." She pauses. "Of course I can come over, but I hardly expect to be able to do anything about it, other than to talk some sense into the workmen, and they are not the type to listen to me . . . no! I really do not need any more 'backup,' thank you very much, Aldo. I can handle this, solo."

My ears perk up. If there is something to be "handled," and if Miss Temple Barr is insisting to someone else that she can do it "solo," my special skills will definitely be needed.

It sniffs as if something is up at the Crystal Phoenix Hotel and Casino, where Miss Temple's grand plan of renovation is even now coming to fulfillment, now that the classiest little hotel and casino in Las Vegas is her biggest client. I have a major stake in the Crystal Phoenix from the old days. Back before it was remodeled into the elegant joint it is today, it was a derelict hotel along the Strip, like the Aladdin was now and then for years until it finally fell like the walls of Jericho a few months ago. The Crystal Phoenix is where I began my career as dude-about-town and unofficial house dick. That was before I met Miss Temple and we decided to share digs here at the Circle Ritz apartments and condominiums.

I glance at the television screen and wrinkle my nose. That was before Mr. Matt Devine came into the picture, or even before Miss Temple came to Las Vegas in the mysterious company of Mr. Tall, Dark, and Debonair: Max Kinsella, a magician known as the Mystifying Max. He lived up to his billing by vanishing without a trace for several months, leaving a vacancy with Miss Temple at the Circle Ritz that I slipped into like an eel on ice. But now Mr. Max is back, an ex-magician, but not ex-enough in other departments, which both Mr. Matt Devine and yours truly are not exactly gleeful about, if you get my drift.

But why should anybody get my drift? I know enough to keep my ears open and my lips buttoned. What they do not know that I know will not hurt me. If you can follow that, you are welcome to assume you have gotten my drift as much as anybody ever will.

Chapter 2

(You Were) Always on My Mine

("You Were Always on My Mind" was written
for Elvis and he recorded it in 1972. Willie
Nelson's hit 1982 version was named song of
the year in both '82 and '83)

"I'm sorry to have bothered you," Aldo Fontana greeted
Temple in the bustling lobby of the Crystal Phoenix Hotel.

"It's no bother; it's my job. And I've been a little
delinquent of late," she admitted.

Aldo, tall, dark and deadpan, took the opportunity to
look her up and down, all five feet of her, appreciatively.
"I have always considered you a little delinquent, Miss
Temple. But I wouldn't have said it."

"I meant that I've been busy and have neglected the
hotel project."

"That is why I hesitated to disturb you." He shook the
sleeves of his chablis-colored designer suit until the left
cuff brushed the face of his Piaget watch.

What did the Fontana brothers, all nine of them—

excluding Nicky, who didn't run with the pack—do for a living anyway? Temple wondered. After all, the long, liquid lines of Aldo's suit proclaimed it an Ermenegildo Zegna.

Las Vegas was packed with pricey boutiques carrying such exotic and costly goods. Temple, a confirmed window shopper, had long before learned what was affordable and what was stratospheric.

Aldo was likely packing something even more impressive than an invisible high price tag. She eyed the impeccable flow of his wool-silk blend for a bulkier accoutrement beneath the Dairy Queen–smooth exterior. Like a Beretta.

Aldo fidgeted as much as his tailoring allowed. "I called you because I knew the boss lady wouldn't want to deal with this. Not that you're not a very boss lady, only you're not *the* boss lady, if you get my drift."

The only drifts in Las Vegas were sand, so Temple didn't let any grit lodge in her shoes at the notion that she was a mere second banana.

Van von Rhine, who managed the Crystal Phoenix with elegant ease, was also married to its owner, Nicky Fontana, Aldo's "little" brother. Since all the Fontana brood stood around six feet tall, such distinctions were pretty moot outside the family.

"What wouldn't Van like?" Temple asked.

"The, er, nature of the crisis. For one thing, she would have to wear a hard hat that would muss up that neat French roll on the back of her head."

"And you figure I can't muss." Temple ruefully ran a hand over waves of unabashedly undisciplined red hair.

"No muss, no fuss with Temple Barr, PR," Aldo grinned as he parroted the name and title on her business card. "Besides, I need to check this out with a cool head before I report to the management. They tend not to believe me because I'm family, you know."

"I know. My big brothers never did believe me about anything either, but *you* are the big brother here, Aldo."

"And I am up to the job." Aldo patted his breast pocket. Temple suspected he was referring to a hidden vein of lead and steel. "I see you have been eyeing my suit, which shows that you have not lost your impeccable taste since last we met. I wish to assure you that not only my software is first class, but my hardware also."

This statement had a certain sexual connotation neither she nor Aldo chose to notice. One thing about the brothers Fontana, attractive and single though they might be: they always treated Temple with the benign unpredatory tolerance of Great Danes babysitting a Yorkshire terrier. Of course, in the dog world, the tiny Yorkie dominated anything bigger than itself when whatever breed it was . . . wasn't looking.

"So you think there might be dirty work in the mine?" Temple led the way through the maze of moats, fountains, and crystal objects that comprised the hotel lobby.

"Mines are always dirty work." Aldo sighed and looked down. "Your footwear is most attractive, but I fear it wasn't made for underground exploration."

"Listen, these high heels aren't just for looks. They give me terrific traction. You ever heard of pitons?"

"But we will not be climbing, Miss Temple, we will be descending."

"The story of our lives and all human striving, right?" Temple stopped as they moved into the open area around the huge emerald-cut-shape of pool-blue water. Scaffolding draped in dusty plastic hid the entrance to the vast reconstruction project underway below.

"Lucky that all those tunnels from Jersey Joe Jackson's heyday allow the Phoenix to expand below the surface," Aldo mused. "Land along the Strip is going for a hundred grand a square foot these days."

Temple gazed down at the burgundy leather toes of her shoes. According to Aldo's latest statistics, just standing here was awfully expensive.

Aldo offered her a hand, while his other hand swept back a dusty swath of plastic. Temple ducked under it.

They suddenly stood in a shrouded world of long iron rods and lumber stacked around an elevator that was little more than a skeletal crate on pulleys.

Temple stepped aboard the wooden floor and tried not to watch while Aldo lowered the boom, so to speak.

Rays from underground work lights seeped through the cracks in the elevator floor. Soon they were bumping to a stop in a cavernous space housing generators and worktables and machines that resembled sluggish giant wasps, so streaked with black grease were their yellow-painted casings.

The scene was indeed no place for high-rise heels.

"It's time to exchange my hardware for softwear," Temple announced.

She tugged Aldo's sleeve to stop him while she sat down on what passed for a tuffet down here, a newspaper-strewn bench. She slung her ever-present tote bag to the ground. No spiders for Miss Muffet. Unless you considered Aldo. . . .

"I can't imagine what you're packing in that major knapsack," Aldo said, more than somewhat in awe.

"For one thing, tennis shoes." From the wide mouth of her tote bag she delivered a mushroom-pale pair of high-topped sneakers, the massive galoshes that passed for leisure footwear nowadays, and began fighting the laces open.

"These things make my shoe size look like 'number nine,' which is what the miner's daughter Clementine wore in the old song," she grunted as she bent over to lace them up.

"I would assist you," Aldo said, "but I might crease the suit."

Temple waved away his semioffer. "You're the one at real risk down here. That suit couldn't take one amok dust mote, and this place is a sawdust factory." She sneezed in coincidental testimony to her comment.

Aldo whipped a silk square of exquisite design from his breast pocket.

"Save it. You may need it to sit on later, and my handy tote bag has plenty of tissues."

Aldo gazed in admiration as Temple extracted an aloe-soaked rectangle of white and blew her nose. "You are like Indiana Jones; you always have the right tool with you."

In a couple of minutes she was smaller in stature, but better outfitted for mine shaft exploration. Standing, Temple stamped her mushy flat feet on the rough terrain. "They certainly made it seem like an excavation for a mine, so far. But where are the workmen?"

Aldo shrugged as he lifted two yellow hard hats off a rack and handed her one.

"This is gonna fit like an open umbrella," she predicted, and despite the smaller inner lining, it did indeed sink down on her head almost to her nose.

Aldo paused, smoothed back his patent leather hair and subjected it to the encompassing indignity of yellow plastic.

"These dome lights are neat." Temple snapped on the headlamp and waggled her head to watch the beam slash through the dusty dimness like a light-sword blade.

Man-made constellations on the rocky walls flashed in phosphorescent spurts.

"This really feels authentic," Temple marveled. "But where are the workmen?"

"That's just it." Aldo shook his head mournfully, the light atop his hard hat casting a beam that swayed like a rope bridge over the fake rocks. "They're not working much since the . . . incident."

A raised voice down the empty tunnel interrupted them.

Temple couldn't make out the words, but the tone was clear: admonition.

She mushed along on her marshmallow-soled shoes, consoled that at least now they could pussyfoot onto the scene unheard.

The man who was speaking obviously felt no fear of being overheard.

"You gutless wonders," he .was railing. "You call yourselves a work crew? This here's supposed to be an attraction, guys. It's supposed to be scary, huh? That's what we're here for. So why're you all shakin' like a set a gag teeth? Light shows are what made Vegas famous."

Temple and Aldo rounded a bend to find the tunnel had broadened into a cavern. Heavy-duty machinery, use-scuffed, sat idle.

So did the workmen in their yellow hard hats, beams from the built-in lights cast on the ground. Temple had never seen such a hang-dog crew, obviously in need of an "Avast, me hearties" speech.

Which they were now getting from the foreman.

One by one, the hard hats lifted and their beams focused on the newcomers.

The foreman turned, for a moment looking worried. But his expression soon hardened into contempt. "And who are you two? Dorothy and the Straw Man?"

Aldo stepped forward as if posing for an *Esquire* ad in a soldier of fortune magazine. "That's 'scarecrow' to you. We are representatives of the management. What's the holdup down here? Still seeing things?"

The workmen stirred. Some spat. All of them grumbled uneasily.

Temple realized that she and Aldo looked like dudes on a mustang ranch. She eyed the foreman, one of those salt-of-the-earth, sweat-of-the-brow types who wore a tool belt like it sported six-guns. Someone who inspired confidence, and a wide berth.

He was tall, burly, big-bellied, hairy, and grizzled, like a teddy bear gone ballistic.

She decided not to beat around the bushiness. "We heard there was trouble down here." It was hard not to add "in River City."

Everyone shifted his weight, but no one spoke.

"Everything's obviously been going great," Temple

went on. "The mine shafts are a work of art, I see the ride tracks are laid, the phosphorescent walls are as creepy as you could hope—"

All motion, even spitting, stopped on the word "phosphorescent."

Maybe it had too many syllables.

"You know, the eerie, glowing . . . whatever . . . you painted on the walls."

A silence. Then Teddy Foreman spoke with the grumble of a wakening volcano. "That's just it, Miss. We got too much phosphorescence for our own good."

"It's not like, a chemical reaction? An allergy?"

A workman laughed. "That's it. An allergy. We need shots."

"I know the kinda shots we need," another man shouted.

But they were guffawing instead of growling under their breaths and spitting, and Temple counted that a victory. Of sorts.

"So what's wrong?" she asked, straight up.

The foreman removed his hard hat to scratch his bald spot. "It's like this. The set dressers come down after us to paint up the rocks. Like you said, real nice job. Except the phosphorescence detail comes behind us. And we suddenly got a little swamp gas ahead of us."

Temple advanced into their midst, aware of Aldo like a reversed shadow on her heels. Such as those heels were. "What's ahead of you?" She peered into the tunnel's continuation on the cavern's other side.

Teddy shrugged. "Doesn't show up right now."

"Maybe the light's bad," she suggested.

Hard hats shook.

"Lights are what made us see it," Teddy the Foreman said.

"It was weird," another voice volunteered. "It moved."

"These beams of light are always moving." Temple looked to Aldo for agreement. His nod demonstrated how wavery a hard hat beam could be. "Even breathing makes them tremble a little, you know how it is when you look through binoculars."

A man stood up, his beam a tremor in the dimness, like his voice.

"We saw it. We shouldn'ta seen it. It was brighter than those paintings behind us. It was moving. Away."

"Cold lightning." Aldo's voice sounded firm as a firearm.

"Naw. We've seen cold lighting. We've seen blue light arcing. Spark showers. Electricity on a bad trip."

A third man's voice joined the chorus. "This was . . . thin light, but shaped, like those tunnels people who are dying see. Only the light wasn't the tunnel, the light was the man in it."

"Man?" Temple asked sharply.

"Or a woman in pants, or an ape in chaps," an anonymous voice snapped from the dark. "Jeez, lady, I guess we know what a man or a woman looks like in the dark, even when they're gussied up in some strange-fangled halo—"

"Or an aura?" Temple wondered.

"Coulda been this guy here in the ice-cream suit, if it glowed. You know, pale with the pinched-in waist. Don't care what you call it—halo, aura, Day-Glo gasoline, it was weird."

"You think you saw a ghost," Temple concluded.

They were silent.

Temple realized it was more serious than that.

"An . . . alien?"

Another silence.

"Know what I think? I don't think it was really anything weird like that." The foreman nodded, a Daniel come to judgment. "It was Elvis."

The silence went unbroken for a long, long time. The simple rightness of the suggestion had struck everyone dumb.

At last, a consensus.

Like the apparition itself, the inescapable conclusion was very, very weird.

Chapter 3

Blue Suede Blues

(Elvis recorded "Blue Suede Shoes" in 1956,
and sang it at his screen test on April Fools Day
that year)

"Elvis . . . Presley?"

Van von Rhine, an elegant taffy-haired woman in an Escada sueded-silk suit, lifted nearly invisible eyebrows with her voice.

That she should even have to use the last name indicated how bizarre she found the problem that Temple and Aldo had duly brought to her ultramodern office.

Then she laughed. "Really. This is . . . incredible. We'll be accused of angling for publicity if this gets out. Elvis. Presley. Please! That's another hotel. Better that the . . . visitant should be Howard Hughes. Or one of those *X-Files* creatures."

"Aliens," Aldo put in.

Van nodded absently, staring at the transparent surface of her glass desktop as if it were a wishing well.

Temple realized that she had never seen anyone who

kept an office so neat that a glass desktop remained empty except for its carefully placed accoutrements.

Van's fingers tapped the end of a fountain pen on the glass. She looked worried when she glanced back up at them. "Glowing, they say. A man's figure. You don't suppose it could be the—the—"

"The ghost of Jersey Joe Jackson is too much to hope for," Temple interjected. "There hasn't been any . . . unauthorized activity in the Ghost Suite lately, has there?"

"Nothing anyone has had the nerve to tell me." Van threw down the pen with a discordant click. "You do understand that if there is any subject on which the staff would spare my feelings—?"

"Van, your superstitious ways are legendary," Temple said. "But other people eat up the odd, the weird, the eerie. Jersey Joe Jackson is a fabulous legend to build the theme ride around: a poor person's Howard Hughes, a desert pack-rat and miner-nineteen-forty-niner with stashes of hidden assets all over the place, who built this hotel in the old days, went broke, and died here. Anybody that interesting was bound to leave a little eau de ectoplasm behind. I wish I'd seen him hanging around his old suite, seven thirteen, instead of you. I'd have asked him for personal appearances." Temple laughed as Van looked horrified. "But I know you don't want to hear that because you believe in ghosts and other superstitious sightings. I'm amazed you let a black cat like Midnight Louie hang around out back before he migrated down the Strip to the Circle Ritz."

"As long as he didn't cross my path. And his successor, Midnight Louise, is especially good at avoiding me. I wish I could say as much for the ghost," she finished with a mutter.

"You know, a ghostly visitation is not necessarily a bad thing. From a marketing standpoint."

"You're the public relations whiz. Is it possible you arranged for *this* apparition to make a small stir?"

"If I had, I'd be plenty disappointed. I'd much rather have the spirit of Jersey Joe Jackson show up than Elvis Presley."

Aldo interjected himself into their conversation. "You got something against Elvis, Miss Temple?"

"Well, other than the fact that he's irrelevant to the theme of our hotel—"

"Elvis? 'Irrelevant' to Vegas? Hey, he made this town."

Van joined Temple in staring at Aldo. Neither had seen a Fontana brother in such a state of enthusiasm, with the sole exception of Nicky, Van's husband.

"Are you a fan, Aldo?" Van asked in polite amazement.

"Aren't you? Isn't everybody?"

"No!" Temple responded.

"What's the matter? You don't like rock 'n' roll?"

"No," Van said much more calmly.

Aldo looked as if he had been shot in the heart. "This is serious. I can understand the boss lady not liking Elvis. She grew up over there in Europe. But, Miss Temple, you do not look like someone who would not like Elvis."

Under Aldo's wounded gaze, Temple found herself flailing for words, a novelty.

"Well, these things are very personal, Aldo. I never thought that much about why I don't like Elvis. . . . For one thing, he was pretty much a dead issue when I was a teenager."

"And he became so overblown in his later years," Van put in, "so—"

"Fat?" Aldo suggested pugnaciously.

Van remained as cool as crème de menthe. "I was referring to his bejeweled jumpsuits, those World Wrestling champion-sized belts, those sideburns bushy enough to have made a grizzly bear blush."

"I think Van is describing a general air of . . . tacky," Temple added.

"Aw, ladies. You just do not get it. Elvis had to be bigger than life. His fans expected it. He was the King."

"The king of codeine," Van put in.

"The king of groupies," Temple added.

Aldo shook his head. "That's just bad press. He was really, underneath it all, a nice, simple, misunderstood guy."

Temple and Van exchanged a glance.

"I'll say this," Van said, ending all further discussion. "He better not be haunting my construction site, or he'll be the king of dying twice."

Chapter 4

I Need Somebody to Lean On

(The first song by Elvis associate Red West to
appear in a movie, *Viva Las Vegas* with Elvis
and Ann-Margret)

"M-miss Barr? I doubt you remember me, but this is
Merle Conrad. I, ah, really need to talk to you about my
daughter. I don't have an answering machine, so I'll
keep trying to call you."

Temple stared at her own answering machine. She
couldn't imagine someone existing without this essential
artifact of new-Millennium life. Even Matt Devine, Mr.
Non-high-tech Living, had bought one.

Merle Conrad? The woman had sounded upset, but
hesitant. Temple, as a public relations freelancer, seldom
dealt with people who found her—or a mere machine—
intimidating. Yet Temple, who could read stress in
voices like an earthquake meter could detect inner-core
tremors, would have sworn the caller was anxious. Anxious about calling little ole her, who was about as im-
posing as Jiminy Cricket?

She puzzled over the call for a moment, agonizing over her in-and-out schedule. The poor woman would miss more often than not, and Temple couldn't do a thing about it, since the caller had left no phone number. Why not?

Then speculation faded before the nearer stimulus of anticipation. Matt was coming down from his apartment to review his recent national talk show tape with her. Presto! From PR gal to media consultant. At least on a small, personal scale.

She left the spare bedroom that served as her office and skated across the polished parquet floor to the living area, massing magazines and papers into tidier piles as she passed. Piles were still piles. She really had to find some domestic time-out one of these days, whistle while you work and all that. Imagine that the broom . . .

A knock on the door stopped her in mid-tidy and mid-Disney animation nostalgia. Matt never bothered to ring her many-noted doorbell nowadays, and Max always entered without knocking, born second-story man that he was. At least she could always guess who was not coming to dinner!

She opened the door, surprised to experience a frisson of anxiety herself. Why did seeing someone you knew on national television seem to make him more of a stranger than before?

"How'd it go?" she asked as she swung the door wide.

Temple would never make it in a "don't ask, don't tell" world.

"You tell me." Matt smiled ruefully and walked in, apparently looking around for Midnight Louie. "You're the one who saw it."

"Not the only one. Hundreds of thousands, millions of people saw the show."

He winced, standing in the middle of the living room and taking inventory of its furnishings as if to ensure they were still there. "I feel like I've been in another world, even though L.A. is less than three hundred miles away."

"Listen, compared to the rest of the country, L.A. is three hundred light-years away. Scared you off with their manically laid-back ways, huh?"

He shrugged, still looking around.

"Louie's lounging in the other room, and nobody else is here, or has been recently, if that's what you're looking for signs of."

"I'm not looking for anybody," he said quickly. "I'm just trying to make sure I'm on terra firma again. That whole lifestyle there makes you feel as if you're standing on a fault line. The costly clothes, the sleek convertibles, the head-turning blonds—"

"Hey, don't put them down: you are one."

"Toys R Us, huh?"

He sat on the sofa suddenly, and eyed the VCR as if it were a spy machine.

Maybe it was Temple's imagination, but just a few days on the fabled coast seemed to have sun-streaked his blond hair to a beachy sheen. Matt favored clothes in modest shades of beige and sand and khaki, but they just enhanced his brown-eyed, blond good looks.

"So what's the verdict on the home screens?" he asked.

She sat beside him and picked up the remote control. "Obviously the camera loves you to pieces."

"What does that mean?"

"You're ultra-telegenic. Don't have a bad angle. Voice is pleasant. Since this was a panel discussion show, you were in competition with a whole lineup of guests. Interesting."

"I didn't consider this a competition."

"No, but some of the other guests did. They want their moment in the spotlight, their fair share of airtime, which means more than anybody else. You were just there to talk about the issue of the day, and it shows. Shows them up. I'm going to run it, and you look at it like you were the other guests' agent, wanting your client to shine. See what you think of yourself as the competition."

He frowned. "We were there to communicate on a hot-button issue: unwed teens, and kids desperate enough to abandon or even kill their own newborns. I wouldn't have gone on if it was some shallow media feeding frenzy. You told me the *Amanda* show was respectable."

"It is, as talk shows go. Not quite the cachet of *Oprah,* but not everybody can be number one, A. S. After Springer. I'll roll the tape. Just relax and watch. And then we'll discuss it."

This time Matt frowned at his wristwatch, the more formal model his mother had given him for Christmas instead of the drugstore variety he usually wore. He was still dressed for stardom. "That'll take a whole hour."

"No, it won't. I'll fast-forward through commercials, and there are a lot of 'em."

"This will feel silly. Watching myself. I was hoping you could summarize everything. You know, tell me: talk slower or faster, or quit looking at the floor, or whatever."

"Quit looking at the floor and watch the tape," she mock-ordered. Essentially private people could be very obstinate about public appearances. At thirty-three, Matt had the reserve of a man twice his age. Not so surprising. In a few months he had catapulted from newly ex-Roman Catholic priest working as an anonymous local hotline counselor to radio shrink to a national hot property because of one fateful phone call only days ago.

On the other hand, maybe nowadays his diffidence had a different cause: Temple's vanished live-in lover, Max Kinsella the magician, had reappeared to resume their relationship just as Matt was making tentative goo-goo eyes at her. Temple admittedly had goo-goo-eyed back, or probably first. So now that she and Max were again a matched pair, Matt made the awkward hypotenuse of a triangle etched in dotted lines. Darn! Temple couldn't have a lover who wasn't a friend, but it could be hard to have a male friend who wasn't a lover.

She finally hit the right buttons on the remote. AMANDA, a graphic announced over the theme music. Suddenly, a recorded telephone conversation—an interrogation, actually—crackled over close-ups of the hostess clutching a mike, listening intently against a background of sober audience members.

The girl's voice was a numb mumble, quietly hysterical. The man's voice was Matt's, sounding calm, but deeply concerned.

As the shocking sentences faded, Amanda eyed the camera. "Actual audiotape of an almost-tragedy, folks: a teenager having a baby in a motel room called a late-night radio psychologist, convinced the infant was an alien she had to destroy. Only the man on the other end of the line could talk her out of it. And here he is."

Matt entered from stage right, wearing pretty much what he wore now, except for the addition of a blazer and muted tie. Amanda climbed the shallow steps to the stage and joined him in sitting dead center in a row of empty chairs.

"Matt Devine works for WCOO-AM in Las Vegas. When did this happen, Matt?"

"Ten days ago. And I'm not a radio psychologist, just a counselor."

"More than 'just a counselor,' I think. You used to be a Catholic priest."

"Yes, I was." Temple could tell he was unhappy about publicly confessing that ex-identity, but fame demands all the information that's fit to mention, and more, if it can get it.

"So it must have appalled you, this young girl so distraught that she viewed her own newborn as an alien being that needed to be destroyed."

"Most people toss around the word 'denial,' but they don't truly understand it. Denial is an emotional version of hysterical blindness. The consequences of her situation were so unthinkable, she couldn't see them as real. In her case, imagining some *X-Files* type of alien-baby substitution played into her need to deny her condition, to keep it secret at all costs."

"And she was willing to drown her baby in the bathtub?"

"Who can say? She sounded like she might."

"Given your religious background, you show a lot of compassion for her on the tape."

"There's no contradiction. A religious background should evoke compassion. Condemnation never helped anyone."

"Well, Dr. Laurel might disagree."

"Dr. Laurel wasn't there."

"No, but she is here. Ladies and gentlemen, Dr. Laurel Lawson."

Temple hit the mute and pause buttons. "That must have been a bad moment. Didn't you see her in the greenroom backstage?"

"No." Matt stared ahead at the freeze-frame screen. "She was a surprise."

"They call it confrontational television."

"I thought you said this was a decent talk show."

"Well, no talk show is really decent, is it?"

"But she's a veteran. Been at it much longer than I."

"And takes a much tougher stance."

"Tougher? Or just less tolerant?"

Temple rolled some more tape to follow the slim, suited figure as she entered and took a chair on the moderator's right. "Very symbolic placement. You on the left, her on the right. What a media vixen. Spouting holier-than-thou inflexible Ten Commandments stuff, and she had an affair with a married man years ago; even has some undraped photos zipping around on the Internet."

"They ambushed me," Matt agreed, refusing to rise to the bait of his rival's ancient shenanigans. "So I ended up defending myself and my caller."

"I thought it was pretty brilliant when you accused Dr. Laurel of being willing to throw the mother out with the bathwater."

"I was getting angry."

"It didn't show."

"That's when I'm angriest. I never would have gone on if I thought that confused child was going to be used as a bad example. She was simply stressed beyond her fragile defenses. And that dysfunctional family . . . What you're saying, Temple, is that I was out of my league."

"Oh, yes, definitely."

"A good lesson. Don't do this again."

"Oh, no. Not at all."

"What?"

"You're out of your league because you're not playing to the lowest common denominator. That's just what talk TV needs, so I think you should do as much of it as they ask you to."

Matt did not look encouraged.

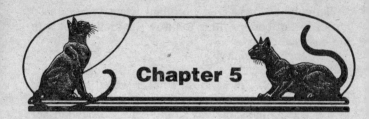

Chapter 5

Help Me

(Larry Gatlin wrote this for Elvis in 1973; his
recording peaked at #6 on the country chart in
1974)

The knock on Temple's door that evening caught her
trying to do something that seldom turned out well:
cook.

She turned the heat down to simmer under a frying
pan choked with softening vegetables and tough shrimp.
If time could heal all wounds maybe it could mend a
stir-fry that was too fried to stir.

She wondered what Matt might have to tell her now.
His life had become a whirligig of news updates, spinning to the tune of a media frenzy.

She opened the door, stunned to find a strange woman
waiting on the other side.

Temple stood there, spatula lifted as high as a homely
wand, one curl of overcooked onion clinging like a
comma to its nonstick surface.

"I'm sorry to bother you." The woman shuffled her

shoes, reminding Temple of a door-to-door solicitor who had suddenly developed cold feet. "You're making dinner."

"That's debatable," Temple said wryly. The woman's voice sounded familiar. Even the face seemed familiar.

Or maybe Temple had just seen too many women like this when she had been a TV news reporter. The expressionless faces of women who were victims of whatever car-jacking/rape-drug/lost child/domestic violence case caught the public's attention for the blink of a battered eye.

"It's . . . I'm Merle."

"Merle!" That rang a bell, even if Merle herself had eschewed using Temple's doorbell. The telephone calls Temple kept missing. Merle Who? Merle What. Above all, Merle Why.

"Sorry." The woman was turning to retrace her steps down the short neck of hallway that led to the circular building's curving central area.

"Wait!" Temple edged into the hall. "I remember now. You wanted to talk to me. So come on in. Talk. Share the spatter."

"Spatter?"

"I'm trying to stir-fry."

Merle's noncommittal face twitched a little. It might have been an infant smile. "Smells more like smoked barbeque."

"Omigosh! That darn controller knob. I can never tell which way is hotter or cooler."

Temple rushed back into the kitchen, where smoke was now billowing righteously to the ceiling. She swatted at it with the slotted spatula, managing only to flip the slimy onion slice onto her cheek.

"Here." Merle marched in, snatched a length of paper towels to use as a makeshift hot pad and transferred the smoking fry pan to an unheated burner. "Do you do this often?" she asked.

"Burn or cook? Obviously not, either one." Temple

watched closely as Merle turned the control a tiny bit to the right.

"You just went past 'Low' to the highest setting," Merle said.

Temple peered at the still-sizzling contents of the pan. "The black charring kind of underlines the faded color of the vegetables. Maybe char-stir-fried is an innovation."

"Whew. Have you got a venting fan in this place?"

"This building is a little old."

Merle leaned over the smoky stove top to press a switch on the charming little copper canopy overhead. With a whirring roar, smoke was suctioned up into it like magic.

"I never knew that was there," Temple admitted.

Merle, speechless again, stood under the glaringly unkind kitchen light, uneasily dusting her palms together as if the crisis, being over, had left her with a case of the willies.

The last few moments had given Temple a chance to sum up her visitor. Besides lank dishwater-brown hair, Merle had nearly invisible eyebrows, wore lipstick in an unflattering shade of coral, and her oversized beige sweater had the same pulled-out-of-shape droop as her shoulders and her spirit.

"Come on," Temple said, "sit down in the living room and enjoy the haze."

"You don't remember who I am," Merle noted as she padded after Temple like a lost puppy.

"Gee. No. I'm sorry."

"We only met for a moment, and I wasn't the main event."

"What was the main event?"

"Not what. Who."

"Well?"

"Crawford."

Temple's face must have betrayed her estimation of the bearer of that name, because Merle hastened on, tripping over her own words like a nervous teenager.

"It was at the hospital. When he was in for that heart trouble. And you took over handling some event for him, I don't remember what."

"You're his . . ." Oops, Temple didn't have a quick descriptive phrase at her fingertips. She should never have started such a clumsy sentence.

"Girlfriend, I guess you'd call it. Insignificant other." Merle's laugh tried for self-deprecating and—like Temple's stir-fry dish—fell far short of expectations.

"I was going to say, Quincey's mother!" Temple coasted on a saving burst of memory, trying to lend the woman a more glorious role than unsanctioned consort to Temple's least-favorite male in the entire world. Accentuate the positive. "How's Quincey doing?"

Merle's crumpled doily of a face collapsed into shattered silk.

"Sit down," Temple insisted, finally hitting her stride. Solving face-shattering problems was a PR woman's specialty, even if stir-fry was not. "I'll whip up what I'm really good at, instant anything, and you can tell me all about it."

"This is really good tea," Merle said enthusiastically about eight minutes later.

"It ought to be. The hot water's the only thing I contributed to it."

"The, ah, lime slices are an original touch."

Temple decided it was better to accept undeserved praise than to give it. "Thank you."

Now that Merle Conrad had shed her shapeless cardigan sweater and had settled into the sofa, she looked more relaxed and less harassed. Maybe it was the comforting pillow of Midnight Louie that had curled up next to her, gazing up at her pale face as if he were all ears.

"What a pretty cat," Merle said, patting his head.

"Pretty cat" did not exactly describe twenty pounds of muscular, vasectomized tomcat, but Temple was just glad Louie was on his best behavior. He apparently got along best with the female of the species, any species.

Having given Louie his due, Merle turned sad hazel eyes back to Temple. "Crawford keeps saying that you should come to work with him at the *Scoop*."

"I left journalism a long time ago," Temple said, politely refraining from mentioning that the *Las Vegas Scoop* was to journalism what lumps of coal are to diamonds.

"It's just a joke. Then, he says, you could have a column called '*Scoop* Snoop Sister.' "

Temple was not amused. "Merle, is this about a . . . criminal matter?"

Merle put her mug atop the morning paper on the coffee table.

"It's about a worrywart mother, I suppose. But Crawford's dragged Quincey into another one of his crazy schemes, and I'm worried about her."

Temple had been worried about Quincey too. The sixteen-year-old had a diffident mother who was under the thumb of a pseudo-stepfather she loathed. Naturally, she retaliated by acting like Biker Chick.

"I got to know her a little," Temple said, "when we were working in the pageant together last fall."

Merle nodded, frowning. "As 'pose-down models.' That doesn't sound too savory, but I supposed if an adult woman like yourself was doing it—"

"You didn't see the pageant?"

"No. Quincey said it wasn't much of anything."

Temple nodded, more to indicate information absorbed than agreement.

The romance cover-hunk contest had been something, all right, even without murder on the menu, which there had been. The pose-downs involved steamy simulated embraces with ninety-nine and forty-four one hundredth percent impurely unclad male cover models. Temple had wondered why any mother would let her teenage daughter participate. As for herself, well, she had been undercover at the time.

"But this new thing Crawford's got her into—" Merle was saying.

Temple jerked her memory back from that close encounter with actual death as well as virtual desire. "What new thing?"

"With the new hotel-casino. Of course they're making a big to-do about it, but Crawford's roped Quincey into playing a 'role' at the opening, and I'm afraid it could be . . . dangerous."

"Wait. What new hotel-casino? There are so many right now, the Belladonna, otherwise known as the Beluga, for one."

"Oh, the really big one."

"There are so many really big ones, as the late Ed Sullivan would point out."

"Huh? Oh, the 'reeely big shew' man from early TV. But haven't you seen the signs?"

"In the heavens?"

"No. On the streets. They're all over town: The Kingdome is Coming. The Kingdome is Coming."

"Oh, those! I thought they were religious billboards."

"Not 'Kingdom.' Kingdome."

"A new sports stadium? At a hotel-casino? Makes sense. The town hasn't fully tapped the sports theme."

"A new arena, all right. But for the King." When Temple looked blank, Merle added, a bit testily, "Elvis."

"Elvis?" That name kept turning up in her life with uneasy frequency.

"Yes. Everybody's been going on about it."

"Well, I was a little distracted, by some other things." Like a few murders and a private life. "So it's an Elvis hotel. High time, sounds like."

"Anyway, Crawford is emceeing the Elvis imitator contest."

Temple nodded. She could picture that. She could

hardly picture it without laughing, but she could picture it.

"And he's talked Quincey into dressing up like Priscilla Presley back in the sixties. The winner of the contest gets a championship belt from the hands of 'Priscilla' and gets a date with her. Except it's Quincey."

Temple kept nodding, although the gesture had started feeling mechanical. She could picture Quincey with Young Priscilla's sky-high-teased dark tresses, wearing enough eye makeup to weigh a Las Vegas hooker down to her knees. Actually, Quincey was a natural for the role.

"And they want to kill her," Merle added.

"What? Kill Quincey?"

"No, Priscilla!"

"But she lives in a Los Angeles suburb, doesn't she?"

"Maybe. I don't know where she lives! And they don't want to kill that Priscilla anyway. Maybe just mutilate her a little."

"But—"

"They want to kill the Priscilla who married Elvis in 1967 and divorced him in 1973. I guess they've always wanted to kill her."

"Wait a minute! I don't know much about Elvis, but who wants to kill her?"

"Everybody who loved Elvis hated Priscilla, Quincey says. Either because they envied her when she married him, or they blamed her for his downfall and death after she left him."

"Talk about a no-win situation. Then female fans are the threat?"

"Sure. And some of the men, too. There was always a power struggle between Priscilla and the Mafia, you know."

"The Mafia's involved in this?"

"Not the plain Mafia. The Memphis Mafia, the guys who were Elvis's bodyguards and gofers, who Priscilla was fighting for Elvis's time and attention."

"You talk like all this was just yesterday, Merle. It was over thirty years ago."

Merle picked up the cooling tea and drank deeply. "I've been listening to Quincey chatter about it night and day. She's gone ga-ga over the whole Elvis mania. She calls it digging deeply into her role. I call it obsession."

"Well, Elvis was an obsessive kind of guy, to hear tell. It's only fitting his fans should follow suit."

"Suit! And that's another thing. This is a very costly show. Those stupid jumpsuits all the imitators wear cost a small fortune. And then the hotel invited all sorts of internationally famous designers to design new fantasy jumpsuits for Elvis, some with real gems on them, and those are on exhibit. I tell you, Miss Barr, the whole Kingdome is a festering circus of the seven deadly sins: avarice and gluttony and pride and envy and lust and— what else was there?"

"Sloth," Temple answered absently.

"That's why I thought of you," Merle said, punctuating this interesting statement with a last swallow of cold peppermint tea.

"Just how concrete are these seven deadly sins getting?"

Merle leaned back to pet Midnight Louie again. He had been as quiet and attentive as Temple had ever seen him. Perhaps he was interested in Elvis lore.

"Well," Merle said, "I don't want to be an alarmist, but Quincey is getting death threats."

"How. Telephoned? Written?"

"Both. And yesterday, when she was in the dressing room alone putting on all that false Priscilla hair and couldn't see, someone sneaked up behind her, grabbed her around the throat, and cut an 'E' into her with a razor blade, right where her neck and shoulder meet."

"Merle, this is a job for the police!"

"They think it's just some Elvis nut."

"Nuts are called nuts because they're dangerous. What do you think I can do?"

"The police are 'keeping an eye on things,' and hotel security swears it's going to be all over the place, but there are so many people in costume and weird get-ups . . . anybody could get around all that officialdom. I thought it'd be natural for a PR woman to be on the site, and you could, you know, snoop."

"This doesn't sound like a snooping job. This sounds like a body-guarding job." Temple's eyes opened wide. Merle leaned forward, hopeful at last. "And that I might be able to arrange."

"Thank you so much. You're such a good example for Quincey."

"I am?"

"Oh, yes. She said you really got down and boogied at that romance cover-hunk pageant. She thinks you're way cool for an old person."

Chapter 6

Blue Eyes Cryin' in the Rain

(Recorded at Graceland in 1976, the last song
Elvis ever sang the day he died, August 16,
1977)

The King eyed himself in the mirror.

His hair. Finally showing the bends from dyin' all these years. Hair's only human. You bend it enough, it'll break. It'll just die.

His eyebrows were refusing to grow, like a cotton crop that had been water-starved too often. Had to paint 'em on now. Mascara on his baby-blond lashes, dye on his head and his eyebrows, and even on his chest hairs now that he was older and those born-waxed-smooth boyish pecs were growin' moss.

He'd gone white when they weren't lookin'. When he wasn't lookin'.

But he hadn't been lookin' for a long time. Too long.

The King blinked. At least his eyelashes weren't fallin' out, but they weren't the thickets he was born with. Born blond. Blue-eyed blond. Wishy-washy. Momma's boy.

Fixed that.

Black. Boot-black dyed hair, eyebrows, lashes. Black 'cycle cap. Black like Brando. Wild Ones. Wild Thing. *Wild in the Country.* One of those damn movies when he'd tried to get serious about bein' an actor.

The King frowned at his reflection. He was an actor now, by God. Actin' like he was alive, still the King.

As long as he could animate this ole bod, he was.

The heart of rock 'n' roll wasn't in no damn Cleveland. Or in Motown, and damn sure not in Nashville. Ever. It was in Memphis. On Beale Street. Always had been, even before he got there. No kings in Memphis, though.

That's why he'd always liked the Luxor Hotel, when they put that puppy up. Even downtown Memphis had its fake pyramid now, a big bow to the Egyptian forerunner.

He liked those Egyptians. Life after death and all that. Very mystical. Sometimes he suspected he was one of them. Death was just crossin' that river. Over Jordan, over Nile. Let my people go. Did the Egyptians have music? Must have. You can't have death or a civilization without music.

Book of the Dead. Hah! He was bigger than any ole Pharaoh. He had collected whole Books of the Dead, mystical books on eastern religions and numerology and all sorts of intriguing things, mountains and mountains of them. Whole pyramids. His entire friggin' life had been a Book of the Dead. Only no one knew it.

Except maybe mama.

Mama.

Without her, nothin'. With her, nothin' and everythin' pulling back and forth until he was a piece of taffy. Blond taffy in a black wrapper; you know, the shiny little papers with the twisty ends. So tasty-sweet, like Krispy Kreme donuts, like young girls. Addictive. Gotta eat more and more of 'em, until you burst.

Guess his end had been twisty enough. Twisted gut, damn near drove him nuts the last few years. Distending his stomach, making his throne room the bathroom, his crown of thorns a chronic case of constipation. His insides kinking up on him, just like his outsides had. And couldn't say it, breathe it. He was the King. No weaknesses. Nothin' snapped, 'cept the hair on his head.

Nothin' snapped in public at least, until two of his oldest friends and a new guy pulled the plug on his peace of mind with their tell-all book. *Elvis, What Happened?* they called it.

The Memphis Mafia reveals everything but what really happened to start it all. What happened was that the weight of everyone on his back had finally gotten too much.

Back can snap too, just like overworked hair.

Chapter 7

King of the Whole Wide World

(Elvis sang this over the credits of *Kid Galahad*,
his 1962 film)

Before Temple would recruit even Boss Banana's boys
as bodyguards, she felt honor-bound to check out the
scene of the forthcoming crime. Before she did that, she
felt obligated to check in with her most gainful employer
of the moment.

Being a freelance public relations person allowed
Temple to handle a variety of special events, bouncing
in and out of projects like a dancing ball on a slide-
projection set of sing-along lyrics. She loved moving
into whitewater-rafting mode for concentrated periods of
time, followed by the lull of tranquil waters. It suited
her employment background: TV news and repertory
theater. Rush and then rest.

Now, though, for the first time she had a permanent,
floating client. The Crystal Phoenix Hotel and Casino
was "the classiest little hotel in Vegas," and it behooved

her to alert the management that their maybe-Elvis sighting had eerie links to another Las Vegas hotel. Temple took the phrase "conflict of interest" very seriously.

Aldo had phoned to report that the workmen were settling down now that they had decided their iridescent apparition had been only Elvis. Elvis, it seems, was the ghost most likely to be welcomed anywhere.

When Temple arrived at Van von Rhine's ultra-modern office, Nicky Fontana, the other half of the marriage and management team, was lounging in a massive leather executive chair that Van allowed to spoil her Euro-sleek decor because he liked it.

Nicky was as darkly delicious to behold as his suite of brothers, but was a hair shorter and much less laid back.

"What's this about the King?" he asked the minute Temple arrived. "Has our underground Jersey Joe Jackson mine ride really got an unearthly infestation?"

"I seriously doubt it." Temple perched on a chrome-and-leather chair. "But Elvis is in the air right now, with the imminent opening of the Kingdome."

Nicky nodded sagaciously. That's what one got to do when one ran a major Las Vegas resort destination.

Temple squirmed in the hard-edged chair. "Odd things are happening at the Kingdome itself. An acquaintance of mine says her daughter, who's playing Priscilla Presley for the Elvis impersonator opening competition, has been getting threats, possibly from Elvis-loving Priscilla-haters."

"What can you do about it?" Van wanted to know.

"Me, not much. But"—she glanced at Nicky—"I was hoping to borrow your brothers. Quincey is only sixteen, and her sort-of stepfather is that 'Buchanan's Broadside' reporter for the *Las Vegas Scoop*. He'll emcee the Elvis competition, and is the same creep who involved the girl as a pose-down model in the romance cover hunk competition last fall."

"Sixteen? A 'pose-down' model? Sounds sleazy," Van

commented with the indignation of the relatively new mother of a baby girl.

"Quincey was actually just fifteen then—"

"Of course you can have Nicky's brothers!" Van was bristling now.

Nicky just toyed with the Rolex watch that kept catching on his wrist hairs as he spun the band.

"Nicky?" Van asked.

"I'm sure they'll be game." He frowned. "And I don't like an icon from their hotel showing up at our hotel just as things are getting hinky at the Kingdome." He eyed Temple. "You could check out this hot new jumpsuit joint. See if there's a reason an Elvis apparition is turning up in our basement."

"That might be dangerous," Van objected.

"Not with Fontana, Inc., on the job." Nicky grinned.

"I do worry about Quincey," Temple admitted. "I got to know her at that romance convention. Her sleazeball stepfather is always using her in his crazy schemes, and her mother isn't the type to stand up to him."

"I bet you are," Nicky said. "We should study the competition anyway."

"The opening Elvis competition isn't for a couple weeks. This Elvis sighting at the Jersey Joe site reminded me that I need to keep an eye on things here now that the construction is underway."

"Aldo said that now the workmen think their haunting is just Elvis, they're flattered. They're working up a storm to impress the King."

Temple shook her head. "I doubt I can take the undiluted Elvis idolatry I'll find at the Kingdome. Besides, I owe the Phoenix so much. That retainer you've put me on is my first steady salary in three years. I could get lazy."

"Forget it." Nicky waved his Rolex wrist. "You aren't consulting just on PR stuff, you dreamed up the whole recreational re-do."

"And," Van added, leaning across her clear glass

desktop, "you inspired that international conceptual artist, Domingo, to design a very arty children's area for us. I've gotten inquiries about the project from *Art Forum*. We're reaching an entirely new and upscale audience, thanks to you and your eclectic friends. Nicky's right. If you feel this poor little Quincey needs a chaperone, you run right over to the Kingdome for as long as necessary. We wouldn't want a daughter of ours in such a high-stress environment at that tender age."

Temple refrained from explaining that there was nothing tender about Quincey but her age.

"I've never really liked Elvis," she confessed in a last-ditch effort to stick to duty and sacrifice satisfying her always-insatiable curiosity.

"You're in good company," Van said, sitting back.

"This is business," Nicky noted. " 'Like' has nothing to do with it."

Putt-putting along the Strip in her aging aqua Storm, Temple drove like the legendary little old lady from Pasadena (even though she was cool for an old person; see what turning thirty does for you!), peering at all the "Kingdome is Coming" signs she'd ignored for so long.

They were everywhere. Obviously, her head had been in the clouds, probably looking for the single billboard advertising Matt Devine's midnight radio advice show. Meanwhile, on ground level, Elvis had been stepping on everybody's blue suede shoes in an attempt to get a little attention for a dead guy.

Temple marveled that the Strip always offered enough empty acreage to support another monument to the Theme-of-the-Moment. The trend had been Euro lately: the suave Monte Carlo, Steve Wynn's artsy Bellagio, and the equally lavish Belladonna, which Temple had nicknamed the Beluga (after the small white whale) for its vast expanses of white marble, not to mention a collection of European masterwork paintings and sculptures, all of buxom, white-skinned naked ladies. Instead of the Naked Maja, Temple thought of the ambiance as the Naked Moby.

But she had never seen the Kingdome coming. How had she missed this Eighth Wonder of the World building? Blink in Las Vegas nowadays, and you missed the Second Coming. Come to think of it, an Elvis Presley hotel and casino in Las Vegas *was* a sort of Second Coming.

Temple pulled into the Kingdome's parking lot and let the Storm throb on idle. Appropriately. This was now the home of rock 'n' roll, wasn't it? Feel the beat? She felt an involuntary frisson of excitement.

Whoever had designed this place, or palace, had not been gun-shy. The Kingdome was a slick, pompadour-sculpted swoop of architecture, mindful of the low, long lines of fifties and sixties cars, and the kinky excesses of seventies fashion. The titular dome squatted like an alien vessel from which Michael Rennie would soon emerge, wearing an industrial-strength silver jumpsuit. Then he would turn into a guitar-licking, foot-stomping, pelvis-swiveling Elvis.

Don't step on my silver-Mylar space boots.

Still, the all-white compound also radiated an air of antebellum gentility that brought Graceland—and particularly dignified funeral parlors—to mind. How appropriately Elvis. Temple remembered reading that he had visited morgues with his entourage, as fascinated by still-life death as he was by death-defying sports like fast cars, 'cycles, go-carts, and hot-and-cold-running girls.

She was amazed, sitting here gawking past her windshield visor, liberated nineties woman that she was, by how much she had unconsciously absorbed of the Elvis legend.

The Kingdome itself implied the wide-legged stance of the King, its nervous pulsing neon reminiscent of his hyperactive left leg. The dazzling white structure even seemed to sweat in the wintery Las Vegas sun and to

gain an otherworldly aura from that very human failing.
Blood, sweat, and tears.

Like the birth of the blues, the King had suffered them
all.

Oh, come on!

She didn't even like his music. Or his looks. Or his
lifestyle. Or his legend.

Still. They'd built a hell of a hotel in his name.

The King is dead. Long live the King.

Viva Las Vegas.

I guess now, Temple thought, *they can call it the
Valley of the King.*

Naturally, you had to pass through the pearly gates to
get in.

The huge gates that split in the middle were covered
in pearlescent paint, with notes and staffs written in
wrought iron.

Walking in as a PR person, Temple was immediately
struck by the immense obstacles to such an enterprise.
EPE (Elvis Presley Enterprises, aka "the estate") must
control the commercial marketing of every item and image connected to the late, much lamented King. No wonder no one had dared to do the obvious and create an
Elvisland in Las Vegas. Graceland had a corner on the
market.

That was why, she discovered, nodding sagely to herself, an interior attraction was called "Raceland," featuring bumper car rides and exhibits of the kind of cycles
and cars the King had collected. The real things remained on display at Graceland in Memphis. Everything
here was ersatz Elvis.

But . . . Elvis himself was ersatz culture, so in a sense,
this place was even truer to the King than real life had
been.

Temple found that sad. All legends eventually become
the living sarcophagus in which their original inspiration
is entombed.

Death Valley of the King. Not a bad way to put it.

She struck out across the valley floor (a custom carpet littered with images of fifties guitars, cars, and 'cycles) for what lay under the dome.

The casino's slot machines chimed with the melodies from a dozen Elvis hits, and Temple spotted blue suede shoes and pink Cadillac convertibles spinning past.

Nowhere, however, was the face of Elvis visible.

While no one could copyright a person's life, or the artifacts he had surrounded himself with, any representation of a likeness that could be sold for a profit would have to be authorized.

So here in the Kingdome, Elvis himself was like an invisible, entombed pharaoh surrounded by all the pomp and circumstance of his life, except his own image.

While Temple was mulling over the symbolism of the Absent Elvis effect, who should come walking toward her but . . . Elvis.

He was wearing a white jumpsuit punctuated with gold metallic studs and gleaming gemstones of ruby, sapphire, and emerald.

Temple had seen a lot of extravagant, outré, bizarre, and dazzling effects in Las Vegas. She had always seen the man behind the curtain: the special-effects wizard who pulled the strings and set off the fireworks and who murmured, constantly, "Pay no attention to the man behind the curtain." Colonel Tom Parker, if you will.

But there was no curtain here.

There was only Elvis, finally, in the flesh-and-blood form.

Walking toward her.

A movement to the side caught her eye.

There was Elvis, sleek in hair cream and black 'cycle leathers.

Walking toward her.

She blinked.

Another Elvis at three o'clock high, this one attired in a martial arts *gi*—white pjs, really—banded here, there, and everywhere in red satin and sashed in black satin at the waist.

On they came, like a mirror image trio of gunslingers: three incarnations of Elvis, the hair and sideburns all of one piece, like a gleaming dark helmet, the garb light and dark, like hero and villain in one and the same form.

Then came the fourth Elvis.

He carried an ornate cane and a flashlight (of all things). His belt and his cloak clasp were swagged in chains of gold, his dress vaguely Regency style, the Emperor Elvis. I, Dracula meets the King of Rock 'n' Roll.

Temple had prided herself on never actually stopping and gawking at anything or anybody in Las Vegas. But now she did both.

She suddenly understood the utter genius of the Kingdome: no image of the King himself was allowed, so the place was crawling with imitators. If No One could be Elvis, Everybody Else was.

While she stood there trying to absorb the existential implications of being, and not being, Elvis, someone had approached her from behind and now spoke.

"Awesome, isn't it, T.B.?"

She whirled. Facing her was someone far more familiar, but a sad let-down from the high-camp presence of the Magnificent Four Elvi.

"You don't seem surprised to see me." Crawford Buchanan sounded peeved.

Let-down could hardly describe the anticlimax that Crawford Buchanan embodied. He was a short, slight man, neat as some scavenger carnivore. His full head of hair, last she had seen it, had been a silver waterfall that curled into froth at his nape. Now it was dyed jet black with moussey aspirations to a pompadour. Not to mention sideburns.

His voice was the same night-radio baritone, oily and suggestive.

His attitude was dyed to match his hair, or maybe it

had always matched his current style: preening sexist smirk.

Temple suddenly remembered why she had never liked Elvis, impressive though his persona could be. She also realized why she felt obligated to help Merle with Quincey. Crawford Buchanan wasn't warped enough to molest a girl, but he wasn't above using Quincey as a nubile draw in his selfish schemes. What an unspeakable pseudo-stepfather for a teenage girl!

"So the place is thronging with ersatz Elvi," she said. "Is that just for the contest, or will they be a regular feature?"

"Oh, the contest is just the opening salvo. The impersonators will be fixtures, a doorman here, a croupier there. That way the customers can get up close and personal with Elvis."

"You actually think a Las Vegas hotel-casino can succeed without anything genuine to its real theme on the premises?"

Buchanan's shrug drew attention to his black mohair suit, white shirt, and narrow black sixties tie.

"Since when did you start dressing like a Jehovah's Witness?" she asked.

"This isn't that look! This is the Memphis Mafia look. Maybe this will give you the right idea." He whipped a pair of ultradark sunglasses with heavy black plastic frames from his breast pocket to his face.

"You still look more like *Men in Black* than Mafia from Memphis."

"And you still look like a million dollars, T. B." Crawford flipped up his shades to leer. "What are you doing over here anyway?"

Temple ignored the leer; it came with the territory when one ventured into Crawford Buchanan Country. "Just checking out the new game in town."

"Then stick around a few days. I'll be emceeing the world's biggest Elvis Presley imitator contest. Well, some call themselves 'impressionists,' and some call themselves impersonators, or even actors, but imitators seems the most honest description."

Temple let her head swivel to survey various passing Elvi from the rear. "Looks like you've got every stage of Elvis from debut to death around here."

Buchanan followed her glance with a sneer. That was C.B.: always a leer for the ladies and a sneer for the guys. She hadn't seen him for so long she'd forgotten how despicable he was.

"There are only Three Stages of Elvis," he was saying—pontificating. "Young Elvis, suits and guitars and pompadour hair; Comeback Elvis, the Man in the Black Leather Suit; and Touring Elvis, otherwise known as Vegas Elvis, the big galoot in the glitter jumpsuits and hernia-truss belts. Nobody much cares about movie Elvis, and neither did E.P. himself when he was alive."

"That's right." Temple frowned as she teased her memory. "I've seen a lot of fifties Elvis, and a lot of seventies Elvis, but what did he do during the sixties?"

"Ran for cover like everybody else in American music when the Beatles came over and usurped Ed Sullivan from our barefoot boy with cheek of sideburn. You know why he's called Comeback Elvis?"

"No, and the answer better not be a dirty punchline."

"T.B.! Would I inflict blue material on a class act like you?"

"Any time you thought you could get away with it." That earned another leer, and an explanation.

"See, the Colonel—Colonel Parker, Elvis's manager and, some would say, Svengali—sold Elvis to the movies for that whole decade. No tours, no live music, just rinky-dink rock 'n' roll romance movies. Travelogues, Presley himself called 'em. Then Elvis went and got himself into the hands of a really good director for a TV special in 1968 that was supposed to revive his singing career. He was poured into this black leather biker suit and really poured on the performance power. That's what launched all those tours in the seventies. 'Course the Colonel soon squeezed the juice out of the comeback kid and got him on the treadmill of a stock touring show again. What a guy! You could always count on the Colonel to give an audience as little as he could get away with."

"I'm impressed. How did you learn all this stuff about Elvis and the Colonel? You must have boned up for the emcee job."

"Naw. I used to be a deejay back when music was on vinyl and only musicians were on drugs."

"A disk jockey? That far back?"

"Ah . . . I worked in small towns, behind the times. Why, how old did you think I was?" Buchanan's crooked smile grew crookeder under his black-dyed hair. Merle Conrad hadn't mentioned Vanity as a deadly sin, but she should have.

"Gee. I dunno. As old as Dick Clark?"

Buchanan paled.

"Isn't that a compliment?" Temple asked innocently. "Isn't he supposed to be extraordinarily youthful-looking?"

"For the mummy of King Tut-tut!" Buchanan's trade-mark snirk (what Temple called his patented combination of sneer and smirk) was fighting not to become a snarl. "That guy's generation and mine are not even kissing cousins. So don't worry, T.B. I'm young enough for you."

He leaned so close she could inhale the noxious scent of whatever goop was making his hair look both stiffened and greasy.

"Well, I'm too old for you." Temple said in farewell, turning and hiking away before he could offer one last parting snirk. Poor Quincey! Someone had to help that girl, and her mother was too much of a victim herself to do it.

She was facing into another trio of oncoming Elvis

imitators, and they were eyeing her like she was a fifteen-year-old fan.

Better to face dead men walking than Crawford Buchanan any day.

Chapter 8

Working on the Building

(A rousing gospel song Elvis recorded in 1960)

Temple finally decided that the Kingdome itself was a cross between the Coliseum in Rome and an Opryland Hotel.

She wandered through a semitropical Southern garden, past pillared gazebos, yet remained beneath an overarching glass dome. On the dome's perimeter, in niches high above the milling crowds, stood white marble statues of Elvis, attired like collector Barbie dolls in bejeweled jumpsuits concocted by the world's most famous designers. The neon role call of names above the designer-doll Elvi read like a mall sign in shoppers' paradise: Donatella Versace, Calvin Klein, Bill Blass, Bob Mackie, Gucci, Dior.

The circle of elevated Elvi regarded the vastness erected in their honor with cataract gazes: the blank white eyeballs of classic Greek statuary. The face of

Apollo (he wasn't copyrighted) stood in for Elvis's.

Actually, the time-tested, white-marble medium used to memorialize long-gone gods such as Apollo and Pan fit Elvis's full-lipped, Roman-nosed profile like an Attic glove, although the ghostly yet solid chorus line of Elvi also (and rather wickedly) reminded Temple of Pillsbury doughboys in candy-decorated astronauts' suits.

Just when Temple thought that Las Vegas had pulled out all of the stops, shown its best hand, exceeded the spectacle speed limit, outgrossed and grossed out, say, the Seven Wonders of the Ancient World, it would concoct another baked Alaska of entertainment: an overdone confection of fire and ice, a high-calorie extravaganza of fairy dust and fever like the Kingdome.

The real wonder was that the Kingdome had managed to evoke Elvis in all his incarnations without presenting one genuine artifact of Elvis Presley's roots, history, performing career, or personal life.

He might as well have been a dead god for anything material of him that survived in this mausoleum of ersatz mementos.

Above the roar of moving, talking people, a sound expanded like an invisible cloud over all their heads. It was not rock 'n' roll, although it was as hard to ignore.

High, piercing female shrieks.

Holy Hunk-a Burning Love! The hotel designers had even imported Elvis's screaming fans!

Temple clapped hands to ears. In this vast, marble-lined stadium, shrieks bounced off every hard surface, and the only softening surfaces here were the plants and the people.

The hubbub troubled no one else. Las Vegas tourists had long since learned to tune out programmed sights and sounds if they were discussing vital issues like the locations of loose slot machines, or looser women.

Temple hurried toward the stage where the sound probably originated, on the theory that it could only be better close up.

But when she arrived at what would be the mosh pit nowadays, she looked up at a dark and empty stage. No show at the moment, no screeching fans.

She released hands from ears. The screams had subsided.

Just when she thought it was safe to breathe normally again, shrieks resumed, so loud that the set of cymbals near the unattended drums vibrated in sympathy.

The sounds were coming from behind, and below, the stage.

Temple knew theatrical geography. She darted up the dark stairs at stage right, then dodged walls of ponderous velvet curtains and the toe-stubbing array of fly anchors in the wings behind them. She flailed in the dark until she found a stairwell leading to the dressing rooms below.

In that narrow, dark passage the screams turned positively painful. Temple burst into the bright light of a deserted hallway and followed the sounds to a dressing room.

And there, dead ahead of her, she found him dead: Jumpsuit Elvis, face down on the bare cement, a rampant rhinestone stallion on his back stabbed through the shoulder with a gold-studded dagger haft.

The screamer was reflected in the dressing table mirrors opposite Temple: a white-garbed Elvira, Mistress of the Dark, whose midnight tresses writhed like Medusa snakes against her long, flowing temple-virgin gown as she continued screaming.

Temple had either stumbled onto the set of a Roger Corman horror flick, or the scene of a crime. Given her past performance record, she'd opt for the scene of a crime.

Chapter 9

Paralyzed

(Otis Blackwell wrote the song for Elvis, and it
was recorded in 1956)

"Thank God you're here!"

Temple had no idea she was expected.

The white witch in the corner stared at Temple
through the black holes of her makeup-charred eyes.
Splayed fingers behind her hugged the wall as if it were
the gates to Hades and the fallen figure on the floor were
King Kong.

Come to think of it, the parallel to Elvis was not far-
fetched.

Temple did not like the way the fallen man's limbs
lay. Living flesh would not tolerate those straw-man
angles of muscle and bone.

She stared at the viscous red liquid pooling between
the winking rhinestones of the horse's bejeweled trap-
pings. Red blood. Fresh.

Then she reached into her tote bag for her cell phone.

This was a job for Crimes Against Persons, not PR persons on holiday.

"What's going on here?"

The newcomer was male, middle-aged, and dressed in faded work-shirt blues. Stage hand or maintenance man.

"Nothing we should mess with," Temple mumbled, scrolling through her computerized directory of key phone numbers, which just happened to include that of a certain homicide lieutenant.

The guy eyed the body, not moving. Then he took a step toward it.

"I'm not kidding," Temple warned. "You could contaminate the crime scene."

He glanced at her, baby-blue eyes puzzled under a worry-corrugated forehead that extended into thinning silver-blond hair. "It's just that I recognize something."

"The dead man?"

"No—"

Before Temple could issue another warning to leave the scene untouched, he darted forward, bent down and snatched something from the end of one twisted arm.

In fact, he snatched a forearm from the end of one twisted sleeve, now an empty twisted sleeve.

"Grooossss!" wailed the vixen impaled against the wall.

Temple couldn't decide whether to (a) scream too, (b) lose her Oreos or (c) jerk the idiot back with a well-executed martial arts move, of which she had mastered very few.

Then he held up his trophy: a long rolled oblong. Bone . . . ? Yuck. Or . . .

"That's nothing but a roll of paper towels," she said.

"Yeah." The guy's voice was taut with anger. "My cart got ripped off yesterday. A whole twelve-pack of goddammed paper towels."

Temple stared down at the spread-eagle Elvis suit. "He's just a straw man? Pardon me"—she glanced at the textured paper cylinder in the man's huge hand—"a Brawny-brand paper-towel man? And the blood?"

"You tell me, lady. Paper products is my job. Blood's another ball of wax."

Temple edged forward, squatted, and dipped a hesitant forefinger into the puddling red. "Fingernail polish!"

"Oh." The girl on the opposite wall waved a bouquet of scarlet-lacquered nails on long, pale-stemmed fingers. "A brand-new bottle of my favorite color, Vamp Tramp, was missing yesterday."

Temple's cell phone received a quiet and dignified interment in her tote bag. She was most thankful that she had not reached her party. "Is this someone's real costume, or what?"

Paper-towel man was shaking his head on the way out. "Don't ask me, lady. Ladies. I'll let maintenance know to clean up."

"No. Wait! This may not be a murder scene, but it is a malicious mischief scene. At the least, hotel security should be notified. And the . . . tableau should be photographed. And probably the components should be preserved."

"Who the heck are you?"

"I handle public relations for the Crystal Phoenix. I know what precautions to take."

"Okay. I'll tell someone who can make decisions. Me, I'm outa here. And . . . if this roll of paper towels might be evidence, keep it. I got plenty more where that came from."

He dropped the roll on the dressing table top and bowed out, quite literally.

"Really?" the woman in white asked in a small, wee voice. "It's just a dead . . . dummy?"

"Nothing but a deck of cards, honest."

The reference to *Alice in Wonderland* was lost on this Babe in Elvis land. Beneath the heavy swags of dark hair, her alabaster brow may have frowned, infinitesimally, as she spoke. "They play cards upstairs. Not down here. This is a dressing room."

"And what were you doing here?"

"Dressing."

"For what?" Temple asked. "And you act as if you know me."

The girl finally pushed off the wall and stepped forward. "Of course I do." She parted the river of long hair that made her face a pale stepping stone almost lost in its rippling brunette flow. "It's me."

" 'Me'?"

"Your posing partner! Well, not your partner. I mean, that would have been a little kinky, even for the cover-hunk pageant."

Temple grabbed the parted hair and separated it more. "Priscilla! I mean, Quincey. Of course! I forgot about you being here during the excitement. Wow. You look . . . unreal. Did Priscilla Presley really look like this?"

"Absolutely." Quincey Conrad patted her borrowed tresses into place again. "I have researched every detail of this role. I'm even wearing the required five pair of false eyelashes."

"Is that why your eyes are at half-mast?"

"I don't have half-mascara on! I have on half a bottle of Daddy Longlegs's Centipede Sweetie from the discount drug store. It's probably a lot more advanced than the stuff poor Cilla had to use, like, in the Stone Age, thirty years ago. It's got little ceramide microns in it. Thousands and thousands."

"I know. Billions and billions. Well. I'm sure the ceramide microns are delighted to be serving on your false eyelashes. You certainly don't look like yourself."

"Oh, honestly. Get with it, girlfriend. I have never looked like myself. What's the point?"

Temple nodded. "You may be strangely right. So. Tell me what happened here."

"You're so good at this . . . you know, calm and collected stuff. Can I sit down?"

Temple eyed the get-up. "That depends on your outfit, doesn't it?"

"Oh, everything was polyester then. Didn't wrinkle,

wears like diamond-dust nail polish. I got it at a funky little shop called Leopard Alley."

"Ah, yes. I remember it well."

"Hey! You know the place. Wild." Quincey pulled out a wooden ice-cream-style chair and stared down at the paper-towel-stuffed costume corpse. "That's probably one of the Elvis imitators' costumes. Poor thing. They pay a fortune for those corny, custom-made pjs, you know."

"I know Elvis must have, but even the imitators?"

"Oh, yeah. Unlike the cover hunks, their job isn't taking it off. Their job is putting it on. The whole schmeer. Suit, shoes, belt, hair, sideburns. Even a girdle, if necessary. People think women are phony when they dress up. Hah! No, those guys pay bunches and bunches to look like a has-been."

"So you don't get the Elvis mania."

"Oh, I get it. I mean, when he was young he knew how to be one foxy dude, once he got over having been a total groadie nerd in high school, but that's no reason to hold anything against him. I mean, a lot of surprising people were total groadie nerds in high school."

"All surprising people were total groadie nerds in high school."

"Really?"

"Haven't you ever felt like a total groadie nerd?"

Quincey curled the end of a false tress around a forefinger. "Maybe. Once. For a few seconds. But I got over it."

"Hmmm. Anyway, you came in here to make up, and that's when you found him?"

"I came in here to check on my makeup bag." She nodded at a quart-size quilted fuchsia zipper bag on the otherwise empty length of communal dressing table. "Sometimes those Elvis boys borrow my stuff, you know? Especially my Daddy Longleg's Centipede Sweetie mascara."

"They use mascara?"

"Oh, girl. He did. Why shouldn't they?"

"No reason. I mean, men in theater use makeup: foundation, eyeliner, but mascara—?"

"Well, what's a poor guy to do when his eyelashes fade?"

"But Elvis was dark-haired."

"Only after a good dose of Lady Clairol. That's why he had to mascara his lashes and dye his eyebrows. I've researched these things. That's why Priscilla dyed her hair jet-black. Elvis wanted her that way too. Her real hair was, you know. Dishwater brown. Yuck."

"What color is your hair?"

"I don't know. Maybe brown or something, but not often. Well, you must know; you do your hair red."

"No, I don't 'do' it. It grows in that way."

"You mean you look like this naturally? Way cool. Some people are born lucky."

"Not many. And none of them like their original hair, believe me. Why was Elvis hung up on dark hair?"

"He decided that dark-haired actors had better movie careers, that they came off better on the screen."

"You *have* researched this." Temple couldn't help sounding impressed.

"Oh, yeah. I even had to go in and apply for a library card so I could take out all the books on Elvis. No way am I being paid enough to buy them. Did you know there were places that had all these books on people's lives, with all the dirty parts left in? Free? Weird. And Elvis was one of the weirdest."

"So I've heard tell." Temple turned to regard the construction on the floor. "It's the wig that fools you into thinking it's a real body at first glance. Somebody worked overtime to fashion this makeshift Elvis. Any idea why?"

Quincey interlaced her dagger-tipped fingers. "Yeah. They all hate me. They want to get me. This was just another warning."

Temple pulled out a wooden chair and sat on it. "I know about that."

"Is that why you're here?" Quincey's posture perked up. She looked like an overdressed puppet whose invisible strings had just been pulled taut.

"Yup. Your mother called me in."

Quincey deflated into a scornful sixteen-year-old. "My mother."

"She's really concerned about you. Okay, that's an old story and you're tired of it. But after what I've seen here, I'm concerned about you too."

Quincey slumped, lipsticked bottom lip swollen with rebellion. "You're not my mother."

"Darn right, I'm not. So I can walk right out on you, and this murdered scarecrow, and my conscience won't bother me one little teeny bit."

"Good!"

"Just what I think."

"Then why aren't you walking?"

"And leave the scene of a crime unguarded? You go ahead."

"Right." Quincey jumped up, shaking out her Priscilla tresses like a spoiled preschooler. "I know what I'm doing, I'm getting paid for it. I'm good at it. I'll be all right."

"Right."

"Okay." Quincey swept—and in a floor-length pink polyester dress with girlish ties at the back it's hard to "sweep"—to the dressing room door.

"Not only that," Temple added grudgingly. "You've even got the screams down real good."

Quincey's back stiffened. Then she turned. "You really think someone wants to kill me? I mean, Priscilla?"

"I don't know yet. Do you?"

Quincey shook her head, no small achievement with about twelve pounds of borrowed hair on her head. "Did you hear about the . . . tattoo?"

"I heard about a razor attack."

"Oh, Mom loves to exaggerate! It was just four little slashes. Really, all the girls at school are so jealous. It's so cool, and I didn't even have to pay for it. And no one can blame me for getting it, like a real tattoo. 'E' as in Elvis. The girls at school are beginning to think even Elvis might be cool. So I didn't tell them the really bad parts about his life."

"I'm sure he appreciates your discretion, wherever he is."

"He really, you know, liked girls my age. Or younger. Even when he was really old, like forty."

"Really?" Despite her acceptably cool tone, Temple felt a stab of what could only be borrowed maternal outrage.

"That's why I'm so perfect to play Priscilla. I'm just like her." She moved to the mirror, stared at her false image. "I even look like her."

Temple didn't tell her that Priscilla in this form was an icon, just as Elvis in his many incarnations was always an icon. That these carefully created images could be assumed by anybody who cared enough to try reasonably hard. Archetypes. Sixties Priscilla the virgin-whore. Elvis . . . the what? Temple could tell by taking one look at Quincey's Priscilla what the image conveyed. She didn't know enough about Elvis to do other than guess. Rebel, maybe, like James Dean. But that had to have been fifties Elvis. What would explain seventies Elvis?

"How did you get this gig?" Temple asked. Merle had told her, but she wanted to hear Quincey's version. Mother and daughter were each at an age, and a stage in their relationship, where the chances of anything about them jibing were nil.

Quincey sighed. "Crawf, who else?"

" 'Crawf?' That's what you call him?"

"Yeah. What's it to you?"

"I call him 'Awful Crawford' myself."

" 'Crawf' sort of sounds like barfing."

"Especially if you have a cat."

"You have a cat?"

"As much as anyone ever does."

"Crawf hates cats."

"I'm not surprised. You can't trust anyone who doesn't like cats."

Quincey's Egyptian eyes lowered to the gaudy faux body on the floor. "Did Elvis like cats, I wonder?"

"Don't you know, with all that reading?"

"No . . . he had a few dogs and horses, but I never heard of a cat."

. Temple nodded sagely. Sometimes the most important things about people never made it into the history books.

Chapter 10

The Hillbilly Cat Scat

(Elvis was called the Hillbilly Cat in tribute to
his mingled country and rhythm and blues
persona early in his career)

Did Elvis like cats?

Does your daddy not dance and your mama not rock
'n' roll? I thought so.

I have made it over to the Kingdome hard on my little
doll's heels.

And my little doll's heels are usually hard on her and
anybody who gets in her way.

So I am discreetly eavesdropping from the hall when
this discussion over the fallen, fake-dead Elvis takes
place.

There are so many fake-live Elvi in the world, not to
mention just in this hotel right now, that a dead Elvis, fake
or not, has by now become a novelty.

Like all of my breed, I thrive on investigating novelty.
That is why I cannot resist following Miss Temple to this
emporium of all things Elvis, and my instincts prove true,

given the shenanigans I am (over) hearing about. While a punctured jumpsuit hardly has the makings of a federal case, a punctured Priscilla Presley impersonator sniffs of nefarious deeds to come. My expert help is now at the service of one and all, whether they know it or not.

And I know a thing or two about the cool cats of the world. That is how I am aware that when Elvis Presley first burst onto the music scene, they did not know whether he was black or white or blues or country, so they called him the Hillbilly Cat. See, hillbilly music was all-white whining, and rhythm and blues were only wailed in black bars then, so combining the two sounds was something daring.

It was so new and daring that it would eventually get that Hillbilly Cat named the King of Rock 'n' Roll, which is what everybody decided to call the new blend once it was rolling off of every radio in the country.

What do I know about music? Listen, I have been a backyard one-man band all of my life. All of us down and out sorts, whatever the color of our coats, like to get together for a good community wail now and then. Not that my breed has ever been much chased by record companies throwing big-money contracts at us, just by irate sleepers hurling shoes and chamberpots. Not everyone has an ear for music. And, luckily, almost no one has a chamberpot these days.

I must say that I am glad to see my Miss Temple getting out of the house and into a new environment. She has spent far too much time around the Circle Ritz these days, worrying about the care and feeding of this one human dude or the other, when there I sit needing a fresh bribe on my dry pile of Free-to-Be-Feline nuggets.

But I see that shenanigans of a sinister sort have lured her from the domestic front to the center of the newest action on the Strip, and that cannot be a bad thing.

As for someone who would find it necessary to create his—or her—own murder victim before plunging in the fatal dagger, what can you expect in a town that is all show and go and no substance?

I see that the age of the Virtual Victim is upon us, especially when someone has gone to the trouble of offing the mannequin of a dead man. Pretty soon there will be a computer game available for this scenario.

But for now, the outré spectacle of a murdered costume is real-time, in the here and now.

Only in Las Vegas, of course.

Chapter 11

Any Way You Want Me

(A million-selling hit Elvis recorded in his
Golden Year of 1956 at RCA)

A head poked around the dressing room door.

"I heard about the deceased jumpsuit and came to see
it if was one of mine."

The face was cherubic under a gleaming helm of high,
wide, and handsome dark hair, with the heavy sideburns
resembling the hinged metal side-flaps on a knight's helmet.

Temple had never pictured Elvis Presley as Sir Lan-
celot, but these stylized wigs sure made the comparison
apt. The hair looked lacquered enough to resist a direct
hit by a medieval mace.

"Hi, Kenny," Quincey greeted him.

The Elvis imitator sashayed into the room, still gazing
at the fallen jumpsuit with fascinated disbelief. "Man,
that's one of those wool-gabardine numbers out of De-

troit. Must be worth three grand . . . or was before the blood got on it."

"Nail polish," Temple said, drawing his attention for the first time.

"Say, this must be a shock for you, kid, coming over to visit your classmate and running into a ruined Elvis suit."

Most gainfully employed women of thirty would be thrilled to be taken for a high-school senior. Temple, at five-feet-three tops in high heels, considered it a declaration of war.

"I do PR for the Crystal Phoenix," she said as crisply as a military officer giving rank. "We've had a . . . manifestation at a construction site and I came over here to look into it."

Kenny frowned, which did not budge his hairline a centimeter. "Why would you come over here to check out a problem on a work site all the way over at the Crystal Phoenix?"

"The disruption was apparently an Elvis sighting."

"Whoo, boy! There's a few of those in town right now, and I bet that's always happening." He nodded at the suit. "Wow. This thing has been laid out, excuse the expression, in the position of a chalk body outline from a crime show on TV. D'you suppose the suit was out for an unauthorized walk, got attacked at the Phoenix, and made it back here before collapsing?"

"Anything is possible," Temple said, meaning it.

Standing here talking to a five-feet-six Elvis clone (the real one had been around six feet, she guessed) with a sixties Priscilla Presley looking on was more than a trip down memory lane, it was a trip, period. And trips like that, Temple had supposed, were mostly of seventies vintage, when LSD was the operating system of choice.

Quincey must have decided that too, because she sat down and returned to arranging her layers of false eyelashes in the mirror, using a straight pin to strip the excess mascara off each one. There was a lot of excess mascara to lose.

Kenny shook his head sadly at the dead jumpsuit. "I'm glad it isn't one of mine. Bet it wasn't insured either. We put a lot of time and heart and soul into our acts, but we put our cash into the jumpsuits. And the hair." He pointed upward, as if anyone could miss the Hair.

"So word about the ruined jumpsuit is getting around," Temple said, encouraging further confidences.

She wanted to figure out if there was any reason an Elvis imitator would make an unscheduled appearance at the Jersey Joe Jackson Mine Ride-in-progress. Or if anyone might have a motive for laying someone's expensive costume low. Anything that touched the Crystal Phoenix was her business.

Kenny pulled out a wooden chair, flipped it around and sat so he could cradle his forearms on the back. He was a bantam Elvis, chunky, with overdeveloped muscles rather than fat, his high hair like a brunet coxcomb. Despite his rounded features, no one would mistake him for a high-schooler. Temple guessed that he was a decade older than she.

"Word gets around," Kenny admitted. "We all watch what the others are doing."

"Paranoid?"

"Naw, eager to learn. After all, there's no one like us, right?"

"How many are running around the hotel?"

"Gosh, maybe a hundred."

"A hundred?"

"This is the biggest Elvis-impersonator competition ever. Everybody's here from the Grand Old Men who invented the art to the rawest new kids on the block."

"And where do you rank?"

"Somewhere in the middle." Kenny grinned. "But anything can happen. It's a competition, right?"

"Competitive enough for somebody to ice somebody else's jumpsuit?"

"Gee, Elvis was red, white, and blue suede shoes. I'd hate to think someone would get petty in his name. None of us would be doing this if we didn't revere the man's talent and what he stood for. So, no, I can't imagine one of us sinking that low. Besides, any competition's a crapshoot. It'd be better to attack the judges than some poor innocent jumpsuit."

"This looks like a pretty spectacular one. I'd hate to duplicate it on short notice."

Kenny shook his head mournfully. "I couldn't feel worse seeing that destroyed there, other than seein' some guy in it. God, I put in every spare minute and nickel for the past three years to get myself here. When I first started performing at karaoke clubs around Philly, I got laughed off the stage until I got good enough to laugh back. Someone who'd ruin any Elvis imitator's mainstay deserves to be stabbed in the back too."

"But your suits are safe."

"Better be. I got two. A lot of guys only got one and they put all their hopes and dreams and their best buddies' cash into it. Families, friends, they gotta support your Elvis habit, or you wouldn't make it this far."

Temple was actually starting to choke up over the ruined jumpsuit.

For an Elvis impersonator, she saw, a jumpsuit was a costly second skin. Designing and underwriting one was the single biggest commitment he made to his avocation. Whoever had thrust the gaudy dagger through the rhinestone stallion had also stabbed a metaphorical blow into the owner's heart.

Malicious mischief wasn't quite strong enough to describe the ruin wreaked here.

"It could be dirty tricks before the competition," she said.

Kenny nodded. "Or it could be someone who hates the King, in any form."

"That would mean you all were in danger."

Kenny's bright blue eyes squinted almost closed. "He did get a lot of death threats when he was alive. You'd sorta hope that would stop when he was dead."

"I thought he was still showing up here and there regularly."

"So the tabloids say. That's always been the big joke."

"What?"

"That Elvis faked his own death because he was tired of all the hoopla. That he's out here somewhere, masquerading as an Elvis imitator."

"He'd be . . . how old?"

"Almost retirement age. Sixty-four."

"Do you think he could pass as himself at that age?"

"I've seen dudes that old pass as Elvis at thirty-five. I even saw a woman do a great Comeback Elvis."

"Why would a woman want to imitate Elvis?"

"Same reason we all do: loved the sound and the songs; loved the King."

Kenny's voice had sunk to a reverential hush.

"What kind of work do you do, Kenny, when you're not doing Elvis?"

He hung his head a little. Maybe he was shy, or maybe the helmet of hair was too heavy a burden to carry.

"Shoe salesman in the mall. And no, they don't make blue suede shoes anymore, least not for guys. Say, those are some sharp heels you got on there."

"That's the general idea," Temple said. A three-inch heel was a portable dagger.

Chapter 12

I Forget to Remember
to Forget

(A catchy song Elvis recorded for RCA in 1956;
record execs were much higher on it than his
next recording, "Heartbreak Hotel")

He'd look at the old photos now and then.

Where had he gone, Young Elvis? And Middle Elvis—didn't those damn Egyptians have a Middle Kingdom or somethin'? He didn't count for much, Middle Elvis. A flash in the developing pan: for a few blinks of the camera's eye lean and mean in a black leather suit. Just a bridge over troubled waters. And then there was Jumpsuit Elvis, and he'd been pretty good almost to the end, except you could see it in his eyes, in the photos. Zonked on pharmaceuticals. So finally he became Ultimate Elvis. Fat and Forty Elvis. Even Johnny Carson on the *Tonight Show* took potshots at Fat Elvis. That had hurt. He watched TV a lot. And he didn't shoot out the screen, either. He was too weary by then to hit back.

Parade-blimp Elvis. Nothin' to hide behind but his own excesses. But were they ever his own? Ever'body owned him. His mama and his daddy, his Colonel Parker and his Memphis Mafia, his playgirls and his maybe-real girls, who touched him just enough to make him not ever wanta get burned that way again.

When he was young, he could eat what he wanted, play with what he wanted, screw what he wanted. Or what wanted him.

And everythin' movin' did.

Oh, yeah.

That's all right, Mama.

The King frowned. It wasn't all right, Mama. Never had been.

No one had told him. He never knew he couldn't just keep on keepin' on. That there'd be consequences.

Consequences! Hell, that was the name of a town in New Mexico with "Truth or" in front of it. He'd never visited that tank town, though the Colonel had him traipsing through every whistle-stop in America. Never out of America, though. Turned out his whole career was driven by what Colonel Parker had to hide. Where were the tell-all books about that? How the Colonel was an illegal Dutch alien, so he kept turning down flat all of the million-dollar offers to play Europe or Japan or Australia, challenging moves that would have kept a performer interested in his own life and career, instead of getting bored to death. Or on the way the Colonel kissed the King off to Hollywood, for thirty-two quick-shoot movies that minimized his performing talent just to maximize everybody's profit. Or how he ran him ragged in Las Vegas with two shows a night because the Colonel owed millions in gambling debts to the International Hotel owner, even when it later became the Las Vegas Hilton. Colonel played and Elvis paid. And paid. And paid, until there was only one way to stop.

No use crying over spilt buttermilk, though.

The Colonel was finally dead now after living to the ripe old age of eighty-seven. And Elvis is still going strong, in one way or the other.

He bestirred himself to open one of the long row of mirrored closet doors.

Time to go out. To see and be seen. Let's see. What would he wear?

His pale, beringed hand reached out for something white.

Chapter 13

All Shook Up

(Elvis's 1957 all-time hit, thirty weeks on the
charts; Elvis's "Yeah, Yeah" here inspired the
trio of yeahs in Lennon and McCartney's "She
Loves Me." Elvis had recorded a song named
"Yeah, yeah, yeah" in 1954.)

Matt Devine was thirty-five minutes into his midnight
radio show, but it felt like he had only spent about ten
minutes at the microphone.

Maybe he was getting good at this.

Or maybe this had been an easy night.

He'd had the usual lovelorn listeners he inherited from
Ambrosia's earlier "music for misery" three-hour show.
"Music for misery" was Matt's name for it. Also "soft
rock for hard times." To be fair, not everyone who called
in was feeling blue; some wanted a sentimental song to
celebrate a new love, or a dedicated parent or sibling.
Still, it added up to a three-hour stint of with-it schmaltz.

Matt and his "serious" talk show was supposed to be
the heavy hitter; the real counselor. But it was hard for
Matt to take the emotional scratches and contusions
of call-ins to WCOO-AM seriously after months of

handling hot-line counseling for ConTact. There the daily owies ranged from domestic violence to drug overdose to suicide, life-threatening problems that were sometimes still in progress.

Still, he had debuted on this station to handle an almost-infanticide, and he'd rather help apply Band-Aids than perform CPR any day.

"So what d'you think, Mr. Midnight?" the tentative female voice was asking for all the world to hear. "Should I ditch Spencer and stick with Kirby?"

Given names nowadays! Hard to imagine what a St. Spencer or a St. Kirby would be like. As for a St. Tiffany . . .

"Tiffany, it's your life. You're only sixteen. You don't have to choose anyone yet. You have a right to tell both guys you want to play the field. You have a right to pick one, or neither. What you don't have a right to do is be dishonest with them, or yourself."

"Right." She didn't sound like the road had become clear and straight ahead of her, or ever would. "I know! Maybe I should find a third guy. That way neither one can blame the other, or me."

"You could try life without a boyfriend for a while."

"Really? I never thought of that."

"Maybe you don't need to know more guys. Maybe you need to know yourself a little better so you can figure out what guys are right for you."

"Oh, that is such a radical idea, Mr. Midnight. Guess what I'm gonna do? Nothing. I'm gonna stay home nights and listen to your show, and figure out what everybody else is doing. It'll be like going to school, right?"

"Maybe." At moments like this, Matt longed to simply end the conversation with some schmaltzy song, as Ambrosia did. With a voice as warm and mellow as her café-au-lait skin, "Ambrosia" was producer Leticia Brown's seven-to-midnight alter ego. Mr. Midnight, unfortunately, sang a cappella. "Whatever you do, do it for yourself first. If you don't know who you are, you won't be able to tell who anyone else is."

"Oooh. That is so right on. Thank you, Mr. Midnight. I'll be here, listening to you."

That's what Matt was afraid of. In the commercial radio counseling game, it seemed that the messenger, not the message, was the big attraction.

Radio was an anonymous medium, but it wasn't a private one, like the hotline. Matt still felt uneasy about the difference.

In the control booth, Ambrosia/Leticia was giving him the thumb's-up sign. Her beautiful, upbeat face was his lifeline. She didn't have to stay after her gig, but she had hired him. She planned on babying him along, especially after his spectacular debut.

"Great, Matt," her deep voice, so like a cat's that had swallowed a brandy Alexander, purred over the headphones. "You're developing quite a teeny-bopper following."

"That's good?"

"That's very good. That's the groove the advertisers crave."

And that's what was happening while they talked: commercials were playing, paying his salary.

Leticia lifted a forefinger like a chorus director. When it descended, another voice was humming in his ears, male this time.

"This, ah, that midnight talk show?"

"Certainly is. The Midnight Hour on WCOO-AM: talk radio with heart." Matt delivered this corny line with as much heart as he could muster.

"I'm just sittin' here, and I heard your last caller. There sure are a lot of lonely little girls out there."

"Tiffany wasn't exactly lonely; that was the point."

"Yeah, well, I got a lot of sympathy for kids these days, with all the drugs and bad folks that are out there. We really oughta do somethin' about that."

"We keep trying. So, what can I help you with to-night?"

"Me? I just wanta help other people. I'm in a position of some influence, you know."

"No, I don't."

"Bein' an entertainer and all. Folks look up to you. Sometimes, though, it can be a pain in the butt. They just gotta come around and get all that attention. I try to give 'em as much back as I can, but it's endless. Just endless."

"Is that your problem?"

"Hell, it's not a problem, son! It's success."

"Seems to me success has been a problem to a lot of people, especially some of those whose acts have played this town."

The man laughed, deep and easy. Matt was having flashbacks to another Vegas celebrity he had unwittingly counseled at ConTact. A light sweat prickled his skin as he remembered that man's manipulative dark side. Their conversations had become antagonistic and deeply personal. Matt wanted to avoid that sort of game on live radio at all costs. It catered to the caller's egocentric needs and did him no good. And it did Matt's psyche not a bit of good either. It was like dueling Lucifer, a being of pride and power and incidental evil. Matt's past as a priest made him all too open to other people's spiritual ills.

"Well, now, see, I'm not just your ordinary performer. I put my whole soul into my shows. And my fans, man, they put their souls right out there, in the palm of my hands. I'm just a wringin'-wet rag when I come off that stage. Hell, I gotta have guys onstage to wipe my brow and bring me water."

Matt was scouring his brain. Who could this be? Who that big was playing Vegas right now? Who that big would call a dinky show like the Midnight Hour?

"These big Vegas shows sure are marathons of endurance," Matt said sympathetically, playing for time.

"En-dur-ance. That is the word, son. I can't hardly sleep until dawn after one of these babies. I can't hardly sleep ever."

"The adrenaline of performance can be pretty hard to burn off afterwards," Matt said, remembering that Temple had often stayed up with Max Kinsella, the magician, until he "came down" after his two evening shows. Even Matt was experiencing trouble sleeping now that he had a midnight performance date every Wednesday to Sunday. "Maybe you need someone around to help you come down."

This time the laugh went on as long as an aria. "I got somebody. I got truckloads of somebodies; always had, always will. I am not alone unless I wanta be. And when I don't wanta be alone, I just snap my fingers and I got people to do whatever I wanta do when I wanta do it: play pool, play football, play footsie and a lot more."

"Sounds like you could do more to do what the people around need and want, instead of just indulge yourself."

"I work my ass off, and they get a lot of privileges workin' for me. It's a rough schedule, two shows a night, night after night. And these shows are all me. I'm not as young as I usta be, gotta have a doctor travel with me, to tend my needs, you know? I give those guys and girls plenty. Least they could do is what I want, when I need it."

"I understand. I'm just saying it might not be good for you to have everyone in your life arranging theirs totally around you, no matter what you pay them. You can't buy love."

"Hey, what're you sellin'? A song title? Been done, son. And you're wrong. You can buy love. I've done it." A pause, for the first time. "Loyalty, though. You can't buy that. I been burned there. All those guys and girls, all blowin' off their mouths after they left me, tellin' the inside story on this and the inside story on that. Makin' me look like a pitiful fool. Makin' money off me even when they're long off the payroll."

"People can betray you," Matt agreed. He glanced at Leticia, wondering if he should lose the guy. She'd like the idea of a celebrity performer calling in, but this guy could be doing stand-up comedy in some fringe club, for all Matt knew. And his voice was slurred with sleep, or with something stronger.

But Leticia's expression was rapt beyond the glass window, and her hand was making the circling motion that meant: keep it going.

"What can I do to help you?" Matt asked.

"Well, son, I came up the hard way, never got much education . . . not that I wasn't plenty sharp. I made me, and don't let anyone tell you different. But it all just hit so fast when I was so young, and before you know it I'm hidin' out from fans. Though I never did manage to hide out from the pretty ones, you know what I mean?"

Matt disliked the complacent womanizing tone. "So you only care about attractive fans."

"No, man! You don't know me. I love 'em all, and they love me back. But there are . . . side benefits, all right? But that was before I got in touch with my spiritual side."

Matt rolled his eyes at Leticia. This guy sounded about as spiritual as a tire iron.

"I had my fun," the caller admitted. "More than any one man has ever had, I'll bet. But I lost my mama when I was young, and we were real close. Couldn't buy her all the things she'd never had, she was gone that fast. Couldn't buy her anything then, but at least she had that pink Cadillac. She didn't drive, but what's money for but spendin'? Wish I'd-a watched who was spendin' what, though. I had to work too hard on my movies and stage shows to wanta do much but have fun when I wasn't workin'. Guess I shoulda been watchin' the purse strings, like they say. I made a lotta money, but a lotta people made too much money off me. It makes me mad, to tell you the truth, when I lie here after a show and everybody's gone and my mind goes round and round, and nothin' can touch that feelin' and I can't sleep no matter what I take. I shoulda watched out for myself more. But I thought I was payin' them to watch out for me. And they did, as much as I'd let 'em. Maybe I didn't let 'em much."

"The problems you describe are very real, except for the scale you live your life on. You're too pampered, that's the problem. You sound too isolated. If you have so many people around taking care of your every want, why do you need to call me?"

"That's just it. Seems like they're not around anymore. First my mama gone, then my little-girl wife and my little girl, then some of the boys turned on me. I don't know what to do. I try to go on with my shows, but they take so much out of me, and it gets harder and harder to live from show to show. Oh, they say, see a shrink, but I'm not gonna have no guy rootin' around in my head where no one can see it. I'm in a rut and I don't know how to get out of it. I need to talk to somebody I don't pay, and you're the only one I could think of."

Matt caught sight of Leticia's flailing arm, hand pointing to her wrist watch. Almost out of time.

"You have big problems all right; more than a few minutes on a phone can solve."

"Maybe I can call again."

Matt devoutly hoped not, but this show was like an old-fashioned confessional: you couldn't stop anyone who wanted to from walking in, keeling down, and confessing all their sins. Here, at least, you could cut them off the air if they took too much time, and this guy definitely had.

"You can always call again," Matt said reassuringly, but he had already grown cynical enough to add mentally, *if anyone lets you through.*

"That's good. That's all right." The man sounded genuinely relieved, and Matt felt a stab of pity for him. "Thank you. Thank you verra much."

Matt rolled his head on his shoulders while taking off the headphones, reducing the muscle tension. The fading rant of a local car dealer commercial was still droning in his ears when Leticia burst into the studio.

When a woman has the face of an archangel, the energy of a whirling dervish, and a three-hundred-pound body, any place she enters is a break-in.

"I know. I let this guy run on too long."

"Too long? Didn't you recognize his voice?"

"Recognize his voice? The only celebrity I ever counseled before was at ConTact, and this wasn't him. This voice was baritone, all right, but with a slurry kind of accent."

"A Southern accent, maybe."

"Yeah, but it was, ah, softened, like he'd been out of the South for some time."

"Oh, he sure has, honey chile. That man has been off the planet for twenty-two years."

"He's that far gone mentally, huh? Sorry, I guess I'm not up on the entertainers at all the hotels. Should I have known him?"

Leticia said nothing, just came over and enveloped him in a smothering, industrial-strength hug.

"Matt, baby, you are the sweetest, out-of-the-loop thing, bless your heart. Don't you even have a clue who that was? Watch our numbers soar now! That was the Hillbilly Cat, Mr. Las Vegas, the King of Rock 'n' Roll, E. the P., the no-longer-late Elvis Presley, or I'm just ninety pounds of soggy grits and chitlin's."

"But . . . he's dead."

"Not on WCOO-AM he isn't. Ohhh, baby!"

Chapter 14

Louie, Louie

(Elvis recorded the 1898-composed "The Whiffenpoof Song," which mentions a Temple Bar and Louie the bartender in 1968; it was used in 1969's *The Trouble with Girls*)

Okay, Elvis never recorded any version of my eponymous song, that venerable drinking anthem that has so enlivened the past couple decades.

But he *did* record "The Whiffenpoof Song," another, far older drinking song in which I and my Miss Temple Barr are mentioned. (Indirectly, of course, but we always were discreet. Or rather, I was. I cannot speak for Miss Temple Barr, especially during her obscure years before she met me.)

The King recorded Whiffenpoof back in '68, and it was used a year later in one of his films, *The Trouble with Girls*. Not that the King had any trouble with girls other than beating them off.

This is how I know so much about the ultimate E. We have a lot in common.

After my undercover visit to the Kingdome, it is natural

that Elvis should be on my mind. I have retreated home to the Circle Ritz overnight, so Miss Temple finds me innocently sitting on her sofa or her bed, whichever will inconvenience her most at the moment, apparently lazing away my days and nights. Like Nero Wolfe, my mind is most active when I appear most physically inactive.

It is clear that any hijinks involving Elvis, whether at the Crystal Phoenix or the Kingdome, will require a vast insight into the man, his life, and times. For me, this is a snap. We have a lot in common.

You could say that Elvis Presley and I are synonymous with Las Vegas.

True, he did not appear to recognize the concept of "low-profile," and I am a master of blending into my environment, but we share a certain raw animal magnetism and a taste for exotic dishes both voluptuary and culinary.

Neither of us went for health food, that was for sure. I am certain all are familiar with E's adoration of burnt-black bacon, hard-fried eggs you could use as blackjacks, buttermilk biscuits, and the infamous fried banana-peanut-butter sandwiches. To him, fruit and vegetables were major abominations, as the Free-to-Be-Feline food pellets that resemble health-store pills are to me.

I do lack E's flair and passion for dressing up, and I do not need the services of his later, ever-present sunglasses. My sunglasses, like my concealed weapons, are built in. I have these laser-fast pupils that contract to shut out too much light. I bet Elvis would have really grooved on my eyes, could he have begged, borrowed, or bought them.

And he would have tried.

Chapter 15

Heartbreak Hotel

(Written by Tommy Durden and Hoyt Axton's
mother Mae, snapped up by Elvis in November
1955, and recorded in January 1956; Elvis's first
million-seller)

"Temple," Matt said to Temple over the phone, "can I
presume on your expertise again?"

"Something to do with talk shows?"

"Just my radio show. Could you come up and hear
my new tape player?"

"Now?"

"Today would be good. Before I have to do another
show."

"That urgent? Well, sure."

Temple hung up, looking through her closet for some
visiting outfit more appropriate than a sweat suit.

As she hopped on one foot hunting the matching shoe
on the closet floor, she did wonder how Max would like
all this semiprofessional hobnobbing between his former
rival and herself. Darn him, anyway! Why did he have
to be off on one of his mysterious missions, which had

gotten mysteriouser after the recent murder of the stripper he had tried to help? Temple froze, transfixed by a stab of real worry. Max ran on an exaggerated sense of responsibility for every ill in the world. His teenaged cousin's tragic death in Ireland had started the cycle so long ago . . . who would end it?

Of course, it was ludicrous to consider Matt anyone's rival. A less competitive personality she had never met, or maybe she'd just never seen him want anything he had difficulty getting. Like her.

Had she been drawn into this help-Matt campaign as a clever way of entangling her emotionally? Matt had shown signs of being seriously interested, also confessing that he had a lot of personal issues to resolve first. She sighed. Ex-priests were so hard to read. She only knew one, admittedly.

By the time she'd worried the pros and cons of both men to shreds in her mind, she was dressed and ready to visit the apartment directly overhead. What Max might think of such neighborliness was none of his business, so long as it was just neighborly.

When Matt answered her knock, he seemed too excited to notice her appearance. "What do you know about Elvis Presley?" he demanded before the door had even closed behind her.

"Elvis Presley?" The weird coincidence knocked her out. "Strange that you should ask, but virtually nothing."

"As little as I'm likely to know about him?"

"Probably not that little."

"Then listen to this." Matt grabbed her wrist—grabbed!—to hustle her into the living room. There he positioned her dead center on his red suede couch.

He then grabbed (grabbed again) the stereo remote control from one of the modest gray coffee table cubes. He pointed it at the shelf unit stereo, which squatted like a technological god on a primitive islander's makeshift altar: a board across two brick pillars.

"Listen!" Matt ordered.

Ordered? Matt?

He didn't even sit beside her, but paced behind the sinuous fifties-style sofa, so she couldn't crane her neck to read his face for some clue to this charade.

A moment later Matt's voice came over the tape, mellow yet intense, that nice combo of styles he brought to electronic media so naturally that seasoned on-air personalities would spit to hear it.

A young girl's voice, vacant and unformed, was fading off.

On came a man's voice, a little mushy but also mellow in its own way.

Temple listened for a few moments, then planted her elbows on her knees and her chin on her fists and listened harder. Behind her Matt paced, his footsteps making the fifty-year-old wood parquet floor creak at intervals, like a scratch in an obsolete vinyl record.

" 'Son,' " she repeated the caller once. "That's an old Southernism."

"Speaking of old . . . how old do you think he sounds?"

"Ummm. Mature. Middle-aged. But with a mischievous, maybe even melancholy boyish quality . . . no, not quite that, maybe a little self-mocking."

Matt aimed the remote and suddenly shot the sound off, either pausing or muting the recording. "So? What do you think?"

She finally turned to confront him. "I think if you hadn't mentioned Elvis, I'd never be thinking what I'm thinking."

"Which is?"

"That it's supposed to be Elvis."

Matt made a noise behind her, then came around the sofa end to perch uneasily on a curve. "What do you mean 'supposed'?"

"I mean the man is stone dead. Been that way since nineteen seventy-seven."

"Is that when he died? That long ago?"

"Yes. Don't tell me you don't remember? I thought it was a Crucial Twentieth-Century Date, like when Kennedy was assassinated, or Martin Luther King, or Bobby Kennedy, or when Marilyn Monroe died."

"We're too young to have lived through or remember much about those other deaths, but I was around for Elvis's death and I don't remember it. I do remember when Pope John Paul the First died."

"Not exactly the same thing, Matt."

He grinned. "That's why I need expert advice. Was that a credible Elvis?"

"I don't know. I'm not an Elvis expert. I can tell you that Las Vegas happens to be crawling with Elvis impersonators at the moment, and I bet a lot of them sound pretty credible."

"Elvis imitators, really? Why?"

"Ever heard that the Kingdome is coming?"

"Kingdom—?"

Temple loved teasing people with the name. "Not the Kingdom, the Kingdome, and not the athletic facility in Seattle that's just been torn down, either. It's the new Elvis Presley-themed hotel-casino."

"How could I have missed that? And you say that a host of Elvis imitators is in town for the opening? So my guy is just some Elvis imitator?"

"That's the best guess."

"But why?"

"Good publicity?"

Matt sighed. "Leticia is really jazzed on that call. Says it'll skyrocket the show's ratings."

"Probably will. And since when have you used a verb like 'jazzed'? Is working for that radio station corrupting you?"

Matt shook off her gentle jibe, still concentrating on what bothered him. "You don't think the radio station, Leticia—?"

"Would arrange for Elvis to 'phone home' without telling you? No." Temple glanced at him, measuring his mood. "But the thing about you, Matt, is you're such a sincere, natural radio personality. If they did want to encourage more sensational news, like that call from the unwed mother a couple weeks ago, they might be tempted not to tell you it was a set up deal."

"I would never approve of a deception like that."

"Of course not, and I'm sure they know that. Besides, if it was a setup, you'd be a whole lot more believable if you really bought it."

"They'd do that? Trick me? Use me?"

"You ever hear the story how some mean director got Jackie Cooper to cry as a child actor? He lied and told him his dog was dead, then shot the scene."

"Well, nobody's telling me Elvis isn't dead. And I wouldn't cry for him anyway. I mean, I know nothing about the man, except for his scandalous lifestyle."

"Right, you were listening to old Bob Dylan instead of early Elvis. Talk about far-spectrum opposites. It is kind of amazing how it all came together in the late fifties and early sixties: Elvis making hard-edged rock 'n' roll out of the rockabilly and rhythm and blues closet, Bob Dylan leaving the Minnesota Iron Range to troll for authentic folk music in the South, then the Beatles borrowing from both and blowing in from England and blowing away both folk and rock for a while."

"Huh? That all sounds like Sanskrit to me. You do know a heck of a lot more about this than I do, Temple."

"No, just the rough outlines. I always had to know a little about a lot in my various jobs."

"That's why you're so invaluable."

"Right."

"So how can I avoid being taken to the cleaners—on the air, yet—by this phony Elvis?"

"Know thy antagonist." Temple bit her lower lip. "There's the library," she said, smiling at the vision of Quincey Conrad being forced to apply for a library card because of her Priscilla assignment. "Tons of books on the subject. And videos too, I'll bet. You could check the voice against your own recording."

Matt frowned. "I don't have a VCR."

"Yet. One more improvement of modern life to invest in, son," she added in a relaxed baritone drawl.

Matt looked at her as if he'd never seen her before. "That was pretty good for a girl who's no Elvis freak. If you can do Elvis that well, how good would a real Elvis imitator sound?"

"Like the real thing. Especially if he had a facial structure that actually resembled the King's. The shape of the facial mask affects how the voice is produced. Ever notice how lookalikes usually sound alike?"

"No."

"Well, they do."

"Come to think of it, there was a priest in Arizona we always used to say looked and sounded like Gig Young, the actor."

Temple giggled.

"Why are you laughing?"

"If you knew Gig Young's wicked, womanizing ways . . . well, him as a priest is pretty funny. Plus, he committed suicide."

"Poor man. But no way would he have been priest material. So I'm still in a pickle: how do I keep from looking like a complete fool the next time the guy calls, if he does?"

"Oh, he probably will. Even if he's just a nut with no motive but exposure, kind of like a psychic flasher, he'll want more attention. Say, I wonder—? May I use your phone?"

"I can't resist anyone who says 'may' instead of 'can'."

"Only every other Tuesday." Temple picked up the heavy receiver. Matt, parsimonious former priest, had ordered the least fancy model. She dialed a number she knew by heart.

"It's not . . . him," Matt mouthed suddenly, glowering as much as one with his sunny blond looks could. He referred to Temple's significant but often missing-in-action other, Max Kinsella. Temple shook her head, unwilling to get into personal differences.

"Hi!" she greeted whoever answered, her PR person's voice set on High-energy Percussion. "What do you know about Elvis? Oh, really? No kidding. Can you get some to Matt's place? Right now? Good."

"Temple, what have you done?" he asked the minute she hung up.

"I've brought in an expert witness: a fairy godmother with a heavy Elvish fetish, it turns out."

"Who?"

"Oh, a music lover of our acquaintance."

"Not Lieutenant Molina." Matt sounded shocked.

Temple couldn't talk for laughing. "Holy Half-note! Not Molina. I wouldn't sic her on you for anything. She not only is convinced Max should be on the Ten Most Wanted List for *something*, but she thinks I'm a pest who couldn't figure out what's in the mystery meat for dinner, much less decode a recipe for murder. Besides, she's into oldies older than Elvis. Can·you imagine her and Elvis together? Ugh! Joan Crawford and James Dean. No way. You'll like your friendly neighborhood Elvis expert. I guarantee it." The doorbell rang. "And here comes—"

Temple pranced to the door·on her mid-heel pumps to flourish it open.

Behind it stood Electra Lark, wearing a subdued black-and-pink muumuu and carrying two canvas bags bulging with books. She assumed the wide-legged and -armed stance of an entertainer as she belted out:

"If your baby done left you,
You've found the right place to dwell.

The bellhop is a black cat,
The landlady's dressed in black,
Down Las Vegas's own Lonely Street,
At Huh-Huh-Heartbreak Huh-Huh-Hotel."

Send in the Clones

(Elvis never sang or recorded the schmaltzy
ballad "Send in the Clowns," but he should
have)

"I feel like a fraud," Matt said, examining the vast white
elephantine bulk of the Kingdome complex shining in
the thin winter sunlight.

"You do have a radio show," Temple pointed out. She
locked the Storm and they started walking into Kingdome World.

"But not the kind of radio show that would ever welcome an Elvis imitator."

"Not knowingly anyway," Temple agreed.

"And what makes you think I could recognize a voice
I heard only once among this horde of burning hunks of
love."

Temple paused to eye him. " 'This horde of burning
hunks of love.' That's good. Very hip. You must have
absorbed a lot from Electra's Elvis books last night."

"A lot and not enough. I've never glimpsed a more

promising or a more poisoned life story before, not even in confession. These tell-all books do tell it all, don't they?"

"I don't know. I never read them."

"Virtuously indifferent to other people's dirt, or just too busy?"

"A bit of both, I imagine. So Elvis's private life was as spectacular as his public success, huh?"

"Both seem to have gone up and down. I can see why the mysteries of Elvis are so tantalizing. . . . What is that?"

Matt had stopped to stare at the four-story-tall tilted guitar in the Kingdome's massive atrium. Heads could be seen zipping along the handle and strings while musical riffs boomed out from everywhere.

"It's a slide. A guitar slide, get it? Popular with kids."

"I guess making noise always is," Matt shouted over the hullabaloo. "Are you sure I can use my radio show as a pretext to listening to various Elvis voices?"

"Who's to challenge you? Publicity-hungry Elvis imitators would cozy up to a scrofulous porcupine if they thought it meant airtime. Speaking of which, Crawford Buchanan will suck up any attention this circus can get him. You are Media now, Matt. You can go anywhere and ask anything and people will trip over their own toes trying to catch your attention."

"I'll believe it when I see it. But at least I might get to see your major crown of thorns in a brand-new hairdo."

"Oh, the Crawf's Elvis pompadour does nothing for him, not that anything would. Try not to laugh out loud."

"The Crawf?"

"His unofficial stepdaughter's term. I had stereotyped her as a rather vacant sleazehead, but it turns out that's just the façade of a typical teenager nowadays. Quincey may not be a happy camper, but she's not such a dim Coleman lantern, after all."

"How could she be a happy camper, with the Crawf

for a father figure? I recall Buchanan as an obnoxious combo of bootlicker and egomaniac, and I don't find that particularly laughable. Those people can be dangerous. That's what some of Elvis's Memphis Mafia turned into."

"Obsequiously overbearing?"

"Well, only obsequious to Elvis; overbearing to everyone else."

"Sounds big-time dysfunctional."

"And what do you call this?"

Temple lowered her eyes from the circling Elvis statues on high to the milling crowds, among whom the Elvis-like black-shag wigs and industrial-strength sunglasses materialized here and there. And this was just the come-as-you-weren't public; they hadn't even encountered any genuine imitators yet.

"You know," she mused, "Las Vegas could be the world's first theme park for the dysfunctional. I never thought of the old town as therapy."

"Or metropolitan enabler," Matt said. "I'm glad I skimmed Electra's books. This all should mean a lot more to me."

"If it means anything at all," Temple agreed. "I thought we'd take advantage of our on-site guide."

"On-site guide?"

"The Priscilla impersonator."

Matt's pale eyebrows lifted. "The cynical teenager. Should be interesting. Can I expect tattooed and pierced flesh?"

"Only razor-burned."

This time no screams led the way to Quincey's dressing room.

In fact, a uniformed Kingdome security guard blocked the backstage route to the dressing rooms below.

A Kingdome security guard uniform was the same *Men in Black* outfit Crawford had affected yesterday: white shirt, black suit, narrow black tie, fedora, and ultradark sunglasses.

"Sorry, folks." He laid down the law with an in-character smirk that wasn't at all obsequious. "This is off limits."

"We're here to see Quincey Conrad," Temple said briskly. Brisk always sounded businesslike and, more important, legitimate.

The guard's head shook.

"Perhaps I should say 'Priscilla.' "

"You may be here to see her, but she's not ready to see you. We don't let in tourists, only people connected to the performers."

"We're connected. Check with Crawford Buchanan, the emcee. He knows the value of publicity."

The sunglasses kept her from reading any loosening of presumably narrowed eyes, but the guy extracted a cell phone from the suit and punched in a predialed number.

"Yeah. Fiorello here. You know a—" During a long pause the impenetrable sunglasses so reminiscent of the latest fashion in alien eyes seemed to wordlessly interrogate them. Then the guard extended the phone so Temple could speak into it.

"Temple Barr with Matt Devine from WCOO radio."

The guard clamped the phone to his ear for the reply.

In a moment he nodded grudgingly and stepped aside, but barely enough to let them pass.

They brushed by itchy-scratchy mohair into the same claustrophobic stairwell Temple had used the day before.

"This is so much nicer without the sound effects," she told Matt.

"You mean Quincey's screams."

Temple nodded, surprised to find the hallway that had been so empty yesterday full of colorful foot traffic.

Elvi in various stages of development (Young, Come-back, and Jumpsuit) and undress (no shirt, open shirt, navel-reaching jumpsuit vee) hustled by, too busy to give them a glance. Matt rubbernecked like someone at a tennis match.

"They sure have the look down," Matt said. "No wonder rumors started that Elvis was alive and well and imitating himself."

Temple darted toward an open dressing room door. "Quincey is expecting us. I told her that I was bringing media and needed an Elvis tour."

She vanished, and Matt hesitated before following her. This place looked like a rabbit hole of the first water. Entering such illogical Wonderland worlds had put Alice through a lot of trauma as well as adventure. He wasn't eager to disappear into another unreal world like talk radio. Investigating Elvis gave the man who had called him more legitimacy. It put Matt in the business of dealing with the lunatic fringe. It meant he was making money off other people's weaknesses. But so was every Elvis imitator in the hotel, and so Elvis himself had done.

Matt shrugged and followed Temple into the room. She was a much more reliable guide than the White Rabbit, not to mention more attractive.

Then there she was, Miss Teenage America, a petite female figure dwarfed by a full bridal-veil fall of jet-black hair. Her eyes played hide-and-seek in a blur of furred lashes, painted eyebrows, and kohl liner. A black Madonna. Elizabeth Taylor as Cleopatra without the aura of seduction. She also reminded Matt of another teasingly familiar image from the sixties, or even the fifties, but he couldn't quite place it. Certainly she was a revenant of the orchestrated image Priscilla Beaulieu had donned when she had lived at Graceland with Elvis from the ages of seventeen to twenty-six, more than half the time without benefit of marriage.

"Quincey Conrad," Temple introduced this apparition. "Matt Devine."

If the eyes beneath the awning of lashes could have narrowed further, they did. "He'd never pass as Elvis," she commented as if Matt weren't there, or were hearing impaired.

Obviously, her current assignment had narrowed her world to the Elvis and the not-Elvis.

"I'd never want to," Matt said. "Elvis had a very troubled life, and death."

"I'm not so sure." Quincey sat back down at the dressing table mirror to fine-tune her mask of makeup.

"That he was troubled?"

"That he's dead."

"Really?" Temple interjected. "What makes you question that?"

"It'd be so cool, that's all." Quincey blotted her tearose-pale lipstick. "Okay. You guys ready to go on an Elvis tour?" She stood up and eyed Matt again. "What's his cover?"

"It's no cover," Matt said a little indignantly. "I've got a radio show. I might be interested in having some of the Elvis imitators on."

"Local?" Quincey's tone dripped boredom.

"Syndicated." Temple sounded like someone laying down a royal flush on a poker table.

"Ohhhh." The exaggerated eyes gave Matt new respect. "National exposure. That's what these guys all dream of." As if she didn't. She rolled her eyes, an athletic feat under the circumstances. "Like *A Current Affair* is the big time."

"Well," Matt said, "they're not likely to get *Sixty Minutes*."

"Not unless Elvis really is alive and well in Las Vegas," Temple pointed out. "Let's go find out."

Matt's few glimpses of life behind stage, accomplished only since he had moved to Las Vegas and in Temple's presence, still hadn't accustomed him to people running around in states of undress.

Here, at least, there were no leggy chorus girls fleeting through like mobile Venus de Milos. No, there were just incarnations of Elvis, elbowing past each other as if encountering mirrored images of oneself in disguise were the most normal thing in their world. And it probably was.

Matt's recent fast-forward skitter through a raft of picture books of Elvis's career helped him identify every imitator's place on the Elvis spectrum. None mimicked the "dirty-blond" natural-born Elvis of the mid-fifties. All were black and beautiful to a degree, depending on age and physical fitness and actual resemblance to the King.

"Ooof!" Even the stage-savvy Temple seemed awed by the proliferation of Elvi. "Where do we begin?"

"These are the community dressing rooms," Quincey said. "Us few girls get separate rooms."

" 'Us'?" Temple jumped on the word. "There are more Priscillas down here?"

"No. I'm the only one. But there are three female Elvises."

Temple's eyes wordlessly questioned Matt.

"I just want to meet the men," he said hastily. "I mean, the voice—"

Temple got his message, so she nodded at Quincey. "Let's start at the end of the hall and work our way back. Show us to the first dressing room and we'll take it from there. I'd love to know whose jumpsuit got axed."

"It's been the talk of rehearsals," Quincey agreed. "Some hotel security guy finally came after you left and took it away, so someone should have noticed it was missing by now. And—" She paused outside an open door before leaving them, suddenly dead serious. "I should warn you. These are nice guys, mostly, but a little bent. I mean, they, like, worship the dead guy. So don't say anything anti-Elvis. Somebody might stick his ringed fist into your teeth, and these guys wear Godzilla-size rings, let me tell you."

With that word of warning, they entered the first dressing room.

A miasma of hair spray hung in the hot air along with a multiscented wave of deodorant. Heavy-set, blue-collar-muscled guys were primping everywhere, patting down sideburns as big as tarantulas, arranging crosses and lightning bolt pendants on springy cushions of chest hair, smoothing shocks of black hair into place, some teasing a few fitful locks down onto the forehead, like the little girl who had a little curl of nursery rhymes. When she was good, she was very, very good. And when she was bad, she was horrid.

That was certainly true of the real Elvis, Matt thought.

The round yellow bulbs that framed the chain of mirrors lining both sides of the long room made the assembled colored stones and gold studs on the various costumes glitter like neon miniatures of Las Vegas hotel signs. Matt recognized several versions of the famous American eagle jumpsuit, the denim-blue and silver-studded model, the Native American motifs. Most were white, or the occasional black version.

For a while during the sixties, he had read, Elvis had dressed in black pants, white shirts: street clothes, but already mirroring the sharp opposites his jumpsuits would embody. The jumpsuits themselves were the pinnacle of Elvis's transference of boyhood needs and loves into popular culture icons. Inspired by Elvis's early love for comic-book superheroes in fancy jumpsuits and capes, they had been tailored to the sixties and seventies fashion explosion of innovations in normally staid men's clothing, like bell-bottom trousers and necklaces for men. Although they looked excessive to the modern eye, they had merely been a show-biz version of the new male peacock emerging. Matt recalled that even Nehru jackets and vaguely priestlike white collars had been popular then, along with crosses of every description.

Although the "Fat and Forty" Elvis of the tabloids had only had a short run at the very end of the performer's career, this version of Elvis was present everywhere in the dressing room. Where else could broad-bellied, middle-aged Everymen find a role model who had remained beloved and sexy to legions of female fans to the bitter end?

Seeing these out-of-shape Elvises reflected in the facing mirrors and each other made Matt understand one reason for the entertainer's life after death: such imperfections and failings had only further endeared him to his fans. Reading of Elvis's Messiahlike appeal had puzzled Matt until today. Here, the degraded Elvis image was embraced as enthusiastically as the idealistic one of endless youth and fitness and energy, most of it running on amphetamines.

Christianity had been the world's first religion to worship a God with a vulnerable face: one facet of the Trinity was divinity made flesh. In a sense, like a shaman who takes upon himself both powers beyond ordinary humans and failings even greater than ordinary humans face, Elvis had become larger than his life. And Matt, from his reading, guessed that he knew it, which explained his thirst for spiritual enlightenment, even his grandiose belief that he could inspire young people to avoid street drugs when he himself gobbled prescribed drugs at a rate that stunned medical experts after his death.

"Awesome, isn't it?" Temple commented under her breath. "The essence of Las Vegas. Or old Las Vegas, anyway, before the Bellagio and the Beluga came along to turn this old town into a literal cultural oasis."

"The Beluga?"

"My nickname for the new Belladonna hotel-casino. Though it could describe some of these guys in jumpsuits."

"That's what's so interesting. Elvis was slim for most of his career, but because middle-aged guys emulate him, he's like a fly trapped in amber or a tabloid photograph: immortalized at his least flattering moment."

"Maybe that was his most average moment."

Matt nodded. "He'd always had a prodigious appetite.

He was almost hyperactive. That's how the performance moves started. His left leg was always jiggling off excess energy even in high school, and onstage it kept time to the music and started the whole pelvis thing when the girls began screaming. He could tuck away enormous amounts of fatty fried food that would send any heart surgeon into cardiac arrest just to hear about it. When he got past forty, he was too used to conspicuous consumption to stop. I think his high metabolism also allowed him to tolerate large doses of drugs. But in a way, fat killed him. The first evidence I can find of him taking any kind of prescription drug was his mother's diet pills; she wanted to lose weight when his career began to take off, and she didn't like her appearance in photographs."

"What kind of diet drugs?" Temple asked. "Like fen/phen?"

"No, no. Amphetamines. Speed. Doctors handed them out to everyone in the fifties and sixties before anyone knew much about the physiology and psychology of addiction. Then when Elvis was drafted into the army, he was given Dexedrine to stay awake on night guard duty—"

"And uppers and downers when he started working in Hollywood, I bet. I have heard about that."

Matt nodded. "I can even sympathize now that I'm on a night 'performance' schedule. It's a lot harder to unwind at two A.M. after the Midnight Hour live, than after anonymous private counseling sessions at ConTact."

"So what do you do to relax?"

Matt laughed uneasily. "Lately? Like last night? Stay up until five A.M. reading Elvis books."

"You know, this is the first time I've ever found Elvis interesting. Who'd think stuff like a nervous tic and a few of your mother's borrowed diet pills could both make you and break you?"

"Yeah. As I read this stuff, I keep wondering, when did it go wrong? What, or who, could have saved him? If anyone could have."

"And if they had," Temple added with a sweeping gesture, "would we still have had all this?"

"I don't know. I don't even know which one of these guys, if any, might be my Midnight caller."

"The only way to find out is to look, listen, and ask a lot of nosy questions. I'll play PR frontwoman. Follow me."

Matt wouldn't have known who to approach. Face it; he wouldn't have approached any of these intent men busy being born-again in the image of a dead superstar.

But Temple just kicked her snappy heels into high gear and clicked over to a neighboring pair of white-suited Elvises who were exchanging a small tube of glue.

On the concrete floor, the heels' approach was as arresting as the sharp stutter of castanets. Temple's predilection for politically incorrect footwear was a subtle way of knocking on people's doors as she approached them. Then they saw her red hair and were as good as snagged by her elfin charm.

Like all small creatures, she couldn't afford to be invisible.

"Hi, fellahs. Lookin' good. Have you a moment to answer some questions? I've got a radio guy here."

Elvi turned their heads in matched-Doberman tandem to eye Matt as if he were raw meat.

"Live?" one asked.

"No, these are just preliminary questions about the competition, about playing Elvis, about the King."

Matt gave Temple an A-plus for avoiding the phrase "Elvis imitator." Exactly what they called themselves, or were called, was a sore point with many semi-pro Elvis clones.

Matt decided the ball was in his court.

"So. How long have you two been Elvis impersonators?" he began.

Like twins, they answered for each other.

"Jerry's been honing his act for three years," said one.

"Mike's been in the biz for at least two."

"What's involved?" Matt asked, pulling over an empty chair.

Mike and Jerry exchanged glances. They were class A exhibits of what Matt saw was the most common Elvis imitator model: short, stocky urban guys with big dreams.

It wasn't that they looked like Elvis very much to start with; it was that they wanted to. He'd guess that they could sing a little, but not enough to forge an independent performing persona. They needed Elvis for instant identity, as much as he needed them to carry on his entertaining legend.

"What's involved? A lot," Mike said. This close, you could see the sand-blasted surface of the cheeks not hidden by the sideburns. Acne scars, but nothing severe enough to be visible from stage. "First we gotta get our act together. Get the right songs for our voices, get the props and costumes, get in touch with the Elvis impersonator network—"

"Get the noive," Jerry added, giving a belly laugh that shook his broad Elvis belt like a rhinestone surfboard hit by a big-mama wave.

Mike wore glasses. Not sunglasses, but real glasses. Elvis looked weird with see-through lenses on his face.

"I, um, ditch these for the show," Mike said, suddenly self-conscious.

"I'm sorry," Matt said. "Didn't mean to stare. I'm just studying everything. I'm new to all this."

Mike stripped off his modern-day frames. "Yeah, well, we're used to people thinking we're nuts. We don't start out anything like Elvis, most of us. That's the challenge."

"You mean, the greater stretch the impersonation is, the more accomplishment?"

"Something like that," Mike agreed.

Jerry leaned forward, intent. He had a TV sitcom Jersey accent, and fire in his eye.

"The thing is, you gotta love the King, or you got no

business even trying to do this. You gotta respect the man."

"A lot of people don't," Matt pointed out. "Didn't they really put him down at the beginning of his career? Call him a white-trash, no-talent hick who had nothing to offer but dirty dancing?"

"Yeah."

Mike was getting pugnacious, twirling his nerdish glasses by one earpiece. He'd be a good on-air interview, Matt was horrified to find himself thinking. Was Temple right? Was he being corrupted by his new media role?

"Yeah. They said all that at the beginning, and it was better than what they said at the end, that he was a drugged-out, used-up fat fool who threw his life away. It's just kinda funny that in between all that bad press the guy reinvented pop music in this country—in the world! He put it all together and brought it on home: rhythm and blues, gospel, country, pop. Man, the Beatles, that Dylan guy, they all were big cheeses after Elvis, and they all said they owed him a lot."

"Yeah," Jerry added. "Elvis grew up poor, but those church folk in the South, they knew how to sing. He heard it at church, he heard it in the bars on Beale Street, on the black radio. No one had put it all together like he did. It was never the same after Elvis. He's the King of Rock 'n' Roll."

The present tense was not lost on Matt. Elvis lives: an eerie anagram of the performer's name that even he had noticed. And now it had come true.

"Are there any black Elvises?" Matt asked. From the corner of his eye, he glimpsed Temple making a startled motion after sitting statue-still and letting him conduct the interview.

He had been thinking of the black churches he had used to drop in on, and the glorious use of music in the liturgy, the most inspired blending of music and worship since the Middle Ages, he would bet.

But Jerry and Mike were bristling.

"We ain't prejudiced," Mike said. "It's just that Elvis mostly isn't a black thing. They got their Johnny Mathis and the old blues guys and gals. They were great, don't get me wrong. But Elvis just isn't a black thing."

"But," Matt mentally riffled through his previous night's reading, "wasn't Elvis accused later of ripping off the black musicians? And didn't he dress black in high school? He was hanging around Lansky's on Beale Street, which outfitted black guys and musicians. He was put down for it then."

"Yeah, yeah. That stuff was there. That's why he was a friggin' genius. But . . . what can I say? We don't get many black Elvises. We don't keep 'em out. They just don't show up."

"What kind of Elvises do you get?"

"We got a Mexican Elvis," Jerry said. "El Vez. One of the top veterans in the business. We got Oriental Elvises. We even got a broad or two. But we don't get black Elvises." He shrugged. "It's just a cultural thing."

"Why do Elvis when you can do Ray Charles?"

Matt nodded. Elvis had been a musical, stylistic bridge from black to white, but it still wasn't necessarily a two-way street, for either race.

"What other specialty Elvises are there?"

The two men exchanged another of their insiders' glances: should we tell him?

Jerry decided to do exactly that. "It's a riot. The Elvises we got. Just when you think you've seen 'em all, along comes a whole new act. Like Velvet Elvis."

"Velvet Elvis?"

"Yeah, man. Very cool. Wears this black velvet jumpsuit with these neon decorations, just like a velvet painting."

"Beeeeau-ti-ful," Mike said, nodding and curling his lower lip instead of the Elvis upper one. "You should see that one under the stage lights. And it's a woman."

"You mean a dyke," Jerry corrected.

"Well, the jury is out on that one, but not the outfit.

First class. Original. There's always room for originality in an Elvis competition."

"But not too original," Jerry said. "There's a certain ranking for the songs and stuff. You got to deliver on the classics. Can't go too far off the path."

"But Velvet Elvis is pretty impressive. Great shoulders."

"Yeah. Velvet Elvis is okay. I don't think she'll win shit. I mean, a woman . . ."

"And then there's Velveeta Elvis."

"Yeah. Cheesy!"

Their raw crescendoes of laughter threatened to split jumpsuit seams. Matt had read that the overweight Elvis had actually done that.

"Styles his hair with Cheese Whiz!" Jerry got out between guffaws. "Dude from Dallas, where I guess Velveeta is the local, you know, cure-all."

"Yeah, they probably use it instead of Viagra there!"

Both men were laughing themselves almost off their chairs.

"Anyhow, Velveeta Elvis is no lightweight. Must go two-seventy. And he has a white jumpsuit and all the stones are this yellow-orange—"

"Like those yellow bulbs they embed in streets. We call him 'Warning Light Elvis' too."

"That guy just won't give up."

Matt hated to interrupt the laugh fest. "Anybody get so serious about impersonating Elvis that they don't give it up—ever? They won't go—" He glanced at Temple. She knew the phrase for what he was trying to say.

"They don't ever go out of character," she supplied.

The two guys barely blinked at her interjection, though they responded to it.

"Oh, yeah," Jerry said. "The Ever-Elvises. These are not professional-caliber impersonators. They never walk away from a gig. They *are* the gig."

"These yoyos show up at Graceland in costume! Tacky, tacky, tacky. We are talking wannabe wannabes.

See, we don't have any delusions. We know we aren't Elvis. We are performers. These guys, they are head cases. They gotta walk like Elvis, talk like Elvis, dress like Elvis, sing like Elvis out there in the real world. Among the public. On the street."

"Sad," Jerry put in for the coda.

"So . . . you don't approve of people like that?" Matt wanted to be sure.

Mike had no doubt. "They give us all a bad name."

"They should be taken out and shot," Jerry said.

"Or stabbed?" Temple suddenly suggested.

The men were too deep in their disdainful duet to notice her, or the sharp relevancy of her question.

"Just drowned, maybe," Jerry conceded, as if one mode of murder were less violent than another.

"Yeah. Elvis is dead." Mike shook his dyed, lacquered head. "It's too bad that creeps like those aren't."

"Amen, brother."

Mike and Jeff, Elvises of one mind under the skin, grinned absolute agreement at each other.

Chapter 17

Turn Me Loose

(Written for Elvis in 1959 when he was in the army; Fabian recorded it first, and it hit the Top Ten)

This is one occasion when I do not have to worry about keeping a low profile while working undercover.

I mean, this Kingdome place is a zoo.

First of all, you figure on dozens of performers milling around in the dressing room area. Not just chorus members, mind you, but all solo acts. (If you can ever consider impersonating someone else as a solo act.)

Then you have the costumes, which are stiff enough with glittering gewgaws to stand on their own, like a space suit. I am beginning to think that these fancy jumpsuits are capable of going out and doing a show on their own power. I mean, in this case it is a very close call as to whether the man makes the clothes or the clothes make the man. Or, in this case, the King.

This makes me sorry to see my little doll and Mr. Matt Devine wasting their time going around and talking to various of these impersonator dudes when it would be much wiser to cultivate a unique source. Talk to one Elvis impersonator, and you have talked to them all, is my point.

So my target is not this plentitude of dudes, but the lone little doll among them, and I am not referring to Miss Temple. Once she has led my friends to the Elvis concession and turned them loose, the subject fades out into the hall, where I am waiting.

A classic line in crime detection is French: *cherchez la femme*.

In plain English, this means tail the frail.

So I pitter-patter after Miss Priscilla, aka Quincey.

Frankly, I do not expect much to come of this. I expect to end up back at her dressing room, where she will resume obsessing about the state of her resemblance to a woman who at least is still alive, even though this particular semblance of her evokes the Bride of Dracula.

I can understand the King's fixation on the color black, however.

No wonder he dyed his wimpy golden locks to the color of soot. I am glad that my rival for the cat food spokespurrson role, Maurice, has not thought to turn his yellow coat black like mine. Elvis, I heard Miss Electra holding forth, dyed his hair because even from the first he wanted a film career and he felt dark-haired dudes had a stronger screen presence. Dudes like Marlon Brando in *The Wild One*, or James Dean. Well, James Dean was a little wishy-washy in the hair color department, but Tony Curtis was another favorite of Elvis, and he was black as Midnight Louie.

Another thing Elvis was into was black leather. I come by mine naturally: nose, footpads and eyeliner, only I do not have to apply mascara like some Adrian Actor dude.

So I cannot fault the guy for changing himself around to look like me. Maybe not me personally, but my kind of cat. We are considered tough hombres, let me tell you, and the ladies really go for that macho look.

Why he wanted his Miss Priscilla to also look black to

the max, I do not know. I myself prefer a bit of variety in my private life. But everyone is entitled to his little quirks, and Elvis, a born collector of everything from cars and 'cycles to girls and horses, was dealt a full hand of little quirks too.

So there I am, only a few steps behind these cute chunky old shoes, and I almost run into Miss Priss's pale hose when she stops at a door that is not hers.

It is all I can do to keep my whiskers from tickling her calves. I do not manage to keep from gawking up her A-line skirt to check out a garter. Nobody wears garters anymore but snakes. Sure enough, Miss Quincey has been accurate enough to Miss Priscilla's era to be wearing a garter belt. I am impressed by her acting verisimilitude.

She does not notice me, though, not even my vulgar surveillance.

She opens this door, darts in, and turns to close it so fast she leaves me standing in the hall extracting my whiskers from the doorjamb. I have just received a most unexpected and unattractive crimp in my facial hair.

Now I am really curious! Just what is so secret behind that door?

I retreat to a nearby trash container, hunker behind its cola-streaked side, and wait.

When Miss Priscilla comes out, I will be ready to dash in, or my name is not Mr. Lucky.

Actually, my name is not Mr. Lucky, but there are times when it should be.

Chapter 18

King Creole

(The title song from a 1958 film)

"And I thought that Mike and Jerry were a twin act," Matt said, staring at the next-door dressing room chock-full of burning hunks of Elvis.

"I guess their dressing room was unusually deserted," Temple said. "Say, wasn't Elvis a twin?"

"Not exactly. He was a surviving twin. His brother was delivered dead about a half hour before he was born. Why do you ask?"

"I just wondered if anyone here did a twin act."

"I suppose it's possible." Matt didn't add that the ever-expanding boundaries of bad taste could encompass almost anything nowadays. "His twin was named Jesse Garon."

"And Elvis was Elvis Aaron?"

"A lot of people in the South used rhyming names for twins, if not first names, then middle names." Matt studied the mirror-magnified mob of Elvises. "Psychologists say that twinship bonds are formed in the womb. Surviving twins like Elvis never seem to recover from the loss of that exact double. They say twins touch in the fetal stage, even kiss."

"Ooh. Creepy."

"And suicide rates for surviving twins are much higher than normal."

"So maybe not just drug abuse killed Elvis?"

"No one was willing to go on record that drugs did it. Heart failure was the ostensible reason, the diagnosis for all sudden deaths. It was also used for his mother, but later sources say her death at age forty-six was caused by cirrhosis of the liver."

"Mother drank?"

"Discreetly, but most of his male relatives weren't in the least discreet. Overdrinking and early death were family traits. Elvis was down on alcohol, forbid having it around, though he tried it out a few times in later years. His instincts were right about booze; his family obviously had a genetic predisposition for the disease, but no one then realized that that kind of thing is genetic, and that drugs are the same bad ticket to ride. Elvis was pretty astute, but he had an odd habit of deferring to people too much. He could have been predisposed to depression, partly because of the loss of his twin, which made him likelier to take drugs."

Temple studied the industrious rows of Elvis clones. "Do you think any of these guys abuse drugs?"

"That'd be taking imitation too far."

"I'd think so, but you never know. Let's check 'em out."

"This isn't a grocery store," he commented.

Insouciant, she grinned back at him while wading into the narrow, gym-bag cluttered passage between big guys in bulky suits spraying their hair and fluffing their side-burns with hair dryers.

"Media coming through," Temple caroled, making

them a head-turning attraction. "No cameras yet, don't panic. Preliminary interviews while you primp."

Matt remained bemused by the sheer wholesale scale of Elvis imitation as an avocation, and perhaps an art form, for all he knew. He was reserving judgment until he saw some of the acts.

Was any of these men his soft-spoken midnight caller? Some shouted back and forth, exchanging tips and valued accessories such as safety pins. Most were grimly confronting their other selves in the mirrors, touching up pale roots with dye-wands, struggling to balance unevenly glued-on sideburns.

A few wives or girlfriends acted as dressers. Everybody seemed to be frowning in concentration, or shouting for an essential something that was inexplicably missing. It reminded Matt of the fevered concentration in dressing rooms before the grade-school Christmas pageant.

"Anybody missing a jumpsuit?" Temple added her voice to the hubbub. It carried like a trumpet when she wanted it to, and she did now.

That shut them all up. Faces snapped from the mirrors to focus on her red hair. And to focus on Matt standing behind her, suddenly wishing he weren't. He still wasn't used to being in the spotlight.

"Seriously, folks." Now that she had their attention, Temple pressed her advantage. "Who would mutilate an expensive costume like that? Any ideas? And whose suit was it?"

"You media," one Elvis finally said, his voice nothing like the real Elvis's. "Always looking for the bad news."

Temple shrugged. "Maybe it was a publicity stunt."

That got them going. A half dozen voices chimed in. No legitimate Elvis, was the consensus, would deface the King's image in any form. And anyway, the impersonators all knew how much money went into the Suit. They'd have to be "lower than Red West" to trash one.

"So where is the ruined suit now?" Matt asked, nonplussed when all those blue-suede eyes focused on him. Apparently colored contact lenses were part of the costume.

"That's a good question," a significant other piped up. "Maybe it was salvageable."

"Someone should ask hotel security," another woman said.

"Maybe the police have it," Temple suggested.

Their glaring eyes returned to her. Matt realized that Temple didn't mind stirring things up one little bit, in fact, she reveled in it, smiling impishly as their voices turned on her as one.

"Why would the police have anything to do with it?"

"Nobody got hurt."

"It was just some Priscilla-hater fan, trying to throw a scare into Quincey to get her out of the show."

Matt found himself with a need to know too. "Why would anyone want Quincey out of the show?"

A pause. He had hit a nerve.

"A lot of us feel she doesn't belong here," began a portly Elvis who wore an outfit Matt recognized from photos: the American eagle jumpsuit created for the *Elvis: Aloha from Hawaii* satellite TV special in 1973.

"Why not?" Temple asked indignantly. Matt could tell she was in her defense-of-the-helpless-and-innocent mode, although Quincey Conrad was neither. "She was the only woman out of gadzillions he actually married."

"Elvis was forced into that," a tall, thin Elvis objected. "Her father and Colonel Parker put the pressure on."

"And look at her now, turned everybody on the staff out like horses too old to pull their weight, snubbed the long-time fans, and turned Graceland into a tourist attraction. She even redecorated the place before it went public. Elvis's Red Period was too tacky for her. Nobody understood that Elvis kept his roots and his tastes; he didn't go Hollywood like Miss Priss. That woman was all bottom-line from the very beginning."

"How 'bottom-line' could a fourteen-year-old be?"

Matt interjected, goaded into feeling some of Temple's indignation. "When she left Elvis in seventy-two at age twenty-six, she didn't even know how to write a check. All of her spending money had been parceled out, and stingily too, by Vernon."

"Maybe there was reason to keep her on a short leash," muttered an Elvis wearing the "claw" jumpsuit featuring Native American designs, dabbing some stuff Matt recognized as concealer under his black-lashed eyes.

"She wasn't kept on one short enough," another man put in with a bawdy laugh.

Matt found his blood pressure rising. He'd read enough about these people, bizarre as their lifestyle was, to feel he knew them somewhat. "Elvis never stopped seeing his rotating harem of women. Priscilla wasn't unfaithful until Elvis stopped having sexual relations with her after Lisa Marie was born."

"Elvis was the King," announced a stocky man with a wig that resembled a nesting duck-billed platypus. "He didn't live by the rules everybody else does. She didn't understand him. She tried to domesticate him. He was born to be wild and free."

"And screwed up," Temple muttered so only Matt could hear her.

"The women who really cared about him," said a quiet voice from a corner, where a man apparently had heard her comment, "they couldn't stay. It wasn't the infidelity so much as his downward slide with the drugs. They couldn't stand to watch him sinking."

Matt was struck by the voice. It wasn't the one on the call-in phone, really, but closer to a genuine Southern accent than any of the Elvis impersonators' natural voices so far. When his searching eyes found the speaker, he wasn't surprised, given his conversation with Temple not long before. Something of Elvis lurked in the bone structure beneath the baby face.

This guy was not primping, just sitting jiggling his

dark-booted foot enough so that the forelock curlicued onto his forehead trembled like it was caught in a fan draft. Something about his relaxed, pensive posture reminded Matt of some of the moody black-and-white photos of Elvis in his early and mid career.

Matt didn't know much about performers, but this guy's very sobriety suggested he could uncoil as hard and fast as a rattlesnake onstage.

A dark horse in the glittery Elvis sweepstakes, but who knows?

Temple was trolling for more obvious prey than potential winners.

"So," she said more loudly into the lingering silence the distant Elvis's comment had caused, "does anybody here have it in for the Priscilla clone?"

"Us?" A yip of indignation from an Elvis in the opposite corner. "We don't have to like the real one, but this girl's part of the grand finale. She hands out the authentic imitation gold belt from when Elvis broke the Las Vegas attendance record at the Hotel International in nineteen sixty-nine to whoever wins the competition. No way we're gonna short-circuit a moment of glory for one of us."

"Only one of you can win," Matt pointed out. "Maybe the other ninety-nine wouldn't mind a sour ending note."

"Nah. We're not like that. We compete, sure, but we know you're up one time and down another."

"You mean there are no leading candidates for the grand prize?" Temple asked.

Silence and shrugs infected the room. A wife, or girlfriend, paused in teasing a pompadour, then one finally spoke.

"Oh, there are guys who've won before, and might again. El Vez always has a good act, and other guys are tops too. But we've been at dozens of these competitions, and there's always some upset, or some new guy winning out of the blue. You can't count on winning, no matter who you are, and you sure can't do anything about it except to do your best when it's your time on-stage.

"But surely," Temple persisted, Matt feeling almost embarrassed by her dogged pursuit of a point of view so strongly denied, "some one contender is particularly strong, someone who won last time, or whatever."

Again, the silence, during which blue eyes courtesy of Bausch and Lomb consulted each other. The fragile wooden ice-cream chairs creaked under the shifting posteriors of nervous Elvi.

"There's KOK, of course," said a fellow so diminutive only his voice could be heard.

"KOK?" Temple was perplexed, and Matt had never seen the initials in all the Elvis books he had skimmed, including those on impersonators.

A huge Elvis stood, and it wasn't hard to look huge in those white, flared-bottom jumpsuits.

"KOK," he repeated. "The King of Kings. Guy named . . . what? David something."

How appropriate, Matt thought.

"No, no, no. His name was Ken-something. Peebles maybe," another Elvis suggested.

"No, Perkins."

"Purvis. Ken or Kyle—something Purvis," the Elvis in the corner contributed again, warily.

"Perkins," the second Elvis said firmly. "Man, he was something. Didn't think he was Elvis, mind you. But he played the part like a reincarnation of Elvis. Eerie, that guy was. In fact, that's what some of us nicknamed him. Eerie Elvis. That's with two Es at the beginning, not like in Erie, Pennsylvania."

Another ladyfriend stopped combing and teasing. "Yeah, I remember that guy. Looked a lot like Elvis before his final downslide. You know, pretty damn good, really, considering all the pharmaceuticals he was downing. That guy was so particular about every detail, more like a fan than an actor."

"Yeah. There was something . . . ritual about him. Had

to have the music played just right. Real nervous before he went on—"

"Just like Elvis was."

"Hell, we're all nervous!"

"Anyway, he was something. I never seen anybody so into Elvis. Like it was his . . . career, or something."

"Grim, yeah. Offstage anyway. Like his life depended on it."

"But he's not registered for this competition," a cheeky chipmunk Elvis put in optimistically.

This Eerie Elvis guy was sounding, even to Matt, like the ghostly gunfighter riding into town at the last moment and blowing everyone else away: Lee Van Cleef at his most smoothly sinister. Part hero, part villain. Not much different from Elvis, really.

"Maybe it was charisma," a hairdressing wife said dreamily. "Elvis had it by the bushel. Some people have that air about them."

The guys were quick to dismiss the mystical approach, just as Elvis's Memphis Mafia had loathed his explorations of Eastern mysticism with L.A. hairdresser Larry Geller.

"Nah, this Kyle-whoever was just damn good at being Elvis."

"But he's not registered for the competition," Chipmunk Elvis repeated.

"No. He dropped out of sight a couple of years ago. Fast."

Elvises nodded in mirrored multiples.

"Like something had caught up with him," Distant Elvis said slowly.

"Maybe the Memphis Mafia," one joked.

"Yeah, John," Chipmunk Elvis goaded Distant Elvis with an air of long practice. "The Memphis Mafia is on the loose and taking out bad actors. We better watch out."

"What do you think of those guys?" Matt asked.

More shrugs. "The Memphis Mafia? They were okay.

Too many relatives riding on Elvis, though. And the Mafia boys, they added a lot of pressure to his life for all they took care of things for him."

"Squabbling like jealous two-year-olds," a significant other added, shaking her sheenless strawberry-blond fright wig. "Boys will be boys, and Elvis's entourage sure proved it. From that standpoint, I don't blame Priscilla one little bit for trying to get the guy to settle down into a normal domestic life."

"Tame the King? No way!"

Matt could see that these adult men weren't much different from the employee-pals who became known as the Memphis Mafia. They were lost boys too, trying to preserve a Never-Never Land of adolescence that was a far cry from what it should have been. They needed their Peter Pan, even if it took fistfuls of amphetamines to keep him flying. No matter that he'd crashed and burned and died alone in a Graceland bathroom over twenty years ago, he still wasn't allowed to stop.

The King is dead, long live the Kings.

Temple must have felt some of the frustration he did when confronting the self-destructive lifestyle and indestructible legend of Elvis Aaron Presley. "Thanks," she said, ending the mass interview. "You were very helpful. Good luck to you all during the competition."

"Hey! Are we gonna be on . . . whatever show?"

"We'll be back," Temple promised with a jaunty, noncommittal wave.

So they all turned back to the mirrors and the job of becoming the best damn Elvis they could be.

Temple was quiet until they were opposite Quincey's dressing room again, and had no chance of being overheard.

"KOK. This Kyle Purvis guy sounds like one hell of an impersonator." Temple eyed Matt soberly, then wiggled her eyebrows for comic relief.

"It's hard to tell how good these guys would be onstage. The one who talked about Priscilla's reasons for leaving Elvis, he struck me as having the natural equipment, maybe the temperament for the role."

"Seemed kind of low-key for the King of Rock 'N' Roll."

"Okay. Let me have it," Matt said with resignation. "You think he is Elvis."

"I think somebody wants somebody to think Elvis is walking these halls. It could be this Kyle Purvis."

"Kyle Purvis. King of Kings," Matt scoffed. "Somehow, I don't think so."

Chapter 19

You Ain't a Hound Dog

(Sales of the Elvis version of "You Ain't Nothin' But a Hound Dog" exceeded six million copies in 1956 alone)

Every time I turn around in this Kingdome joint, I hear someone say that they owe it to Elvis.

I have never heard of a dead dude before with so many IOUs still out.

I owe nothing to no one, but that is the advantage in being nothing but an alley cat. Nobody expects anything of me, so I have an unlimited range of astonishment.

Right now I am determined to get into someplace where I should not go.

My only hope is the Marie-Antoinette hairdo on this little doll Quincey. If it is sufficiently cumbersome, she will be so occupied in getting it safely through the open door that she will not notice me flattened against the floor and wall next to the door. Like Elvis in his latter years, I do not flatten as well as I used to.

But these thoroughly modern misses have no idea how cumbersome big hair is, and I am counting on this as my advantage, since I have watched the Divine Ashleigh sisters try to sashay their Persian fluff through various apertures. They cannot pay too much attention to the surroundings.

I must wait a long time before the door opens again, during which time I hear the distant strains of "Suspicious Minds" being hummed by an awful lot of guys with no ear for music. At last I hear something from within the mysterious room. It is little Miss Quincey intoning, "Bye-bye, baby. Be good now."

And then she is backing out of the doorway, bent over with the weight of her vertical coiffure.

I slither inside on my belly like a snake, or like Little Egypt shedding her veils when performing, wondering if I have solved all the mysteries rolled into one: Elvis is alive and well in a storage room in the Kingdome.

The door snaps shut behind me, and my strategy to use my dark coloration as camouflage has never been so successful. I am in the utter dark, invisible to all, including myself. I cannot so much as see my tail in front of my face, not that I should ever want to do any such thing.

Tails belong in the rear, where one cannot trip over them.

Now who can Miss Quincey have left in the utter dark, locked up, and still call "baby"?

A ghost comes to mind. I do not believe that normal physical deprivations, such as light and companionship, would harm a ghost. Still, even a ghost is no one unless he or she is seen in the right places, and it would seem cruel to condemn a spirit, no matter how restless and in need of containment, in dark isolation.

On the other hand, Elvis had Dracula tendencies: staying up all night and going to bed at dawn; tinfoiled bedroom windows, whether at home or on the roam, to keep the light out; luring young, beautiful girls to his bedroom, where he engaged in much of what humans call "necking," no doubt resulting in what humans call "hickeys" and what vampires call faucets.

This would certainly explain the "Elvis is not dead" notion. If he really were a vampire, all he would need is some native earth—in his case, Mississippi mud—and a nice hidden, dark location in which to stash a coffin. His documented midnight visits to Memphis mortuaries certainly lend credence to the vampire theory. If only I could go on talk shows without a mouthpiece! But since I do not deign to speak to humans, my media career will have to be confined to cat food commercials.

So I crouch just inside the door, envisioning rooting out a six-foot vampire with a depilatory problem.

Faint heart never won a fair fight. I guess I can go fang to fang with anything living or undead. I silently pad deeper into the dark. The floor is concrete, as it is in all backstage dressing room areas. It is also cold on the tootsies. In fact, it is cold and it is damp, which lends weight to my theory that Elvis is a vamp.

I hear a sudden machine-gun burst and flatten to the floor. Elvis kept those on hand, too.

Odd, though, no fire flashes have lit the dark.

My heart is pounding against the cold concrete to which it is pressed. In the restored silence, I can hear every beat, but little else. Another raucous outburst shatters the silence. I had hoped a vampire would stick to the gentlemanly and Old World weapons of fang and nail.

In an odd way, the sound effects resemble the chattering of an extremely noisy and noisome bird. Of course, this bird would have to be the size of a private jet to make such a racket. . . .

This is when I first seriously begin to get nervous about my situation. We all know that it is eat or be eaten in this predatory world. And there is nothing that so upsets an ace predator than the notion that there is a variety of one's usual prey that is big enough and hungry enough to turn the tables on the natural order.

Let us just say that I would not like to meet up with the

likes of a bald eagle without the intervention of an avarian enclosure at the zoo.

Scrabbling sounds echo off the empty walls. Now, scrabbling sounds are an interesting phenomenon. It implies something animal (or at least avarian) rather than vegetable or mineral. It implies some rudimentary intelligence, but nothing human. The scrabble could be as small as a mouse, or as big as a housecat, or an elephant, I suppose.

So what scrabbles in the dark and also carries a machine gun?

Although smell is not one of my primo senses, I put my nose into action. I sniff things that I do not consider eating material but humans do: fruits. Large birds will snack on certain fruits, I believe.

My blood chills. I hope the fellow inhabitants of this room are not parrots. They are not likely to eat me, but they can have nasty tempers and their beaks can do a lot of damage. But Quincey said "Bye-bye, Baby," not "Bye-bye, Birdie." And—by the way—was that not the title of the Broadway musical satirizing Elvis?

I keep coming back to Elvis. Maybe Elvis just keeps coming back to me. Who could blame him?

I cannot stand it. Ghosts are made to be banished. I am tired of having this specter hanging over my head, which it very well may be. I return to the door, guided by the hairline of light underlining it. Then I veer right and leap straight up, and repeat the maneuver, batting out a mitt on my descents. I am not fumbling for a doorknob in the dark, though I might be able to turn it if I got the right spin on my pinkies. I am going for a simpler feat, but the object of my gymnastics is like looking for a needle in a haystack, or a button in a Burlington Coat Factory. Or a single stud on an Elvis jumpsuit.

Then my mitt strikes something on my downward swing. There is a faint crackling above. Light winks on before I land. The naked flare of overhead fluorescents casts an eerie blue-white glow on the piled crates and concrete.

The scrabbling sound has stopped, and so has my heartbeat . . . almost.

I scan the premises for my fellow inhabitant, who should now be visible, unless—

I frown. One crate is made of chicken wire or such, and it is as big as a doghouse, if the dog in question were a mastiff.

Dogs do not eat fruit. I slink over, reassured by the sight of a huge padlock through a sturdy hasp.

My pupils are still needle-sharp slits, thanks to the downpour of fluorescent light, but I make out a huge, shambling shape scrabbling inside the construction.

I have found the King, all right. King Kong. I mean, Elvis's face was furry in his heavy sideburn years, but this guy is wearing hairy all over his jumpsuit.

When he spots me he starts jumping up and down and screeching. He must weigh forty pounds. He bounces to the chicken wire and sticks his hairless fingers through, still chattering up a storm.

I cannot make out a word of it, but there is no doubt that I am facing an ancestor of Homo sapiens, the hairy little ape known as a chimpanzee. On the side of his cage, hanging off the top strut, I spy something shiny. A white jumpsuit, fit for a chimp.

Now I have seen everything.

Chapter 20

Walk a Mile in My Shoes

(Recorded during an Elvis show at the
International Hotel, Las Vegas, 1970)

Temple leaned against the hallway wall.

"If I'd have known it was going to take this much hoofing to visit all of the Elvis impersonators, I'd have worn track shoes."

Matt held up the wall beside her, even though it was painted institutional gray and liberally smudged with fingerprints, makeup, and the occasional billboard of graffiti. He glanced down at her feet in the begemmed J. Renee high heels she wore in honor of the jumpsuits, as she had informed him earlier.

"Haven't you got something to switch to in your tote bag?"

"Yes, but that's for really rough terrain. I refuse to get down and get sloppy when we're paying calls on men who are more lavishly attired than I."

"You have strange standards."

"So I've been told." Temple eyed him a little cautiously. He was really out of his element. "You did some pretty heads-up interviewing in there."

"Maybe I'm getting good at my new job. But . . . all these guys, they start looking like clones after a while. Can you tell one from another?"

"It's hard to see the person behind the persona. I bet that caused Elvis a lot of problems too."

Matt nodded. He looked like someone who was tired of talking about Elvis, seeing Elvis, interviewing Elvis.

"Now he's giving *me* problems," Matt went on. "I'm obligated to take this caller seriously. Whatever else he is, he must be a very troubled man. Maybe he's as likely to overdose any day now as Elvis was back in seventy-seven."

"Yet," Temple pointed out with her usual insouciance, "if you take him too seriously, you could end up a laughingstock."

"Exactly. I don't know what to do. I know what Leticia wants me to do: ride the radio Elvis for all it's worth. But if the man is not just a joker, if he's really convinced he's Elvis, that could be dangerous."

Temple pushed herself off the wall's welcome support. "Let's do this. Let's forget about interviewing Elvis imitators; let's cherchez le suit."

"It's true that these guys don't talk like Elvis until they're onstage, and then they use mikes, so my chances of recognizing a voice are nil. But no one so far has missed a jumpsuit."

"We've only hit a couple dressing rooms."

"Of forty guys."

"Tell you what. Let's find the girl's dressing room. I for one am eager to glimpse Velvet Elvis."

They trekked back down to Quincey's dressing room, but it was empty.

"Too bad," Temple said. "She's the one most likely to know—"

"The girl most likely to know what?" a voice behind them asked.

They turned.

The woman was fashion-model tall, in other words, about six feet. Her jet-black hair was cut short at the sides and back, and full on top. She had the wide shoulders of an athlete on a willowy frame. She wore a T-shirt, jeans, and cowboy boots. With two-inch heels.

"We were looking for the women impersonators' dressing room," Temple said gamely, a feat, since at five-foot-nothing she looked upon model-tall women as a form of goddess. They always seemed more grown-up than she. She knew her attitude was an illusion and a throwback to her squat and powerless childhood, but she couldn't help it. That some girls could actually grow like Jack's bean stalk all the way to Giant World . . .

"You must be Velvet Elvis," Matt said in a cucumber-cool fashion that only made Temple dislike her own awe all the more.

Tall men didn't intimidate her. Tall buildings, horses, even elephants didn't intimidate her, but tall women . . . at least this one didn't carry a badge. Oops! Elvis had carried lots of badges. Maybe his impersonators did too.

"How'd you guess?" the woman asked with a grin. She was also disgustingly lean. Temple gritted her teeth, vowed to let Matt handle it, and repeated to herself three times: this is a media-designed, unhealthy role model; get over it.

"Shana Stewart." The woman extended a hand first to Temple.

All right!

Matt shook her bony hand in turn.

"My digs are right next door. I'm the only Elvisette here. There were a couple other girls, but they chickened out."

The dressing room was a mirror-image of Quincey's setup. Everybody pulled a lightweight chair from under the slab of dressing table that lined the walls, and sat.

"What are you interested in?" Shana asked.

"We're interested in costumes. Jumpsuits," Temple began in a crab-sidling manner. No sense telling her too much.

"I'm a radio talk-show host," Matt said, giving his name, rank, and station call letters. "Someone's been calling me, acting and sounding like Elvis. I'm trying to figure out if it's a gimmick to promote the hotel and the Elvis competition, or if I'm dealing with a really sick person."

"If you are, it sure could be Elvis," Shana said ruefully.

Temple stared at Matt. He had blown his own cover, told this interrogatee everything, but he didn't seemed worried about that at all.

Maybe Shana Stewart *was* a goddess, or at least a witch.

"How did you become interested in impersonating Elvis?" Temple put in, since frankness was obviously the order of the day, and she was frankly curious.

"Lily Tomlin. You ever see her do Tommy Velour, the quintessential lounge singer? Fabulous! Shows you what a woman can do when she cuts free of gender stereotypes. I'm a model." As if Temple, ace amateur detective, hadn't figured that one out! "I'd like to be an actress, but no one takes me seriously. I'm hoping for some coverage from this, maybe a career boost."

"It's quite a stretch," Matt said. "You'd be hard to picture as a man."

He sounded nauseatingly admiring to Temple. What had happened to all his ex-priest's issues, like whether he could relate well with women after all those celibate years? That last line sounded like, well, a line.

Shana stretched back against the dressing table as if emulating Matt's figure of speech. "That's the point. If I looked butch to begin with it wouldn't be as impressive an impersonation. And Elvis was a very pretty man, you know? That's why he toughened up his image with black hair and black leather. Didn't want anyone to see the mama's boy under the swagger. A shrink could have a field day with Oedipus complexes and repressed homosexuality with Elvis, but I think the guy was straight, that way at least."

Temple thought it was time to assert her presence as expert interrogator. "I understand you have a very original costume and act."

"Oh, the boys have been talking about me, have they?" Shana smiled conspiratorily. "That's what you want: preperformance buzz. I let 'em see just enough to get agitated about what I might be doing."

"You're a velvet painting come to life?" Matt asked.

Shana suddenly stood, which was quite a production at her height. She went to close her dressing room door. Temple was glad she was here as chaperone. Poor Matt wasn't used to dealing with upfront females like this.

Shana turned, holding the door shut with her body. "You seem like a couple of decent people. I'll show you my outfit if you keep mum about it. Oh, you can mention it and roll your eyes in front of the other Elvises, but that's all."

"We have become very good at rolling our eyes in front of the other Elvises," Temple said demurely.

Shana's raucous laughter bounced off the facing mirrors. "I bet you have!"

She went to a niche with a rod running across at shoulder height, but no costumes hung there, just a blue satin boxer's robe and a big sweater. A long portable locked case, like sports equipment or a big musical instrument is carried in, leaned against the niche's far wall.

Shana rotated the dial of a padlock, then cracked it open. The interior was lined in black felt, but something else black took up the space.

Temple and Matt came over to see better.

It was a black velvet jumpsuit. Heavenly bodies—constellations, planets, nebulae—decorated the flared bell-bottom pants, the wide sleeve-bottoms and the front.

A dazzling asteroid belt six inches wide hung at the hips. Rather than being gemstones or studs, the celestial landmarks were laid out in something Temple, the glitz freak, had never seen before: aurora borealis rhinestones, only in chalky neon colors of lime green, hot pink, turquoise, and yellow.

"I've got special gels for the stage lights, kind of like black-light gels."

"Oh," Temple blurted, "like the strippers use."

"Right on." Shana eyed Temple with new respect, as if she had grown a half foot in her estimation. "It casts this white-purple glow and then this thing comes alive like a landing strip in Oz. Unbelievable."

Matt nodded. "So they know you're 'Velvet Elvis,' but they don't know yet just how spectacular you are."

"Right. Not until dress rehearsal. The thing is, the jumpsuit is everybody's secret weapon. Some of the veterans don't care, but the rest of us keep our outfits under wraps until we have to show them off."

"So any number of you could have a costume no one's ever seen before?" Temple speculated. That might explain why no one had claimed the mutilated jumpsuit.

Shana nodded.

"And that's why us asking about jumpsuits might get the cold shoulder."

Shana nodded again.

"Isn't it hard," Temple asked, "being the only woman?"

Shana shook her head. "No. And, after all, I've got a pal in Priscilla, right?"

"You and Quincey get along?"

"She's an okay kid. Notice I did not say 'good.' That girl's got a lot to prove and no one to show her the right way to go about it. But we get along. I haven't shown her my Elvis suit, though."

"Why did you show us?" Temple asked.

Shana shut and locked the case and resumed her chair by the mirror before she answered.

"Doing an impersonation is different from any other acting job on earth. You're not digging into a character through the lines the playwright gave him; you're digging into a real person through the life he lived, and in this case, died. It's a commitment. It's an education. If you're any kind of actor, it's a transformation. Even if you're a bad actor, and there are a bunch of those here, you get caught up in the challenge, and maybe the privilege. You are an interpreter, and you want to be the best damn one you can be. So, you've got a vested interest, in the end."

She leveled a glance at Matt, and Temple noticed that her eyes were a clear, strong, undrugged Elvis blue. Contact lenses, again? Ever the cynic.

"Whoever you're talking to," Shana went on, looking hard at Matt, "even if he thinks he's a fraud, is in trouble. Elvis-sized trouble. King-sized trouble. I'm riding on his image. So I owe it to Elvis to help."

Chapter 21

Ya-kitty-yak

(Elvis never recorded "Yakety-yak," but it was
written by Jerry Leiber and Mike Stoller, who
wrote other songs Elvis did record)

I guess I never paid attention when those Tarzan movies
came on.

I find jungle life fairly boring, not to mention hard on
the ears: all those exotic birds and monkeys shrieking in
the trees, the stampeding elephants trumpeting like they
have just been drafted into a mariachi band, natives
jumping up and down chanting, drums beating to beat the
mariachi band . . . not my scene.

Still, now I wish I had picked up a tip or two on relating
to the most intelligent life form outside of Homo sapiens
himself (and that is not saying much). See, these things
chitter. They chatter. They screech. It is very hard to decode their ravings. Oh, they have those big brown eyes
that everyone finds so expressive. So do dogs, and you
know how many of their lightbulbs are on permanent dim.
They also are blessed with those blasted opposable

thumbs that have become the sine qua non of civilization. (This means that you are nobody without them.)

But most of the time those flexible digits are only good for curling around the bars of a cage, and I do not see how that makes the species so intelligent. You will not find my pinkies curling around the bars of any cage. They will instead be kneading in fascinating rhythm into whatever soft surface is available: a mother's milkwagon, a pillow, or whatever human epidermis is most unprotected by distracting layers of clothing.

It is while gazing on the almost-naked ape (this critter is wearing the obligatory diaper) that I happen on the discovery of my life. Why are cats superior to all other species? We know that they are, and that they have attained this high station despite lacking the prized opposable thumb or even the disgusting bark so hailed in the canine species.

I have it. Call me Darwin! (But only as a middle name. It is an extremely wimpy name and I only claim it in the abstract sense.)

The chimpanzee before me betrays the clay feet of the entire human race.

Diapers. This creature is wearing that so-undignified banana bandana that marks a creature who is hopelessly retarded in its elimination. The feline, on the other hand, is notable for its neat personal habits indoors or out (unless subjected to intolerable emotional stress). This has made us a boon to humankind from time immemorial. No other animal species is so remarkably tidy. This makes us King of the Beasts. Or Queen, if Midnight Louise is listening in.

Once the innate inferiority of the creature before me is clear, despite its agile fingers and brain, I sit down and take charge.

"All right. Settle down, Chiquita-chomper. I suppose I should know if you are a dude or a dudette. Well?"

The thing chitters at me in monkeyese. I scratch my nose in puzzlement. It repeats the gesture.

What a silly mug! Naked as a slug, despite the hairy coat that would do honor to a goat. And the thing smells to high heaven. No wonder it is locked up far from human sniffers.

I speak slow-ly and clear-ly. "Me Louie. You . . . well? Me Louie, you—"

"Chitter, chitter, chitter, chatter."

"Enough of the chit-chat. Me Louie, you . . . ?"

The big ape starts pounding itself on the chest. Big hairy deal. If I had wanted a drummer, I would have asked for one.

Then I finally tumble. The critter is trying to use sign language. He is not saying "chitter chitter bang-bang" on his chest, he is saying his name. So I listen harder during the next outburst and come to only one conclusion. Am I a seasoned investigator, or what?

"Or what?" may describe my role as translator for a juiced-up monkey.

"Chatter?" I say, not believing my own words. "That is your name? Chatter?"

"Chitter chitter." Head nod.

By George, I think he has got it. "All right, ah, Chatter."

Grin grin, nod nod. Show teeth. Ugh! So square and dull and regular, no interesting predator peaks and valleys. No wonder humans seek out orthodontists. I would too if I had *that* in my family tree. Fortunately I go back to Ole Sabertooth Tiger, and there was nothing filed down about that Jurassic dude.

"Okay, Chatter. Goooood monkey-wonkey. Ah . . . can you explain why you are locked up in here?"

Chitter chitter, blink blink. What is this guy, a hairy semaphore? I see that there is nothing to do but for me to forsake the sophisticated signaling system of my breed and descend to sign language as well. These crude charades offend my feline soul, but the dedicated investigator must sacrifice even dignity in the pursuit of an honest answer.

So I walk to the door. I walk back to the cage. I lean

my forelimbs up to the padlock, and pantomime a twisting motion. Then I sit down, do my best to impersonate an owl and force my purr into a trilling "Whoo-whoo-whoo."

The big monkey tilts his ugly head and eyes me inquisitively. I am not about to repeat the performance, but I do repeat the question: "Whoo-whoo-whoo."

Suddenly light dawns in those ancient brown eyes. The creature leaps up, assumes a bow-legged stance, and begins playing the air guitar as if he were auditioning for *Saturday Night Live.*

Naturally, I am startled by this unsuspected talent and leap back, in case this is St. Vitus dance and it is catching. Of course the conclusion is obvious. An Elvis imitator has incarcerated this poor benighted being behind these cruel chicken-wire walls.

Verrry interesting.

But why was Miss Quincey Conrad paying surreptitious visits to the imbecile and calling him Baby? Is she perhaps acquainted with the hairy little fiend? Might there be some plot involved.

Ah-hah!

I remember my detective antecedents, born in the USA, even if they were first practiced on French soil.

I refer, of course, to what mystery readers of all ilk must inevitably be reminded of when confronted with a crime, a primate, and a mysterious motive.

Cherchez le chimp, bébé.

It is very possible that the individual who attacked the costume so senselessly, scattering nail lacquer and paper towels about, was this very creature I share confinement with. A chimpanzee is quite strong, and even more unpredictable. Elvis kept one, as a matter of fact, by the name of Scatter, and it drank beer and looked up girls' skirts, much to the amusement of Elvis and the refined gentlemen of his entourage. Then the novelty wore off, and the animal, after being the life of the orgy for some time, was consigned to a solitary cage, where it died alone and unmourned. I cannot condone treating even a silly antecedent of humanity so callously.

Seems to me some son of Scatter would be very interested in laying some version of Elvis low.

Chapter 22

Help Me Make It Through the Night

(Recorded by Elvis in 1971)

"Elvis alert!"

The phrase, bellowed out, made Matt start and look behind him.

Almost midnight, but he was alone in the studio, and the alert was only on his headphones.

Leticia was grinning at him from the other side of the glass window, a vision in an orange and turquoise-trimmed silk tunic and pants. Matt imagined she was the kind of vision Elvis would have had after eating one of those nightmare meals made from his four favorite food groups: lard, sugar, salt, and carcinogens.

"You're expecting that guy to call again?" Matt asked through the mike. He was relaxing into the radio routine: commercials were blaring to the outside world while the staff took a break before they were back on the air.

"I'm hoping, honey." She winked.

Matt wasn't hoping for another visitation from the Tabloid Twilight Zone, but he was prepared if it came. He'd not only read a lot of books about Elvis, but he'd made notes. Maybe he could trip the King up. Prove him the fraud he needed to be revealed as, in order to come to terms with himself. His real self.

This was Matt's show, after all, and he wasn't here to be made a fool of. He grinned at the shakiness of that assertion. Anyone who stuck their neck out with a live call-in show like this was in imminent danger of public folly.

But no tin-star Elvis was going to be his downfall. . . .

Of course, the worst nightmare for a live call-in show was not a bizarre guest. It was the absence of any callers. Leticia had been known to assume other voices and call in herself, if need be.

That wasn't necessary tonight. Calls came pouring in, including three referring to the previous night's Elvis sounding (as opposed to sighting). Two callers were irate that the station would use such a blatant gimmick to hype the new Elvis attraction in town. One caller wanted to know if Elvis had been in the studio for the interview.

"It wasn't a live interview, no," Matt said, tongue deeply in cheek. "He called in just like you did."

"Oh, wow," the woman said. She sounded too mature to be making this call or saying "wow." "Then he could be dead too."

"You're claiming to be dead?"

"No! I meant, it could have been a voice from the grave."

"In that case, I'm very glad it wasn't an in-person interview."

"It's not a gimmick, like that man said before, is it?"

"If it is, it's not a gimmick that's originating here at WCOO. We were as surprised as anybody."

"Too bad you didn't have an expert witness there when he called. Someone who knew Elvis, who could say if it was really him."

"I'm afraid I was pretty much alone here, except for a technician and my producer, and we're all too young to have heard much of Elvis."

"Hey, everybody's heard of Elvis. My little niece, she does the cutest version of 'Teddy Bear.' She could come in and do it on the air. Or, over the phone . . . Brianna, honey, come to auntie—"

"No, uh, thanks. I just do counseling, not auditions."

"Well, what if Elvis wanted to sing on your stupid show?"

"I don't know. I imagine"—he glanced at Leticia's eager face through the glass that reflected his distinctly uneager face—"that he would sing if he wanted to. We don't catch too many live performances of his nowadays."

The caller was gone, disconnected before adorable little Brianna could toddle to the phone to lisp her way through anything of a musical nature.

Matt had time for one deep breath of relief before another voice boomed into his ear.

"You this here Mr. Midnight?"

"That's right. What can I help you with?"

"It's me that can help you, buddy. Lots of us remember Elvis real well. We can tell a fake five miles off. That guy who called you, he was a piker. I'd know Elvis anywhere."

"A rabid fan, huh?"

"A rabbit what? I'm no rabbit!"

"I meant that you're an expert on the King."

"Oh, yeah. That's mah era. Cherry Cokes and unfiltered cancer sticks rolled up in your T-shirt sleeve. Man, either one of 'em would sear the rust off a tailpipe. I can tell you right now: that weren't Elvis last night. No way. You've been took in, or you're trying to take us in."

"No, sir, we're not. That call was totally unexpected. But it's good to know that expert listeners out there are keeping us from being bamboozled by phonies."

"Right. Happy to help out. I guess this is one time the counselor needed counseling."

"You've got that right, brother," Matt said fervently. As an Elvis-detector, he was a King-sized bust.

To his relief, the next caller was a disgruntled in-law who disapproved of how the newlyweds had spent their wedding money. This was a snap; as a parish priest, Matt had handled every conceivable pre- and postnuptial problem that three hundred-some unions could produce.

He glanced at the big school clock on the wall. Only five minutes to final commercials and no Elvis. Leticia was looking deflated, but Matt was feeling even more relieved. Mr. Show Biz he'd never be, if laying yourself open to every nut who could punch in a phone number was part of the job description. Give him ordinary people with dull, ordinary problems, superstardom and self-destruction not among them.

"Um, Mr. M-m-midnight?"

Matt's muscles seized up as if he had turned into an instant corpse.

"Are, uh, you there, sir?"

Leticia had come alive like a football fan whose team had just scored two points by running over the goal line from a faked point-after position. Her smooth cappuccino features all tilted up, as if her head was a helium-filled balloon that would lift her entire 300-pound body out of her chair.

Matt had become enough of a media personality to realize that the sight of such an ecstatic producer was nothing to trifle with. He surrendered to show biz.

"Yes, I'm here. You wouldn't be Elvis again?"

"Well, sir, that's kind of a funny way of puttin' it. I've always been Elvis, so I don't have to be him again, if you get my drift. Once has been enough, let me tell you."

"You had a lot of good times."

"Oh, yeah. But before and after . . . they weren't so

hot. You know, a guy gets to thinkin' when he's all alone—"

"Are you all alone, Elvis?"

"Guess so. Ain't seen nobody around lately. 'Course, they know enough to leave me alone when I want to be alone, and to be there for me when I want 'em to."

"Sounds handy. Like a light switch."

"What do you know about my flashlight?"

Matt hadn't been referring to a flashlight, but he recalled a famous photo of Elvis carrying one like a baton. "Oh, saw some photographs of you with one dangling from your wrist. That would be in the seventies, wasn't it?"

"Uh, yeah. Sounds right."

"Why did you carry that flashlight, Elvis?"

"Well, I got eye problems. One-eye problem, I guess. Had to wear dark glasses. And I liked to know what was going on. Out there, in the dark."

"You were being vigilant."

"Yeah. That's it."

"You were something of a lawman, in a way, weren't you?"

"Hey, you musta been a fan, Mr. Midnight, is that right?"

"I guess everybody was your fan."

"Not ever'body. I had my naysayers. You can't do anything unusual in the world without naysayers. But I could handle that. Hell, I had 'em in high school; didn't like me wearin' my hair long or dressing like I did, wanted to beat me up. They weren't gonna beat me up when I had law enforcement badges from almost every place in the country. Even one I got from drug enforcement, through President Nixon. He was very happy to meet me. I was a Jaycees Outstanding Young Man of the Year in seventy . . . one. Two? Somewhere in there. Didya know that?"

"I knew that, Elvis," Matt said soothingly.

The caller seemed not to have heard him. "Naysayers.

Naysayers who sit in your own living room and then go out and take money from some New York publisher to make you look like a fool . . . make you look bad to your little girl . . . those kind are hard to take."

Matt was silent for a moment too long. Dead air time was the bane of talk shows. But the man had sounded genuinely upset just then. Poor soul, did he really believe his own impersonation?

"That was rough," Matt said. "When those guys got fired and wrote that tell-all book about you. You got . . . pretty sick after that."

Pretty sick? He had died only a couple of weeks after the release of the scandalous *Elvis, What Happened?* book in 1977.

"Daddy done fired 'em. First definite thing my Daddy ever did in his life, and it ended up gettin' that awful book written. I talked to Red. He called, and I kinda asked him to stop it, but he said he couldn't. He even tape-recorded me without my knowin' and put that in his damn book! I couldn't believe one of my guys would do that to me. Red was with me from high school. Why'd he do that, Mr. Midnight? Why?"

Matt glanced at the clock, pointed a forefinger at his wrist so that Leticia couldn't miss it. She didn't. Past one A.M. They were in overtime. But she just kept rolling her fingers in the gesture that meant keep going. Apparently, to continue the football metaphor, they were in sudden death overtime. Matt mentally scanned his skimmed reading material for the relevant response.

"Well, Elvis, he was mad, and Red always had a hellacious temper. He couldn't believe he'd be fired after all those years with you, and his cousin Sonny had been fired too."

"But to say those things in public, those private things—"

"You were rough on the people around you. Demanded all their time anytime you needed them."

"I had to! Good God, man, you don't know what a

performing schedule I was on, from the earliest days when me and my two band guys was driving ourselves around, doin' up to three shows a day. Then later, it was the movies, and those are long, long hours. Then later the tours. Colonel kept me hoppin' with those two back-to-back Vegas shows a night, and road tours night after night, week after week. It's a wonder I made it as long as I did."

"As long as—how long, Elvis, until—?" Matt thought he had him.

The King sounded confused for the first time. His words slurred slightly. "Until I-I I just wore out, and, and I . . . I took some time off."

"Nothing happened, did it? Nothing bad?"

"Well . . . I got kinda sick there. Real sick. Collapsed, you might say. It's pretty . . . fuzzy. I was takin' these sleepin' pills, see, could never sleep. Had too much energy when I was a kid and it carried over. And I'd sleep-walk, you know. People had to be there to watch me. That's why I needed 'em there for me, once Mama was gone. I'd just stroll out the door of the house and walk on down the road and Mama and Daddy would get all upset. That's why I had to sleep with Mama all those years, so I wouldn't wander outa the house, get run over or something."

Matt hesitated. Here was an opening, should he take it? What was he, a counselor or a coward?

"You had a special relationship with your mother, didn't you, Elvis?"

"Yes, sir, I did. I didn't know it at the time, I guess. It just seemed natural. But we were real close. Never had no one close as her again. She was my best girl. Not that she was perfect. Kinda tried to hold me back when I got out on the road and ran into all those pretty girls. But mamas are like that. They want you be upright and clean, and, man, that's hard with all those pretty little things screamin' and carrying on. She liked some of my early girlfriends, though. June. And Anita. Just warned me about the blue-eyed ones. She had real dark eyes, my mama. Dark eyes. Dark hair."

A pause lasted so long Matt thought they had lost him. He made a shrugging gesture at Leticia, who shook her head in mystification.

" 'Course my mama's hair was dark later on because I got her to dye it black like mine. I figured we should match, you know. Like me and Cilla. My mama's eyes got real dark towards the end there. She had these black circles around her eyes. Like bull's-eyes. Poor little Mama, it like to have killed her when I was drafted and sent off to Germany. I think she died before I went so's she wouldn't have to see it."

"But she would have gone with you. Your father did, and your grandmother, and Red."

"Yeah, but . . . she hadn't been well, my little Satnin'. To tell you the truth, though she wanted my success more than anybody and was tellin' me I could do anything, she hadn't figured on me bein' gone so much. I'd never slept away from home until I had to go on the road with Scotty and Bill. And then I could afford to get a car or two, even my first Cadillac . . .man, was that a charge! And then I could take out girls, and Mama, she'd never figured on all that screaming stuff and girls tearin' off my clothes and rioting and comin' to my motel room doors. So she kinda felt she lost me, I guess. And I guess I was like any young guy, everythin' was tumbling my way like apples off a tree, and I was gonna pick up a few and bite 'em, you know what I mean? Mamas don't like to think of things like that. They're on a higher plane."

"You mean in heaven?"

"Oh, yeah, my mama's in heaven. If I hadn'ta believed that, I could never have gone on without her as long as I did."

"And how long was that?"

"Well, my whole life."

"And how old are you now?"

"Uh, oh, I don't like to think about them things. When you're a performer, you're supposed to stay the same as you always were forever. Forever Young. It's the name of a song. Just not my song, I guess. Never recorded it. Never sang it in concert. By that Dylan guy. Did a few of his. Pretty good songwriter. Couldn't sing worth a rat's ass, though. Nobody can nowadays. *Elvis, What Happened?* shit! What happened to the music world, huh? I had almost a three-octave range, and I used it. I did all those ballads. I sang good, like Lanza. And all of us guys who could sing, we're history. These so-called singers today, they rasp, they screech, they shout, but they don't sing, man. That's the book they should have written: *Elvis, What Happened to Good Singers?* Makes you want to . . . well, that's the problem these days. Isn't anything much I want to do. I was getting that way before I, um, retired."

"And what made you come out of retirement?"

"Huh? What's that you said? Mr., uh, Midnight, isn't it?"

"That's right. Mr. Midnight. And I asked why you came out of retirement."

The laughter came then, long and trailing off into weary, high-pitched sounds, like he'd laughed until he'd cried.

"I dunno. I just can't sleep. Never could. It gets old. And the pills don't help anymore. Finally, the pills don't help. I don't know why, Mr. Midnight. I don't know if I ever really retired, or if I'm coming out of it. I'm just all alone in this hotel room and it's dark so I can't tell if it's day or night, and no one's out in the other room, I guess, but there's a phone in here, and a radio and an alarm clock, and I heard you talkin' and thought I'd call. That's all right, isn't it? You got the time to talk to me, don't you? They're finally all gone, Mr. Midnight. You're the only one I can reach anymore. It's all right, isn't it?"

"Yes. It's all right, Elvis."

But the line was also, finally, dead.

Chapter 23

Stranger in the Crowd

(Winfield Scott wrote this for Elvis, who
recorded it in 1970 and was seen rehearsing the
song in the documentary *Elvis—That's the Way
It Is*)

Pools of lamplight lay on the pavement like the spotlights Hercule Poirot walks through during the opening
credits for his series on PBS's *Mystery!* Matt enjoyed
the various characters, particularly Miss Lemon, Poirot's
tart spinsterish assistant, who reminded him of many an
efficient parish secretary.

The opening sequence always stirred memories of a
cane-carrying Charlie Chaplin jerk-stepping out of the
frame of some black-and-white silent film.

Matt felt he was moving under the stop-motion influence of a strobe light too. He always felt stiff and tired
leaving the radio station, as if he'd been doing physical,
instead of psychic work.

When someone appeared from the dark in front of him
like a ghost, he stopped, alarmed.

"Mr. Midnight?"

She was young enough that his first instinct was to ask what she was doing out alone at this hour.

But she wasn't alone. Another figure edged into the puddle of light ahead of him. Another young girl.

"Can we have your autograph?" the second curfew-violator asked.

"On what? And I haven't got a pen."

The first girl mutely extended a rectangular sheet.

Matt was shocked to gaze at his own image, a black-and-white version of the color photograph used for the single billboard the station had mounted in his honor.

"Where'd you get this?

"We called here earlier today to ask about autographs, and they said they were having some photos made up."

Oh, they did, did they? Since when?

But here was a rollerball pen extended by fan number one. Matt looked around, finally spotting a newspaper vending machine. He went over and placed the photo on its slightly corroded metal top. Barely enough light spilled from the parking lot to show where the photo was pale enough to write on.

And what would he say?

He looked up, smiling uneasily at the sober-faced girls . . . they had become three.

He felt surrounded, as if they were the brides of Dracula and he had stumbled into their grim, encompassing midst.

What would he say? Write, rather. Uh . . . best wishes. Dull. Ah . . . good listening, regards . . . ah, Mr. Midnight? Or Matt Devine. No, Matt Devine wanted nothing to do with this charade. The pen took over for his vacillating mind. "Good Listening, Mr. Midnight." What did that mean? Who knew?

"Could you put my name on it?"

"Name?"

"Up there, over your shoulder. 'To Cheryl Baker.'"

"Cheryl Baker." He began writing it.

"Uh, no. With two r's."

"Huh?"

"There are two r's in Cherryl."

"Oh. Well, I'll make the upper part of the 'y' into an 'r' and . . . how's that?"

"Great! Thanks, Mr. Midnight. You were really super with that poor girl. Is she okay?"

"As okay as she can be at the moment. I think she'll get better with time."

"That was so awesome." Fan number two crowded closer to extend a second photo.

He knew right where to sign this time. "And what's your name?"

"Xandra with an 'X.' "

"You'll have to spell that."

She did, letter by letter, as if she'd done this before.

Fan number three advanced in turn.

This was no slip of a girl, but a heavy-set woman in the whimsical cat-print scrub-clothes that nurses wore nowadays. She must have come on her way to—or from—the night shift at a hospital.

This fifty-something veteran of such interchanges knew exactly what he was supposed to write. "From Mr. Midnight and Elvis, to Diane."

"I don't know if I'm entitled to sign Elvis's name."

"You've talked to him, haven't you?"

"I'm not sure. Are you?"

"Oh, yeah. I have listened to everything Elvis for years. I've been to Graceland three times for the August memorial."

"Wouldn't it be . . . pretty amazing if Elvis really were alive, and after all these years started calling some obscure radio show in Las Vegas?"

She shook her shoulder-length hair, which had once been springy and black but now was frosted with broad brush strokes of white. Matt guessed she'd worn the same haircut for three decades, and had worshipped Elvis through every one of them.

"Nope," she said matter of factly. "I mean, not that

it's not amazing, but Elvis was pretty amazing himself. He wouldn't give up on his fans. And if he did get too tired and sick to go on, he might have arranged to disappear. He had the money to go anywhere or be anybody."

"So why would he come back via live radio, over twenty years later?"

"He knew how to make an entrance." She smiled and snapped the gum she was chewing. Matt caught a faint, nostalgic whiff of Juicy Fruit. "You can just never tell what Elvis might do."

Matt recognized pure faith when he saw it. He had never seen it shown to anything other than a religious figure. Maybe the shrinks who identified Elvis as a shaman, a primitive holy man, weren't all wet. Didn't the faithful visit the burial shrine at Graceland every August, and every day of the year, making it second only to the White House in annual visitor count?

"From Mr. Midnight, who listens to Elvis," Matt wrote. Anyone with a stereo could listen to Elvis. "Happy-ever-after listening."

She read the inscription, pulling the photo close to her lenses. "That's all right," she said, grinning and nodding. "Elvis would have liked that."

None of Matt's autograph hounds (hound dogs?) were ready to leave, but stood shifting from foot to foot, grinning.

Matt looked up for some reason, beyond their imprisoning semicircle.

A fourth figure stood silhouetted in the light of a distant lamp.

Its wide-legged stance made clear that it wore bell-bottom pants. The night was chilly, maybe fifty-five degrees. Matt assumed the bulky but truncated outline of a classic 'cycle jacket. The outline of the figure's hair made its gender murky.

Disturbed, he stared, trying to read recognition into what was little more than a cardboard cutout. For an instant he wondered if a fan had brought along one of those lifesized standup celebrity cutouts. He had seen them in various models: Marilyn Monroe, Captain Kirk and . . . Elvis Presley.

Someone tugged on his sheepskin jacket sleeve for attention. "Could you autograph a photo for my friend Karen who couldn't come?"

"For Karen-who-couldn't-be-here," he wrote, already showing the cautious sensitivity to double-meanings of someone who thought his least act might return to haunt him.

Return to haunt him.

He glanced up again to the inadvertent spotlight cast by the street light. The pool of light was vacant. Elvis has left the parking lot.

Matt shook off the eerie speculation and his own superstition. The only ghost he recognized came and went with the adjective "holy."

As he was signing the Mr. Midnight name, he heard a motorcycle cough into life and roar away. Fast.

Chapter 24

Tutti Frutti

(Raucous rock 'n' roll number Elvis sang on the
Dorsey Brothers TV show, 1956)

"You're as bad as my mother!" Quincey complained. "I
don't want my big chance ruined."

"Being a harassment victim is a 'big chance'?"

"Show business can be rough."

Quincey turned back to the mirror to fluff up her already high hairdo. Instead of wearing half of the hair up
and the other half down her back—with one coy lock
flipped forward over her shoulder—Quincey had teased
the hairpieces into a mound as high as her face was long.

Her face was especially long now with teenage angst.
"I don't need 'bodyguards.' I'll look like a kid or something."

"Or something," Temple agreed, surveying the bizarre
child/whore façade Quincey had perfected, just as Elvis
had ordered it done more than thirty years ago, partly to
make his teenage houseguest look old enough to avoid
dangerous gossip. "Frankly, bodyguards will only add to

the illusion that you're the real Priscilla. Besides, these aren't the usual type of bodyguards. Believe me, they'll blend right in."

"Oh. 'Blend in' how? Are they the reincarnation of the Memphis Mafia? Fat old guys in dark suits and hats and sunglasses. Gross."

Temple sighed. She knew everybody over twenty was ancient to a teen angel-vixen like Quincey. Still, she had gone to some trouble to provide low-profile protectors for the kid, and would have liked a smidgeon of credit for being cool for an old person. Apparently, having concerns for someone's safety had cost her the "cool" credentials.

"Shall I ask them in to meet you?" Temple said.

"Them? I'm gonna be trailed by *two* fat old guys in glasses? Double gross."

"Not exactly." Temple pushed herself out of the chair, her high heels clicking concrete all the way to the ajar door, and sounding just a tad miffed. "Fellas, you can come in now."

Come in they did, two by two, just as the animals had entered the ark. Two, and then four, and then six, and then eight, and then the company's lone last member.

They filled up the mirrors and the dressing room, six feet tall and nine strong. They loomed. They glittered. They were all Elvis, Elvis to the ninth power. They were, in a word that Quincey would respect, awesome.

She had almost knocked over her chair as she jumped to her feet to take in this manifestation. "What is this? Who are they?"

"Meet Full-spectrum Elvis, a new and original act for the competition."

After a long pause, during which Quincey scanned every incarnation of Elvis: the raw fifties kid in the pink-and-black pants and shirt, Gold-Lamé-Suit-with-Rhinestone Lapels Elvis, Tuxedo Elvis, Motorcycle Elvis, Blues Brothers Elvis, Karate Elvis, Cape-and-

Cane Elvis, Jumpsuit Elvis, and, last but definitely not least, Oversized Elvis.

Seen in this historical perspective, it was obvious that the many overweight Elvises on the imitators' circuit portrayed a minority version of the superstar. Only the last Elvis, Oversized Elvis, could be described as "gross." Temple credited this man with a true actor's devotion to a role for donning the required fat-suit beneath the jeweled jumpsuit.

The rest of them were trim, foxy-looking dudes with their naturally dark hair moussed, fluffed, and tousled, wearing their blue suede shoes or miniboots, and their various intensity of sideburns, from eyelash-thin to Bigfoot-sized radiator brush.

"How are more Elvis imitators going to do anything to guard me?" Quincey asked a bit less sullenly. She was the age when somewhat older men were intriguing. In fact, at sixteen, she was already a bit old for the real Elvis.

"That's easy," Motorcycle Elvis said, stepping forward so his neck-to-ankle black leather suit squeaked. "We are muscle first and musicians second."

"And," Cape-and-Cane Elvis added, sweeping aside the cape with his cane to reveal a sidearm, "we follow Elvis's sterling example in accessories. Or perhaps I should say 'steel-blue' example."

Quincey's pale hazel eyes widened enough to push back the raccoon rings of eyeliner surrounding them. "Elvis was a gun nut. You guys could get into trouble for carrying concealed weapons."

"Only if you tell on us, little lady," Fifties Elvis said with an off-center smirk.

"Now." Gold Lamé Elvis made a fingernail-buffing gesture on his rhinestone lapels that must have scratched his knuckles. Maybe they itched. "At least one of us will be with you at all times. The others will blend among other Elvis types and see what they can learn about whoever might have gone after your lovely neck with a razor blade."

"I guess that's all right," Quincey allowed. "You guys don't drag down my Priscilla outfit. Some of these Elvis costumes are so cheap and cheesy." Then a girlish storm threatened. "Except him." She pointed a perfectly manicured pale pink fingernail at Oversized Elvis. There was an awkward pause. "Really, Priscilla was out of the picture by the time Elvis got so gross. I'm only pointing this out for reasons of historical accuracy." She eyed every one of them except Oversized Elvis. "It's not like I have anything against Old Elvis."

Of course she did, Temple thought. And so had the millions of people who voted a few years ago for the Young Elvis postage-stamp image, not the Mature Elvis likeness.

Oversized Elvis ebbed diplomatically to the back of the entourage. He also serves who only stands and waits.

After some discussion, it was decided that Fifties Elvis and Motorcycle Elvis should share the first-shift duties of shadowing Priscilla.

Temple retreated into the hallway with the remaining seven Elvi.

"You look terrific, guys!" she told them. "How did you rustle up such high-class King duds so fast?" She hadn't a prayer of telling who was who behind the assorted Elvis façades and decided to refer to them as their costumes dictated.

"No problem," said Tuxedo Elvis, his curly shirtfront ruffles matching the boyish wave in the locks that brushed his forehead. "We had the hair already, Superglue provided the sideburns."

"Hair is easy to duplicate. What about the costumes?"

There was much blue-suede shoe shuffling.

Fifties Elvis bashfully tapped his shoe-toe on the concrete, then shrugged. "The hotel has this 'see yourself as Elvis' photo booth. They have everything but the suit he was buried in."

"That would be tasteless," Oversized Elvis said. "Even Elvis wouldn't have liked that pale suit with the blue shirt and white tie."

Temple was not assuaged. "Wait a minute! A photo booth does not explain how you all got duded up in period so fast."

Karate Elvis launched himself into a fighting pose. "It's like this, Miss Temple. We know the operator and know how to encourage cooperation."

"Moolah." Cape-and-Cane Elvis nodded knowingly.

"And then we got Minnie the Miracle-worker to fit everything and gussy up the outfits—"

"The theatrical seamstress, Minnie Mabel Oliver. I remember her! I met her during the Darren Cooke case."

"Was that a case?" Gold Lamé Elvis asked. "Or was it an accident?"

"The jury's still out," Temple said grimly.

"Just like it's still out on Elvis's death." Karate Elvis executed a leap that landed him nearly on top of Temple.

"I don't think so, boys. Besides, we don't have to worry about a dead Elvis on the premises. It's 'Priscilla' I'm concerned about. Apparently everybody around Elvis disliked her."

"Well, she wasn't one of the boys, was she?"

Temple stared at Blues Brothers Elvis, whichever Fontana brother he was. "That's very true. It was a primal battle for control of Elvis: would his shy, sensitive private side win, or the adolescent bad boy that the world idolized?"

Motorcycle Elvis executed a pelvis move that left no doubt which side of Elvis he was voting for.

"Either way, I guess he was charming as a prince."

"You got that right," Cape-and-Cane Elvis said. "A Prince of Darkness."

"Well, you guys are all princes for taking on this bodyguard detail. You're not actually competing, I hope."

Motorcycle Elvis managed a devilish grin that lifted

his upper lip, left side, just like the original's. "Why not? Where else can we learn who might be pestering our little Priscilla? Elvis wouldn't like that."

"He was very protective of her."

"She was his bird in a gilded cage, and that chick was not gonna fly away on him."

"But she did," Temple said. "And a lot of people blame her defection for his decline and fall."

"Enough to kill even her image?" Tuxedo Elvis asked.

"That's what Elvis was all about, wasn't it? Image. In that kind of world, even a jumpsuit isn't too inanimate to hate."

They nodded soberly.

Someone who would stage the killing of a costume was not operating with all hinges screwed in tight.

Chapter 25

Fame and Fortune

(The first song Elvis recorded after leaving the
army in 1960)

"I can't do it," Matt said. "I can't play games with a
sick man."

He was staring at the front-page headline on the *Las
Vegas Scoop* that lay across Temple's coffee table: IS IT
ELVIS, OR IS IT EYEWASH?

Matt had brought the tabloid journal here. It was more
of an advert than a newspaper. Temple's coffee table
wouldn't be caught dead upholding the sleazy daily that
took Las Vegas's pulse at its most diseased. Other cities
had their artsy "alternative" weeklies that covered the
arts. Las Vegas had the *Scoop* (what she considered short
for Pooper Scooper) whose motto could be: "All the dirt
that's fit to sling."

The subhead was even worse: "Talk Jock Shoots
Breeze with the King." Then the story:

Hot new after-hours air-head Matt Devine at WCOO-AM has held a couple post-midnight tête-à-têtes with the purported King of Rock 'n' Roll, worth mentioning only because said purported King is also purported to be dead.

Elvis, don't be cruel! Tell us if it's really you waxing melancholy at length—at Long Playing length, maybe; remember those good ole LP days?—in conversation with Mr. Midnight.

On the other hand, our spies (and we have countless spies everywhere, thank you, loyal readers) tell us that local radio's recent hero—he talked a homicidal new mama into sparing her infant until the cavalry could get there—was seen hobnobbing with the Elvis imitators in town for the Kingdome's gala opening next week.

Could our local hero be craving more publicity and making sure that he gets it with the collusion of an out-of-town Elvis? Makes you wonder. But then maybe that's what the radio shrink and WCOO-AM want: all of us wondering and tuning in.

How about opening the air waves to the skeptics, Mr. Midnight? Viewers should call the Midnight Hour with some hard questions for the show's most famous (and surely phony) guest. Think you're enough of an Elvis expert to stump the supposed King himself? Call WCOO-AM from midnight to 1 A.M. and put Mr. Midnight to the test. Maybe you'll be a local hero for putting a faux Elvis to rest.

They regarded the story silently, until Matt spoke again. "You're the media expert. What should I do now?"

"I bet this is Crawford Buchanan's work, even though the story doesn't have a byline. It's tawdry, cheap, and despicable . . . but I think it's a good idea."

"Seeing that the so-called Elvis is kept off the air?"

"No! Letting the listeners call in and try to stump him. Bet Leticia could kiss the guy who wrote this article, even if it is the Awful Crawf. It's great marketing."

"That's just it! I don't think we have a right to 'market' a sick man."

"Maybe not, but maybe he's not so sick."

"How can you say that? I've heard genuine hurt in what that man says."

"Then help him. Help him understand himself; that could do him good, whoever he is. And maybe connecting him with his 'fans,' even indirectly, will help him more."

"Listen to yourself, Temple! 'His fans.' That's what I'm worried about, people being so crazy themselves wanting to have the King back that they'll buy any scheme or delusion."

Temple shrugged. "That's the great American public at its best. They want to believe, even if they know deep down it's a snare and delusion. That's what all entertainment is about: erecting illusions, fulfilling wishful thinking. Build it and they will come. You know there's a whole world of Elvis worshippers out there hoping he isn't dead. Maybe he can live a little, love a little again, through your show."

" 'Live a Little, Love a Little . . .' Even you, Temple, have sold out! This is insane. I can't counsel a dead man through a delusional go-between. This guy might be suicidal, and if the 'fans' call in grilling him, who knows what he might do?"

"Good point." Temple frowned down at the *Las Vegas Scoop.* "You should be the go-between for the fans. Don't let them call in directly, just relay their questions, or bring up the issue when you talk to him."

"He might not ever call again."

"I doubt it. The King performed up to the very end. That's the only thing that kept him going even as it destroyed him. He'll call again."

"I don't like it," Matt said.

Temple frowned again. Saleswomen at cosmetic counters cringed in agony if they caught her doing it, but it was one of her best expressions. Anyone who couldn't frown couldn't express uncertainty, and anyone who couldn't express uncertainty in this world was doomed to disappointment.

She sighed. She knew Matt was terribly sincere, which made him such an excellent foil for the insincere of the world. If he had sensed honest turmoil in his caller, then it was there. Therefore the caller wasn't a cynical user, at least not totally, no more than Elvis had been once the bloom had blushed off the rose of his naive country-boy youth and upbringing.

"It wasn't your Elvis"—Matt groaned at her use of "your"—"that brought me to the Kingdome, you know. This whole Elvis thing does involve me, professionally, in a way."

"What way?" Matt was sounding suspicious and hard-nosed. Good; progress. Lesson one from Life's Large Instruction Book: Trust no one, especially those you trust most of all.

"There's been a construction holdup at the Crystal Phoenix. I went over to investigate, then ended up at the Kingdome."

"What could an Elvis attraction have in common with the classiest little hotel in Las Vegas?"

"That was the construction holdup. They're excavating the Jersey Joe Jackson action attraction mine ride."

"So?"

"The workmen were balking at digging any further."

"More money?"

"Less shock waves."

"Shock waves? Underground tremors?"

"Of a sort. They were seeing things."

"Well, it is a ghost attraction, isn't it?"

"Yes, but not for this ghost."

"What ghost?"

"They're convinced it's Elvis."

"Elvis has gone underground? At the Crystal Phoenix?"

"Do you see any reason someone trying to hype the Kingdome would put in a guest appearance at an underground attraction at another Vegas hotel?"

"Only if he was trying to tunnel his way out of a crypt, and Elvis is very definitely buried in Memphis, at Graceland, in the Meditation Garden, along with his mother and father, and grandmother."

"If he's dead."

"Temple! Things are weird enough without you jumping on the 'Elvis lives' bandwagon."

"I agree that it's unlikely, but let's give Elvis a chance. Let his fans, or detractors, call in with itsy-bitsy facts about his life that could trip up an imposter. You relay them in a nonchallenging way, crediting the person who asked the question. Maybe the station could give a trip to Graceland to whoever comes up with the question that stumps the King."

"Temple, that's so tawdry, cheap, and despicable. If I weren't looking at you right now, I'd think you were a Crawford Buchanan imitator."

"I agree. But . . . this kind of bad publicity in the *Scoop* could put your newborn career in jeopardy. You have to demonstrate somehow that this phone-in from Elvis isn't a put-up job. You have to give the public a shot at proving that he's a phony."

Matt ran his fingers into his Fantastic Sam's low-cost haircut.

"My career," he said as if naming a new enemy. "Suddenly I'm getting some decent money. I seem to be naturally good at this talk radio stuff, I'm getting a following, I'm getting criticized by the press—"

"Oh, puh-leeze."

"By the tabloid press, such as it is. Everybody has a stake in me, Leticia, the station, the public who believes I'm a good guy because of the baby incident, only now

I'm maybe a bad guy because I might be a colluding fraud. I don't know what to think and do."

"Ever think that's how Elvis began to feel?"

"No. I've never really put any effort into thinking how Elvis got the way he got, until now. If this is just a taste of the price of fame, it's pretty bittersweet."

"That's why you can't stop now. It's not just the public you owe something to. And the story doesn't really have to have a pat ending. Let me put it another way: you have to give this man who sounds like Elvis a shot at proving he's who he says he is."

Chapter 26

Let Me Be There

(A "sugary pop confection" says one biographer,
that Elvis sang in a 1973 concert as he began to
retreat from the musical ground gained during
his post-comeback touring schedule)

"Have you considered the advantages of an expert assistant?"

Temple considered Electra Lark first.

Her landlady had rung the bell and spent the past fifteen minutes sitting on her sofa bruiting about her qualifications as an Elvis expert, ranging from attending the vital February 14 concert in Carlsbad to avid perusal of virtually every Elvis book published.

"I know, I know," Temple finally said, interrupting the flow of fannish enthusiasm. Electra was looking more like a toy troll than an Elvis freak today, with her white hair tinted a clownish carroty red.

"Have there been any more manifestations in the Crystal Phoenix underground zone?" Electra asked eagerly.

" 'Manifestations' implies an incorporeal presence,"

Temple said uneasily. "All I had for witnesses were some workmen more likely to see Elvis in a shapeless blob of light than Princess Diana." She squinted her eyes at Electra. "It's hard to picture you in a poodle skirt with a ponytail and anklets, screaming over Elvis. Now that's a manifestation."

Electra surprised Temple by blushing, very faintly. "You never saw the man perform live. He put his whole heart and soul into it. You could see it. It was like he was singing just for me, and even if he wasn't, you felt united with everybody else there. I guess the word for Elvis live was electric."

Temple was unconvinced. "And if the fifties were such a sexually repressed time, how could all those girls line up outside his motel rooms? According to your own books, Elvis was hooked on adolescence, and adolescent girls, and he followed through. How'd he get away with it, and why were so many of those sweet little fifties girls so available?"

"Simple. The parents were uptight and repressed. The kids had the same hormones that propel rock groupies today, and they were really desperate to break out. Why do you think Brando and *The Wild One* and rebel-actors like James Dean were so popular?"

"Didn't Elvis idolize those actors . . . or, actually, idolize those rebel roles they played?"

"Yeah. And Elvis brought that rebel persona off the screen and into the performance halls. Live. You could touch him if you got up close enough and rushed the stage. You could be invited into his motel room if you hung out by his door and got lucky."

"Wasn't anybody worried about venereal disease and unwed pregnancies then?"

Electra thought about it. "Oh, we worried, but we didn't know much what to do about it, so we took our chances." She smiled at Temple's shudder of disbelief. "It was a superstitious era. You know, if the time of the month was right and you used a Coca-Cola douche right afterward, nothing would happen. Besides, Elvis was into necking and snuggling more than the actual act."

"Must have burned off all his night moves on stage."

"In some ways he was an innocent teenager just like us. That's what we saw in him. He was from the same uncertain, kept-dumb mold as we were, overprotected for our own good. So for us to get out there and rock, and drive all the adults crazy with the suggestion of sex . . . it was heaven."

"It ended up being sheer hell for Elvis. Not even his most loyal fans could deny that."

"No." Electra settled into the sofa pillows, contemplative, her usually cheerful and plump sixty-something face sagging into seriousness. "In a way, Elvis paid the price for our innocence, and we were innocent, even when we thought we were being daring. People just didn't know back in the fifties and sixties what sex, drugs, and rock 'n' roll could do to you, performer and audience. But, good golly, Miss Molly, it was great to be there. And great to get out alive."

"Elvis didn't."

Electra inhaled deeply, then held her breath. She spoke in a long, strong rush. "Temple, that's why I want to go over to the Kingdome with you. I think I could really help. I've been listening to Matt's program."

"Every night?"

"Sure. Haven't you?"

"I'm a working girl."

"Or has Max been commandeering all of your time?"

"If only. Max has been out of town."

"Ooooh."

"What does 'Oooooh' mean? Never mind. I still haven't the time to stay up nights and listen to the radio."

"Well, I don't sleep as well as when I was a wildly innocent young thing, so I've been faithfully listening to the Midnight Hour. Matt's doing very well, isn't he?"

"You can't argue with success."

"Have you heard his anonymous caller?"

"You mean the undeclared Elvis? Yes. Matt brought me a tape."

"You two whippersnappers are too young to realize this, but that's a very credible Elvis on that phone line."

"The town is packed with very credible Elvises who are gambling a lot of time and money on winning the title of best dead Elvis around."

"Still . . ."—Electra picked a few stray Louie hairs off the sofa seat—"I was there from the beginning. I've seen the documentaries, the movies, the retrospectives." Electra nodded. "That's a very credible Elvis. Too credible to just write off and forget."

"Electra! The story that Elvis is alive is the cheapest, most obvious tabloid news rag staple of the past two decades. Even Awful Crawford is using it in the *Las Vegas Scoop*. Even Awful Crawford is debunking the idea. He's challenged listeners to call in and play Stump the Superstar with Matt's midnight Elvis."

"What a great idea!"

"Yeah, that's what I told Matt."

"I could come up with some great questions."

"Call 'em in, or slip them under Matt's door."

"But I still want to see the scene of the crime."

"Electra, there's no crime here but malicious mischief: violent trashing of an empty Elvis jumpsuit and the more serious act of etching an 'E' into Quincey's neck. From what I read about Elvis and his redneck bully boys and flunkies, they perpetrated a lot of malicious mischief themselves on movie sets, in major hotels, and at Graceland."

"Exactly." Electra's eyes narrowed, and that's when Temple noticed that she was wearing violet-colored contact lenses. What a chameleon! "You've heard of mischievous spirits, haven't you?"

"So now you're resurrecting not only Elvis, but his whole band of merry men?"

"You said that the girl playing Priscilla was attacked, didn't you?"

"Yes."

"I rest my case. Priscilla and the Memphis Mafia had a major power struggle."

"And she won, because Elvis is dead and she's running Graceland."

"Especially interesting when you realize that Elvis left her out of the will and left everything to Lisa Marie."

"Then how did she—?"

"Lisa Marie was a minor when Elvis died, that's how. She gets nothing out of it, just builds an inheritance for Lisa Marie."

"Who married Michael Jackson." Temple shook her head. "Another victim of rock 'n' roll."

"Lisa Marie or Michael?"

"One, or both. I don't care!"

"It really makes sense that she married him, you know. He led the lifestyle her father did: the forced isolation from fans, turning his home into an eternal playground, renting amusement parks to entertain his family and friends."

"Why did they both do that? Too much time and money?"

"Too much fame, and too many fans everywhere they went. They needed the entourage to beat off the fans. They couldn't go to public places to enjoy themselves. They had to become isolated and make their own worlds. And everybody around them got hooked on the idea."

"Sometimes being ordinary is a boon, isn't it?"

"Being ordinary is always a good place to hide," Electra said, nodding. "Now. Can I go along to see all the Elvi? Please, Mommy, puh-lease?"

Who could turn down a whining sixty-seven-year-old teenager?

Not Temple.

"Sure," she said. "Friends and relatives of the performers are always hanging around the dressing rooms and house during rehearsal. Welcome aboard, and consider yourself a preview audience."

Chapter 27

Where Do I Go from Here

(Recorded in a 1972 session where producer
Felton Jarvis fought Elvis's depression and
torpor)

The King was feeling restless.

He knew he should be out there, performing.

The times they were a-changing.

Other performers were catching up to him. In the early days, he had the whole stage to himself. No rivals.

But then he had to leave home, leave his family, go off to a far place, and prove himself all over again in a new role.

There, he was supposed to blend in. You're in the army now. Be a regular guy. It would be dangerous to stand out. Just be the same, simple, polite country boy everyone from Ed Sullivan to the general press had taken a shine to when they weren't blasting him for being a scandalous influence on the youth of America. An aw-shucks, apple-polishing country bumpkin.

He wasn't as simple as they thought, never had been. First in his family to finish high school. That meant a lot to his mama. She hadn't liked him striking out on his own after high school much, or some of the people he'd gotten mixed up with. Traveling people. Drinking people. Girl-chasing people. But that came with the lifestyle, and, heck, he'd enjoyed those first deep breaths of freedom. He wasn't the high-school loner anymore. He was the man with the power. Every guy wanted to be his friend. Every girl wanted to be his girl. Man, those were the days. Nobody worried about AIDS or anything serious. Everybody just had fun, staying up all night.

After all, his new career called for late hours, so why not party the whole night through? And, heck, he'd always had nightmares and would try to walk away from them . . . right down the road from the little house in Tupelo. Mama had kept him sleepin' by her until he was twelve, though he'd figured out not to mention that much, or how she walked him to high school every day. No wonder the hoods tried to beat him up, especially when he started wearing his hair long before anyone had even dreamed of the Beatles.

But once he broke free, he knew just where to go for inspiration. Music first, then Lansky's second, where the colored rhythm-and-blues singers bought their fancy duds. Before he knew it, he was on the road, and that's when he discovered girls as a lot more than a prom date. He never stopped discovering girls. That's what he liked, the discovering.

His mama, she about had a fit. She'd always doted on him when she wasn't raking him over the coals for some misdeed or other. Now here he was off with strange men, meeting strange women who really, really wanted to meet him, and more. Then when that army thing came up, he was gone far, far away, like he'd been kidnapped or something, from her point of view. Taken away. Over Jordan, only this river was an ocean.

He knew deep in his heart that his mama just feared for him out in that big, funky, weird world. She grieved for him so. And it killed her. He knew that. In some ways she was right. It was way more dangerous out there than he had thought. *But it was dangerous in here, too, Mama,* he told her for the hundredth time. He talked to her sometimes, yeah, but it was like talkin' to a dead twin. Kinda natural, after all, to talk to someone who was that close for that long. You'd think people could understand his losses. Uncles and aunts and cousins dyin' left and right. He always said *please* and *thank you*, like she taught him, and *sir* and *ma'am*. These were words of respect, and you got to respect other people no matter who you are. Or were.

Ma'am is just Mama moved around.

The King sighed. Mama had moved around plenty in her lifetime. From Mississippi to Memphis, Tennessee. From one mean little house to another. There was no phone or running water in the house where he was born and Jesse Garon had died, or maybe had been born dead. He wasn't sure which. He just knew that he sometimes could hear Jesse's voice, so far away it sometimes seemed inside himself. He had a lot more inside himself than anyone gave him credit for, even when they were heaping praise or blame on him.

There were many times when he got tired of it all, when the music seemed the farthest thing from the center of his life.

First they couldn't say enough good things about him. Then they couldn't say enough bad. He just never really got taken seriously. They even made fun of his fans. And it was worst after his . . . collapse, when he had to leave his world and disappear.

Then all the books came out saying how strange he had been, from what he ate to how he slept with girls to how he played, even his spiritual aspirations. He was the butt of the whole world. And they never saw, never could or would see that everything he did, everything he became, came about because of the life he lived, because his fans loved him so much they could have almost torn him apart. And, in the end, maybe they had.

But they were keepin' the legend alive now, for good or ill. Whether he wanted to get up, get dressed up, and go out and do it again, or not. Whether he could carry around this ole body anymore, or not.

They kept him movin', that's the truth.

The King got up from the bed, went to the wall of closets

and began sliding mirrors away from his own image, until he confronted racks of pale ghosts: an endless row of empty, glittering jumpsuits.

Which one tonight?

Which one was fit for a King?

Which one was fit for a King to go out and die in?

Chapter 28

Don't Be Cruel (to a Heart That's True)

(Elvis fell in love with this 1955 Otis Blackwell
song; it was the first of three of his recordings
that were number one on all three charts:
country, pop, and rhythm and blues)

Matt was beginning to hate his new job.

Every Midnight Hour was now a suspense show:
Would "Elvis" call or not? And when?

Matt couldn't help bracing himself for each new
caller, breathing relief when it was just some ordinary
person on the line, yet feeling a frisson of disappointment deep within. Was he becoming hooked on celebrity
too? Or was something else going on here?

He understood that he had a cohost now. A ghost
cohost. Everyone in the studio mimicked his own cool
excitement. Pros under pressure, loving and hating it. All
performance was a two-edged sword that way, and Elvis's weapon of choice had been particularly sharp because of his extreme fame and fans.

Matt now kept a cheat sheet in front of him. A list of

questions for Elvis, with names attached. His fingertips spun it on the tabletop. This move turned the counseling game into a quiz show. How could he claim any pretenses to serious counseling when his client had to play games to prove he was who he implied he was? Of course, Elvis had always loved games, arrested adolescent that he was. Still, Matt's ministerial past demanded that he do more than play media games. Was this bizarre charade damaging or helping the man who called on him for help? Maybe, Matt hoped and prayed, exposing Elvis's dysfunctionalism via a voice in the night would help everybody: the caller, Matt himself, the audience. Everybody, of course, except the dead man talking.

Poor Elvis! The weight of his family history and his fame had become as massive and ungainly as his dying body. Elvis had stood on a slippery mountain of uppers and downers, thousands of pills, and ultimately hypodermic injections, a year. His favorite reading was books on spirituality and medical textbooks. He knew the *Physician's Desk Reference* better than most doctors; armed with erroneous authority, he hooked his entourage on the same pharmaceutical seesaw of manic depression that he rode.

Another call was waiting.

Matt punched the button to release a voice. It took a heart-stopping moment to realize it wasn't the one he expected every time he answered.

By then, the caller was well launched, eerily echoing his conscience.

"—you've got a nerve. Playing with the reputation of a dead man. I hope all the Elvis fans out there get together and protest. Can't you do something on your own, without riding on a dead man's coattails? Elvis means something to a lot of people, and this cheap radio trick doesn't fool us, no, sir. You oughta be shot."

"Wait a minute. We just take the calls that come in, like yours."

"Yeah, and some of 'em are put-up jobs. Come on!

This actor you've hired is so cheesy, my twelve-year-old kid could do a better Elvis imitation. And don't think we all don't know that a bunch of these imitator guys are in town for the Kingdome opening. Hell, we Elvis fans just might boycott that big opening—how'd you like that, Kingdome people?—if you don't cut off this corny gimmick with that phony Elvis. Leave the man to rest in peace. Show a little respect. Get a life!"

Matt gave Leticia a stunned look through the glass. She was as shocked as he. But this was a show, and it must go on.

"Obviously," Matt commented into the foam-headed mike that had begun to feel like a friend, and maybe an only friend, "this caller is more in the mood for giving advice than asking for it."

Another call. "I've been listening all week, and that last guy is right. That Elvis thing is taking the air time away from normal people. We got problems with bills and kids and all sorts of things superstars wouldn't know anything about. I never liked Elvis when he was alive, and I don't want to hear about him, or from him, now."

"Believe it or not," Matt answered wryly, "Elvis grew up in a house—several houses, because the family was so poor they kept losing places—that was full of problems like bills and yelling parents, just like everybody else."

"Yeah, but he ended up with money to burn. That's sure not like everybody else."

"He ended up with dozens of people—family and friends who worked for him—to support, including the federal government, which is all of us, because he never took business deductions. For most of his career, he was in the ninety percent tax bracket. And he paid it, without complaint."

That floored this caller. Matt blessed Electra's supply of Elvis tomes.

"I love Elvis," came a faded, female voice next. "I'll take every chance I can get to see or hear him again, even if he's not real. You keep talking to that man, Mr.

Midnight. He seems like he could use a friend. Elvis always had more friends than he knew."

"Oh, I think he knew. That's why he was able to perform when he was really ill. He kept going despite a lot of physical problems, and enough psychotropic drugs to stop an elephant."

"Psycho-what?"

"Heavy mood-altering medications."

"They all came from doctor's prescriptions, didn't they?"

"Yes, but Elvis manipulated the prescriptions. He had feel-good doctors in L.A. who would write him what he wanted."

"Elvis wasn't the first one. Look at Judy Garland. I took diet pills when I was in high school, back in the . . . well, back when Elvis was doing it. Our family doctor gave 'em to me, these pink-and-white capsules. Made my mind race, made me think so much, think about all the things I was going to do. And I never wanted to eat. 'Course, I couldn't sleep a wink for the first month I was on them. And, then, after I lost ten pounds, I could sleep better, but they didn't work to stop my appetite anymore."

"What did you do then?"

"Nothing. Stopped taking them."

"That's the difference. Elvis and his entourage never let the party stop; they just increased the dosage."

"But the pills were legal."

"They aren't anymore."

"Why did Elvis do it? Why didn't he just stop when they wore off, like I did?"

"He came from a family with a tendency to chemical addiction. He led an upside-down lifestyle as a performer that was hard to maintain without artificial energy. He thought they were harmless if a doctor prescribed them."

"So did we. Then. We all thought Doctor Knows Best."

"Doctors didn't understand the many faces of addiction. Oh, they knew morphine and heroin were bad, but other stuff . . . And Elvis was coming into the sixties and seventies, when a lot of people started experimenting with all kinds of drugs. He was a man of his time."

"You know, that's what really bothers me. It was the drugs. I don't understand why nobody stopped it."

Matt shook his head, even though his caller couldn't see gestures. "You can't stop a person who's addicted to drugs. It's truly the hardest thing in life to overcome. It's the last thing in life that person has, and so often the only exit from addiction is death. Elvis may have been a superstar, but when it came to drugs, he had no edge over anybody else. And that's sad, no matter who it happens to."

"I'm just so glad I was smart enough to quit taking diet pills all those years ago." Her voice paused. A deep, trembling sigh. "I'm still fat, though."

"You're still here," he said gently.

The commercial break gave Matt time to contemplate his unexpected—unwanted—new role as an Elvis apologist. From a lifestyle point of view, the man had been everything he wasn't.

Leticia's orange-painted lips were mouthing "poor baby" at him through the glass. Matt took a swig of lukewarm spring water. He felt as if he'd been wrung out and then hung out to dry. And this hadn't even been the main event: the night's Elvis appearance.

At least the phone lines were jumping, and in talk radio, that was the name of the game.

Chapter 29

Return to Sender

(Otis Blackwell's song was the only quality
number on the soundtrack of *Girls, Girls, Girls,*
a 1962 film)

Temple hated to admit it, but Electra's notion that the
spirit haunting the Kingdome backstage area was more
likely a vengeful Memphis Mafia member than the King
himself made sense.

Of course, she didn't for a moment believe in spirit
manifestations. In the two incidents, flesh and blood had
been attacked in actuality, or in simulation. As if the
whole thing were a show. A production number.

It was possible that some Elvis advocate was so
caught up in the past that he, or she, needed to protest
the presence of an ersatz Priscilla.

Temple found the razor attack the most disturbing.
Despite Quincey's tough teen bravado, the act had been
cruel and personal. If whoever did it had an opportunity
to approach the real Priscilla . . . but that was the point.
He didn't, or he wouldn't have bothered Quincey. And

anybody that could do that to a sixteen-year-old girl—!

Temple had paused under the soaring dome, which played endless footage of Elvis in concert. Evidently, running pre-existing film was estate-approved. Most of it was in black-and-white, so the effect was eerily like storm clouds clashing above, a pre-Technicolor twilight of the god.

Electra had temporarily abandoned Temple to make a round of the domed chamber's vast perimeter, admiring each designer Elvis in its niche.

Around Temple, gawking tourists thronged, often bumping into her, the lone stationary object, as they gazed up at Elvis in 3-D surround.

Somebody bumped her and didn't back off.

A half-second later she shook off her thoughts enough to become annoyed. "Hey!"

"Hey, hey, hey! You ticklish, T. B.?"

"Get your hands off my ribs, or you will be corned beef hash."

Crawford Buchanan backed away just enough so that she could focus on his abhorable face. It was grinning.

"What is that dreadful smell?" Temple demanded.

"My cigar." Buchanan swaggered the small brown cylinder to the side of his mouth. "A Tampa Jewel, like Elvis used to smoke," he said through his cigar-clenching teeth, just like a melodrama villain. "Got it in the gift shop."

"He smoked cigars, too? Not my type."

"All of us big shots smoke cigars. It's a guy thing."

"That's what I mean."

"So what are you doing here alone?"

"I'm not alone. Just because I look alone doesn't mean I am."

"Oh, come on, T. B. You don't have to pretend with me. You haven't always got some guy on a string, like you want me to think. Afraid to admit you could use an escort? I don't see any rings."

"You would have, but I lost it."

"That 'lost ring' excuse is as old as Elvis."

"It happens to be true in my case." Temple felt a jus-
tifiable stab of self-pity. Not every woman lost her en-
gagement ring to a traveling magician's sleight-of-hand.
She'd barely had it for two weeks, and, presto! Gone
forever.

"Now, don't pout. Crawford's here to turn every salt-
water tear to pure cane sugar."

"Yuck!" Temple said.

He leaned close. The more she expressed her distaste,
the more he felt compelled to force himself on her. She
wondered for a wild moment what would happen if she
actually encouraged him . . . but she couldn't count on
an equal and opposite effect.

"You'd cheer up if you were sitting on what I'm sitting on," he whispered in sing-song, taunting tone.

Temple didn't want to know what he was sitting on.
"I doubt it." She scanned the crowd, looking for the loud
beacon of Electra's muumuu—chartreuse, black, and orange today.

"I am on to something so big it'll rock this town right
off its blue suede shoes."

"That's hyperbole even for you."

"It's the biggest story of the century."

"Isn't that premature? The century isn't quite over yet.
I believe 2001 is the actual date."

"And it won't be over until I break this story. Believe
me, this is the Big One. I can write my own ticket when
this gets out." He leaned closer, radiating cigar stench.
"And you can ride it with me."

"Why should I want to?"

"Because nobody can resist a success."

"I can, very successfully."

He blew a thin stream of blue smoke over her right
shoulder. "Tut-tut, T. B. You talk a good game, but
you'd fold like everyone else if you knew what I'm sitting on."

"Well, I guess nobody will until you get up."

"Oh, I will, when I'm ready. And then everyone will notice me. The story of the century. Want a clue?"

"No." ·

Leaning to whisper in her ear. "It's the biggest, hairiest hot flash since Abel axed Cain."

"Cain killed Abel."

"Details."

"So what have you got? King Kong?"

"Even better." Buchanan's smile wrapped itself around the soggy cigar end. "But you'll see. You'll see."

At last he moved on, a small poisonous cloud of Tampa-jewel cigar smoke hanging over his head like a visible miasma of bad news.

Hot story, ice-cold heart, Temple thought. As if all someone had to do to earn her interest was have a career conquest. King Kong! Well, the Elvis dome was big enough to hold a mythical beast of that size, but even Elvis couldn't live up to that scale.

Electra returned from her circuit, flushed and impressed.

"Those jumpsuits· are fabulous. I can see why they have to keep them so high up for security purposes— they must be worth millions, altogether—but I'd love to see them closer up."

"Have you ever been to Graceland?"

Electra lowered her pale eyelashes demurely. "I'm afraid so. It was years ago, of course. I happened to be in the neighborhood." She answered Temple's unspoken question. "In Atlanta. Distances aren't that far in the East."

Temple nodded at the non sequitur. Obviously, Electra had gone considerably out of her way to visit Graceland. "I've seen pictures. Graceland is not that impressive."

"It is when you think it's what a dirt-poor teenage boy was able to buy for his mother in three short years of performing music· that nobody had ever heard quite that way before. And that two-story, pillared portico reeks of Southern dignity. Of course the inside is decorated in got-rich-quick kitsch, but Elvis was a musical genius, not an interior designer."

"What I find impressive," Temple admitted, "is the performance records he set in this town. Did you know that he outpulled them all in terms of audience numbers—Sinatra, Streisand, Dean Martin—and that was after he made his comeback in the late sixties."

Electra nodded, as somber as Temple had ever seen her. "That time I saw him perform live back in the late fifties. He was pure heat lightning, energy and music and raw sex branded white-hot onto that stage and searing out into the audience."

"A hunk-a-hunk-of-burning-love. Stupid lyrics."

"Not when Elvis sang them. He got more feeling out of a song than you believed it was possible to put in. And he was always so charming and gorgeous."

"Electra! You were a groupie."

"I wasn't always 'of indeterminate age,' you know. And I've had a few husbands."

"A few!"

Electra's shrug made the flowers on the muumuu shoulders do the hula. "A few," she repeated, and said no more.

Temple let her gaze drift to the surrounding Elvis statues. "It's all so garish, so gross."

"That was the seventies, kiddo. It's just that Elvis is so famous his image is frozen in time. If you'd seen his contemporaries then you'd realize he wasn't that over the top. Don't you remember the glitter rock 'n' roll crowd, Elton John with his huge glitzy sunglasses, David Bowie, KISS . . . ?"

"I was just a kid; they were antiques."

"Besides, he was inspired by Liberace. When they met and he discovered Liberace was also a twin, they really hit it off."

"Now Liberace I appreciate. A master of high camp. Liberace turned glitz into a gold mine. He could make those glitter rock stars look like they were wearing tin-foil."

Electra nodded. "You have something there. So explain to me again how the hotel is able to exploit Elvis-dom without violating the estate trademarks."

"It is fascinating," Temple said, much more turned on by marketing magic than dead legends. "Everything here is 'Almost Elvis.' Nobody can copyright anything in its generic form, so that's what the Kingdome homed in on. Like selling Elvis's favorite brands of things in the gift shop. And capitalizing on his love of fast vehicles of any description in all their indoor/outdoor rides, calling the whole thing Raceland."

As she talked, she guided Electra past the blinking, buzzing, neon-lit entrance to Raceland. A bumper-car attraction in which all the vehicles, modeled after Elvis's favorite cars from pink Cadillacs to black Stutz Bearcats to Mercedes, clashed at the behest of their drivers aged eight to eighty.

"There's a pink Cadillac tunnel of love farther in." Temple gestured past the busy casino areas that acted as a river of commerce between the theme-park attractions, the machines burping out electronic versions of the apparently hundreds of songs Elvis had recorded during his twenty-four-year career.

"And of course they can play his music, as long as they pay for the privilege."

Electra shook her head in wonder. She suddenly stopped and pointed. "Look! There's some Memphis landmarks. Ohmigosh, 'The King's Clothing Emporium.' Elvis shopped at Lansky's Clothing Emporium in Memphis from the time he was seventeen years old. He wasn't afraid to sing black or dress black. Do you realize how gutsy that was for a poor white kid to do in the early fifties?"

"I knew he was the bridge bringing black music into the mainstream. Those books you lent Matt pretty universally agree on that, if on almost nothing else." Temple stared at the simple storefront now glitzed up with neon signs in the windows and above the door. "Yup, they have Elvis clothes for sale there, blue suede shoes and pink-and-black pegged pants, ascots, karate *gi*s, Hawaiian shirts, inexpensive but noisy jumpsuits in sizes infant to 4X."

"Oh!" Electra stopped to stare as tall, square white pillars loomed out of the neon mist pulsing above eye-level all around the Kingdome. "Gladys's Home Cooking. This place is like Wonderland, slightly kinked. Graceland is a restaurant here."

"Clever marketing," Temple agreed. "You can have anything you want at Gladys's Restaurant: fried-banana-and-peanut-butter sandwiches, even burnt-black bacon, some of it really only low-fat turkey. Would that Elvis had access to such healthful food! That's how they got around duplicating Graceland. They used parts of it and called it Gladys's."

"The gladioli are a nice touch. Elvis loved puns." Electra paused to admire dramatic stands of the vibrantly colored tall flowers massed around the restaurant's sloping "front yard." "But they always make me think of funerals."

"Not inappropriate here. You should see the Medication Garden."

"Medi-*ca*-tion Garden?"

"All herbs, you see. Not like the Meditation Garden at Graceland, where the family is buried now. This garden isn't officially on display yet. It'll open the night of the Elvis competition, when the winner comes over here to cut the ribbon."

"Oh, Elvis loved the Meditation Garden. Can't I peek now?"

"Security would get its nightsticks in a tangle over that."

"Were they able to suggest the family graves at all?"

"I don't know. I didn't look into this area, just backstage."

"Please," Electra begged, voice quivering. "The garden is the best part of the real Graceland. I'm dying to see how they evoked that without violating any estate prerogative."

"Well . . ." Temple looked around. The discreet path that led to the Medication Garden would probably be lined with spotlights by the formal opening night, but now it was definitely a path less trodden. In fact, it looked like a dead end.

She herself was dying to know how the hotel would produce what people expected to see without treading on a copyright or a trademark. How do you construct a Disneyland without Mickey Mouse?

So she led Electra past the DO NOT ENTER sign and through a winding, foliage-edged route that reminded her of the Enchanted Forest in Oz.

"The Meditation Garden is so impressive at Graceland," Electra was still recalling. "Do they have the lovely stained-glass panels and fountains here?"

"I did hear that there's a pool, but no graves. I guess graves aren't considered commercial in Las Vegas. I heard they did something spectacular so you can visit and meditate on the many stages of Elvis."

The path flared like a bell-bottom pantleg into a semicircular stage scene. A kidney-shaped pool whose waters were that ultrasweet pastel aqua-sky color Matt Devine had called Virgin Mary Blue lay in the background like a parenthesis curving around a colonnade of white pillars. Between the pillars, jewel-toned stained-glass Elvi shone like Saturday-night saints. Amid the flower beds offering an incense of pungent herbal aromas lay a smaller semicircle of what, at first glance, resembled a quintet of Sleeping Beauties in their glass coffins.

Temple gazed down on the display, at first not aware that instead of actual figures, jewel-emblazoned jumpsuits lay in state. Despite the priceless opportunity to see the costumer's art so close at hand, Temple had the sudden, sinking vision of the man who had once worn such creations. She saw him melting like the wicked witch in Oz, until only these empty suits, these abandoned carapaces were left. He had probably died long before he had ceased to wear and perform in them.

"These jumpsuits are even more exquisite than the ones in the dome." Electra bent to study the jewel-encrusted emblems. "Are these real gemstones—?"

"Careful! Whatever they are, there are probably pressure alarms all over the place, like in museums. Stay on the path."

Temple felt a chill beyond the mere worry of tripping some exotic security system. She had recognized the middle suit, a simpler, street-model suit: It was covered in solid white rhinestones, like one of Liberace's grand pianos dressed in mirror tiles, but the shirt beneath it was pale blue, and a white rhinestone tie dissected the vacant chest like the bottom Y of a coroner's autopsy cut. Strip the suit of its skin of glitter, and Temple recognized the simple ensemble Elvis had been laid out and buried in almost twenty years to the day after he had hysterically seen his mother to her own rest: the white suit Vernon had given him, blue shirt, white tie. Temple suddenly thought of the dead twin buried in an unmarked Tupelo grave forty-one and a half years before Elvis was laid out in Graceland; what had he worn to be buried in, Jesse Garon?

Electra grabbed her arm and squeezed hard. "Look! What can they be trying to do there? Why is that jumpsuit floating in the pool?"

Because one was, front-side down, floating like a giant dew-begemmed lilypad riding the azure of Hawaiian coves, sparkling and spinning in the gentle current of recirculating chlorinated water.

Only this jumpsuit was inhabited. A man's dark hair floated free above the high Napoleonic collar.

And a man's bloated white fingers, choked with

chunky gold rings, spread like dead starfish at the ends of the glittering jumpsuit sleeves.

And a man's bare heels protruded from the flared, floating bell-bottom pantlegs.

Electra shrieked, but not at the sight of the dead man.

Temple stopped herself from following suit, also glimpsing a long rope in the water. No, not a rope, just the pool creepy-crawler, an automated vacuum on a length of hose that kept the water clean.

Then the hose twisted up as if animated and entwined with the real beast that had been loosened on this garden of Elvisian Eden. Temple finally joined Electra's vocalizations.

A huge, mottled snake coiled around the floating corpse and dragged it down into the crystal-clear water, a snake as big around as a fireplug, as long as a living room.

A snake right out of Graceland's Jungle Room, a South American constrictor as big as the Ritz, the Circle Ritz.

Chapter 30

Crawfish

(A highlight duet from *King Creole*, 1958)

There I am, the intrepid investigator, pinned belly-down in the dirt by an allergy attack.

An overwhelming scent of lemon and mint (not my odors—or colors—of choice) has hit me like a wall of Kryptonite blocking Superman's heroic powers.

This place looked like an ordinary, innocent garden of Eden. How was I to know it was packed with pharmaceutical flower beds? All I need to fully incapacitate myself would be a wave of coconut-scented tanning lotion. Luckily, no human hide is sunning near the swimming pool, and the chlorinated fumes it dispenses act on me like smelling salts did on ladies of yore. Nothing like strong chemical odors to disperse a fit of the vapors one can ill afford.

Meanwhile, my two lady friends—imagine seeing them here!—continue to caterwaul.

In Miss Temple's case, I am sure the appearance of the gigantic reptile is far more responsible for her unusual screaming fit than the mere presence of a dead body floating in the pool. Miss Temple is on familiar terms with dead bodies. Even the fact that this one is so garishly attired should not be sufficient to launch the current hysterics.

On the other hand, that is one big mama of a water snake. No doubt it has done body-double work for Nessie of Scotland fame. Me, I am not afraid of snakes unless they carry concealed poisons. Otherwise, they make charming playthings. I do love how they slide across the floor like a bit of yarn dangled to challenge my mitt-eye coordination by humans hoping to amuse.

Still, despite my high opinion of Miss Temple's intrepitude, I have never told her of the family of garter snakes that found their way under the French doors while she was gone. Of how I discovered them rooting in her assorted sundries drawer and was forced to herd them off. It took the better part of the afternoon for me to escort them to the patio and then down the palm tree trunk. Since these were mere . . . what does one call baby snakes? Snakelets? . . . youngsters, I delicately nipped each one up by the neck and transferred it to the tree trunk, from where it wiggled down into the waiting, er, presence of Mama.

But yonder ophidian is not on quite the same scale, excuse the pun, as a string of garter snakes. I have not seen such a large specimen since the movie *Anaconda!* came and went faster than a whipsnake.

Yet despite the presence of a snake capable of strangling King Kong and the debilitating weeds contaminating my immediate area, I realize that I have an emergency job of herding to do: my two dear ladies had better shut up and skedaddle before they are caught raw-throated at the scene of a crime.

Ere I can leap from my cover, sneeze for their attention, and drive them out of this wonderland of weirdness,

I spy the suspicious character I have been tailing emerging from behind a stained-glass representation of Elvis crucified against a cloak of gold.

The newcomer has not the mythic appeal of Elvis's concert pose, despite being appropriately dressed in black from fedora to his suede shoes. All I can think of is that the Circle Ritz ladies must not be discovered alone with the corpse, whoever or whatever it is.

The figure in black is headed right toward their unsuspecting backs, so I head right for its unsuspecting feet.

This is what they call a "sacrifice play" in certain sports. I sacrifice my well-being and get a good kick in the ribs, while my opponent plays right into my hands, or feet, and goes tripping toward the edge of the pool without even a pause to doff the sunglasses.

Into the chlorinated drink the thing in black goes, with a yowl that would do a Siamese queen in heat proud.

In one agile move I have accomplished two things: I have distracted the newcomer from the presence of my lady friends, and I have managed to achieve their instant silence.

My distraction thrashes in the water, screeching in panic. This unfortunate shortly realizes that it is sharing a small, artificial body of water with a corpse and a giant snake, not exactly the human's idea of a picnic. Apparently, it is also howling because of something it knew, and I did not realize. The creature cannot swim. Oops. That snake will owe me one.

Of course all my heroics are for naught. Once the Misses Temple and Electra realize that a live person has joined the bridge mix thrashing up the waters, they go into action.

Miss Temple kicks off her shoes. For a dreadful moment, I fear that she is going to do something utterly foolish like leaping into the feeding frenzy now boiling up bubbles in the water like something from *Jaws* you really do not want to see up close and personal.

But instead of diving in, she kneels at the pool edge

and stretches out her hands, while Miss Electra sits down and grabs her ankles.

I am still recovering from my self-sacrificial loss of breath and cannot lend assistance, although I do not for the life of me see how I can be of any further service. No doubt the individual in the water (the one who is not dead) would agree with me. Certainly the anaconda, or the boa constrictor, or whatever variety of overgrown jungle snake it is, would second that opinion.

I hear grunts, howls, groans, and then coughs.

I also hear the onrush of feet pounding the sodded path. The imitation Memphis Mafia, otherwise known as Kingdome Security, has arrived in a panting pack.

One can only conclude that too many unauthorized personnel are cluttering up this crime scene already. I retreat back into the herbal hothouse, smothering uncontrollable sneezes. Miss Temple will just have to talk herself out of this one without me.

Chapter 31

In the Garden

(Recorded at Elvis's first session with Felton
Jarvis as producer in 1966)

"He's dead," Temple sputtered, shaking off the water the
rescued drowning victim had shaken on her the moment
all three had hauled themselves back from the pool's
edge on hands and knees. "Why did you rush in to rescue him?"

"Ohmigod!" shouted a Memphis Mafioso who had
just arrived poolside. "That jumpsuit is ruined. We're all
in the soup."

Publicity-phobic hotel security staff in Las Vegas always possess a big heart.

Other men in black fedoras and suits were arriving,
bearing aluminum pool hooks like lances. They began
gingerly hauling the resurfaced suit, and its contents, to
the pool's shallow end. Other men in brown work jumpsuits arrived, bearing bigger metal hooks, and began fish-

ing in the deep end for the coiling ropes of agitated serpent.

"I tripped," the soggy person in their grasp admitted. "I wouldn't have gone for a dip with that sea monster to save my life."

"Who are you people?" a disgustingly dry Mafia man asked, looming above them. "And what happened to the man in the suit? Did he fall in?"

"And how did the snake get loose?" another Mafioso demanded.

"The snake is supposed to be here?" Temple asked, amazed.

"Not here. Nearby."

Electra cleared her throat. "Could you gentlemen lend me a hand to get up? Thanks." They grunted, whether from effort or acknowledgment of her gratitude it was hard to say.

Temple scrambled up on her own power, despite skidding on the wet pool coping. Her emerald-leather J. Renee sandals were so water-spotted they resembled snakeskin.

She watched the security men lift the thoroughly soaked figure that had dashed into the pool. She was getting an awful feeling that her shoes had been ruined for naught. That choked, water-logged voice had a familiar ring and now she knew why . . .

"Let me go! I'm all right," Crawford Buchanan spat, quite literally, so damp was he from head to toe.

"But he sure isn't." A workman with a hook gazed on the snagged jumpsuit. "No point in even trying CPR. This guy's been floating here long enough to turn colors. Don't look, ladies!"

Temple and Electra stared avidly toward the pool, but Crawford Buchanan averted his face, pushing his sunglasses more firmly onto his nose.

"So he's been dead for some time?" Temple asked. "And how long could the snake float? Swim? Hang out?"

"The police coming?" the workman asked, ignoring Temple. "We can't hold this guy against the side forever, and I guess they won't want us bringing him out of the pool."

"What about Trojan?" a workman across the pool asked plaintively. "I don't want him getting contaminated by any, uh, decayed stuff."

"That chlorine would purify a cesspool," a Mafioso suggested.

"Oh, God," wailed the Crawf. "I can't believe what I might have inhaled. I'm going to puke."

Temple minced back, leaving Crawf to the disgusted mercies of the Memphis Mafia.

Electra had retreated to a curved concrete bench from which one could contemplate the glorious lucite-entombed suits, so Temple joined her.

"I guess we're witnesses." Electra couldn't conceal a slight tone of pride.

"Yeah. Also suspects."

"Oh. I hadn't thought of that. Why did that foolish man blunder into the pool like that?"

"I don't know, other than 'fools rush in,' and Crawford Buchanan is certainly one not to suffer gladly, in both the passive and active grammatical sense. What I'd like to know was why dear old 'C. B.' was lurking around here."

"Also the snake."

"That is so bizarre. Elvisdom can embrace almost any eccentricity, but I don't see why massive South American serpents would be among them."

"It's the other exhibit." A brown-jumpsuited attendant who was not busy holding something against the pool wall with a hook had overheard them, and now approached. He lit a cigarette.

"Better not do that: contaminating the crime scene," Temple warned.

"Who are you? The coroner?"

"No, but unless you don't want the police to think

that you were lurking here smoking cigarettes until your victim showed up and you pushed him into the pool with the snake you had brought in, I wouldn't smoke around here."

This was obviously a guy born to trample *Don't walk on the grass* signs. "I'll take my butt with me when I leave," he said with a sneer.

Temple didn't point out that everybody usually did that, and other people took their heads with them too. "You'll leave ashes, trace DNA maybe, who knows what? The police love that sort of high-tech evidence nowadays; saves them from doing a lot of legwork finding the perp. Now, what 'other exhibit'?"

The man, busy jamming his cigarette back into a half-empty pack, jerked his head to the left. "Over there. It's not open yet. 'The Animal Elvis,'" he declaimed sarcastically. "Duplicates of the horses at Graceland: Rising Sun, the palomino horse he rode. Priscilla's Domino. Then there's Elvis's chow-chow. And Priscilla's poodle."

"And an anaconda named Trojan?" Temple prompted. "How does that fit into the Elvis bestiary?"

"Wow, lady. Elvis was into a lot of strange things, but I didn't hear he was into that."

"Never mind," Temple said. "I'm asking how the snake fits into the Animal Elvis exhibit."

"I just handle the stock. Must have some connection. Maybe Elvis dated a belly dancer."

"They don't work with snakes."

"I don't know. All I know is that scaly mother is gonna be a truss-buster to fish out of that water. Whoever got it here didn't work alone."

Temple allowed the information to sink in. An interesting observation. But who would go to all this snake-toting trouble to off an Elvis impersonator? A jealous rival, or several? A crazed fan, or several? Animal rights activists?

And why the snake? Such a cumbersome set dressing. Or was it the murder weapon?

Or, if it was just set dressing, what was the message?

A twenty-foot-long anaconda named Trojan.

Oh.

Temple finally got one message.

Why the anaconda was named Trojan.

And that gave her one connection to the King right there. As Electra had just pointed out, Elvis had loved puns.

Was Somebody Up There laughing at them?

Or was Somebody Not Up There who should be?

Chapter 32

I'm Gonna Sit Right Down and Cry (Over You)

(One of the first songs Elvis recorded for RCA
in early 1956)

Crawford Buchanan was shaking like a willow in a windstorm.

He looked worse than a drowned rat, huddling under the "Kingdome" decorative blanket that had been rushed in from the hotel gift shop.

He sat alone on his own Medication Garden bench, teeth chattering too much to talk. Thank goodness, Temple thought.

She preferred the bench she and Electra occupied outside of Crawford's talking range, where she could catch phrases of officialese when the interior air-conditioning drafts were right.

". . . least it wasn't one of the damn display jumpsuits," a Mafioso muttered.

"Bet they'll be checking the Elvis impersonator roster," another speculated.

The body lay by the pool edge, clothed in a garbage-bag-green body bag. Temple wondered why that deep black-green color was considered appropriate for disposal of everything from orange rinds to corpses, and who decided such things.

Perhaps it wasn't quite as chilling as dead black.

The site now teemed with uniformed Las Vegas Metropolitan police officers, latex-gloved evidence technicians and video camera operators, some plainclothes detectives scouring the scene, and the gathered hordes of early arrivals. None of them looked remotely familiar, and for that Temple was grateful.

Eventually, the inevitable happened. A man ambled over to them, laminated police ID clipped to his suit coat lapel, and flipped open a notebook. He rested a foot on the empty end of their bench and took down their names, addresses, and phone numbers.

"You two found the body?" he finally asked.

"Not so much 'found' as turned around and noticed," Electra said quickly.

"You mean you had been here a few minutes before you noticed it?"

"Yes," Temple said, having learned through her dealings with Lieutenant Molina that interrogation sessions were like a dance class: it was better to let the police lead and the witness follow.

"I understand this part of the hotel wasn't open yet."

Temple and Electra nodded in tandem.

"You two don't look like scofflaws."

"Thank you," Electra interjected.

The detective was not interested in bestowing compliments; he just wanted to know the why and wherefore.

"I've . . . been involved with the Elvis pageant," Temple said. "Electra was, is, an Elvis fan and was curious about how the hotel was going to evoke the Meditation

Garden. We figured we wouldn't hurt anything if we took a look."

He nodded and took notes, allowing Temple to take her own mental notes: nice-looking in a bland way, probably a family man with two kids and a wife and a minivan. Quietly intelligent, preferred pencils to pens, maybe an artistic streak. . . .

"What did you think when you first saw the body?"

"That it wasn't a body," Electra blurted out. "Well, we'd been looking at all these Elvis jumpsuits around here, out in the dome and in these display cases here, and then there was that murdered jumpsuit in the dressing room the other day."

"Murdered jumpsuit?"

Electra, cow-eyed, glanced toward Temple. It occurred to her too late that she might have said too much.

Temple answered. "An Elvis jumpsuit was found with some red nail polish splashed on the back and a dagger pushed through it."

"Was this reported?"

"I was told that hotel security was alerted and that the police would be keeping an eye on things, but that was just hearsay."

"Hearsay." The yellow pencil was held poised over the pad like a strike-threatening snake. "You a lawyer, ma'am?"

"No way. I'm just saying what I heard. You'd have to check with the hotel and the police department to find out exactly what was reported and what was done about it."

"What is your occupation?" he persisted.

"I'm a public relations specialist. Freelance."

He glanced to the knots of people strung around the pool. "In your professional opinion, is this good, or bad, publicity for the hotel?"

"Sudden death is always bad publicity for a hotel."

"Sudden death of a guy in an Elvis suit?"

Temple sighed. "That's iffy. Some people can't get enough of Elvis, alive or dead, living or dying."

"Could it have been a publicity stunt gone bad?"

"I don't see how. If the area was open to the public, maybe. You know: see Elvis wrestle an anaconda in the Graceland pool . . . but that doesn't make any sense! Aside from his Jungle Room, Elvis didn't have anything to do with snakes. Unless it was some of the people who surrounded him."

"Oh?"

"I didn't have any particular snakes in mind; just the general show-business variety."

"What about that Buchanan guy?"

"You noticed the affinity."

"You know him?"

"Only as much as I have to. He's a local writer, I suppose you'd have to call him. For the *Las Vegas Scoop.*"

The detective nodded with that patented noncommittal expression they must go to police academy to master. "And why do you suppose he was here?"

"I have no idea. He just came barreling out of the bushes and rushed straight into the pool. He claimed he tripped over something."

The detective flipped his notebook back a couple of pages. " 'Some kind of animal, low and furred, like a weasel.' The brownsuits say that there's no weasel in the Animal Elvis exhibit."

"The only animal we've seen here," Electra put in, "is that awful snake. Did they finally take it away?"

"Yes, ma'am. Quite a struggle I hear. Too bad a snake doesn't leave tread marks."

Electra shuddered at the implication.

The detective slapped his notebook shut and took his foot off the bench. "Thanks for the cooperation."

"Like we were gonna take the Fifth," Electra muttered as he left. "Can we go now?"

Temple looked around. "I guess so." She frowned at

Buchanan, still shivering on his bench. "Apparently they're hanging the Crawf out to dry. You know, keeping him waiting until he cracks and comes up with a good excuse for being here. I'd almost feel sorry for him if I didn't know his biggest regret is not being able to get back to the *Scoop* to break the story."

"Temple, control yourself! Everything you've told me about him makes him the most venal, obnoxious man in Las Vegas, and that's a hard title to earn here."

"Yeah. Think about the competition he's up against. Colonel Tom Parker. I'm going to breeze by the dressing rooms and see if there's any reaction there."

"Think they've heard?"

"This is a pretty bizarre event to hide. Besides, I just directed the investigation toward the Elvis pageant. I bet those impersonators will hunger for my hide; they don't want to break their concentration for anything."

"They should be glad you're here to protect their hides. If someone wants to kill ersatz Elvi, there's a whole menu to choose from."

"I suppose you'll sacrifice your time and your best interests to accompany me down into the heart of Elvisdom?"

"You do need a witness to prove the innocence of your intentions. Just how many Elvi did you say are on tap downstairs?"

"It's a regular microbrewery of megalomania."

"Oh, goodie!" Electra rubbed her hands together and put her muumuu in motion.

Chapter 33

Bad Moon Rising

(Elvis sang this Credence Clearwater Revival hit
in some of his 1970s concerts)

Matt shrugged on his faux sheepskin jacket, but he
didn't pull on his leather gloves.

He knew by now that a straggle of fans would be
waiting outside the radio station for him to autograph a
motley assortment of ephemera: his photographs, their
autograph books, even the occasional T-shirt.

Leticia Brown encouraged this departing ritual. He
dreaded it.

For one thing, he couldn't help feeling defeated at the
end of every show. The Midnight Hour had turned into
the Elvis Hour. The phone lines bristled with calls from
pro-and anti-Elvis listeners. The list of stump-Elvis questions had grown to three pages.

As if sensing this mob excitement building, the mysterious caller had remained mysteriously silent last night.
Matt was being upstaged by a no-show.

He was annoyed with himself for not liking it, for wishing the sonofagun would end the suspense and just call, even it was to admit the whole thing was a hoax. Which was what it had to be, of course. Better to be revealed as the butt of a sick joke than to be stood up by a phantom.

They were always female, his fans, and they made him nervous. They looked at him with such fevered, hungry eyes, especially the Elvis groupies, as if he were an artery to the heart-blood of the King. He had a feeling they would slit his throat if they thought that would re-vivify Elvis.

Why else were they standing out here in the chilly dark collecting worthless autographs from the pen of a pseudonym?

Still, they flocked to him when he exited the building with the touching excitement of residents of a home for the mentally challenged welcoming a rare visitor to their world.

And maybe he was more than slumming in the alter-nate universes of talk radio and media idolization. Maybe if they didn't have this outlet, this hope, their lives would implode, or explode.

Matt smiled and signed, won over despite himself by their enthusiasm. Of the six fans tonight three were stu-dents and three were middle-aged. The twenty-five-to-forty-five-year-old age group seemed to have better things to do than fandom.

He glanced beyond their crowding shoulders to the distant street light.

No ambiguous silhouette stood in wait.

Matt wondered if he had become caught up in Elvis fever, had imagined that witness to his first encounter with fans. Was this how Elvis had started? With a paltry few? No, they had come in droves from the first. Evi-dently Matt didn't have that animal magnetism.

The very notion made him laugh, and the fans laughed

with him, delighted that he seemed happy to give them attention.

Attention. That was the key. Every human, and every animal, craved it. At times. Now he'd had his fill.

The street light had a running mate tonight: a full moon that hung above it like a hovering UFO. Blue Moon of Kentucky. Something Elvis had sung, or some amalgam of song and memory that Matt had made up?

He wished them good night and mounted the English-made motorcycle called a Hesketh Vampire, so well named for nocturnal jaunts.

They eyed it with satisfaction. Elvis had loved motorcycles.

I hate this thing, Matt wanted to shout at them. It was borrowed, once-removed, from a man he at best disliked and at worst envied and feared. It was as obvious and noisy as it was spectacular and fast. Spectacular and fast had never been Matt's speed.

He hated the ostentatious way you had to rev the engine before kicking off onto that aerial act of balancing a thousand-pound machine like it was an English bicycle. And the thing tilted like a pinball machine on curves and turns, defying gravity.

Elvis had loved the rush of speed, at first in any wheeled vehicle, than in any kind of mood-altering pills by the fistful.

Matt only felt safe being sober, maybe sometimes in the worst, humorless sense of the word. He really had to look into buying a car, when he had a minute, now that he had the money. At least motorcycle helmets guaranteed a measure of anonymity, as well as safety, he thought, fastening his. He felt instantly cocooned, muffled, disguised, and glanced back at the dark knot of people gathered against the station building's lit panel of glass door.

Then the Vampire swooped him away on a rush of air, sound, and motion, a magic carpet that roared.

The motorcycle thumbed its chrome tailpipes at the

deserted streets as he made his way toward the lights and the main thoroughfares. Its Vampire whine lifted into the wind and then skittered away like an echo.

The full moon rode over his shoulder, almost as if it was an unborn twin to the silver 'cycle . . . a high, shy shadow of the machine clinging to the ground. Matt could hear a distant howl borne by the wind. They kept pace, the moon and the motorcycle.

And then the second whine accelerated.

It was gaining on him.

The moon hung in its same position, eternally fixed to match the Vampire's speed.

Matt checked the side mirrors.

A single moon of blinding light flared in his right mirror.

Either a car with one defective headlight was behind him, or another motorcycle was taking this same route.

He couldn't make out much beyond the reflected Cyclops eye of light tailing him. Whatever sped behind was black and cloaked by the night itself.

He swerved suddenly left at an empty intersection with no stop signs.

The light swerved with him, showing up in his left mirror.

No car could maneuver that quickly.

Matt accelerated, the lighted dashboard dials seeming to intensify with the increased speed, as if the Vampire, given its head, was grinning like a Jolly Roger and showing neon teeth.

He knew the route; otherwise he wouldn't have dared hit . . . fifty, fifty-five. The area was industrial, not residential, at least.

He didn't know why, but he felt impelled to shake the shapeless form behind him.

It was like being a kid again, this visceral panic, this unshakable sense that something ugly was gaining on him.

Basements sometimes did that to you. Dark places

symbolically and implicitly connected to the blackest regions of imagination and primal fear.

Usually open streets had no potential for terror, not to men who thought they knew how to defend themselves, or at least to avoid obvious trouble.

But this burr of light that kept to the same, tail-gating distance, waltzing with the Hesketh Vampire in a dance nobody had requested or assented to . . . he had to lose it.

Matt recalled an abandoned service station coming up at the next intersection.

He would zip into it, through the empty gas lanes, around back and out the other side, onto a small road leading to an office park with a maze of buildings. He'd lose the thing that followed him there.

Islands of gas pumps looked like totems in the sick light from too few street lamps. He zoomed between them. A hard right almost had him reaching a foot to the ground to keep the cycle from overbalancing. But the Hesketh held, or he did, and the perilous, semihorizontal turn was history.

He fought the inclination to slow down as the maze of one-story buildings hunkered ahead like a Monopoly-board Stonehenge, lacking all rough edges and romance, but still a complex trap of confusing turns and dead ends.

He'd never navigated this place, but at least he knew it was there, and what it was. Whoever hid behind that single eye of light behind him couldn't know even that.

A few security lamps spread a thin layer of light between the buildings. Matt turned left, and then right and right and left, angling for the complex's opposite corner.

He lost the following light on the first turn, but the noise from both machines boomeranged from the glass-and-stucco canyon they shot through.

He recognized that losing someone else meant risking losing himself, but by now his hands were sweating inside the leather gloves, and all pretense was lost. Someone was following him who didn't mean to let him escape. He must escape.

Simple.

The tight maneuvers were making him breathless. This was insanely dangerous, to him and his menacing shadow. It had come down to who would survive the insanity first, and last.

The Vampire spurted out onto the empty freeway access road, jolting over potholes left by the searing summer heat. Matt's teeth and bones were starting to ache from the grinding pace, from tension.

He decided to head for Highway 95 and the Strip. Maybe a crowd would be the best place to lose himself. His mirrors reflected empty, black night.

He couldn't tell anymore if the noise thrumming in his head was the Vampire's or another motorcycle's or his own adrenaline-driven body's magnified function.

The lights of Highway 95 flowed as slow as lava ahead. Above, a hunk of canary-yellow rock as big as the Circle Ritz mooned Las Vegas. His mirrors remained black and vacant.

He glided onto the entry ramp alone. No need to accelerate to freeway speed; he was already doing it, and then some. He couldn't believe the needle: eighty.

And then . . . a pinprick in the mirror. A firefly. Growing.

Ninety.

The light clung, then grew again.

Matt tried to gauge the oncoming traffic. It was suicidal to enter the flow at this speed.

The moon in his mirror was swelling as if to duplicate its sister in the sky.

Crazy, crazy, crazy. Plus, he could get arrested.

He swerved onto the freeway, racing to beat a huge semi lit up like a Christmas tree. He was going way fast enough, but the semi was too close to cut in front of.

He did it anyway, feeling the tremendous wind-drag of the behemoth trying to suck him into its vortex. Past it, he slowed his speed, clinging like a moon to the obscuring planet of a double-long trailer.

He glimpsed the driver's face in the semi's left mirror. A dirty look, maybe an obscenity. At least this rider of the night had a face.

Only double-eye lights flared in his mirror, solid rows of them.

After a couple of minutes, he allowed himself to drop back until the semi surged ahead at its steady sixty miles an hour. No motorcycles shared the crowded lanes with him.

On the parallel access road, though, a single red taillight skated away at an oblique angle until it became a tiny infrared laser dot fading into the absolute darkness of the surrounding desert.

Chapter 34

Playing for Keeps

(Recorded in 1956, when Elvis was taking
control of his sessions with great energy)

ELVIS DIES!

The headline was the usual supermarket tabloid
screamer in tall, 72-point Helvetica bold type . . . except
that the news reversed the usual claim.

Invariably, the tabloids announced that *Elvis Lives!*

Temple was willing to bet that some blasé copy editor
had jumped up and down for joy at the chance to write
Elvis Dies! for a change.

Of course, this was the *Las Vegas Scoop*. Apparently
Crawford Buchanan had finally dried off and coughed
up what the police wanted to know. Then he had scurried
back to the *Scoop* to paint a breathless account of the
gruesome discovery in the Medication Garden.

The one fact he managed to ignore utterly was how
he happened to be on the premises at that particular place
and time.

Temple was intrigued to read that "busybodies-about-town PR woman Temple Barr and justice of the peace Electra Lark" had "stumbled over" the body (pretty hard to do unless she and Electra had a hidden talent for walking on water), "sending up a wail that would do an electric guitar proud."

Temple cringed to imagine Lieutenant C. R. Molina reading that line. Then she brightened. Molina would not be caught dead reading the *Las Vegas Scoop,* although Elvis might.

The account was full of lurid grace notes, including the design of the victim's jumpsuit (Fourth of July explosions) and the anaconda's exact length (eighteen feet), but it contained remarkably little news.

The morning *Review Journal* had been put to bed too early to report the murder. Instead, their feature page headlined: "Seeing Double?" Elvis, that is, a story on the multitudes of Elvis impersonators in town. Velvet Elvis had made it into a photograph. So had several more conventional male models, none of whom much resembled the King of Rock 'n' Roll except for the uniform hair, sideburns, and jumpsuits. Reviving Elvis was an imprecise art.

The *Sun* had the full-meal deal: it identified the dead man as an Elvis impersonator, so far unidentified. The jumpsuit, it mentioned, was an expensive version, not the usual costume-shop model. The victim's hair was not only high, wide, and handsome, but also costly, and had clung throughout the impromptu rinse cycle in the pool.

As for the snake, it had "escaped a nearby animal exhibit." An autopsy would determine its role in the death, if any. The authorities had no evidence that the death was a drowning, and there were no witnesses, except for two Las Vegas residents who had discovered the floating body while visiting the hotel's herb garden.

Temple felt relief soften her muscles. This was such a ridiculous death to have discovered. It didn't seem real.

At least her name wasn't on it in a respectable newspaper. Yet.

She tapped her front teeth with the eraser end of a long yellow pencil. She knew the backstage area would be abuzz with gossip today. More than other performers, these men were not islands. Their whole existence was a form of denying death, so any Elvis death would diminish them. They would not go gently into that dark night.

She really needed to return to the Kingdome and view the aftermath of the articles herself. First, a phone call. She glanced at the clock while punching in numbers to make sure the hour was decent.

"Matt? Oh, I'm fine, but you sound like I woke you up. Oh, didn't get to sleep until six A.M.? Whyever not?"

His answer was vague, saying the ride home had been windy and cold. He really had to get a car.

"Terrific. What kind?"

"Something reliable and economical."

"Oh, phooey. You're no fun. Listen, I'm off to the Kingdome, and I wanted to know what call-in Elvis said last night."

"Nothing."

"Nothing? Don't tell me he sang instead?"

"Not a note, not a peep."

"That's . . . odd."

"We don't have a date every night."

"Well . . . it's really odd that he was mum last night when you know that an Elvis imitator was killed yesterday."

"Killed?"

"Not necessarily murder. Could be a bizarre accident. Electra and I found the body."

"I'm not going to ask how."

"Just by being the usual nosy. I'll spare you the lurid details. It's in the evening paper if you want to read it when your baby browns are open wide. You do sound beat. How can radio chit-chat be so draining?"

"Waiting for someone to call who doesn't can be a strain. And . . . other stuff."

"Other stuff. Life is full of 'other stuff.' It'll be really interesting to see if your call-in Elvis stops calling now that this guy is dead."

"Why do you always see a death as linked to any nearby remote connection?"

"I don't see. I suspect. What does your gut tell you?"

"That I got to bed way too late this morning and need something to eat."

"You want me to breeze upstairs and whip you up something?"

"No breezing, no whipping, and I would hope no snooping around the death scene."

"Can't promise anything. I'll let you know if anything fascinating turns up."

"It probably will. It always does when you're around."

"Thank you!"

"Temple. Be careful. There are odd people out there."

"Sounds like you've had your fill of talk radio already."

He didn't answer, an ominous reaction.

"Let me know if Elvis calls again," she said.

"Temple, that's a fantasy."

"Matt, this is Las Vegas."

Temple thought about Matt while she drove to the Kingdome.

He was usually as easy to see through as a crystal ball, but now, she sensed, he was trying to keep something from her. She couldn't tell if he was feeling worried—not a new emotional state for him—or jaded. Jaded definitely would be a new emotion. How could he be Down when so many Up things were happening to him? A new media career, a modicum of fame and fortune, hero status . . . what more could any normal American boy want?

Of course there were no normal American boys, or

girls, just people muddling their way through the sweet mysteries of life. And now that Temple had ended the unhappy state of being torn between an ex-lover and one not-yet-and-maybe-never lover, she had no business being in Matt's life. What did a fallen-away Unitarian have to offer a recovering Roman Catholic celibate anyway? Temple smiled to recall Matt's astonishment at hearing that she had dropped out of a religion as broad-based and tolerant as the Unitarian Universalists, whose name said it all. Unification. Universality. She had neglected the Sunday sermons, that was all. The lessons stayed with you in spirit whether you were there in body or not. And she'd become so busy when she and Max began living together. A performing magician kept ungodly late hours, which didn't lend themselves to keeping godly Sunday mornings.

When Max had vanished a year ago, everyone had been so ready to believe he was just another skedaddling scoundrel. Not Temple. And Max finally had returned, to confess that he'd left to safeguard her from the secrets of his dangerous undercover past. Matt and Max. Light and dark, quite literally, and both dogged by the darkness of that eternal mystery, their own tangled family relations. At least her family was pretty uncomplicated, if a bit overbearing. But now Max the performer had been forced into hiding, and Matt the modest priest cursed with matinee idol looks had been pushed into the limelight. And wasn't sure he liked it! Did everybody get exactly what they *didn't* want? Was that the sweet-and-sour mystery of every life? Maybe even hers?

Temple felt a rare nostalgia for her fleeting television reporter stint. Maybe she should have persisted in TV, found another on-air spot. Hosting a local talk show, say. Cohosting. She was so good at talking to people, at finding out things about them. Gee, if she had Matt's current opportunity, she'd be jumping in the air and clicking her heels, even if that did scuff good shoe leather.

But she wasn't Matt, she wasn't a talk-show host, and

her off-campus assignment right now was to check out the Elvisfest at the Kingdome. Which was good, because she felt sorry for Quincey, and responsible for her in a weird, big sister way. And in that regard, she really needed to follow up on her Grand Plan.

Half of her Grand Plan greeted her when she reached the dressing room area.

They were attired as sea-to-shining-sea Elvis: from East-Coast glitter Mafia to Hillbilly Cat metallic-thread rayon to Country Crooner rhinestones to Western Swinger to West Coast glitz tux to Hawaiian neon.

"Fetch my rhinestone sunglasses, boys," Temple teased in a Mae West voice, hefting her forearm up before her eyes as if bedazzled. "So what's the status quo?"

"Vadis?" Hawaiian neon Elvis tried.

"I just need to know the basics: who died, who cares."

"Nobody knows yet—I'm not kidding." Hillbilly Cat Elvis was so cute in his fifties muscle shirt and narrow belt that Temple wanted to pinch his arched upper lip. "Somebody says he was from Chicago, I think."

"I suppose the Elvi come from all over," Temple observed.

"Not many Italians." West Coast Elvis twitched his shoulders in his sharkskin dinner jacket with the black velvet lapels.

The Fontana brothers may not have possessed Elvis's facial features particularly, but at a universal six feet even and all imperially slim, they gave Temple a pretty good insight into just how gorgeous Elvis must have been in his prime. Dude-licious, one might say, to go with babe-licious, phrases Quincey would no doubt approve. Or "dig." Or rock with.

"I imagine you hear all the gossip, being part of the show."

"Hey, we're more than that," Oversized Elvis sounded distinctly aggrieved.

"Yeah," said Fifties Elvis, "the management is using

the pageant as an employee screening system." He executed a swivel-pose onto the balls of his blue-suede-shod feet. "Several of us have been offered permanent positions in the hotel," he added importantly

"Oh, really. And how would your brother Nicky at the Crystal Phoenix like that?"

Hillbilly Cat Elvis pouted. "He doesn't have nothing to say about it. He never offered any of us a job."

"I didn't know any of you were pining for jobs."

"We're not, but it's nice to be asked."

It turned out that various brothers Fontana had been plucked from the mob, so to speak, for positions as gift shop sales clerk, parking valet, health club waterboy, floor show usher, waiter, bartender, and blackjack dealer.

"The idea is that every guest will get a young Elvis working his way up to serve them."

"He had a lot of different jobs even in high school," Karate Elvis put in. "That kid was no slacker."

Temple shook her head. "Do you have to sing at any of these jobs?"

"Not a requirement. We can hum a little, though, and fidget our left legs." Fifties Elvis demonstrated with a slacks-shaking shiver.

"That was the birth of the Delta boogie, you know. Elvis was a nervous-energy kind of kid and was always twitching something, particularly his left leg. That's what really got his pelvis going. Who'd ever think a nervous tic would be the key to all those teen angels out there?"

"He caught on fast, though," Motorcycle Elvis said.

"You guys are sounding like fans. Did you start out that way?"

"Heck, no, Miss Temple. Except for Aldo, we thought he was this square old guy in Liberace leftovers who liked to blast out songs like churchy stuff and 'Dumb Coyote.' "

"I know 'How Great Thou Art' was one of Vegas Elvis's staple hymns, but what was 'Dumb Coyote'?"

"You know, 'I am I, Dumb Coyote—' "

Temple stared, dumbfounded. These guys were her age, but they didn't have her broad background from doing public relations for a repertory theater. "It's not 'dumb coyote,' "—she had to pause to keep from laughing herself sick—"it's 'I am I, Don Kee-ho-tay.' Don Quixote. From the musical, *Man of La Mancha*, based on Cervantes's eighteenth-century novel."

"I don't think that *Man of La Muncha* has played Vegas, Miss Temple."

"Well, not the hotels. I'm sure a touring company played the civic center at one point, years ago. During Elvis's heyday. Anyway, that's the show-stopping song from the musical play, and Elvis sang that."

"We didn't really think he'd call himself a dumb coyote."

"He was too cool a guy."

Temple nodded, reminded how fast the plays and songs of the one day fade into the fads of the next generation, and how remarkable it was that no one was letting Elvis turn the same sepia-brown of memory.

Not while anyone was alive to don a jeweled jumpsuit and another man's dream, anyway. Another man's dream-turned-nightmare.

"Hey, Miss Temple, don't look sad. I got some news that will perk you right up."

"What is that?" she asked. They answered serially.

"The scuttlebutt."

"Around here."

"Snake's off the hook."

"Didn't do it."

"Naw, the guy was throttled, all right, but the snake would have crushed his chest, not his throat."

"So the snake is as innocent as a lamb."

"Who's guilty then?" Temple asked.

"We don't know."

"We do know that the so-called Memphis Mafia is crawling all over this place."

"Hotel security." Temple nodded.

The Fontana boys shook their heads until Elvis fore-locks drew cocky, dark commas on every brow. They gathered even closer, lowered their voices to a softer, conspiratorial level.

"See, we know a bit about Mafia guys."

"Just comes with the territory."

"What territory is that?" Temple wondered.

"Being Italian, of course."

"So what do you know?" she persisted.

"There's Mafia here, all right. The real thing. Blend-ing right in."

"Since the death?"

Their weirdly inappropriate blue eyes exchanged fur-tive glances.

"Since before. It's a good thing we're undercover. Otherwise, some wise guys would be giving us guff."

"And we'd have to give it right back."

"Guff, that is."

"Guff." Why did Temple think that "guff" came with a caliber?

"The way it is, we're in a perfect position to watch them watching everyone else."

"You're saying these are heavy players," Temple tried to clarify.

"Yeah. Not any of Boss Banana's local muscle-heads. These are outa-town dudes. Guys from the garbage and cement-mixing business. Old school."

"Bet they could dig up Jimmy Hoffa in two minutes flat if they wanted to, and dump him on the main stage of the MGM-Grand to do a soft shoe."

"Oooh." Temple's active imagination was about to make her sick.

But the brothers Fontana pressed so close they held her up, stiffened her spine, and maybe her upper lip, which had never been known to sneer.

"We also think—"

"Some of the suits—"

"Are passing as hotel security—"

"But are into security in a lot bigger way."

"Like for the whole U.S. of A."

Temple blinked. She thought. She thought like a gangster, which was a stretch a custom limousine would aspire to.

"Feds?" she whispered in disbelief.

Six blue-black helmets of Elvis hair nodded. "She's fast for an amateur," one said.

"What kind of feds? ATF? Alcohol, Tobacco, and Firearms?" Elvis had drunk occasionally, had always smoked little cigars, and was a major gun collector, and carrier, during his later years. "DEA? Drugs were really his Waterloo. IRS?" He had overpaid his taxes, to a ridiculous point. "Um, what else is there?" Or maybe it had nothing to do with Elvis at all.

Their faces were impassive.

"We don't know exactly. We just can smell shills on both sides of the law among the usual dopey hotel muscle. You know, you put on one of those uptight black suits, a white shirt and shades, and you could pass for a Blues Brother or a presidential bodyguard or an enforcer out of any northern city like Chicago."

"Used to be a big Chicago connection to Vegas. Who do you think did in Bugsy Siegel?"

"But that was really decades ago. Way back beyond Elvis," Temple objected.

"The Mob has a long memory," Blues Brother Elvis said, his eyes hidden behind his shades.

"And so do we." There was nothing hidden about Oversized Elvis's expression.

Chapter 35

Animal Instinct

(This song was cut from 1965's *Harum Scarum*
and never heard or seen again)

When a really heinous crook is characterized as too evil
to live, usually all and sundry describe him as "an animal."

That is human nature for you, always looking for some
other part of nature to take the blame for the bad stuff.

Sometimes they will call the offender "an insect," but
that is usually for piss-ant, penny-ante stuff.

I have long taken exception to the human tendency to
attach their own kind's worst actions to the animal world.
It implies that we of the furred and haired and hided sort
have no morals. And we do not. Morals are a cross that
humans give themselves to bear. We merely have "behavior" and "instinct."

And more brains and nicety than we are given credit
for.

So I realize early on that the unfortunate serpent who
was dunked into the pool with the corpus delecti is now

a suspect du jour. I also realize that the usually tongue-tied snake (and it has the forked tongue to tie) might have something relevant to say, and that I am the very one—the only one—ready, willing, and able to unlatch this snake's two-way tongue.

Now this is no easy assignment. I have not conversed with serpents before, although I have had words with a lizard or two. Snakes are notoriously tight-lipped, as well as being a clannish sort. I can only imagine what a lone tropical snake imported to the concrete-and-neon jungle of Las Vegas might wish to keep to itself.

There is no good way to cozy up to a snake.

But I thrive on challenge, and Chatter has lived up to his name and been full of palaver but not much solid information, so I hie myself off to the Animal Elvis exhibition area behind the Medication Garden that proved so unhappy an experience for the two little dolls from the Circle Ritz, and for some benighted Elvis wannabe before them.

My little dolls need my usual stalwart assistance, though they do not know it, which is also usual. Besides, I am catching Elvis fever just like everybody else. Enquiring minds want to know who is messing with the King's new playground.

I am not sure what I should expect besides dogs, horses, and the serpent. I have never interrogated a zoo before. With horses I am on good, if somewhat distant, terms. I am a city lad and more inclined to hitching a ride on a passing pickup than on a horsehair hammock.

Dogs are always touchy. I have been chased for my very life too many times in my early days as a gentleman of the road. Although my species is adept at bullying the bully-boys, when we are young we are often not aware of our powers and may be intimidated. I am sorry to say that my forays with canines have left me with an understandable disdain for the breed. I will have to proceed delicately with the dogs, so as not to betray my natural dislike.

Luckily, the attraction—although I cannot see how a

compound of animals not including any felines could possibly be termed an "attraction"—is not open for business yet.

I should have free run of the place.

I decide to hie up top to interview the noble equine first. I have never known a horse not to talk sense, and find it outrageous that such a mild and useful breed has been so badly misused by humans. Although I have been known to dream that I am the size and incisor-level of the awesome saber-tooth tiger so faint in my ancestry, I have never regretted being too small to ride or to bear or to drag burdens. It is one supreme advantage the domesticated branch of my species has.

The animals are kept, of course, in an outdoor park that I imagine evokes Graceland's rolling acres.

I find Rising Sun, a handsome honey-blond stallion of the type called palomino, munching oats at an outdoor drive-up stand. I hop atop the feeding station. Poor critters are cursed with these big, square teeth and hence are condemned to chew leaves of grass until their enamel turns green. I do not understand how they can keep those huge bodies going without any good red meat in their diet.

"You are new," the horse notes succinctly between mashing vegetation.

"But not green," I add quickly, just in case he mistakes me for a hank of rye grass or something. With their eyes on the sides of their heads, sometimes horses cannot see every little thing clearly. Like me.

I explain my mission, during which Sun nods and munches judiciously.

At least I assume it is judiciously. Horses have that considering air about them, like trial judges. They may be contemplating deep matters, or they may simply be chewing every bite one hundred times, as advised by the health books.

I look around the meadow. "I can see dogs racing over yonder hill, but I find it hard to picture an anaconda in these happy fields."

The horse stops chewing to regard me with a brown eye as velvety as whipped chocolate. Miss Temple may be a wimp for brown-eyed blonds, but not me. There are no brown-eyed cats, obviously another clear sign of superiority.

I decide I need to shave off a little erudition. "The snake," I repeat pointedly.

Sun whinnies and shakes his head until his platinum blond mane shimmies. I am beginning to think that in the brain department, he would be similar to an actor found on *Baywatch*. This boyo is all muscle and sun-bleached locks. And health food.

But he snuffles out a sigh and resumes our fitful conversation. "If you meant the snake, why did you not say so? When you said 'Anna Conda,' I thought you were referring to an attendant I do not know."

"I mean the snake."

"I am not much afraid of that snake," he boasts.

"It is one of the biggest in the world."

"But it is not poisonous. I can take care of it with my hooves. No, the kind of snake I avoid like a briar patch is the small, poisonous sort that could strike my hock before I knew it. This Anna Conda snake is too big to miss, and no danger to me."

"You have any idea how it got out of this area into the pool?"

He shakes his glamour-boy mane again. You would think he was Fabio. "They kept the Conda under glass, in a special area with tropical vegetation. I assume the snake would have to wait for a keeper to come and free it."

"But you know nothing about yesterday afternoon, when it would have been released?"

"I was off for a canter with Domino." He nods to the distant dark form of a horse, head bowed to the imported grasslands. "The tourists like to see us cavorting, you know."

"There are no tourists yet."

"There will be."

He returns to his feedbag.

That is the trouble with these ruminant animals; they think with their stomachs. And sometimes they have more than one.

So I hop down and go on the lookout for dogs.

This whole field setup reminds me of those cheap science fiction movies where the small set in front is supposed to fade into a painting at the back that is intended to depict the surrounding countryside. Only you can see the brushmarks even from the back row of the Lyceum.

I frankly do not find this bucolic scene thrilling, but I suppose Elfans who have or have not been to Graceland relish the country squire look of the place. I am rounding the corner of the small barn when I come face-to-face with a snub-nosed, bristle-ruffed, purple-tongued creature that resembles an unsanctioned union between a giant radiator brush, an Eskimo, and a wild pig.

A growl is the only clue that this sixty-pound critter is merely a dog.

"Get low!" a human voice shouts.

I do not need encouragement. I immediately dive behind a bale of hay.

Sure enough. A brown jumpsuit soon makes the scene.

"What are you growling at?" she asks the bristled pig who had been accosting me. "You know all the stock. Just pipe down and don't scare the horses."

The creature backs off and the lady animal tender moves on.

"I am glad the Jumpsuit warned me," I say to all and sundry who remain around, which is Rising Sun, the head of the lovely Domino, who has now munched her way to the stable area, and, uh, this Brillo pad of pale hair which I discover is sitting right next to me. I have seen wads of hair bigger than this removed from washing machine lint traps.

But the wad turns to me and I spot a pair of beady black eyes amid the permanent wave.

"Nobody warned *you*, silly," the lint trap says. "The keeper was calling the chow-chow off."

Okay. I have heard of chow you can eat and *ciao* you can say "hello and good-bye" in Italian with, but I have never heard of a chow-chow you can call off-off.

Since the fuzzhead speaks with a funny French accent, I restrain myself, play the sophisticate, and merely reply, "Par*don*," with the accent on the second syllable.

"Getlo is the dog's *name*," fuzzhead says, "as mine is Honey." With the accent on the second syllable, I might add.

"Getlo? What kind of name is that?"

"I agree. It is silly. But that was what Elvis called his chow dog in 1957 until it died in 1975, and that is what this edition must be called, as I am called Honey, after Priscilla's poodle that Elvis gave her."

I am relieved to know what species I am dealing with. I was having my doubts.

"Thank you for the clarification, Hon-*eee*." (I make her name rhyme with "Paree," with the accent on the second syllable so as to sound French.) "Why did you not say that the creature is merely a common chow dog? I am familiar with that breed, or at least their reputation for fierce guard work." I do not mention that they also have a rep for going off half-cocked.

"These working dogs are so serious about their roles in life," she adds with a blasé sigh. "I understand that my role is merely to decorate and entertain, hence do not have to throw my weight around like the savage Getlo."

"You do not have much weight to throw around," I note.

Any dame takes that as a compliment, and this one practically purrs. "I heard you nuzzling up to Rising Sun. Are you playing the detective?"

"I do not 'play' at anything," I say in a growl.

"Oh, so serious. Do not bother asking those big *chevaux* anything. They are too high off the ground to know what is going on, particularly in regard to snakes."

"Oh? So what do *you* know?"

She plants her slender forelegs with the wide, Persian-lamb cuffs emphasizing her delicate bone structure, and tosses her curled and perfumed tresses. "What should certainly be sufficient for you, *mon ami.* How are you called?"

"I am not called, as I do not come when called. But my name is Louie." A rapturous squeal interrupts my spiel. "Midnight Louie."

"Louie! So you are French!"

"I am whatever nationality it suits my purpose to be."

"A man of the world, no?"

"I get around. Now. Did you notice any people who were not keepers creeping around here yesterday? Any keepers acting odd? Did you see Trojan escape, or was he removed bodily?"

"I did notice a flurry of activity among the humans, which I attributed to the imminent opening of our attraction. More importantly, I detected several alien scents. If you like, I can lead you to Trojan's quarters and tell you what scents remain."

"Just the thing. You go ahead. I'll follow."

Well, that was a mistake. The poor kid's tail has been shaved to the skin, with only a ridiculous pompon sticking on the end like a skewered mushroom on a shish-kabob tine.

But she puts her long, pointed French nose—leave it to the English and the French to sport the biggest noses in the business, no wonder they do not get along with each other—to the ground and soon we are in sight of a huge glassed-in aquarium sort of setting, except it is all bushes and vines and only a little water.

Honey is making tiny circles all over the ground, calling out scents as she goes: "Jenny the Keeper. Carlos the Keeper. Stranger. Stranger. Getlo. Domino. Stranger. Jenny. Dennis the Keeper head. Stranger."

"I make out four strangers. Just from yesterday?"

"*Oui.*"

"Hmm. And that is all you can tell from the trail?"

"Unless I cross paths with any of these strangers again."

"How do I, uh, break into this glass menagerie?"

"That is your job."

"And I do not see the resident."

"That Trojan! He is very, how you say? Torpido. He is digesting somewhere behind all the leaves."

"Seems like a snake that size should be more visible."

"Oh, he curls up like the big ball of yarn. It is so cute."

I am not convinced, but thank her politely for her help and check out the aquarium's perimeter for possible entry.

The back wall is solid wood instead of glass, and soon I find a nice little doggie door through which the staff inserts Trojan's lunch, which is probably South American rodents about my size and in my condition, alive.

Naturally, the doggie door is just my size, and it is not hard to shoulder my way through.

It is still and humid inside the minijungle that forms Trojan's housing environment. Amazing how a few tropical plants can make the air so heavy it hurts to inhale. For one used to the sere Las Vegas atmosphere, as high and dry as a fine French champagne, this instant steam room is enough to dampen my fur and my spirits.

My first task will be to find my prey in this place so in need of a weed-whipping. My second task will be to convince my prey that I am not lunch, despite appearances. No, my second task will be to figure out a way to communicate with the prey so I can tell it I am not lunch.

A good thing I cannot sweat, because if I could this hothouse air and my perilous situation would have me dripping like a leaky faucet.

First thing I notice is that the vines, trunks, and foliage in this snake pit all have a lot in common with the resident-in-chief. The vines and trunks are as thick as the arm on a sumo wrestler, and the foliage is mostly green-brown and mottled.

I could be eaten by an errant leaf before I even know it.

Slinking around in this primordial feeding station is too dangerous. I decide on the bold approach, brushing my way past rubbery leaves toward the front display window.

On the other side I view the horses at their elevenses, and the topiary-trimmed form of little Honey watching me with bright, avid eyes.

Behind me is the heart of darkness, the jungle as even Elvis never knew it in his Jungle Room. There is a still, heavy silence holding Bast-knows-how-many-pounds of pulsating reptilian predator.

It is a good thing I do not have a snake phobia.

Positioned now, plainly visible, I begin a low croon not unlike the kind of blues us fellows like to improvise off the top of our fences during mating season.

It is halfway between a growl and a purr, or a hum and a howl. It is the blues like you hear it down every dark back alley in every big city from here to who-knows-where. It is the St. Louie Blues, and the Las Vegas Blues and the Appalachia Blues and the Harlem Blues and the Globetrotter Blues.

My rear member begins to itch, then twitch, then beat back and forth like a metronome. Back/forth back/forth back/forth tick/tock tick/tock and underneath it all I keep that eerie hum-croon going, with an occasional yowl for interest.

This Hillbilly Cat is cooking!

I think Siamese and Burmese and Tonkinese and Balinese and Javanese, so there's a little minor-key Asian wail to the tail-beat too. I envision cobra heads swaying in rhythm, rattle tails shaking up the maracas in the back section, asps etching figure esses like Olympic skaters. I envision Cleopatra and Little Egypt boogieing across the tropical wallpaper. They both look like Cher if her hair were a Medusa-do of funky snakes.

We are all percolating to the whine and the wail and the rhythm and the rock 'n' roll.

And then along comes Trojan, winding down from the big tropical what's-it plant, his massive head nodding like it can't stop, his thick coils pulsating to the beat.

In no time he has thumped to the floor of the case coil by coil, his eyes slitted to obsidian slivers, his body bobbing to the sound and the motion.

I let the wail wind down and keep the purr going strong.

Then I slip in a significant question or two.

And it works like a charm.

Chapter 36

Little Sister

(Blues number Elvis recorded in Nashville in 1961)

"It is so creepy around here. I can't believe I gave up singing in a grunge band for this."

Quincey hunched over the long empty dressing table, her white go-go boots dispiritedly turned out at the ankles, her sleeveless A-line pink polyester dress seeming to hold her up by its severe architectural lines alone.

"I didn't know you sang," Temple said cheerily.

Quincey's eyes gazed rebuke through her black holes of mascara. "I don't. That's why I would have been so perfect for the job. Are you sure Courtney Love started this way?"

Temple took in the outfit and the lonely ambiance of the deserted dressing room. Being the only peahen in a clutch of male peacocks couldn't be described as fun. "I'm not sure anybody started this way, including Priscilla Presley. Have there been more threatening notes?"

"To me? No." That fact seemed to further dispirit Quincey. "I am the forgotten woman at this thing," she announced, "now that somebody has offed an Elvis."

"The death hasn't been labeled a homicide yet."

"What else could it be?"

"An accident. A suicide."

"Suicide. Now that I can buy. This whole gig is suicidal." She threw a tube of Daddy Longlegs's Centipede Sweetie mascara onto the scuffed tabletop. It rolled all the way to the other end, like a ball down a bowling lane, where it crashed into a bumper of scratched Formica. "I mean, I am bored to death! It's all sitting around, waiting for the guys to get ready to run through their acts. Like, I've been forced to bring homework and even look at it here."

Temple eyed a slim book with one lined sheet of notepaper stuck askew between its pages. This did not look like serious study.

"That's show biz," she said matter-of-factly. "Waiting for your time to come. In fact, Michael Caine once said he got paid nothing to act, but a very lot of money to sit around and wait."

Quincey stared at her, as if riveted by this gem of theatrical wisdom. "Who's Michael Caine?" she finally asked.

"Oh, nobody. The Brad Pitt of several generations back."

"Brad Pitt. Yuck. Totally retro. He's really let himself go."

"Oh. I guess Elvis holds the record, then. He kept his fans for over twenty years, and even death did not them part."

"But they're all crazy." Quincey sighed. "I guess crazy fans are better than no fans."

"You could quit, you know. They can find another Priscilla."

Quincey seemed to consider the idea. "It is a drag going to school during the mornings and then coming over here to sit around in case someone needs me to stand there while they rehearse the awards ceremony. Like anyone cares who wins best scarf-tosser and biggest belt buckle." Her eyes grew suddenly calculating. "But if I quit, I wouldn't have a chance to meet any cute Elvises."

"I didn't think there were any."

"Well, the bodyguards aren't bad."

"The Memphis Mafia? I thought those old guys in hats and suits creeped you out."

"Not those guards. The ones you got me. They're the best-looking Elvises in the place."

"Ah. They're still a little old for you."

"Please, moth-ther, give me a break. I like older guys if they're not really old, like thirty or something."

Before Temple could get into basic arithmetic with Quincey, obviously a subject she'd skipped in school, the dressing room door banged open against the wall. A phalanx of suits filled the doorway.

Three abreast, this particular outcropping of the Memphis Mafia resembled Siamese triplets. The black suits melted into one vague blob, and their three pale faces protruded like mushrooms under three very black caps . . . that is, fedoras.

"Okay, lady," one addressed Temple. "Up against the mirror. What is your business here?"

"Ah, I'm Quincey's manager."

When they looked blank as well as menacing, she pointed to the seated Quincey, managing to impale her finger into a rat's nest of Clairol's blackest embrittled with hair spray. Yuck.

The Mafia guys were not distracted.

"You haven't been around before," one said.

With their eyes narrowed into tough-guy slits, the guys looked even more like Siamese triplets. Temple couldn't tell which one had spoken. Of course they spit out their words between almost immobile lips, like Bogart on a laryngitis day. Must have been that damp and foggy ending of *Casablanca*. Poor guy. Paul Henreid got the girl, and he got the upper respiratory infection.

Temple coughed discreetly. "Managers come and go. I have other clients, you know."

"That right? She got a right to be here?" one asked Quincey.

A rebel glint brightened the tiny eye-holes between Quincey's quintuple-strength false eyelashes. With one word she could rid herself of a voice for maturity and prudence.

Also a cohort in a hostile world.

"Sure." Quincey punctuated her casual response by snapping her bubblegum. It echoed in the empty room like a gunshot.

The boys stiffened and clapped hands to armpits. Then they began clearing their throats, shuffling their feet, and backing out of the room before they looked even more foolish. Pulling firearms on two lone women would look like overkill.

"Were those the real Kingdome Memphis Mafia, or shills?" Temple wondered aloud.

"You mean there are fake hotel security guards?" Quincey paled a little. "Who can you trust around this place?"

"Regard it as the real Graceland, and trust no one."

"You know, that's true. Elvis had closed-circuit TVs in his bedroom so he could watch people around the house and decide whether to come down and play. So many people came around, it got so he couldn't see them all."

Temple shook her head. "Was that in his later years? Paranoia seems to be the last stage before complete breakdown."

"Maybe I'm being paranoid." Quincey clasped her narrow white arms and shivered. "I'm sure not going to be voted Miss Congeniality here. Do you suppose the guy in the pool had his throat cut? With a razor?"

"No! Definitely not."

"How do you know?"

"There would have been blood, for one thing."

"In a big pool like that?"

"Good point, Quincey. The large amount of water would dissipate any blood. But why slit someone's throat and throw him into a pool? Overkill, if you ask me."

"Las Vegas is an overkill kind of place," Quincey said earnestly. "I mean, I wasn't going to freak because of some funny notes, and whoever wrote the 'E' in my neck could have just as easily slit my throat, but didn't. But now there's a really dead guy—and I'm getting a little worried."

Temple leaned against the tabletop. "So that's why you were so cool about that razor incident. You'd already figured out it wasn't a serious attack."

"I figured it was some publicity stunt. And hanging around here hadn't gotten so boring yet."

"Well, hang in a little longer. As your 'manager,' I'm going to visit the other dressing rooms and see if they're talking about you."

Quincey tossed the immovable edifice of her hair and used a pick as long as a chopstick to torture the topmost strands even higher. "They better be talking about me. I'm not wearing this creepy crepey polyester dress just for my health, you know."

Temple nodded and left, refraining from mention of the seventies urban legend that polyester caused cancer.

Quincey had enough to worry about.

Chapter 37

From a Jack to a King

(One of Vernon Presley's country favorites,
recorded by Elvis in 1967)

"Gotcha!"

"You idiot! Get your hands off me." Temple had pulled away from whoever grabbed her and adapted a battle-ready martial arts stance.

Crawford Buchanan, dry but otherwise as slimy as ever, was leaning against the wall where he had suddenly appeared.

"What's the matter?" he taunted. "Snake got you a little nervous?"

"No. Not that snake, anyway. Why are you here pestering me, anyway? I thought you had major news stories to write. 'Elvis Dies!' Really. Are your trying to build the death in the pool into some kind of Elvis legend?"

"I'm not here to pester you," he answered, shoving himself off the wall and batting his naturally dark-lashed eyes. Temple thought unhappily of Daddy Longlegs's

Centipede Sweetie mascara. "I'm here to keep an eye on Quincey."

"The way you were doing when she got slashed."

"I can't be around here every second."

"I haven't seen you around here at all, until now." Temple glanced down the empty hall beyond him. Nothing that way but storage rooms. "And what were you doing up in the Medication Garden? And why the twenty-foot dash into the pool?"

"You sound like the police. I'm a reporter as well as an emcee, right? So I have to check things out. My being in the Medication Garden when the corpse turned up was just a piece of good luck. I tripped over one of those damn critters from the Animal Elvis exhibit when I saw the body after you and the landlady noticed it. Believe me, I had no urge to share a pool with that snake and its prey."

"I see you've got your followup article written."

Crawford grinned. " 'Giant Snake Gets Elvis All Shook Up.' How does that grab you?"

"Not much better than you did just now. The autopsy results aren't even in. It's irresponsible to blame the death on the snake."

"Maybe, but it's sure spectacular. My next piece will be Elvis's resuscitated career all washed up now."

"You're not going to try to turn the dead man into the real Elvis, are you?"

"Why not? Any dead Elvis could be the real one in disguise. Why do you think Elvis is the story that won't die? It's classic. It's beautiful. You can speculate on anything and it's impossible to prove different. It's even better than Amelia Earhart."

"It's the story that won't die because irresponsible so-called journalists like you keep beating a dead horse."

"Irresponsible? You think I'm irresponsible?" He edged nearer again, his anger turning him from a laughable pest into a sobering threat. Temple retreated despite herself, until her back was hugging the wall. "I'll show you! I'm sitting on a story so hot that it'll make me the journalist responsible for the biggest story of the Millennium."

She didn't know what to say in the face of Crawford's angry but impressive conviction.

She didn't have to say anything. Jumpsuit Elvis had appeared behind Buchanan like the Caped Crusader. He caught up the Crawf by the scruff of his black mohair suit coat and practically lifted him off the ground.

"Hey, there, son," he intoned in a passable imitation of Elvis's laid-back jovial country drawl, "you don't want to scare the ladies, and you sure don't want to make me mad."

When he let Crawford's black wingtips touch concrete again, the toes did a nervous little tap, like a puppet's whose strings were too short, before the soles came down solidly.

"You phoney bozos!" Crawford's invective spit and hissed. "You're laughable, get it? But no one will be laughing at me when I'm ready to move. Get outa my way."

Crawford shoved past Temple and surged down the hall toward the other dressing rooms, soon lost in a milling crowd of Elvis impersonators.

"I shoulda smashed him while I had him. You okay, Miss Temple? He tried to use you as a discus."

"He was really hot under the mohair. I've never seen him like that."

"Mean as a wolverine."

"I guess." Temple shook her head. Dead or alive, Elvis certainly brought out strong feelings in people.

"I'm sorry I deserted my post." Jumpsuit Elvis nodded to the dressing room door. "There was lots of talk down the hall, and Miss Quincey said she'd be all right."

"She was fine. The Crawf apparently isn't worried about her at all."

"Why should he be?"

"He's her mother's boyfriend, for one thing. And it

was his idea to have her play Priscilla. He's the emcee for the pageant."

Elvis's face had grown darker and darker of expression as Temple had explained the status quo. "She's an awful pretty little thing to bring into this crazy place."

"Ah . . . which one are you? Ernesto? Julio?"

"Um, Ralph."

"Well, 'Um Ralph,' I hope you're not digging too deep into the Elvis mythology. Quincey is only sixteen. You wouldn't be getting inappropriate ideas?"

"Sixteen! What kind of rat would bring a sixteen-year-old girl into this? Um, you think maybe I'm getting into my role too much, Miss Temple?"

"How so?"

"Elvis had a hangup for real young girls. Do you think someone else's spirit could take over a guy?"

"How so?"

"Well, I notice a lot of the guys here, the impersonators. Some have named their kids after Elvis or Lisa Marie. They get so into their roles it's a good thing there aren't TV sets around the backstage area."

"TV sets?"

"I'd expect some of these guys to shoot out the picture tubes when they get a little frustrated. Elvis was kinda crazy that way."

"From what I've read, Elvis was drugged out of his mind, all on doctor-obtained prescription drugs, of course. Any of the impersonators seem to be taking drugs? There might be pressure to use speed to better imitate his energetic performances. The guy who went into the pool might have had a drug overdose."

"When you get down to the other dressing rooms, send a couple of my bros back, and I'll start asking around."

"Has anybody mentioned which Elvis impersonator died?"

"Naw. I've seen the police all over the place asking questions, and even these Memphis Mafia hotel security types, but you know what me and my brothers think of them."

"That they're more than who they pretend to be. But what else can you expect at a gathering of Elvis imitators?"

Ralph struck an Elvis pose and sang the opening of "T-R-O-U-B-L-E."

Temple nodded her approval. There was an Elvis song for every occasion. Despite his increasingly calamitous lifestyle, the man had been a singin' fool.

She was relieved to see that Crawford Buchanan had disappeared from the dressing room scene before he could make another kind of scene.

Elvis certainly brought out strange passions in people.

Not her. She was merely masquerading as an inquiring reporter, not in the trying and true C. B. gossip-rag mode.

"You covering this?" a friendly voice called out. "What happened to your on-camera guy?"

Temple smiled wryly at the assumption that she was an off-camera producer and Matt was the upfront reporter. Guess she'd been right to leave TV news.

Mike—or was it Jerry?—came barreling out of a crowd of his twins to say hello.

What a perfect situation for murder: a confusing mob of potential victims/killers all done up to look like each other.

"Wow." Mike seemed out of breath. "This is a media frenzy. It's great for the pageant and us guys, but kinda hard on the hotel and the dead guy. I just got interviewed for *Hot Heads*. You know, the entertainment world TV show? I got to do a minute of "Suspicious Minds" for their cameraman. They want to use the song as a theme for what might be going on here."

"Clever. And good exposure for you. Say, has anybody figured out which impersonator died in the pool?"

Mike bit his bottom lip, which emphasized the slight curl in the upper left lip. Just like Elvis.

"Mike, before you answer, how do you do that?"

"Do what? Besides being cool and being Elvis."

"The lip curl. Isometric exercises?"

"Naw. Too hard." He leaned so close that Temple could smell the Dentine on his breath. "Trade secret. Promise you won't use it."

"I look like I could imitate Elvis?"

His laugh caused smooth dark heads all around to turn their way. "Guess not. Liquid latex. Used for years by old-time stage actors. Guess the special effects wizards have higher-tech methods nowadays."

"Oh, yeah. That's the stuff that tightens the skin and makes realistic scars."

"I use just a little. If the spotlight catches the shiny part, it looks like sweat."

"Sweat is good?"

"Sweat is great. Elvis perspired like a sprinkler system. It showed he was giving his all. Had guys onstage bringing him water and towels. In with one, out with the other. Did you know that some of his costumes weighed thirty pounds?"

"Figures. Opera costumes are awfully heavy, and Elvis was his own opera company, wasn't he, with the elaborate costumes, and giving away scarves and kisses?"

"His jumpsuits were made of wool gabardine from Milan, Italy. Most guys here, we can't afford that, not even for what it cost Elvis twenty years ago."

"You know, the more I hear about Elvis, the more I get this sense of a heavy weight pulling him down. Literally, like the costumes, but also in the retinue he collected, the superstructure he had to support of people and debts, and then his own spending sprees."

"You're right. The man just finally sank under the weight of everything everyone put on him, and everything he needed to keep himself going, holding up the movies and the tours and the relatives and the fans and the employees. Like that world guy, you know—?"

"Atlas."

"Right. Atlas. And the biggest thing to hold up was mostly the expectations, including his own." He glanced down at the white silk scarf around his neck. "A lot of people have the real thing of these, not just soaked with Elvis's sweat, but in a way his blood and tears too. When I do my act, this ends up wringing wet. I'm a basketcase. High, too, but a basketcase. I can see it myself, just pretending to be him. It was just too much for any one person to do alone. And Elvis was alone. He always kept lots of people by him, but he was always alone."

"No one from the pageant is obviously missing, though?"

"One of us? Not that we can tell. There is one rumor going around. That it was KOK. You remember, the King of Kings we were talking about the other day? Nobody's seen him around, and since he lives in Vegas that's kind of unusual. Frankly, a lot of us were worried about the competition. He usually makes all the major Elvis events. Not that anybody would want the dead guy to be him. Still, we figure if he hadn't shown up yet, he probably just wasn't going to. So . . . the man in the pool could be anybody, even a fan who just wanted to wear an Elvis suit to the hotel opening. Of course a thing like this attracts a lot of wild cards. Real amateurs, first-timers, craaaazy folks. Hey, I know what you're thinking: as if the rest of us Elvi weren't."

Temple absently watched the flood of Elvi in the hall ebb and flow. "No one ever claimed the suit that was trashed either, right?"

"I haven't heard that anyone did."

"Heard what happened to it?"

Mike shook his head. "Remember. *Hot Heads*. Probably tomorrow night. I should be on."

He waved and dove back into the multitude, the jewels on the back of his jumpsuit flashing like a semaphore that turned red, yellow, and green all at once.

"Mine eyes dazzle," Temple muttered.

Elvis had died young, but he certainly hadn't stayed that way.

She wandered among the many faces of Elvis. Most of them didn't look like they had started out resembling Elvis. No, first had come the admiration, then the imitation.

She would bet that most of them hadn't done any more performing than at a local karaoke bar before donning sideburns and low-slung belts like glitzy holsters.

A slight Asian man danced through the crowd, on his way somewhere in a hurry. Five-feet-three, lean as stir-fried chicken, he caught the look of the young, mercurial Elvis better than the heavyset Caucasian men who outnumbered him forty to one.

Someone tapped her on the shoulder. Temple spun around, ready to snarl.

"Electra! What are you doing here?"

"I got invited back," Electra said smugly, shaking her shoulders. "By Today Elvis."

"Today Elvis?"

"You must have seen him around. The only guy with white hair, like Elvis's father Vernon had before he died. He's the same age Elvis would be today: sixty-four. Poor Elvis, he won't have to wonder if we'll still need and feed him at sixty-four. Anyway, Today Elvis was pretty impressed by my Elvis collection. Course, you don't know with these guys if it's you or your sweat-stained scarf, but I never could resist a younger man."

"Elvis would be sixty-four?"

"Don't look so amazed. He's still pretty young. Clint Eastwood is pushing seventy."

"It's just that I've been looking at the photo-bios and you get to thinking that's reality. So you have a, like, date with Today Elvis?"

"He invited me to watch the rehearsals."

"Really. I should do that."

"I'm sure you can hide behind my muumuu when I present my pass. If anyone spots you, I can say you're my twelve-year-old granddaughter. Just wear your hair in pigtails."

"And ditch the high heels. I know, Granny. Did you hear anything from Today Elvis about the identity of the dead man?"

"No one here has a clue. They counted noses and they know it's not one of them, that's all."

"So when's the rehearsal?"

Electra checked the hot-pink patent leather watch on her chubby, freckled wrist.

"Is that an—?"

"Elvis watch from the fifties. Yeah. My mother screamed at me for a week for spending my money on junk. I don't wanta tell you what it's worth today. Even you might mug me for it."

"You've never worn it when I've been around before."

"I don't wear my souvenirs. But these guys appreciate this stuff. Makes me the queen of the hop again." Electra primped her hair, which had been rinsed a tasteful lavender. "The rehearsal is in twenty minutes, and only the media is allowed in. Besides friends and family of the performers, of course. Which is we. Us?"

"Whatever. I can't be grammatical without a pencil or a keyboard in my hands. Let's duck into Priscilla's dressing room so I can change into my tennies, and then it's off to see the weird wolves, Granny."

Quincey was absent from the room, so Temple did a shoe-change, and in forty seconds flat her feet were level instead of inclined.

"You do look awfully young," Electra commented, "without those high heels."

"Don't even need pigtails, huh?"

"A bow on one side of your head would help."

"Argh! I don't do bows."

On that declaration of independence, they left the dressing room and climbed the backstage stairs.

At the top stood a man in black, legs spread, hands

clasped in front, poker face shaded by a snap-brim early-sixties fedora.

"You okayed for the rehearsal area?" he asked.

Electra flashed her yellow pass card. Temple flashed what she hoped was an eager teenage grin.

With a grunt, the guard nodded them past.

"This reminds me of the security the real Elvis had," Electra grumbled as Temple led her through the clutter of the wings to the steps leading down into the vast theater's house.

"I can't believe you actually lined up and screamed. Those girls in the photos look so—"

"So uncool. Sweaters and bobby socks, and those circle skirts that swept the floor when you sat and that everybody stepped on. That's what Elvis should have sang, 'Don't Step on My Pink Poodle Skirt.' "

"Hardly suitable for Elvis."

"He did love pink, though. Had teddy bears all over his bedroom to the end, and his first bedroom before Graceland had pink bedclothes. Black and pink were high-fifties-chic colors."

"Teddy bears. He was just a big overgrown kid, wasn't he?"

"In some ways. In some, not. You know, not all us teen fans were pimply and awkward. The good-looking ones got invited to meet Elvis. He had his pick, believe me."

"Groupies." Temple made a face. "Why do those young girls sell themselves so cheaply to a bunch of egocentric drunk and/or drugged guys old enough to know better and not much worth bragging about as human beings?"

"It's obvious, my dear girl, that you have never seen an authentic sex symbol in action." Electra's face assumed a beatific look as she pulled down a plush fold-up seat and plunked her middled-aged heft on it.

"From what I read, Elvis wasn't born bad and beautiful; he deliberately modeled himself on his favorite actors, those urban bad boys Marlon Brando and James Dean and Tony Curtis. And he started putting those bumps and grinds into his act when he saw the girls' reaction to the moves he probably picked up from black performers he saw on Beale Street."

"That's the thing. Underneath the act was this shy guy our age who was acting out what we all wanted to be: independent and bold, and rebellious and, hey, even rich and famous. Teen dream. Didn't your generation have something like that?"

"We had a choice between satanist rockers and TV-show family sitcom guys who sang a little. Elvis's bad-boy act was minor-league compared to the decadent rock that came along after."

"It was a time. It was a place. It brought city and country together, white hillbilly music and black blues. It brought black and white together before the Civil Rights movement made it official. Elvis usually had black groups in his band." Electra looked at Temple over her reading glasses. "But then you don't know a thing about the Civil Rights movement either, do you, whippersnapper?"

"I know, I know! I'm just a shallow yuppie. I missed all the major social upheavals of the sixties. I couldn't help it. I was just a baby."

Mollified that Temple had admitted total ignorance of her life and times, Electra settled down and gazed happily toward the huge empty stage. "The Colonel always sent Elvis to the funniest out-of-the-way arenas when he was on tour, even after he became a megastar. Places like Portland and Buffalo and Baton Rouge and Wichita."

"Maybe it was a strategy to make Elvis available to more than his big-city fans. Where did you see Elvis?"

"Carlsbad, New Mexico, February fourteenth, nineteen fifty-five. I weighed a hundred-and-eighteen pounds for probably the last time in my life. The waist of that circle skirt I wore would hardly fit my thigh nowadays.

They dis Elvis for getting fat, but who doesn't?"

"Gods, supermodels, and rock stars aren't supposed to. And maybe they take all those drugs to make sure they don't."

"We never even dreamed about taking recreational drugs back then. Cigarettes and whiskey and rock 'n' roll music, they were the wicked ways teenagers wanted to get into. If we took anything, it was the officially sanctioned uppers that Elvis started with, his mother's amphetamine diet pills. My mother had some too, and I 'borrowed' 'em."

"And it was all so innocent."

"Yup. Magic pills from Dr. Family Physician."

Temple gazed toward the stage. The fifties seemed so quaint, like they really were lived in black-and-white. On stage, a band was assembling. Drummer, a real piano man, guitarist, backup singers, they all dressed in some amalgam of fifties–sixties clothes.

Electra leaned over to whisper in Temple's ear, even though no one sat near them. The rows of empty seats were sprinkled with guests of the performers who took pains to sit as far away as possible from each other. Maybe they thought they might give away the trade secrets of their Elvis, like Mike's lip trick with liquid latex.

"Most of these guys started singing along to karaoke machines, or used their own tapes. Performing with a live band is a major step up for them. They're beginning to understand what Elvis was up against for the hundreds of performances he gave from nineteen seventy to seventy-seven."

Temple absorbed the information. She didn't sing a note, didn't ever want to do more than hum along to "The Star-Spangled Banner" or "Happy Birthday to You," all a loyal American or decent friend should be expected to do. Molina, though, the humming homicide lieutenant, she could stand up on the Blue Dahlia stage and belt out a melody to whatever riffs the backup band was ruffling. Took nerve. And if the nerve wasn't there anymore, maybe it took pills.

Then a bouncing baby Elvis was bursting into stage center, his fringe jiggling and the gemstones winking like a drunken fleet of sailors on shore leave. That's what Elvis's white jumpsuits reminded Temple of, not comic-book superhero uniforms like the books said, but little boy's sailor suits, wide-legged, jaunty, innocent, only Elvis's had been embroidered with glitter. Suddenly the teddy bears that lined his bedrooms made sense.

She watched the heavyset guy who resembled every repairman who'd ever been sent to her apartment to fix something, down to the swag of heavy belt at his hips, tool-belt-as-gunslinger-holster substitute.

Elvis was not only blue suede shoes, he was blue-collar superhero. The guy who went from high school into the navy or the army. The average Joe, not Joe College. And his garish onstage taste celebrated the common person's idea of glamour, half Hollywood, half gas-station fire sale.

The music, though, that was timeless, classless. The words were nonsense, the beat was liberating. Gotta dance. Elvi came and went, a lot of them the chunky sailor-suited model so endearingly kiddish despite so many being on the other side of forty. The sleeker ones did Comeback Elvis in black leather biker suits that shone like silk-velvet tafetta in the spotlights. Velvet Elvis made a spectacular entrance in her midnight jump-suit. Temple knew that the costume would light up like a gasoline-slick rainbow under the actual performance's special light gels, but even underlit the look was dyna-mite.

Oddly enough, the sole female Elvis impersonator was also the only contestant to evoke Elvis the sleek young sex symbol. Electra, not knowing Velvet's gen-der, grabbed Temple's forearm and hung on as Velvet Elvis strutted, purred, and stomped through "Tiger Man."

"That's it!" Electra cheered Velvet Elvis on, under her breath. "That's it!"

That's it, all right, Temple thought, a good part of the young singer's appeal, only then the phenomenon hadn't been noticed and named. The Androgynous Elvis. Clairol on his hair, eyebrows, and sideburns, mascara on his lashes.

The fifties were more decadent than they knew.

Temple found herself getting a kick out of the proceedings. Some of the impersonators were so nervous they shook (so had Elvis) but they had brought an innocent, sincere, raw energy to their acts that overcame the sophisticated theater-goer's expectations.

She leaned back in her seat, scrunched down on her tailbone, and let her right tennis shoe noiselessly tap the carpeted floor.

Beside her, Electra sat transfixed, her features lit by the reflected stage lights so she glowed like a, well, a thirty-six-year-old, anyway.

Elvis was gone, but his fans lived on, and they would never see him again. Only imitations.

Temple scoured her memory for some performer whose absence from a stage or the planet would deprive her. All she could come up with was the Mystifying Max, and that wasn't a fair comparison. Maybe she just wasn't born to be a fan. . . .

The onstage musicians must have been tiring of backing up such an endless parade of Elvises, who were beginning to blend one into the other. Even what they excelled at seemed lost in the sheer repetition.

You could hear the musicians' feet shuffling during a lull, and those of the backup girl singers—and they were no more or less than girls in their fluffy outfits and hair.

Then she became aware of a figure, a ghostly figure lost in the dark at the back of the set.

The drums started pounding in deep, bellowing alteration: drum/drum drum/drum drum/drum. "Thus Spake Zarathustra," the universe-opening theme music from

2001: A Space Odyssey that live-concert Elvis had taken for his opening theme.

It was melodramatic, it was egomaniacal and pretentious, it was terrific theater.

The man at the back lifted his arms slowly to the pulsing throbs of the drums, a short cloak he wore spreading like wings. Then he turned and strode forward into the lights, a dead man walking.

He came onward. This was Edwardian Elvis of the early seventies. This was the mature, recharged Elvis who had resumed live performance tours after nine frustrating years of inane movie-making, all engineered to provide the most money and exposure and least star satisfaction by the inimitable, pseudonymous, and bogus Colonel Tom Parker, carny confidence man turned theatrical manager. Some said Parker had mismanaged Elvis to death.

But he wasn't dead now. He was in complete control.

Temple quite literally sat up and took notice. His steps, timed to the thundering drumbeat, seemed to lift her off her seat.

He came right to the stage's very brim. If maddened girls weren't jumping up and down in the orchestra pit, screaming, they should have been.

The band suddenly revved up and the still figure exploded into searing song and mind-bending motion. First came "Jailhouse Rock" as delivered by a pneumatic drill. Then "Blue Suede Shoes" and "Don't Be Cruel."

Women started screaming in the audience. Temple stared wide-eyed as Electra jumped up on her seat and began clapping her hands. Temple blinked at the spectacle on stage. Images of Elvis in performance were emblazoned on the collective popular memory. The impersonators had the patented poses all down, wide stance, swiveling hips, knees flexed, tippy-toe balance, dipping almost to the stage floor. Elvis fan or not Elvis fan, everyone had images of Elvis branded into their brains.

This guy made it all new, reinvented the moment as if twenty-some years had never passed. Evoked the same primal screams.

Temple felt herself about to surrender to the mass hysteria that welled up around her like a ground fog filled with shrieking horns that happened to be people.

She clenched her fists and crossed her ankles under her seat.

By sheer willpower, she forced herself to stay calm in a monsoon of recognition and disbelief and ear-blasting nostalgia.

And then the performer suddenly stilled, and clasped his mike like a sinner would a cross, and sang a sweet, aching version of "Love Me Tender" that had the hysterics in silent tears.

Some people wanted to see Venice and die. This crowd only had to glimpse Elvis to go to heaven.

Chapter 38

Jailhouse Rock

(A Jerry Leiber and Mike Stoller song for the
1957 movie of the same name, a hit on several
U.S. charts and the first single in the history of
British music charts to debut at number one)

It is a good thing that every dressing room door in the
backstage area is open, and that every dressing room
wall is lined with mirrors.

This is how, despite the fact that the floor is full of
milling boots and blue suede shoes, I can make my discreet way along the crowded hall. These Elvis impersonators are always checking out their hair and clothes in the
nearest mirror.

A crocodile could be twining through their ankles, and
they would never notice.

And I am far less noticeable than the average croc,
especially when I am not snapping my incisors and growling.

So I slink on my belly like a snake of my great and
good acquaintance along the joining of floor and wall,
hoping that the one person who could spot me in a coal

cellar (my devoted roommate Miss Temple Barr) is not in the vicinity.

You can bet I breathe a huge sigh of relief when I arrive at the end dressing room occupied solo by Miss Quincey Conrad. I almost sound like a dog. (Have you ever noticed that dogs are very big sighers, especially when they are settling down to sleep? My kind, however, avoids the extravagant gestures, especially overt begging. You will not hear huge happy—or unhappy—heaves from us. Just another of the many little ways in which we differ from the inferior species.)

I cannot resist peeking in. I have never seen a human hairstyle that reaches the height and hubris of Miss Quincey's Priscilla-do. I believe that I could curl up in it and remain unseen for some time. As well as keep quite toasty-warm, if a bit tipsy on all that hair spray.

She is at the dressing table, doing her fingernails and looking very bored indeed, despite the handsome gentleman in a caped white jumpsuit who has one foot up on an empty chair and a guitar in hand and is serenading the lady fair with "Love Me Tender."

I have to admire the dude's courting technique. You cannot beat a good melancholy howl for making points with the ladies. Sometimes, if you are lucky, they will howl right back.

But Elvis, despite all the onscreen lovelies he serenaded in his thirty-two movies, was better off singing to them, as he continued to do with great results up to the bitter end.

So I slink away down the hall to the pleasant strains of song and story.

I am hoping that the object of my quest is a little easier to reach this time. When I arrive at the door, it is shut. Since it is made out of painted steel this is a severe setback, although not unexpected. Here my native ingenuity leaps to the four. I mean, fore. And to the four-on-the-floor I am equipped with.

Since there is nothing so formal as a threshold, I am

able to thrust a mitt under the steel door, pads and shivs up. First I move my limb to the left and to the right, then I stretch and strain, and stretch and strain with all my might. I do the pokey hokey and turn my leg around, and that is what breaking in is all about.

Naturally, I feel nothing but air, empty air. No one has considerately dropped a key on the other side of the door that I can paw onto this side (so then I can go get Miss Temple and get her to open the door for me, which is the last thing I wish to do, because my investigation is not yet ready for another operative's messing with it).

I am so exasperated it almost crosses my mind to sigh, although that is entirely too doglike a thing for any self-respecting dude of my sort to do.

And then . . . I feel a flutter light as a moth in the palm of my pads. Eek! It tickles!

I do not do giggles either.

So I steel myself against the teasing sensation and keep my mitt still. Smooth pad leather strokes mine. Playing footsie through the door might be a toothsome experience were the Divine Yvette or some other lissome lady on the other side, but I know what is on the other side, and I do not want it getting overfriendly with my pads.

So I pull my questing limb back under the door. Sometimes what is denied is what is most desired. Face it: what is denied is *always* what is most desired, a fact which accounts for the success of several crime families all over the globe.

I hear a soft pressure on the door's other side and fix my gaze on the locked doorknob above me.

I know the Stare will not be sufficient to get me to the other side of this door, given the circumstance, but I also know that Someone on the Other Side Likes Me.

The silver steel knob jerks. Then jerks the other way. I heard the sweet snick of a deadbolt being drawn. The knob rattles.

And then the door cracks inward, and I am again almost overwhelmed by the fruit-salad odor that sweeps out the open door.

I hold my breath, drag the cracked door open just enough to admit my svelte form, and dart into the darkness within.

I am welcomed with a raucous chatter and a crushing embrace.

Chapter 39

Guitar Man

(Featured in the '68 Comeback Special, this
Jerry Reed song was given a new Reed
instrumental background by Felton Jarvis in
1980, and become Elvis's last number one song
on any *Billboard* chart)

It was as if Elvis had risen from the dead.

All the other Elvi's nearest and dearest stood in tribute, applauding wildly. They left their seats and stormed the orchestra pit, reaching up to this sudden embodiment of what the Kingdome was created to memorialize.

He stayed down on one knee near the stage rim, shining with the holy sheen of effort, head bowed, both the humble knight-to-be awaiting the icy touch of the naked sword, and the prideful acolyte accepting richly deserved acclaim.

Only the fact that Temple sat on the aisle kept Electra from charging out of her seat and doing likewise.

"That was incredible," Temple said. "This guy is good!"

Electra flashed Temple a glance. "He's only about a tenth as good as the real Elvis." She sat back, and her voice shook a little. "But he's the best make-do I've ever seen."

"He must be KOK, and that means that the dead guy isn't."

"KOK?"

"The King of Kings. The other impersonators were talking about him like he carried the Holy Grail. I can almost see this guy justifying rumors that Elvis is alive and masquerading as one of his own imitators. How old do you think he is?"

"Does it matter? Temple, we just glimpsed something that no one has seen for over twenty years. It's like breathing the air of a pyramid that hasn't been opened since the time of the pharaohs."

"Electra, I know you're a fan, but breathe deeply. Think. Elvis isn't a pharaoh. He isn't eternal. Maybe he had extraordinary performing charisma, but . . . we all die, and he lasted longer than Jimi Hendrix and Jim Morrison and Janis Joplin, the other rock-star drug casualties of the seventies."

"Elvis wasn't like them. He didn't get into the drug culture from that disaffected counterculture. He was like us. He got into it because no one told him it was dangerous; it was prescribed."

The degrees of difference in drug addiction didn't cut any cocaine with Temple. She was impressed by good theater, by how totally a performer could absorb the persona of another. She was thinking how perfectly playing a dead man might challenge the gods, how it might seem to demand death as its perfect, true-to-life ending. One thing had really struck her about the performance, besides the impersonater's passionate perfection, his own true compelling charisma.

It was the design embroidered on the back of his martial arts *gi*: from where she sat, it looked remarkably like a rearing stallion. (She had read enough about Elvis by now to sit back and free associate. Rising Sun was the name of Elvis's horse, and also a bow to Eastern mysticism and Japan, the land of the Rising Sun. It even could refer to Sun Records, his first recording house. He had called the ranch where the horses were kept the House of the Rising Sun.) Around the equine rampant radiated stylized sunbursts of gilt and red embroidery: fireworks, if you will, also an Eastern invention, whence came the rising sun every morning. And of course dawn was the symbol of rebirth.

Just how old was this guy under the iconistic disguise? Could he possibly be a fit sixty-four . . . oh, Temple, get a grip!

Still . . . his performance had given her chills.

And she didn't even like Elvis, or his music, or his looks, or his lifestyle, or his legend.

Chapter 40

Bossa Nova Baby

(From *Fun in Acapulco,* another of Elvis's
"travelogue" movies)

My first notion is to panic. Here I am, entrapped in the dark by person or persons unknown.

Except that I have a pretty good clue to the identity of my captor, especially when I inhale deeply to keep from having the breath squeezed out of me, and smell banana breath.

"Well," I growl, "you have already answered one of my questions. I now know that you like to wander at will if your master forgets to latch your cage."

I am dropped like a hot potato, or more accurately, a mashed one.

"You not human," the creature manages to spit out between indecipherable syllables of high-pitched chatter. "Human come. Feed. Human come. Talk. You not human."

"That is good to hear." I shake myself to repair the

flattened hairs. My coat of choice may not be Memphis
Mafia mohair, or Elvis jumpsuit wool gabardine, but it is
a decent set of threads, even if they are home-grown. "I
had thought you had to exist here alone in the dark all
the time."

I get a long drum-roll of chatter in its native language.
Then it settles down to tell Louie all.

"Only for surprise," Chatter says. "Chatter big surprise.
Must wait in dark. Be patient. Be patient." I can tell the
poor monk is repeating the mantra some human has put
in his head. "Chatter perform soon."

I suddenly have an inspiration. "Hey, Chatter. Jump up
at the wall there next to the door. Yeah, right there. See
where the crack of light from the outside ends. Right.
There is a small switch on the wall. Pull it down as you
descend." No use exerting myself when there is someone
else around to do the dirty work, that is, any work at all.

Amid screams of excitement, Chatter manages to follow instructions, and after several upward bounds hailed
by arpeggios of awful squawking, fluorescent light suddenly floods down on us like a jungle rainstorm.

Chatter's hairy little form is now in full display. I examine his long arms and the naked fingers at the end of
his large hairy hands. His naked face is repellent to one
of my breed. Chatter is like a halfway house between the
animal and the human, and I find this cross-species appearance and behavior unsettling. One should either be
four- or two-footed, I feel, but Chatter proceeds to canter
around the storage space, his legs doing the leaping and
his dragging forearms dipping now and then along the
ground like oars.

"What is it that you do when you perform?"

"I play the . . . the—" The chimpy chump makes
sounds like a machine gun gagging.

After about five minutes of close interrogation, I determine that Chatter plays a musical instrument. Yuk-yuk-
yuk-yuk.

I finally realize that Chatter is not doing a bad Curly of

Three Stooges fame imitation, but is trying to articulate the name of his instrument of choice. A ukulele. What a word! He plays this tongue-twister instrument wearing, of course, the miniature Elvis jumpsuit I spied hanging from his cage on my first visit.

Now that we have light, I head for the cage, jumping atop some piled boxes and then climbing the chicken wire side to inspect the costume hanging high above the concrete floor.

I am not thrilled about performing this high-wire act, but I need to investigate the ape suit. I had noticed that this jeweled jumpsuit included a built-in diaper, which would not have been a bad idea for the original wearer, given the sad state drugs had put him into during his last months. To my expert eye, and I have in the past discovered smuggled diamonds, the stones begemming the suit are purely glass and plastic. I bat at the low-slung seat to see if the built-in diaper is suspiciously heavy. (It would be an excellent hiding-place for smuggled goods, since who is going to inspect a chimp diaper but the keeper?)

Nothing but the usual absorbent padding.

And, by the way, if chimpanzees are supposed to be the next thing to human, give or take an australopithecene this or that discovered hither and thither, how come they have not the basic elimination skills you can find in an alley cat? A much overrated species, in my opinion, and Chatter is doing nothing to change that conclusion.

"Louie climb good," he comments, leaping up and down on his knuckles from below.

"When I have to." I let my built-in pitons relax and drop back onto the box top.

Then I turn my attention to Chatter's cage latch. No doubt about it, the critter has excellent motor control in his fingers. And that damnable opposable thumb . . .

"I see you've figured out a way to let yourself in and out of confinement," I note.

Chatter jumps up and down, screaming, which I assume is his way of taking the Fifth.

I jump down to the concrete to join him.

"I like visitors," he screeches. "I like Cilla."

This is not surprising. I knew the beauty was sneaking in to visit the beast, but I never knew why.

"Is she your friend?"

"Friend. Cilla pat Chatter. Cilla talk Chatter. Cilla bring presents."

"Okay. "Fess up. Who is your master? Who brought you here?"

"Master?"

"Do not play dumb. I am not your usual gullible human. You are an impersonator as much as all those Elvis clones running around out there. You represent Elvis's pet chimp Scatter. You were brought here for a purpose. Was it just to play second banana to some Elvis impersonator? Or something else?"

Chatter hides his ugly mug behind his funky fingers, just his bright beady eyes peeping out, looking oh-so-coy. "Chatter play tricks."

"I know. The ukulele."

"More! Chatter run around."

"So does a gerbil."

"Chatter run around and look up the lady skirts. Big laugh."

"Nasty trick. I bet the original Scatter was a peeping Tom too. Is that all you can do, act like a deviate?"

He may not know the word, but he is smart enough to recognize an insult when he hears one. Chatter screams at me, monkey invective. "Chatter clever. Chatter smart. Chatter open cage and no one knows."

"Hah. Louie knows."

"Not just here."

"Not just here? Then where?"

Chatter's marble-round eyes squint shut, just like a human suspect when he is feeling shifty. "Upstairs."

"You got loose upstairs?"

"I get loose."

"And did you let anything else loose?"

Chatter plays peekaboo through his fingers again.

I quash a spasm of annoyance. I am getting the picture. This lethal weapon with the opposable thumbs is a loose cannon on a very big deck.

"Did you let Trojan out of his container?"

"Trojan?"

"The big snake."

"Biiiig snake. Jungle creature like Chatter. Big snake like to get out of cage."

"So who put you up to it?"

"I not put up. I jump down to open latch."

"But who told you to do it?"

"No human tell Chatter to do anything."

"A human tells you to put on your Elvis suit and strum the ukulele."

The chimp shook its head. "Not same. That work. Other play. Chatter play."

"When did you release the snake?"

"When Chatter did it, Chatter did it."

I question the creature further, but it has no sense of time other than when it is performing "work." Sometime before the anaconda was discovered doing the backstroke in the pool by my lovely roommate, this devious chimpanzee was on an illegal scouting expedition and released the snake from confinement. Chatter would have me believe that was merely a mischievous prank.

It does not have the brains to realize it might have been used. If its unknown owner did not encourage this stunt, perhaps Miss Quincey Conrad did, for reasons of her own.

I have never trusted dames who play the submissive sort, and the young Priscilla Quincey impersonates is certainly one of that ilk. Are all these resurrected Elvises strolling around reviving old vendettas too? Maybe against Priscilla, as my roommate fears, and maybe against one particular Elvis, whoever or wherever he may be.

Chapter 41

Moody Blue

(Recorded in 1976 at Graceland, during a period
in which Elvis could hardly be dragged into
recording sessions, it made three charts, reaching
number one on the country chart and number
two on the easy-listening chart)

For the first time in her life, Temple ran nose-first into
what it was like to be a fan, and, indirectly, what it was
like to be a star.

The backstage area thronged with shouting, milling
people, all bent on seeing the Elvis of the moment.

And these were not amateur fans; these were professional fans with a personal stake in other Elvis impersonators. Their presence here was flagrantly disloyal.

But they didn't care. The entire object of the Elvis
imitation exercise was to evoke the presence of the King,
and this man evidently had.

Not only did his rehearsal hall performance and its
rapt reception skew the very idea of a competition, it
made every other Elvis impersonator into excess bag-
gage. Who could hope to compete with this triumphal
performance? Maybe not even the real Elvis.

"Having trouble, Miss Temple?"

She turned, looked up, smiled to see Oversized Elvis looming behind her. "I'd like to get into the dressing room to see that incredible Elvis impersonator," she told him, "but everybody else seems to have the same idea."

"No problem." Aldo turned and whistled sharply once, as if hailing a cab.

In a couple of minutes eight tall Elvi converged on them both.

Then they made like the Memphis Mafia, surrounded her and wafted her through the mob, through even the narrow birth canal of the dressing room door, and into the room itself and the presence of the new King. She could get used to this.

Tuxedo Elvis handed her a tiny tape recorder.

"Miss Temple Barr," he announced to a man sitting before the mirror. "She is doing a feature for, ah, *Vanity Fair*. The hotel would appreciate your cooperation."

The brothers Fontana ebbed back to the door, serving as a phalanx to keep out the rest.

Temple felt a stab of guilt about standing between a man and his true believers, but she squashed it like a bug. She had finally become utterly fascinated by the Elvis legend then and now. She also still wondered why an Elvis apparition had visited the Crystal Phoenix excavation, and why a man seeming to be Elvis was calling Matt on the radio. Something was going on, and it was more than it seemed to be. She couldn't resist a mystery, and Elvis was a double mystery. There was the man himself, and there was how someone could be using him, or his persona.

The performer seemed exhausted now, as well he should. He was oddly passive, going along with whatever promised an island of calm in the frenzy his performance had created.

Right now, that was a phalanx of Elvis Fontana brothers guarding the door, and the fraudulent notion that a major national magazine reporter was asking for an interview. Actually, Temple was thinking, having a tape recorder meant she could maybe write an article about this phenomenon and sell it to *Vanity Fair*. Well, perhaps some more modest magazine. She didn't have the connections to sell to a major rag.

So by the time she asked her first question, Temple was actually feeling quite honest and justified. Amazing how easy it was to impersonate someone and, even more incredible, to be believable in that role.

"I know you're exhausted," Temple said. "Do you need anything? A glass of water? Something stronger? I can have one of the ersatz Elvises get it."

He glanced to the door, and smiled wearily. "I've never seen a multiple Elvis act before, except for the Flying Elvises they concocted for that *Honeymoon in Las Vegas* film. No. I'm fine. Actually, I could use a quiet conversation to take me down." He lifted the white terry cloth towel hanging around his neck and patted at his sweaty face, as actors will who don't want to smear stage makeup.

A pro, Temple thought. What else? "Did you expect to make such a sensation here?"

"Not at the rehearsal."

"You're the 'King of Kings' Elvis, aren't you? The other impersonators were wondering why you weren't registered for the pageant, especially since you live in Las Vegas."

He nodded. His eyes were dark blue. Temple tried to catch a glint of colored contact lens edges shifting on his eye whites. Of course, if they were soft contact lenses, they would be harder to spot.

"I . . . debated coming out for this. I'm basically retired. I've had my hour in the sun."

"Ken . . . is that your name?"

Another weary smile. "Fleeting fame strikes again. My name is Lyle. Lyle Purvis. I'm from Alabama originally, ma'am. I don't know where anybody got the idea my name was Ken. Guess Lyle's a different name. Parents like different names for their kids, and then the kids spend the rest of their lives living it down. That's what first made me feel for Elvis. That was even worse than Lyle. At least there was this actor, Lyle Talbot. There wasn't no Elvis Talbot, that's for sure. Now, of course, there's Lyle Lovett, the country singer."

"I know what you mean about names. Temple?"

"It's real fine for you."

"Thanks. So is that what impersonation is all about, feeling for the person you're evoking?"

He thought, dabbed sweat, drank from a half-empty bottled water container. "Maybe so, yes. Most of us started as Elvis fans, plain and simple. And, for me, it helps to have a Southern soul to understand Elvis."

"When did you become an Elvis fan?"

"Well, now, ma'am, are you tryin' to find out my age in a nice way here?"

"Maybe. We reporters like to pin down hard facts like age."

"And name, rank, and serial number, right?" His laugh was loose and infectious. "Can't help you there. Never served my country in the military. Not that way. Not that I wouldn't have, if it had worked out. I'm a loyal American."

"Does being an Elvis impersonator require being a loyal American?"

"Yes, it does. That boy, he was Mom and apple pie personified."

"What about the rest of it? Babes and barbiturates?"

"Aw, now, Miss . . . Barr. The boy was under tremendous pressure. Sure he went overboard, but those girls were throwing themselves at him. He was young, he was breaking free from a very strict religious upbringing . . . you know, he didn't touch a lot of those girls. Sometimes all he wanted was someone to sleep with, like those teddy bears he collected. In a lot of ways, he was just a scared seventeen-year-old country boy."

"In some ways, he was the wicked, rebel King of Sex."

"Yep. He had that charisma. But that type of thing works better from the stage and. screen than it does in real life."

"You have some of it."

"Very kind of you to say that, a sophisticated professional lady like yourself. But it's a stage thing. It isn't real. That's where Elvis went a little haywire. He thought he had to live up to his stage image. See, Elvis only felt really free when he was onstage. That was his biggest love affair, with the audience. Nothing else could live up to that. It's hard to explain. I've heard dozens and dozens of other people who saw him perform live. He was like nothing else they ever saw. Some folks like to make fun of him, or put him down, but they were fighting against the tide. Even in their hardest hearts, they must of seen the phenomenal pull he had on people. It was like one big mass—can I say this? If not, please don't print it. I'm tired and I'm not thinking sharp enough to defend myself . . ."

Temple nodded. "I won't use anything harmful, that you don't mean to say."

"It was like one big mass orgasm, is what it was like. Only spiritual. An emotional release like you've never had before."

"You obviously saw him perform live."

Lyle nodded. "In the seventies, of course. I came late to the banquet." He paused. "I even saw him in the last couple years, when he was just pitiful. He was like a puppet on those drugs. It made grown men who knew him cry. The fans cried, but they never stopped loving him. Unconditional love, isn't that what you call it? It was like he couldn't do anything to make them not love him, and sometimes I think that's what he was trying to do, putting himself onstage when he was too drugged to stand up, or to remember lyrics or anything. He was trying to make them give up on him, so he wouldn't have to bear the burden anymore. If they would just stop loving him . . . but they couldn't, any more than he could stop hating himself at the end. He was ready to leave. That I know. He was ready. Everybody around him knew it. He died standing up, with his boots on, not in that bathroom at Graceland. That was just the actual fact. The real death was earlier. We were all watching a dead man walking for a long time."

"What did you do then?"

"Do?" Lyle shook his head as if to shake off a nightmare, Temple thought.

She glimpsed the tiniest flash of white roots at his left temple. His face was lightly lined and tanned, the way Elvis liked to look after a trip to Hawaii. Temple was miserable at guessing ages. Because she felt she looked so ridiculously young, she tended to underestimate other people's ages too. She would put Lyle Purvis in his forties. In fact, Elvis's hair had gone white by forty-two. It was weird to picture a snowy-haired Elvis.

While Temple was dallying on top of old Smokey, all covered with snow, Lyle had come out of his own fog reliving Elvis's last performances.

"What do you mean 'do'?"

"Do for a living back then?"

"I don't even remember. I was just a kid."

"What's your day job now?"

He laughed, uneasily. "It's pretty unglamourous." When she waited in silence, he added, "I work for a messenger service."

"Around town here?"

"Right. Have car, will travel."

"None of the Elvis impersonators have performance-type jobs that I can tell. Unless they're the ones who make a living at it."

"There are a few of those," he agreed.

"Why not you? Everybody talks like you're the best."

"Because I don't want it to be that serious, all right? I want it to be something I can do if I feel like. I don't want to end up like Elvis, having to go through the motions to make enough money to get everybody off my back, and then get so depressed I blow the money myself and have to dig myself in deeper to keep the whole cycle going."

"It's hard making a living as an entertainer," she agreed. "What brought you out of hiding for this show?"

"Hiding? Who says I was hiding?"

"I didn't mean hiding, exactly. Just that the other Elvises see you as some kind of mysterious figure that comes and goes without notice."

"There's nothing mysterious about me."

"You certainly wowed them by showing up on the stage."

"Okay. Maybe I like theatrical entrances. Elvis did too, and that's who we're supposed to be impersonating. These offbeat Elvises oughta be drummed off the stage. The idea is to honor the man and his music, not come up with the funkiest interpretation. Cheese Whiz Elvis. Where's the respect?"

"Didn't Elvis mock himself and even his audience sometimes?"

"Yes, he did." KOK sat forward and fixed Temple with a stern look. "And he was wrong. It was a gesture of surrender to his own vulnerabilities. In the end, his self-esteem was so low he looked on his audience's love for him with contempt. Instead of seeing them as forgiving friends, he saw them as fools and dupes he couldn't force to turn against him."

"You're saying he wanted to be martyred."

"He wanted to end what had become too hard to keep up. He didn't see any honorable way to desert the field. So he performed himself to death."

"What about the Colonel's role in driving Elvis into mediocre movies and debilitating tours?"

"Oh, Colonel Parker. The villain of the piece. Everybody was responsible but Elvis Presley. Did you ever notice how the least likely suspect in a murder case always turns out to be the killer?"

"Who's the least likely suspect in the Elvis saga?"

Lyle's tiny shrug made the gold threads on his *gi* shimmer and shimmy. His lower lip curled up before he gave a half smile that lifted the left side of his upper lip, just like Elvis's.

"How about the victim himself?"

Chapter 42

Elvis and Evil

(Elvis recorded the song, "Adam and Evil," for
the 1966 film, *Spinout*)

"What a weirdo guy," Temple reported to Electra, after
Full-spectrum Elvis had escorted her through the throngs
waiting to bedevil Lyle, aka the KOK.

They all made proper farewells—bows, kisses, caressing scarf moves—and left, leaving Electra in an even
greater girlish tizzy.

"How can you say that about the Elvis of the nineties?" she demanded of Temple when they were alone.

"What's the Elvis of the next decade going to be: the
King of Zeroes?"

"I thought you had seen a bit of the magic that made
Elvis the biggest star of the twentieth century. I thought
you were becoming converted."

"Converted to a particular impersonator being good,
yes; to Elvis, no. Besides, this Lyle guy said something
so bizarre at the end of our interview. He implied that

another Elvis impersonator killed the Elvis in the pool."

"Professional jealousy?"

"How could that be? The dead Elvis isn't even missed. If it had been Lyle Purvis himself, okay. But a nonentity Elvis isn't worth killing. Besides, Lyle sounded about as clear as Elvis was during one of his spiritual meanderings. It was like he was describing some mystical sort of murder, as if Elvis somehow had killed himself."

Electra's sweet-sixteen sixties face—today Temple had glimpsed the madcap teenager inside the not-so-dignified matron's exterior—grew radiant with inspiration.

"Temple! Elvis could kill an Elvis . . . but only if the real one is out there somewhere."

" 'Out there' like 'the truth' on the *X-Files*? Over the edge and into Paranoid Country? I'm sorry, Electra. I will never buy that 'Elvis lives' scenario."

"Oh, you little hard-headed cynic! That notion doesn't have to be taken literally."

"What other way is there to take it?"

"If you need to ask, I don't need to tell you."

"Huh? Oh, that this too, too solid delusion would melt, dissolve into a dew—"

"When you're done spouting, could we meet somebody else?"

"I'm sorry you couldn't go in to meet KOK Elvis. It would have blown my cover."

"Well, I can meet one pseudo-celebrity without blowing your cover." Electra took Temple's arm firmly. "Now. Show me Miss Priscilla."

Quincey was in and receiving visitors in her dressing room. "Hi," she tossed over her shoulder and around her flowing hair at Temple. "I heard a whole lot of stomping going on upstairs. Did somebody off Elvis onstage?"

Electra stepped around Temple, which was never hard to do. "No, dear. We just saw an Elvis performance that rocked the roof off the Kingdome. A pity you were confined down here."

"I'll see plenty of Elvis acts at the real show." Quincey's long, pale fingernails poked at her towering hair, which leaned a little to the left, like the edifice at Pisa. "I'll have to sit there for hours and hours, dying of boredom. But my gown arrived, thanks to the hotel. Isn't it cool?"

She led the way to the costume niche, where a white column of silk and lace and beading hung like a frozen fountain.

Temple, who had been known to glance at a bride's magazine gown layout when killing time in front of a magazine stand, was stunned by the high-necked, long-sleeved design of Priscilla's wedding gown, a world away from the strapless bustier styles modern brides preferred.

She was stunned that Quincey, with all her teenage eagerness to equate beautiful with bad, actually liked this virginal froth of fabric.

Quincey lifted an empty sleeve as if introducing a friend. "It's not a perfect replica. I guess the estate owns that. I'll wear it when I present the winning Elvis with the championship belt."

"That's scrumptious, dear," Electra said with naked envy. "Oh, my. I could have fit into that, once for fifteen minutes in nineteen fifty-two."

Quincey laughed. "Don't worry, Everybody gets their fifteen minutes of fame, and I guess everybody gets their fifteen minutes at fitting into an impossible dress."

Temple formally introduced Electra, then thought of something. "By the way, you two, with all the Elvis trivia you must have stockpiled, was there ever any mention of a pet snake?"

Electra and Quincey exchanged coconspirators' glances: Was Temple off her rocker?

"You have to admit a huge snake is a pretty bizarre prop for a murder," Temple said. "It has to mean something, it being in the Medication Garden . . ."

"Oooh." Quincey was waxing theatrical. "Like in the Garden of Eden."

"The snake is a universal symbol of evil," Temple agreed, "through no fault of its own except the usual human superstition."

Quincey giggled. "A big snake is the symbol of something else humans are pretty superstitious about."

Electra collapsed onto a dressing table chair, laughing. Her muumuu turned even more fluorescent in the makeup lights. "You got that right, girl. Say, now that we're on the subject. I do recall something about a big snake."

"The only strange animal I can think of was the mynah in the basement," said Quincey.

"That was at Graceland," Electra said. "The snake was not there. Somehow . . . I know!"

Temple and Quincey came over to Electra like an audience gathering for a revelation.

"Felton Jarvis," Electra said portentously. "That ring any bells for you, Quincey?"

The girl dropped her jaw, rolled her eyes, and otherwise pantomimed deep thought, or what passed for it in her set. She shook her head.

"Nothing?" a disappointed Electra wailed.

Quincey tried, God love her. "Uh. Felton. Kinda like Elton. And the last name starts with a 'J.'" When Temple and Electra continued to stare blankly at her, she added defensively, "Elton John. His name's kinda like Elton John's."

"Not really," Temple said. "And what about the snake? Where's the snake in all this?"

"Felton Jarvis," Electra intoned, as if she were channeling the man, or calling up her memory. She smiled like Buddha. "Felton Jarvis! He was a record producer who actually did a good job for Elvis in the sixties and early seventies. Worked out of Nashville. And he had a

pet anaconda he took swimming with him in his apartment pool."

"Did he call it Trojan?" Temple asked.

"I don't know what he called it, dear. All I know is
you're lucky that I remember that much. Can't you
check this out with the Animal Elvis attraction manager?"

"Yes, I can, now that you've remembered something
concrete." Temple glanced from Quincey to Electra. The
effect was like a time machine. Over thirty years ago,
Electra had—what color hair?—and maybe had dressed
like Quincey's Priscilla in white go-go boots and teased
hair. On the other hand, the real Priscilla, who was at
least a decade younger than Electra, didn't look anything
like the older woman, and probably never would, not
with all the anti-aging services Hollywood had to offer.

"Fel-ton Jar-vis," Temple intoned, mimicking Electra.
Southern men's names had a certain elegance when they
weren't the usual countrified Billy Bob and Bobby Joe:
Rhett Butler. Lyle Purvis. Ashley Wilkes. Elvis Presley.
Felton Jarvis.

"She's thinking," Electra whispered to Quincey. "It
doesn't always come easy."

"Hush your mouth!" Temple mock-snapped. And then
the subtlety that had been nagging at her snapped back.
"Ohmigosh! Elvis's name is in Fel-ton Jar-vis. El-vis.
Do you suppose that was a clue? Is that why the snake
was let loose in the pool with a dead man? Because it
had a personal connection to Felton Jarvis and therefore
Elvis himself? Was Lyle right? Did an 'Elvis' have
something to do with the mock Elvis's death?

"Or did his anaconda?" Quincey threw in, looking excited. She turned to Electra. "Where did you read about
that anaconda?"

"I don't know. In one of my books."

"You actually own books about Elvis?"

"Dozens."

"Can I come over to your house and study them? If I

missed something as way cool as the snake, I need to."

"I did loan some to a friend, but I'm sure you could look those over too. When do you get off here?"

"The rehearsal's over, so I can split."

"Great." Electra stood. "Temple, coming?"

"No. I need to find out more about Trojan here. There must be a keeper for that miniature zoo somewhere."

"Hope he isn't a miniature keeper," Quincey said with a giggle.

She and Electra exited left, laughing.

Chapter 43

Too Much Monkey Business

(A song Elvis recorded—and never released—
during a truculent 1968 recording session, the
first time his musicians noticed a puzzling
personality change)

I am beginning to develop a deep sympathy for those
forced to make their living as nannies.

This conclusion comes home to me when I escort the
ingratiating Chatter on an outing to the local zoo and garden, both happily uninhabited yet by humans, save for
the staff.

Chatter, it seems, would like to hold my hand.

Apparently, the chimp is used to being treated like a
child and likes to cling to his escort of the moment.

It cannot have escaped anyone's observation by now
that I do not have a hand.

Oh, I have useful forelimbs, aka arms, and clever pads
and shivs. But hands they are not, and they must double
as walking extremities. When I am afoot, they belong to
no one but me.

So Chatter, being an inventive, clever chimp, settles for tightening his long fingers around my tail.

Oh, the indignity!

Fortunately, this is a clandestine outing.

We have made our surreptitious way from the dressing room area, keeping to shadowed halls, handy walls, and hiding behind the lush landscaping once we enter the Kingdome itself.

Our situation is made even worse by the fact that I did not care to take Chatter out undiapered, so he is wearing his jeweled jumpsuit, which he was only too happy to don at my request. I do not know how humans with offspring keep their sanity during these terrible Wonder Years. Perhaps they are called that because parents are always wondering why they became parents in the first place.

But Chatter is happy to have a stroll, and keeps the chit-chat down, also at my request.

I breathe a big doggy sigh of relief when we reach the Animal Elvis exhibit unremarked upon. This has been one of my toughest undercover assignments yet.

"Now, Louie, now? Chatter sing. Chatter swing. Now?"

"Not yet," I tell him, trying to release my rear member from his tight grasp. "First we need to talk to Trojan on redirect."

"Huh, Louie, huh? How we talk Trojan? I no talk Trojan. What redirect?"

"Lawyer talk. I do not have an Esquire after my name for nothing."

"S-cried? Who S?"

"Never mind."

I manage to ease Chatter around Rising Sun and Domino. He is all hot to crawl up on their backs and hang onto their "hair."

I have never seen a critter so interested in hanging onto the appendages of other creatures. What he made of Trojan, who has no appendages, I cannot imagine.

When we get to the snake pit, I let Chatter open the lunch slot and bounce in first.

If Trojan is in the mood for food, I am sure monkey

meat is much more nourishing than a few scrawny feline limbs.

But the big snake is pretty much where I left him yesterday, doing the usual drowsing and digesting routine. In fact, he may still be hypnotized by my soothing feline wiles.

Chatter jumps on his back and begins playing ride 'em, Cowboy. It would take only two lazy coils of that svelte muscular body to turn Chatter from a three-dimensional being to a two-dimensional one, and I am tempted to let nature take its course and preserve my tail.

But my Miss Temple has mysteries to solve, so I sacrifice poetic justice and the law of the jungle to serve the greater good.

"Off the furniture!" I tell Chatter.

He yips like a dog and bounds to the cage floor.

Trojan's narrow jet-black eyes blink. I have never seen eyes so black. They are like pools of tar, and I know that if I were not hypnotizing Trojan, Trojan would be mesmerizing me into a menu item.

I begin purring, causing an irritated ripple to pulse down Trojan's long, long scaled and mottled back.

But this is the only way I can communicate with the big fella. That reptilian tongue that doubles as a sniffer does not have a huge range of vocabulary.

"You remember Chatter?" I ask first.

The huge body shifts as if it rests on a nasty tack or something.

"I thought so. Did the monkey release you from the cage?"

"Yesssss." Trojan turns his massive, spade-shaped head the chimp's way.

"Why did you take the opportunity to leave the safety of your, er, artificially accurate environment?"

"To ssssee Vegassss."

Is everybody a pushover for a good promotional campaign, or what? "How about getting into the pool?"

"Pusssshed."

Now this is interesting. "Who pushed Trojan?"

"Men. Men alwayssss pusssssh Trojan around."

"Well, there's a lot of you to push. I imagine they think they mean well."

"Thessssse men not mean well."

"How do you know?"

"They put Trojan in water with carrion. I like fressssh prey."

"So you're saying that the dude was dead before you took a dip in the pool with him?"

"Dude?"

"Man."

"Man dead. Trojan try to play, but man dead."

"How long?"

"In jungle river, piranhassss would eat all."

I love the tropics: giant reptile stranglers, little bitty flesh-eating fish. Before you can take a bite out of them, there will be nothing left but your false teeth chattering like a demented chimpanzee before sinking to the bottom of the Amazon River. Remind me to stay north of the Grand Canyon.

Speaking of the devil you know, Chatter is getting restless and wrestling with the twisted length of jungle vine.

It occurs to me that this is the narrow far end of the mighty Trojan. I flash my shivs across Chatter's knuckles. "Did you not see the signs outside? DO NOT FEED THE ANIMALS. Which is what you will be doing if you continue to toy with Trojan's nether regions."

With a shriek, the chimp desists, going to crouch against the glass.

I remain in the middle, caught between two highly erratic animals.

"So, sir," I conclude, addressing Trojan respectfully, which is the only way to talk to a twenty-foot-long garrotte. "Your accidental dive into the pool had no bearing on the life or death of the poor dude—man—who shared your natatory endeavors?"

"Sssssay what?"

"Never mind. We will be leaving now. Is there anything we can do for you?"

"If you encounter anything edible besides yoursssselvesss, sssshove it through the door assss you leave."

I look at Chatter. It is tempting, but I still need the overactive little Elvis throwback. No wonder I would dearly like to throw him back to Trojan. Another day, perhaps.

Chatter is bouncing beside me as soon as we exit single file through the food door.

"Can see more, Louie? Huh? Huh? Huh? Look up skirts? Huh? Huh? Huh?"

"Sorry, kid. Dames do not wear skirts like they used to. You will have to get another hobby." I do not mention that I took a peek for Miss Priscilla's garter belt just before entering Chatter's storage closet a couple days ago. That was purely investigational.

I lead the way to my former hangout, the Medication Garden.

I have to stop the action right here to say that I do not understand the great contempt in which Elvis is held for liking a mood-altering substance. My kind has a similar weakness for a little herb called catnip in our honor. It is true that when we indulge in catnip we are transported to moods beyond our normal range. We become kittenish and clown around and roll around and generally cavort around, to the amusement of all and damage to none. Apparently the nip that Elvis used was less innocuous. Perhaps if he had tried catnip, he would have had all the enjoyment and none of the ill effects. Instead of "just say no," perhaps humans should just say "hello" to catnip. What could it hurt?

"Have you been here before?" I ask Chatter, not hoping for much in the way of lucid reply.

He takes a lope around the pool, those disgusting knuckles brushing the pavement all the way around. He stops, sits, and shimmies the lower half of his face from side to side, as if sniffing the air.

"No," he finally says.

I gaze around, disappointed. This was where Crawfish Pukecannon—as I renamed him long ago in honor of his disagreeable personality that begins to smell three minutes after you meet him—met up with me last. Or do I mean three seconds? Anyway, where C. B. is lurking I smell a rat. It would help my little doll no end if I could do the dirty work and dig up this rat without her mussing her dainty little high heels.

I admit to being disoriented in this garden. Someone has seeded the place with attractive but stinky plants. It smells like the respiratory infection remedy shelf of your local discount pharmacy.

I mean, menthol and mint, lemon and licorice, and not a snippet of catnip.

I am not at my best when getting a sick headache from innocuous medicinal herbs.

But does this atmosphere bother the affable Chatter? No way.

He bounds around, jumping from the top of one see-through plastic coffin to another, gazing at the garish suits within and shrieking with laughter.

I cannot blame him. Compared to the modestly jeweled jumpsuit he is wearing, these laid-out ones are over the top and around your block. They shine under the artificial dome light, a shifting sky of white clouds that take on the faces of the principal players in the Elvis Presley saga . . . Mama Gladys, Daddy Vernon. Baby brother Jesse Garon is a cute little unformed fluffy cloud attached to Mama and Daddy, I guess. There's a big blue thunderhead that is either Colonel Parker or the three Memphis Mafia members who wrote the first tell-all book, Red and Sonny West and Dave Hebler, all melded together to *look* like Colonel Parker, another villain of the piece. There is a Priscilla cloud, an all-white thunderhead that must be all hair, and a whole bunch of babe clouds who are pretty fluffy in all the right places.

Of course, this is a subtle effect, and I do not spy Lisa

Marie's cats among the heavenly cavorters, although I spot a few horses.

Chatter has been silent for a while now, so I get my head out of the heavens and back down to earth.

And I do mean earth.

In the two minutes I have let my attention wander, my chattering charge has been up to major mischief.

I gaze aghast at the ground.

This is the damage the unfettered opposable thumb can do.

Chatter has worried at the ground opposite the tasteful Elvis funeral suit display, tossing foul herbal plants aside like weeds (I cannot blame him for that) and uncovering something buried just deep enough to need a demented chimpanzee to unearth it.

It is a pale limb. It is soft and limp. As I stare, bemused, for I have never witnessed the de-burying of a body before, I see that it is not bone, but the flared sleeve of a white jumpsuit, encrusted with faux gemstones embedded in genuine dirt.

Speaking of dirt, Chatter has got it all over his own white jumpsuit.

And I think he has become a little too excited at the discovery. My sniffer tells me someone should change his diaper.

I will leave the disposition of *that* to the proper authorities.

As for the jumpsuit in the herb garden, is it Elvis or is it Memorex?

Chapter 44

Also Sprach Zarathustra

(The Richard Strauss piece whose thundering drum overture was so effective in 1968's futuristic film, *2001:A Space Odyssey;* Elvis used it to open his live concerts beginning in 1972, and on many albums)

"Two nights running, no Elvis." Leticia's mellow voice sharpened with disappointment.

She had just finished her five-hour on-air shift as Delilah and now was switching her performer's beret for a producer's hard hat. "I don't get it," she added.

"We play the passive part in this charade," Matt pointed out. "We sit here and wait. People choose to call in. Or not."

Leticia's frown carved no parallel tracks between her brows, merely a fleeting ripple in her mocha skin. "What's not to call in for? We're a feel-good station. You're a feel-good radio shrink. That Elvis guy was getting a lot of reaction, not to mention ink."

"He was getting us a lot of reaction and ink. Maybe

'Elvis' is tired of notoriety. Or maybe . . . maybe he can't call."

"What do you mean? Someone is holding him prisoner?"

"Leticia! You're buying into all those Extreme Elvis scenarios. As if he's really still alive and out there, and no theory is too wild about what might have happened to him or what he might be doing now. This caller was just a guy with an Elvis fetish, indulging his mania and getting lots of the attention he craves."

"So why'd he give it up then?"

Matt sat at the desk and took up the headphones she had abandoned. The schoolhouse clock said he had less than a minute to contemplate the absence of Elvis. Then he'd have to get on with what he was here for: talking to real people. "Maybe he died."

"Funnee man."

"No, really. A guy in an Elvis suit was found floating in the Kingdome pool the day before yesterday."

"I haven't heard anything; how did you?"

"I know the two women who found him. And there was an obscure article in the paper. Oh, and for the weird set, a huge anaconda was floating in the pool with him."

"It was dead too?"

"No, quite alive. In fact, it's a suspect."

"What the hell's an anaconda doing in a Kingdome pool?"

"There's an exhibit of animals associated with Elvis. Apparently an anaconda was one of them. Don't ask me why."

"An anaconda . . ." Leticia's dark eyes glittered with possibilities.

"Don't tell me: if a snake calls tonight, I'm to keep it on the line as long as possible. Even if it lisps."

The first three callers wanted to know the same thing Leticia did: Where was Elvis?

"He doesn't give me his touring schedule, you know,"

Matt answered wryly. "And it's a bad idea to believe everything you hear."

"You call him 'Elvis.' "

"I call him what he implies he is. We're strangers. I owe him at least that courtesy."

"Howard Stern would be calling him a sicko ghoul who needs to ride on a corpse's reputation, and a lot worse."

"Maybe that's why he didn't call Howard Stern."

The next caller was less accusing. "Just tell him that we miss him and would like to hear from him again."

A third caller wanted to get into the Existential Elvis.

"You know, everybody is either ready to believe it has to be Elvis, or angry that it can't possibly be Elvis," she said. "What if it's something in between?"

"Semi-Elvis?" Matt asked.

"How about semisolid Elvis? He was a recording artist, after all. Maybe the airwaves were always the best way to deal with Elvis. It doesn't matter what he wears or how much he weighs, it just matters how he sings."

"That's the beauty of radio. Image is nothing."

"It's the perfect medium for Elvis: voice is all. And that's what he really cared about—the music and how he sang it. The rest was just distraction."

"The rest was destructive. But even today a rock star has to tour to keep the fan base. We want our performers live and in person."

"They say by the year twenty-twenty we'll have Virtual communication. Like the holodeck of *Star Trek*'s starship *Enterprise*."

"Maybe by then you can visit with Virtual Elvis at Graceland."

"Are you sure this whole 'Elvis calling' thing isn't a promotional gimmick for the Kingdome opening?"

"No," Matt said, "I'm not. But who ever is sure about anything connected with Elvis?"

"That's some achievement," the woman mused, "when you think about it. To have made such an impact that even after your death endless scenarios seem possible. At least to some people."

"Elvis struck me as both pretentious and unpretentious, and the ways he was pretentious were the ways we all might go overboard if we had the opportunities he did. That's what's wrong with some people making him into a god. He had such predictably human failings. The same ones teenage sports stars show today. It's more instructive to regard him as a man gone wrong, not a god betrayed."

" 'Instructive.' Gee whiz, Mr. Midnight, do you know how odd it is to hear that word on talk radio?"

"Sorry."

"Don't be. Elvis would like that word. That's what his spiritual quest was, to find some way he could inspire people beyond moving them with his music. Some way to use that remarkable power."

"I have to say that the Rolling Stones don't seem too concerned about using their remarkable drawing power for anything other than what was the darker side of Elvis: sex, drugs, and rock 'n' roll."

"No, Elvis was peculiarly American, both idealistic and egotistical."

"Do you know how rarely the word 'peculiarly' is heard on talk radio?"

She chuckled. "Bingo! I'd better get back to my Elvis-channeling sessions. Say hi to the King for me."

Matt was happy that the audience was mellowing, accepting that the caller, whoever he was, could go as suddenly as he had come. Whatever the so-called Elvis had done or not done, he had certainly kept the phone lines ringing at WCOO.

"Mr. Midnight? Are you still on? I kinda lost track of time. Sometimes I do that."

That familiar easygoing voice made Matt sit up ramrod straight, as if he were on television and had to look alert. "I figured you weren't going to call again."

"Heck, man. Who else am I gonna call? Ghostbusters?"

The caller's hearty laughter faded into worn-out wheezes. He sounded like a punch-drunk kid who'd stayed up late for too many pizza nights in a row.

"Give it up, man," Matt urged. "You're not a ghost. There's not even a ghost of a chance that you're who you claim to be. You don't have to be Elvis."

"Yeah, I do." Rage drove a baritone-deep spike into the soft, Southern underbelly of the tenor voice Matt was used to hearing. "I can't help who I was born as. Can't help that God chose me to be Elvis Presley."

"Being Elvis could be dangerous right now," Matt warned, back-peddling. "You heard about the man who died at the Kingdome?"

"Yeah. Terrible thing. But that don't scare me. I used to get death threats all the time."

Maybe, Matt thought, he could use the facts of Elvis's life to force this deluded man to confront his own fictions. "Isn't that why you were forced into that isolated lifestyle, why you kept an entourage between you and everything else?"

"What do you mean 'lifestyle'? It was my life, man. I guess I gave it some style. That's all."

"Everybody thought you lived a lavish and isolated life because that was what stars did, but most of it was due to the fans. They just couldn't leave you alone. One of your guys says when you made those cross-country train trips to and from Memphis, you had crowds waiting at every stop, like nothing anybody had seen since Lincoln's funeral train."

"Yeah, the fans were always there for me. And I didn't even have to die to do it. At first. At the end—" Laughter again, forced laughter.

"Elvis . . . you don't mind if I call you that?"

"No, sir. They used to think it was a funny name, in the beginning, made fun of it. Now it's all they know me by."

"And they know you all over the world."

"That's right. We're a trinity: Jesus, Elvis, and Coca-

cola. I only drank Pepsi, though. They always get something wrong. I got a few things wrong myself." A pause.
"Wish I coulda toured the world. Kept getting invited,
but Colonel, he always managed to hex any trips like
that. Guess he had reasons."

"He wasn't a U.S. citizen. He was afraid if he put a
foreign tour in motion, that would come out."

"Yeah, but it would have given me new worlds to
conquer, right? I needed that. The old one was getting
stale. It's always more interesting getting somewhere
than being there, you know?"

"I know. And you got there so fast. You stayed there
for a long time."

"A long time. Almost lived to be my mama's age.
Now that was a miracle. I never missed no one or nothing so much as I did her. Still do."

"Don't you . . . see her now?"

"Naw, what do you think, man? Think I'm Superman
or something? Think I'm a swami? I'm just trying to
figure out the world and God and stuff, and why I was
chosen to be Elvis Presley. There must have been a reason."

"There's always a reason." Matt looked down at the
lists on the tabletop, feeling like Judas Iscariot, or like
a chief prosecutor, he didn't know which. "There was a
reason you got a guitar for your eleventh birthday. Your
mother took you and you got a used one . . . how much
did it cost?"

"Eleven ninety-five. Shoot! I wanted a gun! But my
mama said no, so I got the guitar."

"And that was the beginning."

"Who knows what a beginning is, man. Or an end. If
I could tell you that I would really be somebody. It all
runs together, and then we put order on it and say this
happens because that happened. Like they say my mama
dying was the end of me, or Cilla leaving, or, hell, why
not my dog Getlo dying after eighteen years? That dog
was there when mama still was, when my star was shiny

and new. How does anybody know what brought me down? I don't even know it."

"Everybody's an expert on you, Elvis."

"You got that right, Mr. Midnight. Ever'body but me, huh?"

"Haven't you had time to become an expert by now?"

"I've had time to think, that's for sure. If I just hadn't been raised to respect my elders like I was. Maybe I woulda given Colonel his walking papers. I used to threaten to do it, but ever' time I got mad enough to do something about him, he'd sit me down and scare me, like that time in seventy-six when he showed me this bill of millions I'd owe him if I fired him. That man was a wizard with figures. Had mah daddy beat seven times around the block. Somethin' in me just couldn't say no to anybody's face. It was like I was paralyzed."

"You couldn't say no to your mama. Maybe that put the fear of saying no in you."

"That's what they say about drugs now: *just say no*. Heck, they got no idea how hard sayin' no is."

"But you don't take drugs now."

"Ah . . . naw. Mostly not. Hell, I haven't got the money for that stuff now."

"But your estate's been built up again. It's worth millions. Why don't you go back and claim it?"

"See, that's what got me in trouble, all the money, and then the Colonel letting me pay ninety percent taxes on it, then me being a Big Spender. I was needing dough in those last years. Had to work to keep ever'body paid and the planes and cars coming so I had a chance of going somewhere fast some way. So I don't want all that. Finally got away, son; think I'm gonna run right back?"

"What happened to the boy who wanted to be James Dean, who showed up on his first movie set with the whole script memorized: his and everybody else's lines?"

"I was a go-getter then, wasn't I? I still had hope I

could make somethin' of myself, instead of ever'body makin' something on or off of me."

"What happened to those girls you fell in love with back then? Dixie, and June, and Debra Paget, your first costar. You were always falling in love, Elvis. What would have happened if you'd have married one of those girls and stopped letting those fans in the motel and hotel rooms for you and the boys to pick from like a basket of free fruit the management sent? They were just adventure-crazy young girls. What did you or they get from all that?"

"I don't know, Mr. Midnight. It seemed like a new adventure ever' night, that it did. And the guys, they really looked up to me. I was the King. I could have every woman in the world. They could take what I left."

"That's . . . not the way you were raised, Elvis. Not what your mother wanted."

The pause elongated into that one thing dreaded in live radio: dead air time.

"I know it." The voice was soft, shamed. "I know it. She wanted me to be clean-living. No cussin', no drinkin', no wild, wild women. And I didn't let anybody have alcohol around for a long time, or do no cussin'. But then I got used to the hard life of the road, and ever'thing slipped. It seemed like fun. It seemed like I was somebody."

"You were the King. You were everything you weren't in high school, right?"

"Right! It was fun. I couldn't keep 'em away. They loved it. Got to be wearin' on a guy. Too much to live up to. A lot of the time we didn't do anything. Heck, a lot of the girls I was with for a long time before we did anything serious."

"Kind of like in high school, huh? Necking and games, but nothin' you could get in real trouble for."

"Yeah. But you're right. My mama like to kill me if she knew all the messes I got into on the road."

"Maybe she did. Maybe that's what killed her."

"Don't say that! I thought you were listenin' to me. I thought you were one of my guys! There's loyalty, and you don't be loyal to me and say things to tear me down. To bring me down. Damn it."

Breathing, labored, came over the line.

Matt wasn't watching Leticia, or the clock. He wasn't seeing anything but the dark tabletop in front of him. His ears were tuned to his caller's every nuance, every breath. This was a man on a tightrope over a mental chasm, stretched as taut as an overtuned guitar string.

His history was national knowledge. His life was a national resource. His death was history.

He may be delusional, but the delusion was reality-based. If he thought he was Elvis, he was Elvis. He had to be treated as Elvis.

Treated as Elvis. Not just handled, but counseled. Helped. No one could save Elvis the first time around. Did twenty years of psychobabble make it possible to do now what couldn't be done then?

Was "Elvis" finally ready to be saved, or was this Elvis clone ready to die like Elvis? Inevitably? Publicly? Pathetically?

"I think I'm ready to go back to Graceland for good. Graceland," Elvis said, his voice even softer. "Name never meant anything. People thought it did, but Grace was just the first name of the daughter of the guy who first owned the place. He musta loved his little girl, like I loved mine. Just happened to sound like something special, even spiritual, when you put 'land' after it. Like Dixieland. Only now it sounds commercial. Like Disneyland.

"But not that commercial. It had a special sound, Graceland. I bought it to be our home. My mama's home. My daddy's home. My home. That's all it ever was. Graceland. Peaceful sounding, isn't it?"

"You deserve peace," Matt said. "Didn't you tell Dixie, your first long-time girlfriend, when you broke up in 1960, that already the weight of the Elvis empire was too heavy? That you'd like to drop out but too many people depended on you for their livelihoods?"

"That's right. Too many people had a piece of me. Not much left for myself. Best thing I ever bought was Graceland. Up there on the hill. On the highway. Elvis Presley Boulevard, they renamed that part of it. How many people have a piece of highway named after them? I was proud of that. It meant I'd been somewhere. Maybe I didn't stay somewhere. But I'd been there."

He laughed, softly.

"Graceland. That there Simon guy named a whole album after it when he got toney. I always liked the sound of it. Liked those high white pillars. Loved to race around those rolling hills on whatever wheels I could use. Only time I felt free, felt like the world had caught up to me, was when I raced around. I think maybe I was born racing, my whole self, my heart, and my head. Movin', movin'. Always movin'. Only thing'd stop me was them pills. And start me again. Stop. Start. Racin'.

"It was my home. Graceland. Not any of those Hollywood houses on Bellagio and Perugia and all those foreign candy-box-soundin' names.

"Graceland was the kind of place you can go over Jordan from. I still see my mama's chickens peckin' around the yard, as happy there as on any ole spit of land we ever rented and she ever spread chicken feed on.

"And Daddy corralling his donkeys in the dry swimming pool at Graceland. I tell yah, it makes me laugh, and laugh, until I cry. We sat on those white steps, Daddy and me, and cried and cried. Cried for Mama's chickens she'd never feed again. Cried for her bein' gone, and us bein' left and all those damn chickens.

"Neighbors used to sniff at Mama's chickens, and Daddy's donkeys, and my big cars, and later reporters came 'round to sniff at my shot-out television sets and my red rugs. Hell, Mama, she got scared when I got so famous and the girls came screaming. Mama, she got worried for me. Said I should give it all up. Come home to Graceland and sell furniture, I was so good at collectin' it for Graceland. I swear to God, that's what she really wanted me to do. Sell furniture. I swear to God. Mama.

"She was my best girl. I always said that. It's as true today as it was then. What was I gonna do? Turn all them girls away? No red-blooded boy'd do that. But they were just all noise and worry and wantin,' them girls. They didn't really care for me, most of 'em. And those that did, didn't last. Maybe I didn't let them last. She was always my best girl. I even said it on a collection of those bubble gum cards they sold in fifty-six. You know, Elvis answers all your questions. Said back then I didn't like to be bored, and I ended up bored to death.

"See, that's what I gotta wonder about death. Always did. Is it just sleepin'? Or is it boredom? Bore, bore, boredom. Man, that'd kill me!"

"You're not thinking of dying, are you, Elvis?"

"About time, isn't it, Mr. Midnight? Maybe I just gotta let go of this world, even though nobody seems to want to let me go. Just let go, get the answers to all those mysteries for myself."

"You don't want to take your own life?"

"And ain't I supposed to have done that already, son? How can you kill a dead guy?"

Chapter 45

Keep Them Cold Icy Fingers Off of Me

(Traditional country ballad Elvis sang at the
Humes High School Minstrel Show in 1953)

"All right," said Motorcycle Elvis. "We're gonna rock
around the clock until tonight."

Temple admired their energy. They had been rocking
since last night, long after she left the Kingdome, when
an escaped chimpanzee had been found digging up a
body of evidence in the Medication Garden.

She had no idea that Fontana Inc. had her home phone
number, but they did, or they had gotten it somewhere.
She had been rousted from sleep at seven A.M. by an
Elvis singing "Wake Up, Little Susie."

She had no idea whether the song was associated with
him, but he had recorded so many songs that it was
possible. Certainly the song's era had been his heyday.

"We thought we would break the news to you gently,"
the serenading Elvis had explained once her fury at a
wake-up call that implied she was "little" had eased.

"Elvis would do that kind of thing," he added. "Call up a girl and sing an appropriate lyric to her by way of greeting."

"Elvis is dead, so even if he did that, I certainly don't want to be awakened thinking I'm either past the pearly gates myself, or being treated to a tabloid newspaper incident."

"Yes, Miss Temple," the contrite Elvis said, asking her to meet them at the Kingdome ASAP. That's how he said it: ASAP with a long A. Not the full form: As Soon As Possible.

Now her personal guard of Elvi were assembled in the dressing-room hallway in all their glitter and glory.

"So what's the news?" she asked.

"Well, we managed to linger in the area of the, ah, dig, remaining inconspicuous."

Temple eyed them en masse, Rainbow Elvis. She had to admit that in the Kingdome, this was indeed a subtle and soft-spoken disguise: Max's maxim that overdressed is the best camouflage in Las Vegas proved true once again.

"And we were able to see the . . . victim disinterred," Oversized Elvis added delicately.

"Don't tell me! It was Elvis, as fresh as the day he was put to rest."

"We can't tell you that, Miss Temple," Fifties Elvis rebuked her. "It wasn't even a person."

"The suit was empty?"

"Yup."

"You're sure them bones, them bones, them dry bones weren't paper towels?"

"Absolutely. That suit was as flat as a long-playing record."

"And get this!" Rhinestone Lapels Elvis put in. "We saw some of the gemstones and the pattern was of, like, rays around something. Some of the dirt and moss covered the design."

"A rearing stallion?"

"Could be."

"Then that's the jumpsuit that was 'killed' in Quincey's dressing room? Why bury it in the Medication Garden? Listen to me! I'm beginning to go along with Elvisinsanity. Why bother to bury a jumpsuit at all?"

"Wanted to get rid of it," Fifties Elvis suggested.

"Didn't do a very good job of it, did they?"

"Yeah," Cape-and-Cane Elvis said, "but how often is a chimpanzee going to go ape in the Medication Garden? I mean, the tourists weren't about to root up the herb beds like dogs, were they?"

"There's an Elvis fan who carted a toenail clipping away from the shag rug in the Jungle Room at Graceland. Another devoteé went to a doctor who had removed a wart from Elvis very early in his career and—"

"Wait a minute." Oversized Elvis looked genuinely concerned. "The doctor or Elvis?"

"What?"

"Which one was early in his career when the wart was removed?"

"Elvis! Nobody knows where the doctor was then, or now. Or cares. So what does it matter?"

"Timing is very important in these things," Oversized Elvis/Aldo said.

"Anyway," Temple emphasized fiercely, "this other fan bought the wart from the doctor—he'd apparently kept it preserved all these years. It's now a major Elvis artifact. So does this give you any hint of what Elvis fans might try to do in the Medication Garden?"

"Yeah, but the people who buried the suit might not have known much about Elvis fans." Karate Elvis.

"Not like you, Miss Temple, who is always on top of everything." Oversized/Aldo again.

"Yeah. I was even on top of that buried suit. From what you say about its location, Electra and I—and Crawford Buchanan—were sitting right near it when the body was found in the pool."

Temple had a sudden epiphany, which was a fancy

word for insight. Maybe it was an Elvis Epiphany. She could feel her eyes narrow. Rainbow Elvis sucked in their diaphragms in preparation for action.

"Crawford Buchanan!" She could feel the clues struggling to click into place. "Has he been heard from or seen lately? Could he have buried the suit? Could he be buried up there too? Too much to hope for, but he was acting very strangely when Electra and I found the body floating in the pool. Dove right in with it. Was he trying to save . . . the suit?"

"I understand these artifacts are worth a great deal, Miss Temple," Aldo said.

Even Temple could tell he was agreeing with her wild theories simply because he was trying to be kind.

She took a few steps into Quincey's dressing room and sat down, glad that Quin was not there to see Temple flailing for answers. That girl needed a strong role model, and a confused thirty-year-old was not it.

Jumpsuit Elvis stepped forward with the air of a man about to tell a tale or two.

"We have been making some inquiries," he said gravely.

"Of whom about what?"

The brothers Fontana shook their dark-helmeted heads in awe, rendered speechless.

"Did you hear the lady?" Jumpsuit Elvis asked Karate Elvis.

"I did."

"Of whom," Jumpsuit Elvis repeated reverently. "Does anyone here doubt that this is the proper grammatical form?"

Heads shook in unity.

"Of whom." Jumpsuit Elvis regarded her with the fond wonder of Columbo catching a murderer in yet another slick but useless lie.

"Awesome," Motorcycle Elvis added.

Jumpsuit Elvis shook off his amazement to return to business. "We have been making inquiries," he resumed his speech with a politesse equal to Temple's employment of the pronoun "whom," "of those who might know or be able to find out who the stiff in the pool was when he was lucky enough to be breathing air instead of chlorine."

"What kind of people are these?"

"Connections," Karate Elvis said shortly.

"Friends of the family," Rhinestone Lapels added.

"You mean, friends of your uncle Mario?" Their uncle Mario was Macho Mario Fontana, an old-time kingpin of Las Vegas when the only mafia in town had decidedly not been from Memphis.

"In a manner of speaking," said Motorcycle Elvis.

"Let's say they owe him," Tuxedo Elvis added.

Temple nodded. Since she didn't have an in, or even an out, with any official police personnel on this case, it was handy to have sources on whom one could depend on the other side of the law.

"So, who was this guy?"

Tuxedo Elvis shimmied his shoulders inside the formal jacket. "Well, actually, the bigger question is . . . the suit."

"The suit. The jumpsuit?"

"Right. See, it isn't a tourist-shop number." Tuxedo's dark blue eyes made quick contact with his brothers'.

"And it isn't from the big-time Elvis outfitters around the country," Karate said, making a move appropriate to his name.

"Nor is it from the twinkling needles of any show costumer like Miss Minnie." Oversized.

"And it certainly isn't from any collection of the real jumpsuits—" Blues Brothers Elvis.

"So you see our problem." Oversized again.

Temple looked from Blues Brothers Elvis to Fifties Elvis to Karate Elvis. For once Quincey was right: they were all scrumpdilliscious. But they were also all as aggravating as . . . Elvis.

"Let's try another tack," she suggested. "Who's the dead guy?"

"Some loser who used the name Clint Westwood." Fifties Elvis curled half his upper lip at the obviously phony moniker.

"Used the name?"

Karate Elvis shrugged. "He'd been arrested for petty this and minor that for so long that 'Also Known As' was closer to his name than anything else."

"Just a local deadbeat." Tuxedo.

"A nobody." Rhinestone Lapels.

"Rumor had it he ran errands for Boss Banana twenty years ago." Oversized.

"Some old guy. In his sixties." Fifties Elvis.

"Should have been wiped years ago, but he slipped through the cracks." Karate.

Temple interrupted this epitaph for a petty crook. "Kind of like the dead bodies slipped through the cracks of the Goliath and Crystal Phoenix ceilings in the last couple years?"

Throats cleared and cheeks pinked on a ripple of Elvis visages. Sideburns even shifted, as small cigars were moved from one side of the mouth to the other. At least they were all unlit. So far.

"Kind of," Cape-and-Cane Elvis finally said after removing the small cigar from his mouth. Elvis and his Tampa Jewel cigars. C-and-C Elvis resembled a Western novel dude gunslinger and coughed as discreetly as Doc Holliday. "This was a Man Who Did Not Matter, that's the main thing. No one would miss him. Not the police—"

"Not the criminal element," Oversized gave the man his epitaph.

"So why was he given this really classy sendoff?" Motorcycle Elvis asked excitedly.

Temple had to clarify things. "You consider an undetermined death in an ersatz Elvis suit in an Elvis ersatz-garden classy?"

"For a guy like this? Yeah." Motorcycle also twitched his shoulders clad in a black leather jacket.

Apparently the brothers Elvis were itchy-twitchy today.

"The snake," Oversized Elvis added, "that was an inspired touch. Can you imagine what the police are trying to make of that?"

Temple had to admit that the notion of Lieutenant C. R. Molina contemplating an AWOL anaconda, a slightly larcenous corpse of no importance, and a soggy Elvis jumpsuit of original design might be a sight for sore eyes.

Hers.

Chapter 46

Today, Tomorrow, and Forever

(Elvis sang this song based on Liszt's
"Liebestraume" in *Viva Las Vegas* in 1964)

Temple turned the glass canning jar in her hand, worrying about the ring its condensation-dewed sides were leaving on the wooden tabletop.

It wouldn't be the only dark circle on a surface that sported more rings than the planet Saturn.

The dark brew inside was Pepsi-Cola, of course, Elvis's favorite beverage.

You could get anything you want, except Coca-Cola, here at Gladys's Restaurant.

The wooden, high-backed chair was hard on Temple's bony derriere. She fidgeted, slicking her palm with dew drops, and glanced at the long chromed lunch counter with its dotted line of swiveling stools, upholstered alternately in black and pink vinyl.

The jukebox was playing "Johnny B. Goode."

Hokey as the environment was, it made it easy to

imagine a teenage Elvis sitting here, drinking pop and dreaming the dreams harbored by pimply kids with no money and less self-confidence everywhere.

"Hey!"

Temple turned. Electra was waving at her from the door.

Temple blinked.

Electra wasn't wearing a muumuu.

Electra's hair wasn't sprayed a wild and wacky color.

Electra's hair was sprayed brown.

B-r-o-w-n. The one color no female influenced by Media America would ever want to own up to. Plain brown.

It was up in a saucy ponytail, and a hot-pink chiffon scarf was knotted around her throat. She was wearing a black-and-white checked circle skirt and a black sweater. A hot-pink patent-leather belt, wide, circled her less-than-svelte waist.

She looked as cute as a bug in a rug. A jitterbug in a rug.

Next to her towered this tall old guy with snowy, thick hair and one of those elaborately billowing guts atop thin hips and legs that made him an excellent Santa Claus candidate.

He was wearing boots, jeans, and a nylon windbreaker. And Frosty the Snowman sideburns as fluffy as cotton balls.

The two sashayed over to Temple's booth like Saturday-night square-dancing partners: in tune and dressed to charm.

"Temple," Electra said, gesturing to her escort, "this is Today Elvis!"

For a bizarre moment Temple thought she was on a TV show, like *Today* from NBC, or *This Is Your Life* (but It Shouldn't Be).

The old guy stuck out a callused hand that took Temple's and shook. Hard. "Howdy. Nice to meetcha. Call me Israel."

She blinked again. "I beg your pardon?"

"Or my younger friends call me 'Izzy.' Israel Feinberg. I, ah, am in the show. I do Today Elvis."

"You do 'Today Elvis.' Elvis Today. What else?"

While Temple babbled, Electra slid into her side of the booth first, on the power of her unseen crinolines—mercy, but those fifties skirts had Puff Power! Israel slid in after her.

Aside from the gut, he was a handsome old boy with a self-denigrating charm that could either go country or populous urban.

"So you're the legendary Temple Barr," he said, nodding sagely. "Electra here says you're a mean gal to cross."

"Um, I don't know. Nobody bothers to cross me much. So how'd you become Today Elvis?"

He chuckled, a rich, operatic sound. A singer, Temple twanged.

"Born in the USA, the same year as E. Nineteen thirty-five. Heart of the Depression. Up north. Philadelphia. Wouldn't know a guitar from a sitar. But I sang a little. Did a lot of Neil Simon on the amateur circuit in the sixties. You ever see *Come Blow Your Horn*? Ah, it's old, cold stuff now. I was the playboy son in that. Kept my hair. Liked to sing. Suddenly occurred to me: if Elvis were alive today, he might not look, or sound, too different from me. Can you believe it? Elvis had Jewish blood, you know."

"No, I didn't."

"Well, he thought so. Wore a Star of David and a cross together, to hedge his bets. Put a Star of David on his mother's headstone. Gotta love a guy like that, and him studying all those Eastern gurus too. Omni-Elvis. I can dig it."

"So, now you do—?"

"Ordinary Elvis." His arms spread wide to display his middle-class, middle-aged spread. "Unadorned Elvis. How he might have been had he lived to his father's age. His hair was already white at forty-two. Maybe his health problems made his weight worse, but it's the burden male flesh is heir to. He was wearing girdles in his last months. The black hair dye wasn't cosmetic then, it was necessary. Johnny Carson said it: old, fat, and forty. Johnny was blessed with thin genes. Me, I wear jeans, and I'm old, fat, and sixty"—he glanced at Electra— "something. Elvis would be sixty-four today. I figure I've aged and saged and sagged enough to do him justice. So, I 'do' him." He leaned over the table to wink at Temple. "Most fun I ever had in my whole life."

Temple put her hands to her . . . temples and leaned back in the booth. "Thank you. 'Fun.' That's what everyone forgot. Elvis had fun. Even if it was just an escape—"

"Especially if it was an escape! Let the man have a little fun, young lady! He didn't have much while he was growing up poor. He didn't have much after the Colonel got his claws into him. He didn't have as much fun as his fans got out of him. The fun was short and the shit was deep. I play Elvis as if he had outlived and outloved and outlawed them all."

"That's neat," Temple said.

Across the table from her, Electra beamed.

"That's right. That's all right, Mama." Izzy winked.

Temple felt as if she had entered an Alice-in-Wonderland set.

They dined on fried-banana-peanut-butter sandwiches, with burned bacon on the side. She and Electra had cherry Pepsis and turtle sundaes with pecans, butterscotch, and hot fudge sauce. Yummmm!

All she needed was a dormouse and a caterpillar. No Red Queen, though. Skip the Red Queen. Come to think of it, where *was* Molina?

They discussed the buried Jumpsuit.

"Right," Izzy said, munching on a burger. He had skipped the burned bacon. "It's Freudian. Symbolic. If there's any one symbol of Elvis, it's those damn jumpsuits. We impersonators—pardon, according to the estate, we're now 'tribute performers.' La-di-dah! La-di-dah-dah. La-di-dah-dah." He was jiving in the booth, drumming his fingertips on the mint-green Formica tabletop and Temple was thinking Elvis would be sixty-four . . . when I'm sixty-four. Need me, feed me. Fried bananas and peanut butter. Comfort foods, every last one of them.

"Izzy?"

"Yeah, kid?" Drum, drum, drum-drum-drum. Doo-wap, doo-wap.

He was like some uncle she had never had, the one you could ask about anything. He was cool for an old dude.

"Izzy? Would Elvis really be exactly like you today?"

"I hope not, honey." He leaned toward her, his dark eyes set in baggy, wrinkled bezels like elephant knees. "I hope Elvis today would be sleek and toned, flat-bellied, and that his coiffure would be dark and smooth as semi-sweet chocolate. I hope he'd be everything that I'm not. Eternal almost-youth at no more than . . . um, fifty-six, a well-preserved, hale and healthy fifty-six. With lots of plastic surgery and hair transplants and maybe Viagra; you think?"

She laughed. "If he isn't like you, he should be so lucky."

He inclined his snowy head. Like a king. "Thank you."

"Izzy. Could Elvis still be around? If he was, what would . . . could he look like? Really?"

Izzy sighed deeply. "If he didn't look quite like me? What are you asking?"

"Could he pass as himself? Could he still be out here? Somewhere? What would he really look like?

"You tried one of those police department computer imagining things?"

"No, and I don't have access. I only have access to speculation. To you, Today Elvis."

"You're serious. You think Elvis could be out there. You . . . have a notion."

"I have a wild idea."

Electra, who had sat back to luxuriate in Temple's learning to appreciate Izzy, stared dreamily at the grille of a fifty-eight Oldsmobile embedded into the soda fountain. "I'm getting the weirdest feeling. Like Elvis is everywhere, just like Mojo Nixon said. Just . . . open your mind's eye, and see for yourself."

Temple's mind's eye saw senior citizens, even if they used to rock 'n' roll. But who could channel Elvis better?

"Izzy, is there anybody in this competition who could really be Elvis?"

He shook his head. "No contest. I'm probably the closest thing to reality, and I'm a far cry. A far cry. Hey. Young lady. You just reminded an old man how inadequate he is."

"No. I just reminded you how close you are. No one else?"

"Well . . . I've seen most of the acts rehearsing." He shook his frosty head. "Naw. Maybe . . . that guy they call the King of Kings. Maybe him. Maybe. Heck, lil' darling shiksa. He looks too young, but then you kinda hope Elvis would be Forever Young. He's got the power. Part of it, anyway."

"Do you think he could still be out there?"

"Sheesh! Where'd this kid learn to ask questions? No. Elvis is dead. He killed himself after everybody around him let him down, after he let everybody around him down. He's better off dead. He had too much pain. He had too much . . . too much. The man makes me cry. That's why I 'do' him. He makes me feel. That's a luxury at my age."

Electra took his hand.

"I'da saved him if I could," Izzy said, "but no one could. And especially not you, kid. Especially not you,"

Temple, chastened, thought. She thought, rebelliously.
Elvis was out there somewhere, or all of this wouldn't be happening.

Elvis was out there somewhere.

Chapter 47

There Goes My Everything

(Elvis recorded this song about a broken
marriage in June of 1970; it did well on three
charts)

"Isn't Izzy something?"

Electra had scrunched down in her theater seat to stare
at the dark stage of the Kingdome showroom.

"You sound like the teenager you're dressed as. He's
an interesting man—"

"And were you really serious with all those Elvis
questions? Do you think the real King might be around?"

"I don't know what I think, but when you figure in
that Matt is getting very credible calls from a possible
Elvis . . . and that Quincey was seriously harassed, something sinister besides murder is going on, but it seems
so scattershot."

Electra's eyes were still only for her new beau. "Izzy
doesn't really expect to win," she explained. "He just

does this to have some fun. Who's gonna let a realistic-looking Elvis win? Everybody wants Elvis at his peak, even on stamps."

"I guess he was something in his prime, to go by the Fontana brothers." Temple eyed the awesome clot of mostly early Elvi at stage left, near the band.

"They are so cute! I don't know if the judges would let a whole litter win, but I'd vote for those boys any day."

Temple scanned the seats in front of them in the house's raked tier. Shiny black helmet heads pock-marked the burgundy velvet seats like beetle backs.

She spotted Mike and Jerry fussing with their jump-suits in the wings, and the King of Kings watching from the shadows of the flies. Probably sizing up the competition. From what the guys had said, dark horse Elvi were always showing up at competitions, ready to dazzle the jaded Elvis world.

"Even the contestants who've already rehearsed can't stay away," Temple mused. "Guess they want to the see the competition strut their stuff. Look! That's the King of Kings guy down behind the Fontanas. What's he do-ing talking to the band? He's had his time on stage."

"He sounded like a perfectionist," Electra said. "Elvis was. You think he could really be . . . our boy?"

"No! But he is uncannily good. Twenty years too young. Although, if Elvis had cleaned up his act, dumped the drugs, got some medical attention for his ills, lived clean, maybe he could look a couple decades younger. Sixty-four isn't so old nowadays."

"Glad to hear you say it, dearie!"

Before Temple could congratulate herself on her new maturity about advancing age, the onstage band mem-bers geared up with the squawk and stutter of tuning strings and instruments.

Crawford stepped up to the center-stage mike. "Num-ber ninety-nine."

Entry forms rustled in the echoing house, but Temple

and Electra were not among those granted official documents.

A guitar screamed, then twanged. The drums beat their way in and then everything was cooking in the manner of overdone rock 'n' roll, a vaguely dissonant, deliciously anarchist stew of sound.

A dark figure in the wings rushed forward, then slid into a long knee-slide onto center stage: Young Elvis in his fifties suit—loose pants, tight jacket, and energy incarnate.

He rose by pushing his knees together until he was balanced on the balls of his straddled feet, part acrobat, part spastic. The musicians ground down into their instruments as their music mimicked his gravity-defying gyrations. "Tutti Frutti," the newest Elvis was howling like a madman, or a mad dog, or maybe only like a dislocated Englishman in the noonday southern sun.

"Wow." Temple sat up, Electra taking notice with her.

Elvis heads throughout the auditorium and in the wings snapped to attention.

Tutti Frutti Elvis had the right stuff, all right, Mama. His suit shook, he shook, everything had to shake 'n' bake, and rock, rattle, and roll along with him.

When the number ended, a ragged chorus of claps hailed a rehearsal that had been performance-perfect, but already the lacquered Elvis heads were consulting.

Temple could almost hear their judgments from where she sat: too raw, not enough variety; a shot of adrenaline, soul but no subtlety.

She wasn't sure Elvis was about subtlety.

"That young man has drive," Electra said, fanning herself. "Whew."

"But he couldn't really be Elvis."

"Him? Heavens, no! Way too young. Way too... well, Elvis."

Still, Temple could tell from the checkerboard of chatter and silence all over the theater that this Elvis was a new force to reckon with. Acts were being modified even now to meet the challenge.

The next Elvis to rehearse was Jerry. She recognized him as he walked up to give the director his stat sheet and nervously eyed the musicians. She could guess that he wanted to give them special instructions so his set would match the dynamic difference offered by the unexpected Elvis ahead of him.

While Jerry negotiated, the audience fidgeted.

Temple searched the wings for Tutti Frutti Elvis. She hadn't seen his like around this place before. Even the King of Kings must be checking his crown.

Then the sound of an out-of-tune electric guitar shrilled up onto the stage and into the sparsely occupied seats like a dentist's drill hitting a nerve.

The place had terrific acoustics.

Temple realized that she had heard this instrument before, and it was a set of human vocal cords pressed into their worst extremity.

Quincey! Her latest aria in terror lofted to the distant ceiling like a solo from *The Phantom of the Opera*.

Temple bolted from her seat. "Now what?" Luckily, she had her running shoes on, and she put them to good use.

"Wait!" came Electra's diminishing plea behind her. "You don't know what you're rushing into."

But Temple did. Another nasty impractical joke had obviously been played on the piece's much-abused Priscilla. She remembered the puffy, red, razor-etched "E" on Quincey's neck that she had flashed like Elvis flaunting one of his cherished law-enforcement badges when pulling over a cute chick on wheels for a mock traffic citation in Memphis. That girl's notion of self-esteem would have done a sword-swallower proud. And here Temple had promised her mother to watch over the kid.

Other people were rushing toward the sounds, but none of them knew the route as well as Temple.

She got there first.

To find . . .

To find Quincey still in her civvies, with only the swollen brunette beehive on her head, her fingers pressing into her soft, teenage cheeks, screeching like a slasher-movie patron.

No violated jumpsuit lay on the dressing room floor.

No blood dripped down Quincey's neck or hands.

Nothing was wrong.

Quincey pointed, hiccoughing with hysteria when she tried to speak.

"Hmmmph, hummmph," she wheezed, a dagger-long fingernail pointing as if transfixing a killer in a stage play. "It's a ruuu-uuu-uuu-ined. They mur-mur-murdered it. My bee-bee-bee-eueueueu-ti-ful gown."

Temple stared to the aluminum rod suspended across the mostly empty expanse of the dressing room clothes niche.

The white wedding gown hung there, shredded like a toilet-paper mannequin. Cut into ribbons, the gown hung, a tortured ghost. Glittering piles of severed beads mounded like decorative Christmas sugar at its jagged hemline.

Another costume had been expertly assassinated.

Why?

"There, there. There, there."

The 3-D wool poodle on Electra's shoulder was soaking up Quincey's tears. It was hard to tell which sparkled more: the rhinestones glinting on the poodle's collar, or the salty teardrops falling to the fabric in cataracts of distress.

Temple would not have known Quincey had that much water in her.

In the hall, the crew and performers shuffled and commiserated. Even Awful Crawford paced and stewed, more worried about the show going on than Quin's welfare. Preopening theatrical disasters were always exaggerated. Lost costumes were mourned like long-lost relatives.

Temple dared not admit that she was relieved that the cause of Quincey's alarm was so minor. Not that you can tell a sixteen-year-old girl that her destroyed prom-queen wedding gown is a small price to pay for a whole skin and a whole mind.

Memphis Mafia were shouldering into the room to take charge, enough of them to staff a Strip hotel and the local office of the federal government too.

Temple exchanged eye contact with the string of Fontanas penned behind a wall of black wool sleeves in the hall with the other spectators, including the Crawf, thank God.

Best let the authorities, however many and however much in competition, fight for their turf without her.

She eased into the hall, missed by no one. Electra was upholding the distraught girl with a motherly fortitude far beyond Temple's experience.

"What happened?" Oversized Elvis asked in real concern.

"The Priscilla wedding gown was trashed. Pretty completely."

"What a shame. Miss Quincey really liked that costume."

"Guess this sets the rehearsal back a bit." Temple fought her way through a clucking group of sympathetic Elvi to the stairwell leading to the stage. "I don't know what to think," she told whatever Elvi followed her.

"We don't blame you." Karate, downcast, shook his full head of dark hair, reminding her of Elvis gearing up to render one of his more poignant ballads. "Maybe you should sit down."

"Where?"

"Good question."

"Don't worry about me," Temple told them. "You guys stay here and keep an eye on what the officials, and unofficials, are up to. I'm going upstairs to think in peace and quiet."

"That's it, Elvi! Back to the admiring throngs below."

Temple smiled faintly at Cape-and-Cane. She found his air of urbane authority soothing.

So she retraced her steps up to the stage. Theaters also had a soothing effect on her. The dark vortex of an empty stage, the mathematical repetition of rows of empty seats, the becomingness of it all, the silent potential, reminded her of well-designed churches.

She loved to hear her footsteps echo in an empty theater.

She walked onto the dark-painted boards, so different from the warm honey color of most theater floors. This was Vegas. You wanted drama, not hominess. You got Elvis on his knees, not ballet troupes in flying leaps.

She was surprised to see something walking toward her over the ebony boards, not making a sound.

She was completely astonished to recognize Midnight Louie.

Chapter 48

Tiger Man

(Sung in concert, usually in medley with
"Mystery Train")

I am always reluctant to be the bearer of bad tidings, and particularly on this occasion.

I can see that my Miss Temple is both weary and puzzled, and not looking around as alertly as she usually is.

Naturally, when I heard the screams from the belly of the beast I avoided doing the obvious. It is the nature of my breed to do whatever is opposite to what the common herd is doing.

So there I stay in my humble position of unseen observer behind the assemblage of drums onstage.

I do not like drums normally. They are needlessly noisy and are the original blunt instruments, bereft of finesse.

However, though the stage floor is black and excellent camouflage for me, I did feel the need of a better barrier, so established myself behind the percussion section.

The only reason I am here in the first place is to try to

figure out what this hillbilly cat has got that no one will let the poor dude rest in peace. This Elvis character is the only human dude I have ever seen—or not seen—to manage something approximating nine lives. Well, maybe five lives going on six. He is only human, after all.

Still, I had hoped to learn somewhat of the Elvis phenomenon from my onstage watching post. Would that I had thought to cram some cotton into my supersensitive ears. That Tutti Frutti guy could have raised the dead with his high Cs.

Even I did not realize at the time that what was going on was not raising the dead, but laying the living low.

So it is my sad duty to meet my Miss Temple and escort her to the unavoidable conclusion.

"Louie?" she says.

She always acts surprised to see me, when she should know by now that I am expert at being where I am least expected.

But I merely look wise and sad, a habit of my kind, and turn to lead her to the crux of the matter.

I am glad that we are alone. I would not want the world at large to know how much leading my Miss Temple requires in certain matters. Certainly, I do not need the credit. I am noted for being a primo predator by my own self. It is nothing new for me to be presenting a recently live prey to my charming roommate.

I only wish that it was something that might make her scream and faint, like a mouse or a lizard.

I am sorry that it is a guy this time, and one that she has met recently.

He is lying on the floor by the deserted instruments in a most undignified position. In fact, were he still upright, the position would not be unlike the late King's more convoluted contortions on the balls of his feet, as we just saw demonstrated so recently by the newest Elvis candidate.

To put it shortly, the dead guy is twisted like a salted pretzel, and his face is growing red and dark and will soon blacken. I think it is due to the long white silk scarf twined around his throat.

He surely will not sing "Love Me Tender" now.

Miss Temple has obediently followed me over to the latest corpse.

The late dude's dark cloak has parted to reveal glimpses of a most original and splendiferous jumpsuit beneath. Even I must swallow a lump of emotion. The suit is emblazoned with members of the feline kingdom, primarily tigers.

Now no one will see this marvelous jumpsuit in motion. The tiger's rippling muscles of gold-and-black gemstones are forever stilled.

Miss Temple seems unaware of the jumpsuit as she stares down at the darkening face of the dead Elvis.

"Lyle?" she says, as if expecting that he might still talk back, despite the choke hold the white silk scarf has on his epiglottis. "The King of Kings is dead? Then . . . who is Elvis now?"

She looks at me. "Louie?"

Do not look at me, babe. He is not me, and I am not he.

Although I might look very good in the right jumpsuit.

We must talk to the À La Cat people about this, once there is no longer a whole lotta shakin' going on in the Kingdome.

Chapter 49

Suspicious Minds

(One of Elvis's signature songs, beloved by
impersonators; recorded in 1969)

"Why did you come back up here? All the excitement
was downstairs in the dressing room area."

The detective was in his mid-thirties and had a neat
blond mustache. His name was just as bland: Stevens.

"That's why I came back up here," Temple said. "I
wanted to think. So many bizarre things have been going
on around here lately—"

"Two murders are more than bizarre. You knew the
victim?"

Temple nodded, settling into the velvet theater seat.
Forensic technicians were swarming over one corner of
the stage, but otherwise the place was empty.

From below came the moans of anxious Elvi, fearful
that the murder would postpone, or even end, the competition.

Temple found something uncanny in the fact of an Elvis "tribute performer" dying on stage.

"How did you find the body? With that dark cloak, it was fairly low-profile, and the lighting was low."

Temple was not about to introduce her guiding light, Midnight Louie, who had glided into the shadows and disappeared as soon as she gave the alarm.

She managed a sheepish expression. "I used to act in school plays. I can't cross a stage without 'treading the boards' a little. They all have a different sound."

"So you walked your way right into the dead man."

She nodded.

"Did you recognize him immediately?"

"Not quite. First I just saw he was an Elvis. Then I saw something familiar about him. Suddenly I knew it was Lyle."

"Lyle Purvis." The detective pursed his lips. "I'm still not clear what you're doing over here anyway. Are you an Elvis fan?"

"Nope."

"You and this"—he consulted his notebook—"Electra Lark were on the site of the last murder too."

"Just unlucky, I guess."

"And prone to wandering off the beaten path." He was checking his notes again, or, rather, another detective's notes. "The Medication Garden where the drowned man was found was supposed to be off limits."

"We trespassed a bit there."

"And you didn't trespass here?"

"Not that I know of."

The detective shook his head. "You make a lousy suspect for anything worse than jaywalking, but you were at the discovery scenes of two recent, connected murders."

"So the drowned man was murdered? And the murders are connected?"

"By you."

"Oh."

"Frankly, your being just another crazy fan, that would explain a lot."

Temple couldn't quite cop to that rap, but she could offer a hint for her presence. "Well . . . to be frank—"

"You haven't been before?"

"To be fully frank, I'm here because of what's been happening to Quincey."

"Quincey." He eyed her with the baffled suspicion you'd direct at a harmless-looking person who kept turning up corpses. "You mean that old TV show. About the coroner. He was on close terms with corpses too."

"No. I am not some fannish flake or a media nut! I'm just a PR person moonlighting as a nanny. Quincey is the girl who is playing Priscilla Presley for the competition. Her mother was concerned about the threats she was getting, so I said I'd keep an eye on her." Temple could hardly mention the Elvis apparition at the Crystal Phoenix as the instigating event; then he'd really typecast her as a flake.

" 'Keeping an eye on Quincey' took you to the Medication Garden and just now on stage?"

"I ran into those situations in the course of hanging out at the contest."

"The attacks on the girl have been noted. You have any insight on that?"

"Not a clue. Except that this last time, her screams at discovering the assault on the dress did a pretty good job of pulling everybody out of the rehearsal area. Except for Lyle."

"And his killer. Good thing you didn't wander back here too soon."

Temple had thought of that. Lyle must have been killed as soon as the stage was clear: lassoed from behind with the scarf, disabled and silenced by strangulation, and then held in thrall until dead.

It would take a strong, tall person to dominate a big guy like Lyle. A man, of course. Or a woman like Velvet Elvis.

"What do you think is going on with the Priscilla thing? A deranged fan?" the detective asked.

"They do dislike her, but—don't you think it could be some other agency?"

· "It's some other agency that's putting the jinx on our investigation, all right."

Temple detected something besides bitterness in his voice. "You don't mean . . . *Twilight Zone* stuff? Like Elvis sightings."

"Don't I wish." He slapped the notebook shut. "We could all live with a little tabloid ridicule. It's the hush-hush that kills an investigation, not the yellow journalism. Speaking of yellow journalism, you know a guy from the *Las Vegas Scoop*? Crawless Buchanan? He's been chomping at the bit to interview you. I had to have a uniform restrain him, he was that hot to see the body. Some of these guys are really ghouls."

"Crawless. Yeah, I know him. He was at the other death scene too."

"He was?" The notebook flopped open.

Temple nodded solemnly. "He was so eager to examine that corpse he jumped into the pool with it."

"That creep!" The notebook snapped shut again.

This was starting to look like an open-and-shut case, Temple thought.

The detective stood. "Maybe you'd give him an interview. Get him off our backs."

"You're asking a lot." She glanced beyond Detective Stevens's dark coat sleeve to the sight of Crawford practically slobbering with eagerness twenty feet away. "Are you sure you can't pin anything on him?"

Then it struck her. Crawford had not only been at each death scene, he was Quincey's stepfather. He could have popped in and out of her dressing room, spreading havoc, without much comment.

She feared her speculations were running rampant across her expression, but the detective had turned away already, eyeing the Crawf with distaste.

"Pin anything on him? A new haircut would help."
He stuffed the notebook into his side coat pocket and
returned onstage to the cluster of white-gloved people
hunkering over the dead man like abducting aliens.

Crawford sprang toward Temple like a spaniel. "T. B.!
Thank God they didn't arrest you!"

"What would they arrest me for?"

He brushed off the question with a gesture. "It's not
that Purvis guy dead, is it? Tell me. They won't let me
near enough to see the body. It can't be him. He's just
not around downstairs, right? Maybe he didn't come in
today at all. His rehearsal was yesterday. What would
he be doing here today?"

"That's a very good question."

"Then . . . he was here today?"

"Yup."

"But he left."

"Oh, yes."

Crawford slumped into the dark lines of his Memphis
Mafia suit. "Thank God."

"Well, he left, but, like Elvis, he's not completely
gone. Something remains."

Crawford's expression turned sick as he glanced at the
assembled officials. Talk about "ring around the collar:"
a noose of Memphis Mafia suits surrounded them as
thoroughly as they circled the corpse.

"Oh, God."

Temple was actually moved to put out a hand in case
Buchanan folded. "It is Lyle. Why are you so upset? I
didn't know you were friends."

"Friends?" Crawford's normal sneeringly sure look
had melted away like a wax dummy's expression in the
face of a forest fire. "God, no. He couldn't stand my
guts."

When she said nothing, he added, "What's new? Who
can?"

"Whew. You *are* in bad shape, C.B. Here. Have a
chair." She pushed down a fold-up theater seat with her

foot. Crawford Buchanan, in any shape, was not someone she cared to bend over near.

He collapsed into the seat, patting the backs of his
hands over his face as if wiping off invisible beads of
sweat. His normal pasty face had gone as green as spin-
ach fettuccine.

In a moment his face was in his hands, and he was
rocking to and fro.

Temple looked around for witnesses. This was em-
barrassing.

"He's gone," Crawford wailed softly. "My God, my
God. He's gone."

"He seemed like a nice man," Temple said inade-
quately. What else could you say about someone you'd
only met once. "And a damn good Elvis tribute performer."

"Oh, don't use that stupid euphemism!" the Crawf
snapped. "Impersonator is an honorable word. And in
his case, it wasn't even an act. Don't you understand?"

Tears stood in his large, cappuccino-dark eyes.

Temple sat on the seat next to him out of sheer, mute
amazement. "You really cared about this guy."

"Why shouldn't I? I found him. I found him out! And
then he exits on me." The Crawf slapped a palm to his
forehead, so hard that Temple winced.

"Crawford, you don't—You couldn't think . . . It's
crazy."

"He. Was. The. King. I know it."

"That's your story that was going to shake the world?"

"Was!" The word came out half a cry of rage, half a
bawl. "I was so close. This would have made me."

"What about him?"

"Huh?"

"What about . . . Lyle. Did he want to be the means
of your getting made?"

"No, but I could have talked him into it."

"You told him your suspicions?"

"Of course. It wouldn't work unless he cooperated and went public."

"And he didn't laugh you off."

"At first, sure. Why not. He was in denial."

"In denial."

"Wouldn't you be if you'd done such a good job of hiding your identity that no one would ever suspect?"

"But Elvis tribute perform—" Crawford was looking not only bereaved but homicidal, so Temple backtracked. "Impersonators are always suspected of being the real thing. It'd be the worst place to hide, because it's the most obvious."

"You said he was good!"

"Not that good."

"How good does a sixty-four-year-old man who's been out of the limelight except for the odd Elvis contest have to be?"

"What kind of evidence have you got?"

"Him! And now he's dead."

Temple scratched her neck. "Listen, Buchanan, you didn't arrange for those attacks on Quincey as part of some scheme to get Lyle worried and reveal himself, did you?"

"No." He sighed. "I thought of it after the first attack, that seeing 'Priscilla' in danger might shake him out of the denial of his new persona. But, face it, Elvis had gotten over her by now. And Quincey may have a punker's heart, but she's not a very convincing Priscilla."

"I thought she was doing a really good job!"

"What do you know about all this?"

"More than I used to know. So I'd be very hard put to buy that Lyle Purvis was Elvis Presley. Where's your evidence?"

"You agree that he's the best Elvis impersonator you've ever seen."

"I do, but I haven't seen very many, just the ones here. That new guy this afternoon was pretty good, but he's way too young to be really Elvis. So stomping the stomp and shouting the shout are not evidence enough."

"Purvis had lived in Las Vegas for several years, had enough money to afford a pretty big house with a copper roof and a six-car garage. You never saw him except at night. He didn't smoke, or drink, or gamble."

"There's a pit boss at the Crystal Phoenix who doesn't smoke, drink, or gamble, and you only see him at night. That doesn't make him Elvis, and that isn't as uncommon in this town as people think. Las Vegas is famous for churches as well as casinos."

"Okay, but when I first got suspicious about who Lyle really might be, I started checking his background."

"Any good, or bad, reporter starts there. So?"

"So . . . Lyle doesn't, didn't have any."

"You just said he'd lived here for several years."

"Right. Did Elvis gigs around the country, had an act at a small club for a while, but before that . . . zero. The man was fifty years old, at least. He had a driver's license, but I couldn't find a Social Security number on him, a credit record—he paid everything with, get this, cash."

"Maybe he had a history of credit-card abuse."

Crawford's mournful dark eyes sharpened through their residual mist of emotion. "Exactly, T.B.! Once a spendthrift, always a spendthrift. There are certain habits so ingrained you can't ditch them, even if you're living in another place under another name."

"Even if you're Elvis, you say."

"Especially if you're Elvis."

Chapter 50

Big Boss Man

(Elvis swung out in a 1967 Nashville session
that was bedeviled by the usual personal politics
among his associates)

"Mr. Midnight, I presume."

Matt froze.

He wasn't used to getting radio show calls at home.

He wasn't used to getting phone calls at home, period.

But he wouldn't put anything past his mysterious caller. His heart accelerated despite himself. Had "Elvis" become a stalker?

"Don't freak out," the man's voice urged, laughing. "It's just Bucek."

"Ah . . . Frank?" Matt's mind once again had to merge the image of his long-ago spiritual director in seminary with the FBI agent he had become on leaving the priesthood. That always took a leap of the imagination, if not of faith. "I don't get it. Why are you—"

"Calling? Combining business with personal business, I guess. Just to say I'm in town, and to ask a favor."

"Sure."

"I want tapes of your Elvis interviews."

"Tapes. How did you—?"

"Hear about them? You're famous. Or maybe I should say infamous."

"But why do you need them?"

"Don't know that I do, but I can't really say."

"It's about a case?"

"Can't really say. Can you get me the tapes?"

"Sure. I'll call the station right now; ask them to make a set."

"Don't say who for."

"Okay."

"I'd rather go through you. It's more discreet. You could say they're for your mother."

"I will, but I don't think I'd ever send her them. She'd think I had gone seriously weird."

"What's your take on this guy?"

"As a counselor?"

"Anyway you want to read it."

"I don't know. He could be completely immersed in the Elvis personality. He could be self-promoting in some way, not yet clear. If he comes forward and turns out to be a shill for the Kingdome, we'll know."

"But he's credible?"

"He knows his Elvis trivia, but so do thousands of Elvis fans. I pick up a genuine confusion. He may have absorbed some of Elvis's characteristics from sheer obsession. Has he really 'become' Elvis? It's easier to believe that than that the real Elvis could have lived and hidden out so successfully all these years."

"So he's credible."

"Yeah. As credible as a voice over the airwaves can ever be."

"Interesting."

"How will you get the tapes?"

"Someone will pick them up after the show tonight. You have your post-game groupies. One will ask you to sign a tote bag; you can slip the tapes in there."

"Big Brother's been watching me? This that urgent, and that covert?"

"Always, Matt. Always. Elvis mania may be good for a laugh, but we've got some grim business going on here."

"FBI business."

"You said that. Talk to you later, if I get time before I leave town."

A brisk good-bye ended the exchange.

Puzzled, Matt dialed the station and got Dwight, technician and jack of all trades. His request for tapes was met with a belly laugh.

"You and two hundred others. Leticia's working up a sales program, but I'll run you some free. You want more than one set?"

"Yeah. Give me . . . three?"

"Fine. Freebies for you, but Leticia's thinking twenty-nine ninety-five for the public."

"Can you do that, without the caller's permission? Without mine, for that matter?"

"What's to object about? Anyone could have taped you guys from the air. And by calling in, these folks put themselves into a public arena."

"I'd have a lawyer check it anyway."

"Leticia will. She doesn't let much get past her. Including gold mines."

"What a wimp," the caller said. "Holing up in his bedroom like a spoiled kid just because the world wants too much. If he had any guts he'd come out of hiding."

"Why are you so angry?"

"Because if he really was the King, he wouldn't have left us like he did, and if he did survive and go into hiding, then he cheated us another way."

"It's not like you owned him."

"Yeah, we did. We made him."

"A bunch of things made him . . . the music, the times,

his own instincts, all the people who cried 'lewd' and made him notorious, all the people his death shocked into an orgy of mourning. But I don't think he owed you anything. He had a right to just stop."

Another voice had taken the airwaves. "That man is wrong. We didn't just make Elvis, we made him sick. We made him stand in for our sense of rebellion and freedom and wanting to live so high we'd be legends. He was our . . . what do you call it?"

"Scapegoat?" Matt suggested.

"Stand-in," another male voice said. "She had it right. He was our stand-in. But he's gone, and we don't need to listen to any version of him asking for answers on the radio. We don't need stand-ins anymore. You fans who won't get over it, get a life!"

The debate was high-octane tonight.

"Couldn't you tell the poor man is just looking for peace, whoever he is?" The woman's voice was teary. "We can give it to him if we just stop expecting him to be anything any more, even alive. That was so sad, Mr. Midnight. What Elvis said last night. I hope he's all right now."

"He's all right, mama. He's probably calling in from some money-laundering island in the Caribbean, laughing at how gullible we all are. He's probably got a secret deal with the estate to stay dead, so they can milk his image better. Who wants to see Elvis a senior citizen? I hope you radio people expose the bastard who's been pulling the wool over everybody's eyes. If he comes on again, I dare you to let me ask him a few questions."

"You'd scare him away! You probably already have. Guys like you were just jealous of Elvis."

Matt was playing referee tonight. He hardly had to put a word in as Leticia conducted the bristling switch-board like a bandleader.

He sat there, listening, exhausted by the strong feelings pro and con the topic of Elvis raised, growing more concerned that this outbreak of emotion would drive away the one man who really needed to get on the line: the supposed Elvis himself.

These calls had always come independently of whoever else was calling in and what they were saying. Elvis seemed cocooned in his own world, musing in a sometimes laid-back, sometimes manic monologue. Matt almost got the impression that he didn't listen to the radio show at all, that he just dialed during the proper hour and connected.

Two isolated men, talking, with the world listening in.

And the FBI.

Matt shifted in his seat, interrupting a denouncement of rock 'n' roll music. "The music can't talk back. And neither can Elvis."

"Yes, he can!" the next caller argued. "He's been talking here."

"We don't know who that is. Was," Matt said, suddenly sure. "I don't think whoever he was will be calling in again."

"Why, is his contract up?" a snide-sounding man demanded.

"I think he's shared as much of himself as he's going to. Didn't you notice his call last night had a . . . final . . . air to it?"

"Aw, he won't ever go away, not really." The woman sounded more anxious than certain. "You can't mean that was it. That he'll just stop."

"He did before."

But the calls didn't stop. Someone even asked everyone not to call in, "so that the King could get through."

Matt smiled to see Leticia's face solidifying into horror on the other side of the glass barrier. Nobody wanted Elvis to stop calling.

Except Matt.

"It's over," he said, voicing his thoughts.

The big hand on the schoolhouse clock sliced the line that stood for twelve fifty-nine. The roulette wheel of time was running out tonight, and even Leticia's willingness to let the show run overtime meant nothing if the main attraction failed to show.

"He's skipped a night before," a woman's thin voice pointed out just as the minute hand clicked into place on high noon, or high midnight.

Matt heard his rush of closing words. Thanksforcalling, we'llhavetowaitandsee. Waitandsee.

Reluctantly, Leticia's falling hand cued Dwight to run the scheduled ad.

Matt pulled off the headphones before he could hear some inane jingle for a furniture rental place or a car dealership or a Laundromat. Advertisers at the midnight hour expected a young and restless audience in need of credit and consumer goods. What a role model Elvis was for them.

"Sorry," Leticia told him on the way out.

He didn't want to admit that he wasn't sorry.

Maybe his long session last night had exorcised Elvis. He hoped so.

The group outside was bigger than ever, up to nine people. All women.

"He didn't call us," one wailed as soon as she saw him.

"Don't take it personally. If he's standing anybody up, it's me."

"Nobody would stand you up, Mr. Midnight."

Matt stared, nonplussed, into devoted eyes that would look right on a basset hound.

"How did you all get here so fast?" he wondered aloud.

"We came early and listened on the car radio," a pair of plump night-shift nurses said, almost as one, proud of their initiative.

"Maybe he'll call tomorrow." Another woman handed him the usual photograph to sign.

Leticia had given him a pen that wrote in silver, so it would show up on the photo's darker surfaces. She had a whole box of the things, brand-new, and had beamed like Santa Claus bestowing an electric train instead of a producer anticipating many nights of numbing ritual outside the radio station door that would soon become tiring and then an imposition.

Once the novelty wore off, so would the ease.

"You might want to sign this on something solid."

Matt had been so busy autographing his photos that he hadn't noticed the quiet woman come up. She looked more businesslike than the average fan, and her tote bag still had shipping folds in it. Elvis's face on the black background was drawn and quartered right through the Pepsi-Cola smile.

Matt took the thick fabric pen she offered—do their research, the FBI—to the newspaper vending machine, slipping the one set of tapes from his jacket pocket and into the bag.

He wrote "Sincerely, Mr. Midnight" in big loose letters across the rough surface.

Her mumbled "thank you" vanished into the pressing crowd, who weren't many, but who all wanted to be in the first row of his admirers.

"Maybe if Elvis doesn't call any more, you won't have to sit out here at midnight listening to your car radios," he joked, signing as fast as he could.

"Oh, no. We'll still be here for you," they promised in a ragged chorus.

They were fans. They would always be there. For somebody.

Chapter 51

It Wouldn't Be the Same Without You

(A song Elvis recorded during an early Sun
session, without much success)

Temple's phone rang eight times before she answered it,
and it was after noon.

Matt was too weary to have much imagination after a
sleepless night haunted by Elvis clones, but he couldn't
help wondering if Max Kinsella was back in town, keeping Temple up late.

She sounded rushed when she finally picked up the
phone.

"Hell-oo."

"Matt. I wondered if you have a moment for career
consultation."

"Now?"

He felt like the ceiling had rained a bucket of ice-
water. "No, of course not. Not now. Whenever—"

"Matt, don't be so darn eager to oblige. You sound a

little . . . worried. I'm sorry. It's been wild. Why don't we go to lunch, or something."

"What would the 'or something' be?"

"Something fun. I know! We could drive out to Three O'Clock Louie's at, ta-dum, Temple Bar. I've been wanting to patronize the old guys. This is as good an occasion as any."

"But you'll have to drive, as usual, and it's me who wanted to get together. I've really got to find some free time to buy a car."

"Agreed. I could go with you . . . except I've forgotten all the tips on car-buying, it's been so long since I got the Storm."

"Maybe I'll just get a Saturn."

"Sounds fine, but kind of . . . predictable."

"Sorry. Why don't I be unpredictable now? Any reason we can't take the Vampire out to the lake?"

"It's just as far away as my leggings and fifties ankle boots. I can use Electra's 'Speed Queen' helmet. I've been dying to."

"Okay! Twenty minutes?"

"Make it fifteen. I'm hungry, and there's nothing like a nice, cold, bouncy ride to enhance an appetite."

Yeah, Matt thought, hanging up.

Suddenly, it was an expedition.

He felt a little like Elvis going for a motorcycle thrill-ride, putting on his suede half-boots, his faux sheepskin jacket, and getting out his leather gloves. Picking up Temple, who was perky enough to pass as one of Elvis's fifties starlets and even resembled a smaller, less sexy Ann-Margret, who had shared Elvis's love for motor-cycles and had apparently shared a deep love with Elvis before he had begun the final, slow spiral downward. Ann-Margret never opened a show from then on with-out a huge floral tribute in the shape of a guitar from Elvis . . . except for the show she opened the night of

August 15, 1977. No floral guitar, no Elvis after August 16, in Memphis, or anywhere else . . . except here and there and everywhere, like that "demmed elusive Pimpernel" of *Scarlet Pimpernel* fame. The actress-singer-dancer's hair had been a heavier, sultrier red than Temple's, which was even now being dampened by the sleek silver bubble of Electra's helmet.

"Speed Queen" read the cursive letters above the dark visor. The play on words was a late-middle-aged woman's jest and defiance to the world, but Elvis had been a Speed King in every worst connotation of the phrase. And that had not been a joke but a tragedy.

Why couldn't he get a long-dead man out of his mind? Matt wondered. Maybe it wasn't a dead man he was trying to exorcize.

"Did you bring gloves?" he asked Temple. "It gets icy at seventy miles an hour without heating."

She pulled something that resembled wooly udders from her dressy white leather jacket pockets. "Courtesy of a Minnesota girlhood. Will they do?"

"Are you sure you can spare the time?"

"Stop being such a Guilty Gus!" Temple stomped a toy boot heel on the shed's concrete floor. "I've been dying to travel on this thing. Let's do it."

"You had a ride once before."

"But we didn't go anywhere. For a purpose. Not a whole round trip."

She was like a kid; her promised outing had to be the whole enchilada. Matt smiled, unlocked the shed, and rolled the massive machine into the clear winter sunlight. The flat, bright light ignited the Hesketh Vampire's fluid silver lines, reminding him of the slanted, silver letters he scrawled on photographs nowadays.

"Awesome." Temple waited for him to mount the cycle, then struggled to hop on behind him. The seat had been "cut down" for Electra, but Temple was a lot shorter than their landlady.

He felt her hands curl into the side seams of his jacket,

donned his own, unlabeled helmet, revved up the lion's-roar motor, and kicked off. They slid into smooth, chill motion.

Electra, being a solitary rider, had never invested in helmets with walkie-talkies built in. Silence was enforced. The bumpy side streets evened into the entry ramp to Highway 95; soon they were sweeping past the clogged lanes of the city onto the asphalt that slashed through the Nevada desert.

He couldn't know if Temple was nervous, or cold, or having a ball.

He knew the machine enough to enjoy the ride now, though. And he was actually reluctant when they pulled onto the smaller access road to rattle up the deliberately rutted dirt road to Three O'Clock Louie's.

Various vehicles were scattered like dice around the rough-hewn restaurant building: ersatz Wild West on the shores of a lake the brilliant color of a London blue topaz. He'd looked at those stones when buying a Christmas present for Temple, deciding on the black opal cat necklace instead. Opals and black cats had lived up to their unlucky reputation that time, Matt thought grimly; his gift came too late, after Temple's Christmas reconciliation with Max Kinsella.

He felt the idling bike lighten as she jumped off, then he shut off the motor, kicked down the stand, and let it tilt into silence and stillness.

"Gosh. I'm still vibrating!" Temple shook her gloved hands. "I've never had my teeth chatter from motion before, not cold."

"You didn't like it."

"I loved it. Like being in a blender. Makes me want to eat a hamburger with onions on it and a brown beer."

"A brown beer?"

"Yeah, you know. That manly stuff that comes in long-necked bottles. Let's hustle inside."

Matt shrugged and followed her in.

Two steps outside the door they picked up a big black cat with a gray muzzle.

"Hi, Three O'Clock!" Temple turned to Matt. "The critter the place is named after. Isn't that a scream? A name like Louie's and he looks like his grandfather!"

Three O'Clock humped his back, whether in anger or as the prelude to a leg-rubbing it was hard to tell.

"I don't know if he's allowed in," Temple said, hesitating in the open wooden screen door.

"Of course he's allowed in." An elderly man for whom the phrase "old coot" had been invented, down to the handlebar mustache, leaned out to hold the door open for man, woman, and cat. "Come on, Miss Temple Barr. We owe you lunch on the house."

"I can't think what for. We wanted to add to the restaurant's customer base."

"And this fellow is—?"

"Matt Devine, one of Electra's most valued tenants."

"After yourself," the guy said with a bow.

"This is Wild Blue Pike, one of the restaurant owners."

Matt, gloveless again, shook a gnarled hand that gave no quarter.

"Cold hands, warm heart," Wild Blue commented, shaking his fingers gingerly.

"Sorry. We motorcyled out. I guess my fingers are too cold to know their own strength."

"No problem. I like a hearty shake, and a hearty lunch. You ready for a Louieburger, Miss Temple?"

"A Louieburger! What's that?"

"Sourdough bun, almost a pound of prime lean beef with jalapeño cheese, Worcestershire sauce, and cayenne-peppered onion rings."

"Wow. Lead us to it."

The tables were wood with inset tiles, the chairs heavy to match, and sported woven-rush seats and backs.

Wild Blue led them to a corner near a roaring mesquite-wood fireplace.

"This is neat," Temple said as she sat in the chair Wild Blue held out for her, and then pushed way under the table, as if for a child. "I can't believe I saw this place in the making, a sawdust palace."

"All good things gotta start with a pile of elbow grease," Wild Blue said, slapping plastic encased menus before them.

"Forget the menu. It's a Louieburger for me."

"Me, too," Matt said.

"All the trimmings?"

"The full Louie," Temple responded. "And the brownest beer you have."

Wild Blue frowned. "You like dark ale?"

"No, but I'm suited up and ready to ride."

After Wild Blue left, Matt regarded her. "You're in a feisty mood."

"I'm probably in the same state you are: my brain is weary and my spirit is wilted. Desperate times take desperate measures. Bad-for-you food is the answer!"

"I never thought of advising that over the radio. These guys should buy a spot on the Midnight Hour."

"Tell 'em."

"That's not my job."

"It's your show."

"No, it isn't. It's his."

"His? Ohhh, your guest celebrity."

"I think he's made his last appearance."

"Really? Why?"

"We had a real go-round the night before last. I pushed him on all the issues. I feel bad about that."

"You were too hard on him?"

Matt shrugged out of his jacket. The fire was hot. "No. I feel sad about it, that's all. We . . . he reached a kind of closure, I think he's . . . gone for good this time."

"Really?"

"You keep saying 'really,' in that noncommittal tone. Like everything you say has a double meaning."

"It could," she said seriously, drawing back while

Wild Blue plopped a condensation-dewed bottle of dark beer before each of them.

"Should have asked for a glass."

"Easy riders don't ask for glasses."

"Sorry." She sipped, then sighed. "I've been feeling kinda blue too. One of the neatest Elvis impersonators—oops, we say 'tribute performers' nowadays—died yesterday. He was really, really good. Might even have passed as the real thing, if you were inclined to think that way. Had a great chance of winning the competition. I did it again: found the body, thanks to Midnight Louie."

Matt only noticed then that Three O'Clock had settled on the brick skirt of the fireplace and was watching them through slitted eyes.

Despite the half-full dining room, he felt that here even the cats had ears, and lowered his voice. "That's the second guy to die at the Kingdome."

"Don't I know it. The first wasn't a real tribute performer, just some petty crook in a cheapo costume. Not a truly cheap costume, but not up to what Elvis had ever worn. That guy was drowned, as far as the police are saying. Lyle was killed onstage, strangled with a white silk scarf."

"Aren't women usually killed by strangling?"

"True. Maybe because they're easier to overwhelm from behind. That's what bothers me about this murder. Lyle wasn't quite as big as Oversized Elvis, but he was no bantamweight. It would take a lot of force to bring him down with one silk scarf."

"Bizarre. And this happened—?"

"Yesterday."

"The night Elvis didn't call. The night after our big on-air showdown. I hope I didn't drive the guy away to do something foolish. I assume you haven't been following my nightly channeling sessions."

"Not recently."

"I could leave a set of tapes at your door. You think—?"

"I think what you think: something awfully close to Elvis has been going on here. After all those jokes about Elvis playing one of his own impersonators. I must say that Lyle was an impressive Elvis impersonator. He looked closer to fifty than to sixty-four, but plastic surgery nowadays can make even a Savannah Ashleigh look fifteen to twenty years younger. Elvis had already had a facelift when he died, although his associates said he really hadn't needed it. Poor guy, age and prescription abuse were catching up with him and he was trying to stem the tide—he really was a great-looking man, almost to the end. It must have hurt to see that sliding away."

Matt nodded. "You could come to take it for granted."

"Oh?"

He found Temple regarding him with interest and realized that he had never before spoken as if his own good looks were a given. Maybe the midnight groupies had converted him. Maybe he was making as much progress in self-acceptance as the call-in Elvis had been.

"What can you do about this man's death?" Matt asked. "You're not really involved. You should stay away from that Kingdome place. And what was Louie doing there?"

"I don't know. He tends to tail me, excuse the expression."

Matt glanced at Three O'Clock, his forefeet tucked under him like a Chinese mandarin's hands slid into his sleeves. The posture made the venerable cat into a feline sage.

"These cats have a way of looking like they know as much—or more than we do. I don't know if I could live with that. I like dogs; at least they look a lot more anxious and dependent."

"Can't take an equal animal, huh? I love the way Louie seems to get one step ahead of me sometimes. I know I'm reading things into simple feline behavior, but it's fun to pretend."

"Finding corpses should not be fun, Temple," Matt lectured. "What about what got you to the Kingdome? Anything new on the Elvis apparition at the Crystal Phoenix?"

"Not a word." She took a disgruntled swig of beer. "But I feel responsible for Quincey, especially now that her Priscilla wedding gown has been trashed."

"You should get out of the picture. You and Louie should get back to the Phoenix and to harassing goldfish and the ghost of Jersey Joe Jackson. I'd feel a lot better if you did."

"So you think your gorgeous, intelligent, pleading brown eyes are gonna cut it with a cat person?"

Matt shook his head. "Nope. I know your weakness for the aloof and mysterious feline and that, against that competition, I ain't nothing but a hound dog, cryin' all the time. It's just that advice is my business nowadays. I may have exorcized my Elvis forever. Time you exorcized yours."

"Don't be cruel," she answered with a mock pout.

"We could go on forever in Elvis-ese."

"There is an Elvis for every occasion."

"Even murder, apparently. I mean it, Temple. I've only had to deal with Elvis long-distance. You've gotten much too up close and personal. Time to pull back."

She nodded, serious. "You're right. I don't even have a link to the crimes against persons unit this time. Molina could be on the moon for all I'm hearing from or about her."

"You miss her?"

"Lord, no! It's nice to be an innocent, anonymous witness for a change, with the detective on the case just shaking his head at my unsuitability as witness or suspect. I could get used to playing Susie Citizen again."

"Take my advice, and try it."

"Got a Lot O' Livin' to Do," Temple agreed.

"I hope so. It Wouldn't Be the Same Without You."

They both had been studying way too many Elvis books.

Chapter 52

That's Not All Right (Mama)

(Elvis's breakthrough song, recorded during his
first session at Memphis's Sun Records, July 5,
1954)

Temple returned to the Kingdome aflame with righteous
resignation.

Matt had convinced her: she was out of the Elvis business.

Apparently no one else was, because acts were lounging about the vast stage on which Lyle Purvis had died
so recently, rehearsing for the competition tomorrow
night.

In fact, Purvis's death had thrown expectations into
turmoil. It seemed that a whole lotta shaking was going
on now that the King of Kings was out of the picture.
A lot of the other candidates had a decent chance.

Could the Elvis murders be the ultimate answer to
performance anxiety?

Temple also noticed that the Memphis Mafia numbers
seemed to have tripled. Men in black suits were every-

where, watching rehearsals like competing Hollywood agents, and flocking in the hotel's vast lobby.

Temple even expected to see them lurking like Cold War spies behind slot machines, jotting down notes and talking into shoe-cell-phones.

The Kingdome's general air of high intrigue may have been why she wasn't surprised to hear piercing screams issuing from the backstage dressing rooms again.

She joined the stampede to get there, a force divided almost equally between the sublime (Elvis tribute performers mostly in jumpsuits) and the ridiculous (the dudes in black mohair suits).

For once a conservative mode of dress looked far more self-dramatizing than wall-to-wall jeweled jumpsuits.

Alas, the shrieker was the usual suspect.

Quincey, this time wearing civvies (hip-slung black vinyl pants and a skimpy shrink-top in neon leopard-print), sobbed and thrashed like a punk banshee.

This time, the person harassing the much-tried Priscilla performer was . . . her mother.

"I don't care how much faster the world will end if you leave the show. You're leaving it." Merle Conrad finished her declaration by folding her arms over her low-profile chest. Her daughter's high-profile edition, emphasized by skin-tight Spandex, heaved with disappointment.

"This'll ruin my life!"

"Maybe," Merle said, faintly but firmly unshakable. "At least you'll be alive to have a ruined life. This is it. You're out of the pageant. Or contest. Or race. Or whatever it is." Her darting dishwater-hazel eyes fastened on Temple. "It's time, isn't it, to take Quincey out of this terrible place where people are dying?"

"The Elvises are dying," Quincey wailed. "There's only one Priscilla, and all I've gotten is spooked a little."

"A little spooking is too much." Merle grabbed her daughter's skinny arm. "I'll get the hotel to stand behind me, if I have to. Enough is enough. Two men are dead. You have no business being here."

"She's right," Temple told the girl, whose mascara-blurred eyes were desperately panning the hallway outside for supporters. "If Elvi are dying, it's not safe for the one Priscilla among them."

"But they're counting on me!"

Somehow, Merle had dragged her daughter to the doorway. "They can count on some other girl."

"The Crawf is counting on me!" Quincey clawed at the doorjamb, but her long fingernails snapped under the pressure. "My manicure—!"

A man in black stepped forward. "Need some help, ma'am? We'd like your daughter out of the line of fire, too."

"Fire?" Merle stiffened. "There's been shooting too?"

"Just an expression, ma'am. Come on, miss. Your mother's right. This is no place for a teenager."

"Elvis was my age when he started his career!" Quincey was kicking as well as screaming now, and the man in black's mohair shins were bearing the brunt of it. "You don't know what you're stopping here! I'll sue! I'll get my probation officer to go to the highest court in the land. I'll—"

The words, "probation officer" had the opposite than desired effect. Men in black tightened their lips, and their grips. They hustled Miss Quincey down the hall to instant obscurity, and therefore safety, her mother taking up the rear.

"Probation officer," Temple mumbled, awestruck. All she had was one unimpressed homicide lieutenant, and it had taken her until age thirty to attract official attention.

That Quincey was a pistol.

But she was gone, and the dressing room emptied of spectators with the expulsion of Quincey and her mother, no doubt bound somewhere well east of Eden.

Temple, left alone, stared a little sadly at the impressive rows of discount store hair, eyes, teeth, and nail products laid out like leaderless soldiers whose general had been captured. Saddest of all was the gaudy tube of Daddy Longlegs's Centipede Sweetie mascara, and the spidery array of false eyelashes entombed in their clear plastic packaging coffins like Elvis jumpsuits in the Medication Garden.

Enter the cause of it all, the snake, hissing, stage left.

"Psst! T. B."

How could she have forgotten? The last Elvis Exploiter, foiled at first and always. Her eyes met his in the mirror.

They were alone.

Crawford—somehow the title of Elvis's *King Creole* opening number, "Crawfish," came inexorably to mind—crept into the deserted dressing room.

"Glad to see you haven't gone ballistic, T. B."

"I will if you continue to refer to me as an infectious disease."

He ankled over to stand beside her in the mirror. "Why, Temple honey, I didn't know you cared."

She elbowed him in the ribs.

"I'm done," he said, doubling over.

"Come on. I didn't hit you that hard."

"It's not that." He looked up from almost black eyes, large and accusing. "It's my emcee gig here tomorrow. I need my Priscilla."

"Maybe you can talk Merle into doing it."

"Merle? She's all wrong for the role."

"Oh, come on! Anyone can impersonate a Priscilla Barbie Bride. You could do it now that you've shaved off your stupid mustache."

"I'm hosting the competition, much as I care anymore." Without taking his arm from his midsection, he collapsed onto a dressing table chair. "You're right. None of it matters. The King is dead. My career is dead. Quincey will have to go to reform school; I won't have the dough to bail her out."

"Craw-ford! Since when were you going to lift a finger for Quincey anyway? You're always getting her into some gig no teenage girl should do. I'm glad her mother has finally shown some backbone and jerked Quin from the competition. How bad does it have to get before you start thinking of someone besides yourself?"

"About as bad as this." He looked up, his face stricken. Crawford Buchanan stricken looked like a Chihuahua with Montezuma's revenge. Small and obnoxious and big-eyed pathetic. "I really idolized the King. Wouldn't admit it to just anyone, but I did. I was thrilled to emcee this competition. I don't mind the impersonators. Maybe all together they only capture a tenth of what he had, but it's a tenth more than we'd know about today without them. Even lightning needs lightning rods, huh?"

"Maybe lightning bugs," she suggested pointedly.

"I'm not sure I can go on," he sniveled.

Yes, Crawford Buchanan sniveled as well as sneered and leered. He belonged in a bad melodrama, as if there were any good ones.

"You'll live," she said shortly, moving toward the dressing room door.

"No, I don't mean I can't go 'on' on. I mean I don't know if I can go on stage tomorrow night. For the competition. It's not only too soon after Elvis's death"— Temple rolled her eyes and found herself exchanging exasperated glances with a big fat spider on the ceiling; how appropriate; even the insect world had no use for C. B—"but it's dangerous out there. Someone could kill me by mistake."

"Don't worry about it. I can't ever see it happening that someone would kill you by mistake."

"What if the Elvis-killer is another impersonator, mad to win? Or a deranged fan afraid a rediscovered King wouldn't live up to his old image? It could be anybody."

"That's absolutely right." Temple folded her arms over her chest, which even in his extremity of emotion was attracting too much notice from Crawford Buchanan. "Okay. I can provide you with bodyguards, but that's all."

"I need a Priscilla to share the stage. It's a great part, T. B. —Temple."

"Oh, sure. Stand around in the background like an albino Christmas tree and then sling some humongous, heavy belt to the guy who wins, all the time wearing shredding organza and unraveling seed pearls. And maybe while I'm at it, a deranged fan/killer/maniac can rush out and strangle me with a guitar string. Bodyguards."

"Who can you get for that?"

"Experts. That's all you need to know."

"There are enough guys running around here in those funeral-director suits already. They haven't been able to stop a thing."

"Those aren't my bodyguards."

"Who are they then?"

"I can't tell you."

"Then how do I know if they exist and are doing their jobs?"

"You'll just have to take my word for it."

He frowned and squinted, trying to squeeze out a fresh glaze of liquid to his eyes. Apparently he was done crying for the King. He only managed to look constipated, which was also appropriate.

Temple turned to leave.

"Please! I need a Priscilla tomorrow night."

"Rent a department store mannequin, then, and drape what's left of the wedding gown on it; I'm sure no one in the audience will notice. Now." She pointed a forefinger. "Out."

He slunk away like a whipped weimaraner.

Temple sat on the vacated chair, feeling virtuous about heeding Matt's advice to take the sane and stable road of noninvolvement.

He had been right. How satisfying it was to turn C. B.

down cold, although it might have been fun to masquerade as Priscilla. If the dress hadn't been trashed, she might have tried it, but no dress, no Priscilla, and one less Presley persona to worry about.

She glanced again at the many accoutrements necessary for recreating a late sixties woman, including almost-white lipstick. Ick! How had they brainwashed women into these universal "looks" back then? Temple liked to skim a fashion magazine occasionally, and occasionally went after a way-out nail color or a certain article of clothing, but she was mostly immune to the color palette of the season or the next weird Hollywood hair thing.

The soft scrape of a shoe on cement made her look up.

A man in black's silhouette filled the doorway. As she watched, puzzled, he stepped into the room, drawing the door closed behind him.

Maybe the impenetrable sunglass lenses spooked her. They were as shiny and opaque as the bug-eyes on those shrimpy albino aliens who were the official poster beings of the UFO set.

Whatever, the visitor was a tall, impassive guy, born to be typecast as either a mob enforcer or an IRS agent. Temple theorized that they moonlighted as each other a lot more often than people realized.

Whatever his affiliation, government, crime, or out of this world, his presence radiated authority and force, and had Temple absolutely cornered.

She stood and backed up, nervously, feeling her throat tingle and her stomach tighten.

"Why do I get the impression," she asked, "that you're not hotel security?"

He pulled off the sunglasses by one ear bow. "Good instincts?" He smiled slightly, but she had already recognized him.

"You're . . . Bucek. Matt's Father Frank." She didn't relax one bit. "You're FBI."

"Thanks for saving me digging out my ID. Now you can do me another favor."

"Favor?"

He nodded, pulled out the chair she had abandoned, turning it toward her.

"I'll stand." Temple fanned her fingertips on the countertop for balance. Her knees were still knocking slightly from the adrenaline rush of finding herself alone with a strange—and strange looking—man.

Bucek shrugged and sat himself, holding his shades loosely in the hand he balanced on one knee.

"I heard you tell Buchanan that you wouldn't step in as Priscilla Presley in tomorrow's Elvis competition."

"That's right. Two men are dead, and the girl who played Priscilla has endured harassment and even personal attack. I have no business taking such risks because 'the show must go on.' I'm just an innocent bystander."

"Excellent decision. I'm sure Matt Devine would be very happy to hear that."

"How nice for him, but I came to this conclusion all by myself. So you don't have to worry about my 'meddling' in this case. I'm outa here."

He smiled again, to himself.

"I am outa here, aren't I? You aren't going to arrest me, or anything sinister? I didn't do it, honest."

"No, I'm not going to detain you at all, but there is that favor . . ."

"I'm leaving, this very instant. I'll be out of your hair forever." Temple pushed herself away from the support of the countertop in demonstration of her imminent departure.

Bucek shook his head. "I'm afraid we're both about to disappoint Matt. I want you to stay."

"Here? Now?"

"I want you to stay for whatever time it takes to enact Priscilla Presley tomorrow."

"I'm sorry, you'll have to get yourself another bride

of Elvis. I'm absolutely determined to keep out of it."

"Again, an admirable decision, and pretty atypical, from what I've heard from Lieutenant Molina, but you're here. You know the setting, the actors, the costume. We don't have enough time to prep a female agent and get her into place this fast. I don't like it, either, but you'll have the agency's full protection."

"Hah! That didn't help Lyle Purvis much."

Bucek sat forward, alert. "You knew he was a target?"

"It was pretty obvious after I found him dead."

"You knew we were here?"

"The Memphis Mafia security crew make a great cover for G-men, but there were a few dozen too many of you running around."

Bucek's smooth features suddenly roughened with a new insight. "And you had the fabulous, flying Fontana brothers to point out dramatis personae to you."

"They did mention the Mob, and the feds. And they knew that the first victim, Clint Westwood, was a minor crime figure. Where do the bozos get these names?"

Bucek chuckled. "In their own self-dramatizing imaginations. Even the bad guys want to see themselves as good guys."

"Maybe especially."

He nodded slowly and puckered his lips. "Career criminals are just that: upwardly mobile working stiffs trying to climb the ladder. Whoever hit Lyle will expect a promotion."

"And it's the same person who harassed Quincey. Why?"

Bucek tilted back on the wooden chair's fragile legs, making Temple even more nervous. She hadn't relaxed for a second since he'd entered the room, though she was finding the information he was sharing fascinating. Why, he was almost talking to her like a colleague . . . or a patsy.

"You ever read any G. K. Chesteron?" he asked.

Temple shook her head. "Not an Elvis impersonator, I take it."

"British writer. Created the Father Brown mysteries in the nineteen-teens and -twenties. Ever read those?"

"Not that I can remember."

"Guess they're considered old-fashioned these days. Chesterton was a writer with a theological bent. He used Father Brown as a vehicle for his ideas about God and good and evil. Father Brown was this utterly over-lookable little man who just happened to understand the human soul in all its extremes."

Temple nodded politely, as she did at all impromptu lectures, but she was wondering when Frank Bucek would get to the point. She could see him holding forth before a class of seminarians. No wonder so many had left the priesthood.

"Anyway," Bucek said, sensing her restlessness, "Father Brown once asked Flambeau the thief 'Where do you hide a leaf?' 'In a forest,' Flambeau answered. The case involved an officer who died on a battlefield."

"And you think the killer here is hidden among the Elvis impersonators. Makes sense."

Bucek's smile grew patronizing without his realizing it.

Temple felt anger flare, as it did whenever she detected men patronizing her, which they did more than they realized, in no small part because of her petite appearance.

Yet her anger suddenly illuminated the other side of the same equation.

"And someone else was masquerading as an Elvis impersonator! That's redundant, 'masquerading as an Elvis impersonator.' Wasn't there a rumor after Elvis's death that he went underground with the witness protection program because his antidrug stance angered the Mob?"

"That's far-fetched, even for conspiracy buffs. Elvis had nothing to do with illegal drugs, except for some LSD he tried once, and a little pot, also a brief experi-

ment. He loved playing power roles, though; that's why
the Memphis Mafia. But it was all play. Nothing to take
seriously."

"Except as a cover at the Kingdome."

Bucek nodded. "Unfortunately, that works both ways.
We have a few real players running around here in
shades and suits, just enough to confuse the issue."

"So. How long had Lyle Purvis been in the witness
protection program, if he wasn't really Elvis?"

"He wasn't, but he was a lifelong Elvis fan. We went
along with the cover because it was the perfect identity-
within-an-identity for him. It's hard for these guys to
drop out of their previous lives, move, get new identities,
worry about jobs, all that. Lyle was a loner, divorced,
no children. He decided to indulge his secret passion for
all things Elvis. It embarrassed him, but no one knew
about it. He already had the perfect hobby to hide in,
even made pretty good money at it. And the notion that
surfaced now and again that he was really Elvis, well . . .
Elvis is a larger-than-life figure. He makes a pretty good
screen, just obvious enough that everybody looks right
past the impersonator to Elvis. But somehow the players
had figured out where he was. We don't take kindly to
breaches of the witness protection program."

"Poor Lyle." Then Temple snapped herself out of the
lonely life and pseudonymous death of a former crook.
She didn't even want to know what he had done, and
she was sure Bucek wouldn't tell her anyway. "But poor
Lyle is dead. And what about Clint Westwood? He
wasn't in the witness protection program?"

Bucek's head shook. "Remember the question about
hiding the leaf?"

"You were hiding a witness among the Elvises, and
the Mob was sending in their own Elvis impersonator to
find and kill your witness. But more than that, the Mob
was hiding its real target behind a flurry of other incidents. The attacks on Priscilla, the bizarre killing in the
Medication Garden, with a snake in tow no less. You're

telling me they'd kill other people to hide the fact that they had hit Lyle? That's vicious."

"That's why they're the Mob. They don't know we're onto them, and we don't want them to know that until we can build a case not only against the hit man, but against the family that ordered it. So they don't know that there's any reason to stop their original plan."

"Another killing. Turn the whole thing into a three-ring circus: Clint, Lyle, and . . . oh, no!"

"You'll have all the protection I can get."

"It didn't help Lyle, as I so presciently mentioned before."

"We didn't know Lyle was the target. We knew something was up when Westwood turned up dead, and you know that there's an ongoing mob scam in this town tracing back to the Goliath and Crystal Phoenix hotel casino deaths tied to the late Cliff Effinger, our friend Matt's noxious stepfather. If we don't blow our cover now, we may be able to net years' worth of illegal activities, perhaps on an international scale. So we need to catch the killer in the act. We think he has no reason to stop his plan now."

"I have no evidence to believe you guys could stop a flea from biting my cat, much less a hit man from killing me."

Bucek's smile was apologetic. "You have reinforcements, don't forget."

"Reinforcements."

"Full Spectrum Elvis. The only reason they didn't keep Quincey's dress from getting trashed was that they had to be onstage to run through their number. We expect the last murder to occur during the show. We'll all be onstage, and you can have it the way you set it up for Quincey: Priscilla with her personal bodyguard around her at all times. The Fontana brothers are as apt to spot the perp as we would be. Just tell them you're the target of a hitman, and they'll be better than a pack of watchdogs. Plus, we'll be there."

"I don't know. I've been attacked on stage before, but I've never gone on knowing someone was going to attack me. Talk about stage fright!" Temple shivered and looked around the dressing room. All the laid out cosmetics reminded her of a mortuary preparation room. Tomorrow night Poor Priscilla could go from wedding to grave.

"Besides," Temple took a last stab at eluding the role of sacrificial lamb, "poor Priscilla doesn't have a thing to wear anymore."

Bucek stood. "Are you telling me there isn't a fairy godmother in this town who can get you a gown by tomorrow evening?"

"I suppose it's possible."

"You'll be as safe as in your own living room. We're fully on to this scheme now. I wouldn't ask you if I weren't sure we could protect you."

Temple read absolute conviction in his eyes, but no one could promise immortality. She nodded. She had a horrible feeling Quincey would try to resume her role if Temple didn't take it, and Temple had promised Merle to look out for Quincey.

She just hadn't expected to do it in the persona of Priscilla Presley.

Chapter 53

Catchin' on Fast

(From 1964's *Kissin' Cousins*)

Temple poked her head in the various dressing rooms, hunting Full Spectrum Elvis and casting her eye over likely suspects: Velvet Elvis, for instance, looking like the Melancholy Dane. She was big enough to manhandle an unwary Elvis, and big enough to be a transsexual. Now that was a thought. Maybe she was, somebody had found out, and she'd been blackmailed into murder to avoid being disqualified from the competition, though Temple didn't quite see why or how transsexuals would be barred.

Mike and Jerry were still best buddies despite the looming pressure of competition, exchanging grooming essentials, and looking nervous. Wasn't Jerry from New Jersey, a storied if stereotypical Mob bastion? Sometimes stereotypes, like fairy tales, can come true.

Oh, and there was Kenny, eager-beaver Kenny, so

quick on the scene of the jumpsuit murder.

Not to mention a whole raft of other Elvis impersonators.

Full Spectrum Elvis was not in the below-stage area, so Temple was forced to clomp up the backstage stairs to hunt them down.

She found them massed in the wings at stage right, watching a sincere but uninspired Elvis perform the difficult *American Trilogy* medley of "Dixie," "The Battle Hymn of the Republic," and "All My Trials."

"Speaking of 'trials . . .' " Motorcycle jerked his head at the guy onstage as soon as she spotted them. "We gotta run through our act after that. Anything going on downstairs? We heard, ah, whining."

"You heard right. Quincey had another crisis." Elvi gathered around, glittering.

"How so?" Rhinestone Lapels wanted to know.

"The Priscilla wedding gown was slashed to smithereens, well, rags, anyway. Quin's mother had heard about the murdered impersonator and took the attack on the dress as a last straw. She was ready to jerk Quincey from the show."

"Aw," came the chorus. The brothers Fontana, even in unrecognizable guise, at least had the grace to sound disappointed.

"But Quincey talked her out of it," Temple added quickly. "And you have someone more vital to guard now."

"How so?" asked Oversized.

"Your endearing emcee, Crawford Buchanan, is convinced the late Elvis impersonator was really the late Elvis, that someone killed Lyle Purvis because of it, and that now that someone will kill him, Crawford, because he too 'knows' it."

A silence greeted this theory, during which they could all hear a really dreadful version of "Suspicious Minds" filling the stage.

"You want us to watchdog the Crawf?"

Temple laughed at their hound-dog-long Elvis faces. "Guess you heard Quin discussing her adored stepdaddy. Yeah, watch to make sure he doesn't fall apart on stage and ruin the show for all the genuine impersonators who are not Elvis, really."

"Purvis." Cane-and-Cape lifted the former, and tossed back the latter. "Not such a far-fetched idea. The guy had something."

"Maybe, but do you think someone would kill to win a contest, or to keep Elvis dead?"

"In this crowd," Fifties said, surveying his clones backstage, "anything is possible, including the impossible."

"Do not worry," Oversized assured her. "We will watch the little weasel like hawks."

"Are you going to stay now to watch our act rehearse?" Karate asked eagerly.

"I can't. I promised a friend I'd stay out of the field of fire," she answered mendaciously.

Mendaciously was one of those long, not-readily-known words that made lies sound like something naughty but noble. The fewer people who knew who the real fake Priscilla was tomorrow night, the better. That was where she disagreed with FBI-man Bucek.

"Meanwhile, once you get off, do you think you can dig up a new bridal outfit for Quincey?"

"We got these swell costumes in no time flat, didn't we?" Rhinestone Elvis waggled his glittering lapels.

"I want that cut down to my size after this is over," Temple said, narrowing her eyes.

"I don't know, Miss Temple." Oversized twinkled his Elvis-blue eyes. "We might be too fond of our personas to pass them on."

"Just pass on the name of your tailor, which I already know. But I'll see you in all your onstage glory tomorrow night. I'm sure I won't be able to keep Electra from dragging me to the actual show. What exactly is your act?"

"We do a medley of song titles." Fifties struck a guitar-twanging pose.

"One Elvis, one title," said Karate, leaping into a deadly stance.

"Oh, really."

Temple couldn't picture it, but perhaps originality counted. Then again, she thought—waving good-bye to the guys and hustling offstage and through the empty house, gazing at Elvis to the umpteenth power—maybe when it came to Elvis impersonation, originality did not count.

Chapter 54

Double Trouble

(The title song from Elvis's 1967 film)

Temple sat staring at the morning paper.

An illo on the top front above the masthead showed a pseudo-Elvis in full writhe. "Night of 100 Elvises," read the teaser head.

The Kingdome should be happy for this plug for its imminent six-hour opening extravaganza of Elvis, Elvis, Elvis.

But the local highlight of the day wasn't what had riveted Temple's eyes to 9.3-point Roman type.

What had done that was the one-column crime story below the front-page fold that announced "Elvis imitator iced."

The headline was crude and would drive advocates of the term "impersonator," and even "tribute performer" nuts.

But that wasn't what had Temple staring like a zombie at the tiny type.

No, it was Lyle Purvis's name, right there in black-and-white. She was sure the reporter had gotten it right. "Lyle Pervisse." It was too odd to be a misspelling.

A rollerball pen drooped from her nerveless fingers.

She wasn't sure she had done her task right, so tried again: The "le" from Lyle, and the "vis" from Pervisse equaled Elvis. That left the "Ly" from Lyle and the "e" from isse for "Ley. That mean the "Pers" from Pervisse, combined with the Ly and the e, added up to PresLey.

Oh, my.

Lyle Pervisse's name was an anagram for Elvis Presley. Elvis ("lives") Presley had loved anagrams. Of course, everyone who heard the name "Pervisse" thought of the more common, phonetic spelling, Purvis.

Could the unthinkable be?

Had the Crawf been right? Had Lyle Pervisse really been Elvis?

No.

He had been an Elvis fanatic. As a protected witness, he could take any name he chose. He chose an anagram of Elvis Presley. If anybody noticed, he was certified as an Elvis nut, not a rat fink on the run.

And he had to have been a rat fink on the run from the Mob to need the witness protection program.

Simple.

Even a crook could have an Elvis obsession. Maybe especially a crook.

Temple looked up at her computer screen. She was in her second-bedroom-cum-office. One of dozens of Web pages on Elvis was frozen on the screen.

It described a seventeen-million-dollar armored-car heist in North Carolina. The crooks were caught, and their ill-gotten gains were seized and sold at auction. There were more than a thousand items, including fifteen vehicles from minivans to a BMW convertible. There were rows of tanning beds and big-screen TVs.

But the lone star of the auction was a velvet painting of Elvis.

The loot went to prove, said one bidder, that you can steal millions of dollars, but you still can't buy taste.

Still . . .

The item that attracted the most interest, that everyone wanted his or her picture taken with, that made it into the single photo used to illustrate this cornucopia of ill-gotten gain up for sale, was . . . the velvet painting of Elvis.

It went for $1600 to a pawnshop owner who intended to display it with a plaque describing where it came from.

Because that was the point. Elvis did one extraordinary thing with his life of fame and fortune and talent and lost opportunities: he never left his roots. He never stopped being a poor boy from Memphis. He never went Hollywood or St. Tropez, and never reinvented himself as a banner boy of Taste.

An Elvis is an Elvis is an Elvis, as the poet said about the singular and lovely rose.

He was a King even a crook could aspire to.

And maybe more than one had.

Chapter 55

Scratch My Back (Then I'll Scratch Yours)

(In 1966's *Paradise, Hawaiian Style*, Elvis sang
this seductive number with pussycat Marianna Hill)

I am still on self-assigned duty in the Kingdome.

It seems that guys in black suits do the security detail around here, so I figure I might as well stick around too until I see my little doll through her descent into Elvismania and back onto solid ground again.

Despite the overpopulation of Elvi, I have tumbled to some other suspicious overpopulations too. Like three times as many Memphis Mafia members as there should be. Given my unique position in undercover work, I am soon eavesdropping on everybody.

You would be amazed how dudes on both sides of the law are willing to unburden themselves of information that should be kept hush-hush in front of a least-likely suspect like myself. They should be ashamed!

But their indiscretion is my information highway, so I do what I do best: creep around, look innocent as well as deaf, blind, and dumb, and soak up the situation.

One thing going down that I decidedly do not like is the absence of Miss Quincey Conrad and the subsequent presence of my Miss Temple. When I see the Fontana brothers come in early flourishing a plastic clothing bag about eight feet long, I am pretty sure what Miss Temple is up to: an unauthorized Priscilla Presley impersonation. EPE (Elvis Presley Enterprises) will not like this, and I am even more against it.

I am well aware of the climactic role this Priscilla person is supposed to play in the ceremonies up top. And I am well aware that young Quincey was subjected to some sinister tricks that may culminate in something even more sinister . . . death.

Steps must be taken, and it will be hard to shepherd events onstage with 100 Elvis tribute performers milling about among two dozen Memphis Mafia wannabes from the highest and lowest ranks of both law enforcement and organized lawlessness.

I have a strong sense of competence as well as responsibility, but even I know that an operation of this scale is too big a job for the likes of me to make much of a difference.

Unassisted, that is.

So I amble down the hall—no one, and I mean no one thinks much of an ace mouse-snapper like me hanging out in basement dressing room areas—to my least favorite door.

Even from outside I can smell the fermenting fruit, not to mention bodily fluids.

I close my eyes and insert a forelimb beneath the crack under the door. I can only push a few shivs through, but these I wiggle around.

Primates are notoriously hard to teach, especially if they are of a higher order, but this primate is on the primitive side, and I soon bent it to my superior will.

As soon as it hears the scrape of my shivs on the concrete floor inside the storeroom, I hear an answering scrape along the lock of its cage, which I have fixed to never quite close by sacrificing a luxuriant tuft of my own hair-shirt, thrust into the mechanism.

Because the dumb little ape is brown, and I am black, and the storeroom lighting is the usual monkey piss color they use in such places, the human who cares for the odious Chatter was not likely to see my modification of the lock.

So Chatter, using its obnoxious jointed fingers and rotten opposable thumbs, is soon free as a bird on helium. I hear the creature working to turn the doorknob and admit me.

Despite the fancy forelimb appendages, it is a good three minutes before the door is cracked and I eel in.

"Shut it, quick!" I order.

"Why shut? Just open."

"Because I want it shut! Took you long enough."

"The hair got caught under my nails."

"Braggart!" Just because my nails are not broad enough to entrap much of anything . . . I hate one-up-apeship.

I pace, because I am getting worried. "Did you see your so-called master today?"

Chatter sits back on his obscenely hairless rear and rocks happily. "Oh, yes. We had kiwi and banana."

"How terrific. How is your master?"

"Busy. No time. Brings and is bye-bye."

"I bet. Listen, I know you are not a dog, and that you do not have the brains of a cat. But do you think you can sniff, see, find your master in a place crowded with strange people and smells and sounds?"

Chatter lives up to his name and begins gibbering. He goes so far as to bite his nails.

"Idon'tknow. Idon'tknow. Been in dark so long. Scared, Louie. Chatter do tricks. Look up skirts. Can look up skirts."

"There will be no skirts on this scene, except one, and it goes all the way to the ground, and then some. You will have to forget the vulgar tricks you were taught and concentrate on one, very important thing."

"Yes? What?"

The hairy little ape is agitated. Personally, I would not keep anything I was devoted to in the dark like this, no matter what I was up to.

"Now, now. Smooth that savage brow. Nothing to worry about. Uncle Louie is here. All you have to do is clear your mind of all confusion. Just go where I say and find your master."

"No trick? Master like trick."

"No trick. Just find your master. He, she, or it will like that trick plenty."

Chatter hop-slides over to me and puts a big hairless mitt on my paw. His long fingers curl around it as if we were holding hands, had we hands. I control my aversion.

"Scared, Louie. Big place. Noise. People. Like . . . zoo. Like lab."

"Lab? You were in an experimental lab?"

"Big lab. Small cage. Dark like this half the time." Chatter frowns. I am beginning to find his almost-human expressions creepy. "Master take away."

I shift my weight from forelimb to forelimb and do it again. "That is good. You owe master a big kiss for that one. That is all you have to do: find master. I will be there to protect you." Too bad I cannot protect his master.

"Okay." Chatter leaps up and down. "It is game. Fun. Find master. Louie say find master."

"Louie say find master. But first we wait until there is a lot of thump-thumping on the stage upstairs. Then we go, quietly, up."

"Game. Trick. Chatter love trick."

Yeah. I was hoping that Chatter's master would just love this trick to death.

Chapter 56

Who Are You
(Who Am I)

(From 1968's *Speedway*)

"Boys," said Temple in her second-best Mae West voice, "you are the finest fairy godmothers a girl ever had."

"Watch it!" Karate Elvis glowered.

Her hand dropped its instinctive caress of the new wedding gown, a column of shining white fabric and iridescent beads that hung from the otherwise empty rod in Quincey's dressing room. "How did Minnie make this up so fast?"

"Minnie made the first gown," said Oversized. "She loves a challenge, and you and Quincey are the same petite size as Priscilla."

Temple lifted a swath of empire skirt. "Priscilla picked this style herself, off a rack. So much had been decided for her. I think the simple act of buying something ready-made was a statement. After she left Elvis, she ran a boutique with a friend. Picking and choosing, she who had so much picked and chosen for her."

"Elvis could be a little overbearing," Tuxedo admitted, clearing his throat. "Especially with women."

"Elvis could be a lot overcontrolling," Temple said. "Just like his mother. To them, it was a sign of caring."

"I haven't seen Miss Quincey about today," Motorcycle put in.

"She's coming along later. I'll help her get dressed. Now you guys, shoo! You've got wardrobes and makeup and lyrics and moves to tend to. I'll help Quincey."

They scattered, excited despite themselves. Elvis had a way of doing that to people.

Temple confronted herself in the mirror. It awaited her, the impersonation of a career that never was. She went to shut the door, then dragged an ice cream chair from the dressing table and tucked its upper rung under the doorknob.

"Give a girl a little privacy on her wedding night," she whispered to the empty hall.

She went back to the mirror and began assembling her weapons: false eyelashes, false nails, white lipstick, black wig. She couldn't totally say why she was doing this, except that she agreed with Velvet Elvis: someone owed it to Elvis, or to Lyle Pervisse, or even to whoever had so hated to stop the music, but had to do it anyway, despite himself.

There's something about a show just about to go on. You can feel it in the air, all around.

You can sense it in your lonely dressing room, the thumps and stutters of preparations on the stage above, like a dead body being dragged out of a trunk and into the center spotlight.

The audience is sifting into their seats, chattering in the soft illumination of the house lights, deciding whether their location is good or bad, eyeing the other audience members' position and clothes, glancing at the naked, empty stage, almost afraid of catching some lowly set technician doing something overt.

They are listening for the first sounds of the low-profile backup musicians creeping into place one by one. Picking up and adjusting their instruments even though no one is supposed to notice them, these Rumplestiltskins of the gold about to be woven by the main attraction.

Elvis to the hundreth power.

Rich man, poor man, beggarman, thief.

Doctor, lawyer, Indian chief.

Poor man, rich man, beggared by a thief.

Doctored and lawyered, and left to grief.

Victim, hit man, bridegroom, bride.

Singer, survivor, sweetheart, suicide.

Temple finished installing the fountain of illusion veiling over the high, illusory helmet of hair beneath it. Steel within smoke.

She looked as much like Priscilla as Quincey had, as any woman would who erected the same cage of artifice around herself.

Poor Priscilla, who could only free Elvis once she had freed herself from the gilded cage he had made her; only when he was dead, and none of it mattered but the trademarks.

Temple's fingertips trembled as she adjusted the veiling. This was a foolhardy thing to do. She had even deceived her stalwart defenders, but they had their own stage roles to play, and she feared their presence would intimidate the killer. Besides, she had Bucek's professionals looking out for her, promise.

The hair pick so essential to an evenly balanced beehive was clenched in her hand: six inches of pointed metal. Not much of a weapon, but easily concealed.

Bucek was out there.

And the Fontana boys.

And maybe even Agent Mulder, this being a natural *X-Files* case, but Temple didn't believe in that last notion as much as she believed in Elvis.

Because he, the original dead man, had driven every incident that had haunted this hotel opening, and had even impinged on the grounds of the Crystal Phoenix.

He meant something different to every person who thought he or she knew him, or loved him, or betrayed him. Sometimes a legend is so large he cannot be counted out.

This Priscilla outfit was made for entangling. Temple stood, arranged the folds, and floated to the door like a gorgeous ghost.

She was so totally retro. In the spirit, so to speak.

Ready to meet a ghost on a parapet.

Ready to exact revenge. Extract justice.

Hopefully, the villain of the piece would cooperate.

A knock sounded on her door.

She unjammed the chair, swept it aside, threw open the door.

"Quincey! Hey, kid, I'm glad you escaped the JD types to come back to do your part."

"Forget it, Crawf," Temple said, sneering delicately. "I didn't want to waste the neck tattoo for nothing."

She swept past him, heading for the stairs to the stage. "You gonna help me galumph up these stairs in this too-dead outfit? You owe me for this one. I hope you break a leg," she added nastily.

Nothing like family solidarity, right, Elvis?

The heavy hair, the cataracts of veiling, dulled the sounds pounding off the stage. The show was underway.

As Crawford trumpeted the impersonators' names between acts, Elvis after Elvis attacked the ebony wood with his feet and voice and soul.

Temple watched from the wings, impressed, but not moved. All were mostly good. None shook the world.

Then Velvet Elvis came on, her holographic black jumpsuit crawling with phosphorescent constellations as the special lighting gels kicked in. Her voice was high, but clear, her angular moves impeccable.

The crowd roared as she finished her three-minute set and eeled off, tensile as a guitar string tuned to high E.

All the performers nodded to Temple waiting alone in the wings as they exited. She was the prize. The High Princess who would award the Sacred Belt.

It lay near her in an open box long enough to hold roses: a five-inch-wide length of inscribed metal that would look heavy even around Mr. T's 24-karat neck.

Temple felt cultural confusion. In a way the artifact was the Sword in the Stone. In a way it was the National Wrestling Federation trophy belt. It was Platinum Records and Latinum bars, a cross-cultural mélange of trophies both fictional and factual.

It meant nothing and everything, just as Elvis had.

It meant life and death, just as Elvis had.

She was Priscilla, she was Guinevere. Both had feet of clay while they wielded belts of gold.

She was mortal, she was eternal.

The sword was in the lake, the sword was buried in a bejeweled back.

She was a symbol, she was a solver of symbols.

She was nuts to be here.

Then the nine Fontana boys bounced onstage, each to a twanging guitar chord, each in a pose that reflected his version of Elvis.

"Lawdy Miss Clawdy," wailed the first.

"You Ain't Nothin' But a Hound Dog," whined the second.

"Running Scared," howled the third.

"Farther Along," crooned the fourth.

"Find Out What's Happening," urged the fifth.

"Any Day Now," moaned the sixth.

"Love Me Tender," whispered the seventh.

"Crying in the Chapel," blazed the eighth.

"Amen," intoned the ninth.

They got a standing ovation.

Temple was among the clappers who blistered the heels of their hands.

Then someone else was gyrating on stage. Kenny! Looking much larger than himself, larger than life.

"Do You Know Who I Am?" he wailed with savage passion, hips swiveling like a stopped-up pepper shaker on a humid, Gulf-coast restaurant table.

Temple jumped up and down in the wings. "Go, Kenny, go!" An exiting Elvis glowered at her. She wasn't supposed to show favoritism.

Temple settled down to look around. No one much noticed her. She really wouldn't come into play until she awarded the winner's belt.

If the killer was an Elvis freak, and if "Priscilla" was his next target, it didn't make sense to kill her until all the shouting was over.

"Hey!" Oversized paused by her. They had to whisper, which helped disguise her voice.

"You guys did good," she told him.

"Thanks. You okay, Miss Quincey?"

"Fine."

"You want some us to hang out by you?"

"Naw. What's to worry? I'm packing a really mean hair spray."

Oversized laughed. "You always did. Well, if you're okay—"

"Go on. Wait for the rankings. I'm sure you guys got at least an eight."

"It's like the Olympics, right? Ten's the winner."

"But eight's not to sneeze at. Go on."

"You're sure in good spirits, Miss Quincy. I can't see why Miss Temple wanted us to leave you to your own devices, seeing as how your own devices involve some pretty strange stuff."

"I'm fine." She pushed Oversized away, quite a feat given his bulk, and her lack of it. "Quincey" couldn't take too close examination.

She watched him join his brothers in passing behind the black velvet back curtain to the stage's other side, where Crawford held forth as emcee and they could watch him. If only Crawf were the target most likely . . . !

She felt terrible about deceiving them, but the show must go on.

The King of Kings' show wouldn't go on.

Temple lost her sense of time and place as she thought about Lyle. She had really liked him in the few minutes they had talked, and would probably never know what he had done to merit witness protection, or death. Maybe nothing but blow the whistle. Why would a man risk his life for recognition as someone he could never be? If the King of Kings had lived and won, a protected witness really couldn't afford that much attention. Nor could the "real" Elvis, if Lyle had been what Crawford thought he was.

Being Elvis seemed to be an unhappy vocation all around. What was the attraction? Did they all hope to do Elvis better than Elvis had?

No, it was something else. They all wanted to *save* Elvis.

Turn back the clock, step on their blue suede shoes. If they could change something in the Elvis legend, they could change Elvis himself. Save him. Even Priscilla was still engaged in that very mission, through Elvis Presley Enterprises. Redeem the past by preserving it in plastic for the present and future King.

Beam me up, mama.

The stage was sprouting new Elvi like legendary dragon's teeth sowed soldiers.

But the routine—Crawford's slightly lugubrious emceeing, sudden entrance, hard-chord intro, quick and dirty rendering, fast exit—was becoming routine. Repetitive drudgery, as it had been for Elvis, in the end.

Temple heard the numbers work their way to the inevitable countdown.

Sixty-seven. Eighty-three. Ninety-four. She yawned. Gosh, she hadn't seen Electra's new boyfriend, Today Elvis, perform yet. A shock of white hair would be a nice change from all the black. Funny guy. Israel what? Feinberg. Not a likely Elvis impersonator name. Unless . . . wasn't Israel an anagram for Is real? Could it be? Where was he?

The watch she wore under Priscilla's long, dainty Cinderella-gown sleeves read almost midnight.

A rat-a-tat of bass guitar chords preceded a rebel yell.

An Early Elvis in black leather came sliding across the dark stage floor on bended knees, a guitar cocked at his leading hip like an ax.

"(You're the) Devil in Disguise" was the song, and a madman incarnate delivered it straight from Beelzebub's mail room.

Temple straightened up, blinked, and only then noticed a pale satin rope looping down from the heights above her misty headdress.

Every eye in the place fixed on the magnetic Elvis on stage. Tutti Frutti Elvis from rehearsals, Temple realized belatedly. Why did he change his number . . . ?

Her hand lifted to bat at the encroaching stage line. Wait! There were no white ropes backstage, only black—

The dangling bridal rope was looping around her neck.

She twisted her head away, but the pouf of veiling over her exaggerated hairdo made it hard to see. Holy Hound Dog! Someone was trying to strangle her! Bucek had been right.

Her arms flailed so sharply Minnie's shoulder seams ripped like pressed wood in a table saw.

Beads rained past her veiling, bleached poppy seeds falling to the stage floor, but Temple couldn't hear their brittle landing. Everything was pulsing to the song's driving beat; the stage floor was heaving, her throat was tightening and her eyes were losing focus in a pale, many-layered haze.

The corner of her eye caught a compact black form launching at her head, launching beyond her head.

Something was screaming, screeching. Not her, her voice was silenced.

The white satin snake at her neck loosened and fell away just as the on-stage Elvis charged into her vision like a rocket.

He grabbed her elbow.

His grip forced her to duck and run forward. By center stage she had been dragged to her knees beside him, skidding on yards of beaded organza.

They were sliding together like suicidal skiers toward the stage's far corner rim, a satin garrote trailing over Temple's left shoulder like an aviator's scarf, like the scarf that had caught in Isadora Duncan's car wheels and killed her. What a way to go!

Elvis and Priscilla skidded to a dead stop at the very brink of the stage, cheek to cheek, right where a phalanx of photographers in the pit were posed to snap their picture.

Temple coughed discreetly. "Nice timing," she complimented her unknown savior. One of Bucek's ersatz Memphis Mafia men? She never would have credited the FBI man with such flair.

"Rotten planning," he muttered through her smile and his into her almost-kissed lips.

The voice was as unmistakable as Elvis's. "Max!?"

"May I call you Cilla?"

"Oh . . . fudge."

Chapter 57

Won't You Wear
My Ring

(Entered *Billboard*'s list at number seven, the
highest opening position of any Elvis single;
advance orders exceeded one million)

Frank Bucek offered Temple a huge Styrofoam cup of
coffee.

"I'll never get to sleep tonight if I drink this."

"Maybe that's not a bad idea. No dreams. I heard
Elvis had a lot of nightmares."

She was back in Quincey's dressing room with what
was left of Minnie's instant wedding gown.

Bucek tossed an ivory satin rope in a plastic bag on
the dressing table top. "You had a close call."

"More like a close curtain call."

He shook his head.

People still clustered in the hall, but they were alone
for the moment.

"I'm a little fuzzy on what happened," Temple admitted.

"We're still a lot fuzzy on what happened. The Fontana Elvi tell me you told them to guard that Buchanan guy? Why? For God's sake, why?"

"I was afraid no one would try anything with that much Elvis-power around. Those guys can be pretty pervasive."

"Yeah, like garlic. You're lucky that monkey escaped."

"Monkey? I thought . . . wasn't it a cat that jumped up when I was being attacked?"

She was thinking of Midnight Louie, of course, her knight in shining fur.

"Chim-pan-zee." Bucek had the nondescript, chiseled features of an astronaut or a military man or a monk. Hearing him intone the name of the beast that had saved her was too funny for words, but Temple didn't have the energy to laugh. "Named 'Chatter.' Ring a bell?"

"Elvis had a pet chimp named Scatter. He trained it to play all sorts of vulgar tricks. And it came to a bad end, didn't it? It got hooked on straight scotch and bourbon and turned violent. Everybody lost interest and it was caged at Graceland until it died of cirrhosis of the liver. What's gonna happen to this one?"

"Hey, he fingered a hitman for the Mob. We'll have to put him in protective custody. Probably here at the hotel Animal Elvis exhibition. In a big chimp suite. Lots of interaction with the clientele. He should be fine."

"You have a sense of humor," she accused.

"Don't tell Matt. It would destroy him."

"And you too, probably. So . . . somehow the chimp, who belonged to the hit man, got out. So he happened to find his master right when the guy was homing in for the kill. Then the killer was an Elvis addict, right?"

"Right." Bucek still looked amused, like Temple was a trained chimp he was watching. "You're so smart, how come you didn't finger the killer before he laid a finger on you?"

"With so darn many Elvis impersonators here? I'm not totally stupid. I had a leading candidate, but he never came near me all night and I didn't figure he could kill me long distance."

"Then you got a little distracted."

"Oh. Yeah."

"That next-to-last Elvis really got to you, didn't he?"

"He was good."

"He was great. Distracted you from the fact that you were a potential victim. Maybe even made the killer so jealous he decided to interrupt the act with murder. Almost was the death of you, that Elvis. You remember him?"

Temple tried to look vague and helpless. It was hard. "Yeah, but . . . it all mashes together."

"He got you out of harm's way, though, in the end. Amazing how he swept you into that photo opportunity at the last moment. The *Sun* photographer says he's got a shot that looks just like Elvis and Priscilla at their wedding. Yep. That ninety-ninth Elvis made a big impression on the judges. They were going to give him the top award."

"Going to?"

"Couldn't find him after all the excitement."

"Really?"

"Couldn't find him entered in the competition."

"Really."

"The rumor is, Elvis saved you."

"Elvis? That guy was much too young—"

"Not Elvis Now. Elvis Then."

"Oh, Mr. Bucek. The FBI doesn't believe in ghosts, does it?"

"Only on TV, Miss Barr. Only on TV."

"So who won?"

Bucek looked down at the coiled satin snake in the bag.

"Maybe I should ask, 'Who lost?' " Temple said.

"Sometimes you can have it both ways."

She caught her breath. A fitting end for an assassin: triumph and capture at one and the same moment.

"The judges didn't know, of course," he said.

She nodded.

"And you weren't available to award the belt, so they just had Crawford Buchanan hand it to the winner."

"I see." Temple couldn't keep her lip from curling in an Elvis sneer. Crawford's moment in the limelight must have been bitter, having to crown a King who'd slain the man he believed was the real King.

"Hard to hold a belt like that with handcuffs on, but some you win and some you lose."

"You have a true gift for cliché."

"Thank you. Care to guess the identity of the winner and loser?"

Temple took a deep breath. "Is it . . . Kenny?"

Bucek nodded, impressed. "What did you figure out first: who won the competition, or who worked for the Mob?"

"Kenny was good tonight, though not as good as . . . whoever. But I'd already suspected him. Because of the jumpsuit."

"What jumpsuit? The place was crawling with jumpsuits."

"The first jumpsuit. The first victim in all this. The one that was trashed in Quincey's dressing room and turned up buried later in the Medication Garden."

"More legerdemain. Tricks to fool the eye."

"Not really. Because I finally realized that if Lyle the protected witness could be an Elvis fanatic, maybe his executioner could be one too. To catch a thief, et cetera. Like you said about the leaf and the forest and Father Brown. It had to be all about Elvis. So I decided that the killer must have loved Elvis as much as the victim. And I still remember how genuinely sad Kenny was about the violated jumpsuit. Then, when it disappeared and turned up buried—in the Medication Garden, next to all those enshrined Elvis jumpsuits—I realized why."

"Why?"

Temple sipped the coffee, though she'd probably regret it in a couple of hours. "It was buried in reverence, not in guilt and concealment. The killer was sorry he'd offed the jumpsuit. Do you see? The hitman could destroy a living, breathing target, but it almost killed him to ruin any Elvis artifact, no matter how effective the ruse was."

"Interesting theory. You want to test it on the source?"

"Kenny's still here?" She thought about it. "I suppose he didn't know it was really me he was going to off so spectacularly on stage.

"No, he didn't, but it wouldn't have really made any difference. Lucky that his lonely chimp got out and that Elvis impersonator decided to sweep you into the end of his act, or it would have been the end of yours. That backstage was an ill-lit piece of chaos, a perfect murder scene."

Temple lifted the long, slightly worn skirt of Priscilla's second wedding dress. Kenny had murdered two people, and who knows how many before that. Did she really want to see him? Did she really want him to see her? Then she glimpsed herself in the mirror. Odd how wearing a costume can make you forget that you look utterly unlike yourself.

"Sure, I'll see him, since he can't really see me."

Bucek took her elbow to assist up from the chair. Temple wasn't sure whether he assumed she was shaky from her recent veil's-breadth escape or he thought that the trailing gown was hard to walk in, which it was.

Faces in the hall—mostly Elvis faces—peered curiously at Temple as she passed. For the moment, Priscilla had stolen the spotlight from her ex-spouse.

Two grim men in black guarded a closed steel door.

Temple recognized the fruity smell of the storage room that must have housed the chimpanzee, but now the large cage was occupied with a human being.

Kenny paced in his glittering jumpsuit like a big cat in one of those awful confined cages zoos used to have before most of them became humane and provided animals with open spaces reminiscent of their natural environments.

She had always seen him as muscular, but it wasn't until he performed that she had seen how strong he was.

He looked up as she and Bucek entered, and stopped dead.

One leg, his left, twitched.

Two other men sat on folding chairs near the cage.

Under the flat, unfriendly illumination of overhead flourescent lamps, the entire scene had a surreal feeling.

Temple would have liked to have seen her gothic Priscilla figure entering this stark environment like an avenging ghost.

Kenny didn't look scared, just uptight.

A third folding chair, empty, stood near the cage. On it lay a massive, gold-plated belt studded with Austrian crystals, very like the vermeil belt Elvis was given to honor his 1969 appearance that broke all existing Las Vegas attendance records. Elvis had his gold-over-sterling-silver belt inlaid with sapphires, diamonds, and rubies later.

It must have weighed the world.

Curious because she'd never held this less valuable but no less massive belt, Temple bent to pick up the trophy she'd lost the chance to award because the man in the cage was trying to throttle her.

"Don't touch it!" he said.

Temple paused, startled by his vehemence.

"You don't deserve anything Elvis earned," he went on in the same low, loathing tone. "Or anything anyone else earned by honoring Elvis."

She turned and went closer, even though the men on the chairs stirred uneasily. The metal chair feet screeched on the concrete floor.

The only thing that kept this bitter man from calling her "bitch" was the presence of the men in black. For the first time she understood the roots of Elvis's paranoia. He'd gotten death threats for years; so had Priscilla; so had Lisa Marie.

"How could you persecute a sixteen-year-old girl who had nothing to do with Elvis or Priscilla, who was just playing a part in a stage show?"

She didn't bother revealing that she wasn't Quincey, or that he had seen her earlier in her ordinary form. It didn't matter who she was to Kenny. If you were masquerading as Priscilla, you deserved anything you got. Killing Quincey or killing Temple would have been no sweat to him.

"You nailed Elvis when you were just fourteen," he accused back, "and he was away from home with his mama just dead and gone. Snared him like a Mississippi Delta catfish in a net. Like Dee Stanley snagged Vernon. Elvis was never free after he met you. The Colonel and your father made him marry you finally in sixty-seven, and that was the beginning of the end. You broke his heart when you left him."

Obviously, Kenny had imprinted on the image of Priscilla the way a racing greyhound is trained to imprint on the helpless cats and rabbits used as bait to get it running.

"You loved Elvis," Temple said. "You really hated to see that Elvis jumpsuit destroyed. Yet you must have commissioned it, brought it here, and it wasn't even a design that Elvis had worn. It was totally invented."

"Well, you don't want the estate to get its trademarks in a wad, and it owns just about everything Elvis. So some of us make up our own designs. That was a great one. I never planned to trash it, but I needed distractions, and . . . it had to go."

"Why the horse motif?" Temple wondered.

"Why not?"

Bucek suddenly spoke. "Wish we'd known about that earlier. If you knew Kenny's background, it would make sense."

Temple turned, puzzled.

"I don't know whether your big ego or your small brain is more trouble to you, Kenny." Bucek joined Temple at the chickenwire barrier and shook his head. "Now that you mention it, Kenny left a clue the size of horse hockey."

"You mean burying the suit?"

"That, but what was on the suit is more telling." Bucek kept his eyes on Kenny, but he spoke to Temple. "Kenny has a nickname in the Mob. Most of them do. His is 'Kenny the Horse.' Comes from starting out as a mule for heroin deliveries, before he moved up to hit man. No matter how much he was into impersonating Elvis, he couldn't help letting some braggadocio about his Mob connections creep in. Now he gets to take his victim's place, and we get to hide him and protect him and call him our very own, until we can make a good case on the whole organization."

Kenny listened, never taking his eyes off of Temple/Priscilla.

"What happens to my suit?" he wanted to know. "Who gets custody of the suit?"

"What about the chimp?" Temple wondered indignantly. "Don't you care what happens to him?"

"That stupid animal! Blew my cover. He was good for a few laughs, but nobody better step on my jumpsuits."

"Don't worry," Bucek said. "That jumpsuit will be on display like the rest of them, as Exhibit A in court someday. You'll be reunited before a federal judge, but I doubt anyone will sentence a jumpsuit to the prison term you'll get."

Kenny shrugged at this dire prediction of the future. "*Jailhouse Rock.* One of E's best films. He did real well in prison stripes."

Bucek shook his head and took Temple's elbow again, escorting her to the door.

"That man has an unreal sense of values," she commented.

"That's what makes hit men tick."

"So . . . how does this case get settled? Publicly?"

"For now, everything, of course, will be denied, lost, brushed under the rug. There was no one here but Memphis Mafia hotel security. One Elvis impersonator cracked and was . . . institutionalized. A mysterious Elvis impersonator tried to steal the show. Life goes on, murders go unsolved, local police hate the outside agency's guts. We try to keep Kenny alive to testify and bring down the bigwigs behind it all. Are you happy, Miss Barr?"

"I'm happy to be alive," she said when they stood out in the hall again. The onlookers had thinned, bored by the lack of action. "And so, I imagine, is Elvis."

"Right." Bucek escorted her back to Quincey's dressing room so she could change back into herself. "By the way, there's one member of the press we haven't been able to muzzle. Luckily, no one would believe him in a million years. I'm sorry."

He left the room, shouldered through the remaining spectators, and vanished.

The Fontana brothers made a daisy chain in front of the door, but a slight, agile figure dashed through, under their arms.

"T. B., are you all right?"

"Fine," she said.

"Tell me about it." He came close, crouched beside her chair.

"About what?"

"About *Him*! The Elvis who disappeared. I was wrong. Thank God I was wrong." Crawford trembled on the brink of tears. "Lyle wasn't Him. He didn't die. He came, and saved, and went again. Tell me about him, please."

"Well," said Temple. "The first thing I noticed was how blue his eyes were, and how they . . . glowed. Like electricity. In fact, everything about him . . . glowed."

Crawford nodded, at peace. Not even taking notes.

Temple drew in another hit of caffeine from the big cup on the dressing table, even though the contents were stone cold, just like Elvis. She was riding on the high of survival and the joy of imagination. Elvis had saved her, yes, he had. In one form, or another.

Viva Las Vegas.

One-twelve A.M.

Matt was gliding away from the radio station on the Hesketh Vampire. Leticia was annoyed that the results of the Elvis competition at the Kingdome hadn't been available in time to announce at the end of the Midnight Hour.

He was relieved it was all over. Elvis had not called since Lyle Purvis had died, whatever one event had to do with the other. Only three women had been waiting for Matt after the show. Maybe his fans were all over at the Kingdome, cheering the ersatz Elvi on.

Even the Vampire seemed subdued tonight, its motor running smooth and relatively silent for a change. Leticia was busy preparing "Elvis tapes" for sale, but Dwight had raised the issue of the estate objecting to merchandising any unauthorized shred of Elvis.

Matt could see their point.

Matt could almost see Elvis, a distant, lonely figure riding a predestined track, a human being lost in the meteoric dazzle of his own contrail.

Could you ever reach deep into another human being and know him?

Could you ever reach deep into yourself and know him?

Matt glanced in his right side mirror.

Moon at twelve o'clock high.

Moon, or falling star?

He was tired.

He might be tired of himself.

And then he saw that cyclops of dogging light, just like the other night, that phantom in the mirror, that motorcyclist's nightmare, that buzz at the farthest range of his hearing.

The part of himself he could never escape, because it had somehow become Other.

Matt pushed the Vampire, pressed it into higher speed.

It grew throaty, as if growling protest, then it leaped forward.

Still. A light in the mirror.

A pursuer.

A Hound of Heaven.

Or Hell.

Well.

He knew how to ride this thing at last.

He wasn't afraid to tilt almost horizontal.

He didn't fear the noise and the speed.

Speed King.

He wasn't going to get caught.

Not here.

Like this.

By . . . whom?

An anonymous splinter of himself. The eternal judge. The Wild Card Incarnate. Elvis on the half shell?

No.

Sometimes you move and it's zen. The hand, the eye, the soul in mindless syncopation. Maybe it's rock. Maybe it's roll. Maybe it's delusion.

Matt was in that state. The machine moved with him. He moved the machine. The needle said they did ninety. The moon and the asphalt said they were waltzing in three-four time.

But finally the whirr and the scream behind them caught up. The light in the mirror was a star gone nova. Some hounds you can't outrun.

Matt slowed, breathed, pulled over.

In the mirror, the single light focused, stopped, hung there like a spotlight.

The sound of silence was deafening after the rush.

He waited, balancing the weight of the Vampire on the balls of his boots.

Leather creaked in the dry desert air.

Black leather.

A motorcycle policeman advanced in Matt's left side mirror.

A mythic figure, really. Boots, pants, jacket creaking. Hips expanded with a holster of accessories: gun, gloves, baton, walkie-talkie, whatever.

Paper in a notepad shifted like dry bones. "Whoa, son. You were goin' pretty fast."

"Sorry. My shift is over. I'm anxious to get home."

"Home's not worth rushin' to so fast. Let's see here. Ninety miles an hour."

"Guess I didn't look. I'm sorry."

"What this thing do?"

"The bike?"

"Never seen one like it." Boots creaking at each step around the Hesketh.

"It's English."

"English bike? Usually they're those real light bicycles. This is a heavy machine."

"Custom."

"Custom. I like custom. Got to give you a ticket, though."

"I understand, officer. I'm a little nervous. Been working late a lot. And, I thought, someone was following me—"

"Someone following you. That's a nasty feeling."

"Yeah. You get it sometimes?"

"All the time, son. All the time. Comes with the territory." He walked around the Vampire again. "Nice bike. So what'll it do?"

"I don't know."

"Don't know?"

"Never took it up to maximum. It's . . . well, against the law."

"Against the law. We don't wanta be against the law."

The cop leaned close, peered at the dash. "What does it say it'll do?"

"Uh, the speedometer goes to one-twenty."

"You tried it?"

"No."

"Maybe you should."

"I can't. It's against the law."

"Against the law. See this?"

"It's a badge."

"Yes, sir. Now that's not against the law."

"I guess not."

"So I'm not going to give you a ticket tonight, son, on one condition."

"Yes?"

"That you take this thing to the maximum."

"But—"

"Now, go on. I don't want to have to get mean, but if I can catch your taillight, you're not doing as I say."

"No, sir. I mean, yes, sir."

"Go on, then. I want to see you flying."

Matt went.

Into the desert on empty roads, timeless flight.

The moon couldn't keep up.

The motorcycle policeman couldn't keep up.

Finally, finally, the voices in his head couldn't keep up.

He got a ticket anyway.

A ticket to ride.

Temple turned the key in her door, then tiptoed into her own place like a thief. It felt so great to have the weight of Priscilla, actual and metaphorical, off her.

"Meroww," said Midnight Louie, writhing against her ankles and stalking over to his bowl to stand and stare resentfully.

She had thought . . . who knew what she had thought tonight?

"We had some monkey business at the Kingdome tonight, Louie. Good thing you weren't there."

"Merrrroooow!" said Louie. He almost sounded like he was scolding her.

"I know I've been gone a lot lately," she said meekly. "Got caught up in Elvis fever. This whole town did. But it's all over now. Here, have some ocean flounder on your Free-to-Be-Feline."

Louie dug in and Temple tiptoed away before he could scold her further, to the bedroom.

"Meow," said Midnight Max, who was reclining on the comforter, sans Elvis accoutrements.

The stereo was softly playing something Elvis, though.

"You would have won if you'd stuck around," Temple said.

"Couldn't afford to."

She sat at the foot of the bed. "Okay. How? Why? When?"

Max smiled. "I got back in town and couldn't reach you at home, so I finally appealed to Electra for news. She informed me you'd become Elvis's greatest fan and told me all about the dirty tricks going on at the Kingdome. I figured you couldn't resist the greatest mystery of the twentieth century, so I slipped over there to sniff around—apparently Midnight Louie had similar notions, because I kept seeing him around—"

"I didn't."

"He's like me: hard to spot unless he wants you to."

"Hmmmph," Temple said.

"Anyway, I decided that being in the thick of things was the best way to give you backup."

"Did you have to pull me into that too-too hokey knee-slide?"

"The audience loved it."

"The audience loved you. I didn't know you could do that."

Max shrugged. "Neither did I. So who tried to kill you, and why?"

"A Mob hit man with.an Elvis fetish. Priscilla's death was just the icing on the cake. The real target was a man in the federal witness protection program."

"Elvis hitting Elvis. Has a sordid sort of harmony, doesn't it? Are you angry that I turned up?"

"Not at all, Max. I'm just really sorry that I couldn't give you that belt."

"I bet you are!"

He leaned forward to reach for her. "Isn't it time Elvis and Priscilla had a reconciliation?"

"Way overdue," she agreed.

In the kitchen, Midnight Louie howled his objections.

Chapter 58

Mystery Train

(Recorded at Sun Records in 1955 and cowritten
by Sun founder Sam Phillips)

Matt approached WCOO the next night like a surly tran-
sient. He kept his hands stuffed in his jacket pockets,
hoping no preshow fans would accost him for autographs. They'd started showing up before as well as after
his hourly midnight stint now. A. E. After Elvis.

He just wanted to creep into the radio station unnot-
iced, and get on with whatever the night would hold in
store. It certainly wouldn't be Elvis anymore. He hoped.
He had served his time in Elvis's particular variety of
limbo and needed to get on with his own life, as dull as
it was.

His blood chilled when he saw people clustered near
the station entrance. They all seemed focused on something. Maybe he was just jumpy after last night's post-
show encounter, but he couldn't help thinking of the
body Molina had found outside the Blue Dahlia.

Was it his turn to find a corpse on his own turf?

His next thought was even wilder. Had his caller ended the silence with a sudden plunge into depression and suicide on Matt's very doorstep?

His footsteps made them turn one by one. The staccato conversation of an agitated group trailed off word by word.

"He's here!"

Faces focused on him, full of strange excitement. Even Keith who worked the switchboard was out on the parking lot asphalt, looking dazed.

Matt stared past the strangers' faces to what had occupied their attention.

A parked car, that's all.

Keith had bought a new car, and Matt's fans were admiring it. Good, let them bug some guy their own age.

"Nice wheels, Keith," he said in passing, seeing little more than a sleek silver fender. Silver. Keith had openly lusted after the Vampire. "Sorry, I've got to get on the job," he told the girls who were gravitating toward him like mercury finding ground zero.

Matt waved in passing, smiling at the sincere flattery of imitation, and went into the station.

Ambrosia herself (Leticia in full radio diva persona) was sitting on the deserted receptionist's desk like a chocolate Buddha wearing the face of Shiva, gorgeous goddess of destruction.

"You're pretty mellow, man. Considering."

"Considering what?"

She hoisted a dangling plastic tag. "Considering your new car."

"My new car."

"That's what the tag says. Glad to see an employee doing so well. Won't have to give you a raise for a while."

"My new car."

"Sure glad you're not so repetitious on the air, honey.

You better hurry if you're gonna look at it, or before Keith kidnaps it."

Matt took the tag from her hands. It was attached to a set of car keys, all right. And his name was printed on a paper sandwiched between two slices of clear plastic.

Matt exploded out the door, not pausing to ease it shut for once. The crowd of eight women parted like a curtain.

There it sat, illuminated by the nearest parking lot light until it shone like a hologram: an aluminum-silver puddle of metal in the shape of the redesigned Volkswagen beetle.

"Let's see the inside," Keith urged.

Matt tried the key, surprised when it opened the passenger door.

Keith, tall and thin as a soda straw, jackknifed into the seat. "Wow. Cool. Look at this stuff."

"What stuff?" Matt asked.

Keith was caressing the upholstery like it was Sharon Stone. "I think it's suede." He leaned close to the driver's seat, sniffed and squinted. "Blue suede."

Matt forced his mouth to stay shut and walked around to the car's sloping front, looking for a dealer name on the license plate holder.

There was none.

There was a license plate, though,

It read: 281 ROCK

Elvis had just given away his last—or maybe just latest—car.

Chapter 59

Tryin' to Get to You

(Recorded at Sun Records in 1955, probably
with Elvis on the piano)

"I do not see what you need me for," Midnight Louise
complained.

Since we are standing in the bright sunlight near Chef
Song's fish pond, it is especially fitting that she is in her
usual carping mood.

"I told you. As a witness. I do not lay the dead to rest
every day. Especially a corpse as famous as this."

"I do not like dark, enclosed places."

"Neither do I."

"So that is why you invited me along. You are scared
stiff."

"What is to worry about a bit of ectoplasm? I have already glimpsed Elvis in the non-flesh before, at the Halloween séance last fall. Or . . . it could have been a dear
departed Elvis impersonator. It is so hard to tell the real
thing from the sham these days."

"You ought to know about that. I suppose you had something to do with that brouhaha at the Kingdome. Your roommate was in the newspaper looking like a bride of Dracula, cheek to cheek with an Elvis impersonator. She was identified, but he was called 'a mystery man' since he disappeared after his act, even though he was the leading contender to win. This is sort of a Cinderella story with dudes. Maybe he left a lone blue suede shoe on the Kingdome steps.

"This incident and the Mr. Midnight tapes have got the Elvis-sighting machine cranked up to maximum. And your friends and associates are up to their sideburns in it. You know what I would do if we did indeed spot some form of Elvis down in the mine attraction? I would do something more pungent than step on his blue suede shoes. I am not impressed by these dudes that cat around and get away with it. Clear? Are you sure you still want me along?"

"Of course, dear Louise." I refrain from telling her of my key but hidden role in nailing the Elvis killer by loosing the chimp to find his master, in mid-murder, as it happened. "If we do see something, you will make an excellent supporting witness because you are so skeptical."

"Okay, pops. Let us shove off, then."

Unfortunately she is right. The only way to get down in the mine attraction is to take the rickety crate that functions as an elevator.

We wait until the workmen are on a lunch break, all above ground and munching on enough tuna fish to feed a cat colony. Then we dart from islands of shade and finally into the elevator.

Unfortunately, it is firmly anchored in the "up" position, so we must shimmy down the ropes, which are big and rough.

I make a four-point landing from five feet above the floor of the tunnel.

Faint work lights diminish into the dark distance. I

swear I can hear the drip of subterranean water, even though this is desert.

Miss Louise has knocked a yellow hard hat off its rack on the way down; this is not the kit's usual clumsiness, but part of a plan, I discover.

"If we are going ghost-busting," she says, "I want to throw some light on any apparition with the nerve to take us in."

"How do we get it down the tunnel?"

"We take turns pushing. All right by you?"

I privately think this a dim idea; a ghost is supposed to glow in the dark. Who needs light? But together we play kick-the-hard-hat and soon we are down where, I figure, the workmen spotted what they thought was Elvis before.

"Will there not be hologram figures in this exhibit?" Miss Louise asks.

"Yup. Of Jersey Joe Jackson, the founding father of the Crystal Phoenix Hotel when it was the Joshua Tree back in the forties. And maybe of some other noteworthy dead people."

"Sometimes I think all the noteworthy people are dead." Louise sits down and looks around. "They already have painted glow-in-the-dark paint on some of the walls."

"The workmen say that is not what they saw. Nor are the holograms installed yet. They saw a figure in a white suit, shining down the dark tunnel."

"That way?" Midnight Louise stands and begins walking farther down the passage. "Kick on the chapeau light, Daddy, I am going to see Elvis."

I do as she says. A beam shoots down the tunnel at human ankle-height. I can see Louise's swaying hindquarters, tail high, sashaying away into the dark.

I do not think Elvis would hurt her, but I also do not think she is aware what strange forces she flouts. I believe she will soon have a rude awakening, which will be very good for her.

So I curl up around the hard hat—the built-in light provides a nice cozy warmth, and yawn. I expect her back in a sudden flurry of haloed hair and hiss and spit. If ever anyone needed to see Elvis, Midnight Louise is it.

I yawn. I am getting sleepy, very sleepy.

Then I hear a faint noise far down the passage. I force my drooping eyes open and try to focus.

A white human figure is swaying in the distance, arms working, left leg buckling.

Elvis is pantomiming one of his finest moments on stage, just for me.

I leap up. It will be a shame to tell this spirit to get lost, but this is a Jersey Joe Jackson attraction, and his ghost has dibs on the venue. Call it ectoplasmic copyright. He was here first, and it would be interesting to discover who predeceased who. I am sure that they have debates about haunting rights in the afterworld.

Meanwhile, though it is impressive to see Elvis rockin' and rollin', I grow a bit uneasy about not seeing Miss Midnight Louise. No doubt she has swooned, as so many female Elvis fans were prone to do. I guess I should amble down, now that she has learned her lesson, and make sure the ghost doesn't turn any of her black hairs white. She would look pretty silly spotted like a Holstein.

I step into the yellow light road made by the hard hat and follow in Miss Louise's invisible footsteps.

The light fades and the darkness gets thicker as I move along.

I hiss for Louise, but get no answer.

Elvis is still bent over, flailling his legs and arms like a madman, playing the meanest air guitar I have ever *not* heard.

If only I had this on videotape. I could make a boxcar full, just like the Colonel.

Still no sign of Louise. Looks like I will have to ask Elvis to answer for it.

The closer I get, the more the jumpsuit glows, white-hot, with red, green, and blue sparkles. Elvis has his head dropped down so he can see his ghostly fingers hitting his ghostly chords on that air guitar.

Well, no. Elvis does not have his head dropped down. Elvis has no head!

This is not your usual *National Inkquirer* sighting. This Elvis is not rated PG, but R. Too much for my tender offspring.

"Get out of here, you creep," I shout, worried for the first time. Ghosts with major missing parts are usually more sinister than the all-there sort.

Of course he does not listen to me. I am now only a few feet away. "What have you done with my daughter?" I demand. "Unhand her, you phantom."

No answer, not even a pause to recognize my presence and demand. Okay, the Michael Jackson gloves are off.

I spring from my position, shivs extended, planning to hit him in the jerking knees.

My first contact with the incorporeal is the sense of a barrier being breeched, a soft, giving barrier that I push through like the fighting feline I am. In a second, I am right through Elvis and on the other side.

Oops. I hope it is not the real Other Side, like I cannot get back into the living world.

Even as I worry, I land like a bag of nuts and bolts on the cold, hard cavern floor.

Elvis has crumpled into a pale puddle, just like the Wicked Witch of the West went south in a dark pool of ickiness in *The Wizard of Oz*.

But where is Louise?

I stand and call her name, turning in a circle. No answer.

And as I turn back the way I came, I see that Elvis is struggling to rise again. I leap upon his heap of congealing, ethereal atoms.

But Elvis is striking back. I feel the sting of wounds from beyond the grave and soon his jumpsuit is becoming a winding cloth. I spin round and round until I am swaddled and trussed like a turkey.

"Cut it out!" a voice orders.

A familiar voice.

Midnight Louise struggles out from the wadded fabric, which is only too, too solid. It is, in fact, not only material, but a cotton material common to work clothes.

"Here is your Elvis. One of the painter's jumpsuits. He must have been 'putting on the phosphorescent paint along the tunnel corridor and got it all over his white coveralls. So he left it hanging to dry down here. Everybody was too scared to come down and investigate."

"Great. I always thought this was a purely natural phenomenon. What would Elvis be doing down a dark hole, anyway? All we have to do is drag this suit down by the elevator, and even the dimmest bulb should be able to figure out what happened, just as we have."

"We. Right. Start dragging, Dad, and save some strength for the upward climb. I did hear you refer to me as your 'daughter,' did I not? When you thought I was missing?"

"I was, ah, calling for *wa-ter*. Not daughter. I thought you might have fainted."

"Yeah, sure. Well, at least your roommate will have seen the last of Elvis on all fronts. I would definitely say that Elvis has left the building."

I cannot disagree.

We set off down the long, dark tunnel to the elevator shaft. It reminds me of a birth canal, though I do not often think of things like that.

We are halfway there when my left ear flicks back to catch a distant murmur of "Thank you, thank you verra much."

I glance at Louise, whose sour puss is pointed dead ahead, ears unperked.

Naw.

How a Cat May Look
at the King

If you ask me, Elvis, the world's most famous draftee, may have been A-1 to the army, but he was 4F in life: literally crushed to death by fame, fans, floozies, and flunkies.

I have detected several similarities between the King of Rock 'n' Roll and my kind of cat, least of all our propensities to hang out in a streetlight in front of all and sundry and cut loose with sound, motion, and our natural erotic appeal to females of all ages, stages, and wages of sin.

First, we share very humble origins, but extraordinary pizzazz at making ourselves beloved by others. Elvis was never a street person like myself, but we were always loners with a vision of how we could rise far above our kind to become an idol and inspiration to millions. Okay, thousands and thousands in my case, but I am not done yet.

Natural talent can be such a curse, always in danger of exploitation by others. Like myself, Elvis had touching trust in those who purported to assist him in his meteoric rise to fame and fortune. (Okay, so my rise is more mediocre than meteoric; close enough.)

Elvis had his mysterious Svengali, a self-created illegal immigrant who put on a pseudonym and airs, Colonel Tom Parker. The so-called Colonel commandeered the King's career at an early stage and helped himself to a much bigger share of the take than a reputable manager would.

I have my so-called collaborator, Miss Carole Nelson Douglas, who signs our contracts and handles the purse strings and catnip dispersion. It is assumed I have no interest or aptitude for the distribution of my own wealth. In fact, I am treated something like an ignorant and minor child, who must be "managed" for my own good.

Although our associations with our respective "partners" have been necessary and good for us at the onset of our careers, as time goes by our Svengalis have exercised far too much artistic control of our high-energy brand of performing genius that requires constant challenge lest it become boring servitude. Elvis was indentured to films and concert tours. I have my books and book tours, although my front woman takes over even there.

And then there is our endless attraction to the ladies. We cannot help that. We were born with that, although Elvis helped it along by adopting my hair's own natural ebony coloration. So there we are: bigger than life, black, and beautiful. Add in our natural athletic ability and urge to take the spotlight, and you have a potent variety of catnip for dolls of all persuasions.

Speaking of nip, we even share the same failing. I too am mighty fond of a legally prescribed medicinal substance, which, if taken too intensely, can change my kittenish, lovable side so appealing to my friends and fans into cruel, predatory moods during which I lash out and bounce off the wall. I cannot help it any more than Elvis; it is a genetic predisposition.

Elvis always wanted to be a helpful authority figure. Early in life, he wanted to be a policeman, which accounts for his later habit of hanging out with the police and collecting badges—even via President Nixon, during one famous Elvis incident when he was pretty well smoked—and major personal armaments such as guns. Despite his own medication dependence, Elvis hated kids using street drugs and wanted to serve as an example to them.

I, of course, help homeless members of my own species through my Adopt-a-Cat tours. And I too am drawn to police work, although I walk the PI side of the legal beat, not being much of a dude for regulations, just like Elvis. Just like Elvis, I am often loaded with concealed side arms, only mine are of the edged variety.

In karate, which he loved for both its defense and mystical side, his fighting name was Tiger, and for a while he carried a cane with a ruby-studded head of a Big Cat.

Then there's our shared mystical side and penchant for Eastern religion. Elvis was interested in the *Autobiography of a Yoga* and Kahlil Gibran's *The Prophet* and such. I am a follower of Bastet, an ancient and powerful goddess of the Egypt of the pharaohs, where the hot text is *The Book of the Dead*. We both have been ridiculed for exploring fringe religion, but the impulse is sincere, and that is all that is called for in religion. Unlike Elvis, I do not see any necessity for standing up and preaching, but then I have never had access to the amount of catnip he did. Personally, I prefer to keep the mysteries of Bastet just among us nonhillbilly cats.

Alas, I do not share Elvis's enthusiasm for motorized vehicles, although I will resort to them when I must.

Nor do I have a raft of former associates eager to leak every detail of my life and times. Miss CND is bad enough with the occasional personal eccentricity she will detail in my fan publication, *Midnight Louie's Scratching Post-Intelligencer.* Did the world really need to know that Midnight Louie Jr. was taken for a girl when he first came to the shelter? This is a sore point with Elvis and me: we are both such gorgeous dudes that some envious types would use it to impugn our virility. This is nonsense!

We also have been dogged by paternity suits and death threats.

I, of course, am completely innocent and still kicking.

As for Elvis, anything is possible.

Very best fishes,

Midnight Louie, Esq.

Have an Elvis sighting to report, or merely wish information about Midnight Louie's newsletter and/or T-shirt? Contact him at *Midnight Louie's Scratching Post-Intelligencer,* PO Box 331555, Fort Worth, TX 76163, by e-mail at cdouglas@catwriter.com, or visit the web page <http://www.catwriter.com/cdouglas>. Thank you. Thank you very much.

Carole Nelson Douglas
Takes the E Train

For me, Elvis was always inevitable.

His past presence hangs over the Las Vegas landscape like a ghost moon, visible day and night, night and day. He first peeked from behind the curtain when Elvis impersonators contributed to the climax of *Cat in a Crimson Haze,* the fourth Midnight Louie novel.

I was never an Elvis fan. My grade-school best friend and I swore that we'd never join the screaming hordes of teenyboppers making him such a sensation. Our Midwestern upbringing ensured that we'd disdain dangerous icons of sexiness (or sexual excess, or sexual liberation, pick your point of view) such as Marilyn Monroe and Elvis Presley.

Later I realized that Elvis's musical influence had been truly extraordinary, but I still didn't care for or about Elvis, though I knew I needed to know more about him to fully portray Midnight Louie's Las Vegas.

In 1996, while on a Midnight Louie Adopt-a-Cat book tour of the Southeast, I had just enough down time in Memphis to race to Graceland via Gray Line tours. I joined the milling throngs in the souvenir plaza and donned headphones for a self-guided tour, feeling like a fraud among the faithful. The fabled house and grounds surprised me; so ordinary, really. I most vividly remember a painfully thin horse in the pasture behind the grounds; very old or ill, for no tourist attraction would abuse an animal. Was this some frail survivor or descendent of Elvis's horse-riding kick of '66? A last witness to his final spurt of happy (and expensive) enthusiasm before he turned totally inward into a paranoid kingdom of obsessive karate, mysticism, megalomania, prescription drugs, guns, and badges?

At the Meditation Garden Elvis loved, filled with flowery floral and written tributes, I was impressed despite myself by the numbed silence of fans who filed past the engraved tombstones set into the ground. Here lay Elvis, his beloved mother, his ineffective father, and his ever-present paternal grandmother. He called her Dodger. As a kid he once threw something at her and she ducked so it missed. No doubt that Elvis inherited his mother, Gladys's, notorious temper. Even there, though, I remained an unbeliever in the temple of another faith. Not even the sober contemplation of death could make me a pilgrim to Graceland.

In 1994, I was asked to edit a collection of stories about Marilyn Monroe. Marilyn left me as cold as Elvis, but I dutifully delved into the mountains of Marilyn books. I even included my take on M. M., a dramatic monologue about what Marilyn would be doing at age seventy if she had survived: debuting on Broadway. Soon I found myself dusting off my long-shelved performing skills (theater was my college major) to don M. M. "drag." I not only delivered the monologue but on occasion answered questions and related to crowds in the M. M. persona. Moonlighting as a Marilyn impersonator enlightened me enough to finally confront Elvis impersonators, the Elvis phenomenon, and the even greater mountain of books on them both.

Every writer becomes an actor, getting into characters' heads, thinking like them, feeling for them. Any writer who deals with historical personalities becomes a kind of psychic channeler. Eerie how much you come to know about that person beyond mere fact. It happened to me with Oscar Wilde. In a short story, I named his favorite painting, my pure invention. A new, exhaustive Wilde biography was published soon after (as they are every couple years). Two of his favorite paintings were pictured, including the one I'd cited. My prescience was no mystery; the painting was of a religious subject with latent homosexual erotic appeal. I knew my time period, my art history, human psychology, Wilde's writings and biography, and therefore my man.

I never knew Elvis or wanted to. It's not a pleasant process, investigating stunted lives and early deaths. Like a forensic psychologist, a writer reading about such icons' hyperbolic lives can't help wondering what, if anything, would have made a difference to the tragic decline that followed fame. What would have saved Elvis (or Marilyn)? Who killed Elvis (or Marilyn)? I wasn't intrigued in a literal sense, because I concluded neither death was murder, but by the paradox that success so often breeds self-destruction.

Elvis' life and death is an object lesson in the perils of peaking early. Before he was eighteen, he experienced two intensely emotional elements in his life that nothing else could ever duplicate: a singular connection to his mother, an extended and symbiotic twinship, and the artistic and erotic euphoria of a performing charisma that drove his audiences to frenzy. His mother died when he was twenty-three. Nine years of movie-making surgically separated him from his live audiences. Fame and fortune forced him into isolation from overwhelming fan adulation and death threats. Nine years of a return to the manic-depressive performer's emotional seesaw brought him from career rebirth and comeback triumph to a drug-assisted decline and death.

Compare how Elvis and Marilyn were alike:
Both were self-made blue-collar heroes
Both stuttered
Both scorned underwear
Both had birth certificate misspellings of their middle names (Norma Jeane/Jean; Elvis Aron/Aaron)'
Both were overmedicated by doctors
Both created iconic personas that were perpetuated by impersonators and massive merchandising
Both rebelled against the sexual hypocrisy of the fifties
Both sought to be taken "seriously" as actors; Marilyn fought for and got better films
Both were dominated by soulless money men who stifled their potential and careers

The best book about Elvis is Peter Guralnick's two-volume biography. *The Last Train to Memphis* relates Elvis's phenomenal rise up till 1958, when his mother died and the draft interrupted his career, sending him to Germany as an army private. John Lennon later said that Elvis died when he went to Germany. *Careless Love* is subtitled "The Unmaking of Elvis Presley" and covers the twenty-year period after Elvis returned to the United States until his shocking death at the age of forty-two.

Guralnick's books cite the few useful parts of the many memoirs that focus on Elvis's failings and extreme behaviors, and also convey the inborn personal charm and the performance charisma that Elvis cultivated shrewdly before the sheer weight of his popularity (and therefore power) overcame even his remarkable gifts. *The Inner Elvis* by Peter Whitmer, Ph.D., explores the pathology of a surviving twin and identifies Elvis as an abused child whose "lethal enmeshment" by a doting and domineering parent, his mother Gladys, doomed him to the fate he found. P. F. Kluge's novel, *Biggest Elvis*, about Elvis impersonators in Guam, is moving and insightful. Gilbert B. Rodman's *Elvis After Elvis* makes a scholarly case for Elvis single-handedly creating the climate for the sixties' social revolution: youth culture, the protest movement for civil rights and against Vietnam, the sexual revolution and gay rights, and ultimately, the resurgence of feminism that resulted from all the preceding.

Reading many of the dozens of books about a pop icon like Elvis is like listening to conflicting yet buttressing testimony from an endless parade of witnesses in a legal case. You must strain fact from self-serving faction. You read details about the prescription medication dosages, the autopsy, and the theoretical causes of death; you consider forensic psychology and testimony of interested and disinterested parties. You eventually distill the flood of facts and opinions into a theory of your own.

Here's mine: both nature and nurture created and destroyed Elvis Presley. His extended family of aunts, uncles, and cousins had what is now recognized as a genetic disposition to the disease of alcoholism. His mother was never autopsied, and her death at age forty-six was attributed to liver disease, but it is thought to have been cirrhosis of the liver. She certainly drank in her last years. The headstone Elvis put on her grave reads "She was the Sunshine of our Home," and during Elvis's youth she was described as musical and fun-loving, although possessed of a frying-pan-throwing temperament. Photos of Elvis with his parents as his fame grew show a somber, tender symbiosis: Elvis and Gladys always focusing on and touching each other;

Vernon a tangential figure on the fringe of this consuming bond. But Gladys's eyes are ringed with unhealthy black, her expression is dead (or dazed by alcohol). She is not a well or happy woman. Her cherished son's meteoric rise, her loss of contact and control as he was swept away in a fever of touring and publicity and screaming girl groupies, coincided with her decline and death.

Wisely, Elvis disliked and avoided liquor, except for brief experimental periods, and disdained "recreational" drug use even as he escalated into massive doses of prescribed uppers and downers. He had no more knowledge than anybody then of the addictive dangers of mood-altering medications. He educated himself in the medications' side effects so he could prescribe for himself with authority. The seeds of his psychological and physical downfall were not only genetic and familial, but rooted so early in his performing career as to make his "unmaking" inevitable, which is where the word "tragic" enters his saga.

Because of lifelong sleeping problems, including nightmares and sleepwalking incidents, he slept with his mother until the age of twelve. He had never slept away from home until he went on the road in his late teens, to perform. This extended maternal closeness drove him into a confused sexuality: women he became truly close to became mothers, and the sexual side of the relationship became nurture and caretaking rather than passionate. Elvis always had "other women," often actresses or groupies, whom he pursued for shallow sexuality, but were more often needed as bedtime companions rather than lovers.

Through many books, the first reference I found to his using "uppers" was when he was given Dexedrine by other soldiers to stay awake on night guard duty in Germany. He came home with massive jars of the pills for the whole entourage. Although he'd made a few movies by then, Hollywood's tendency to medicate stars doesn't seem to be the culprit in his case. Then I found a reference to Gladys, self-conscious at the media attention Elvis's stardom drew to her. She took diet pills and Elvis borrowed them at the very brink of his career. Diet pills then were amphetamines, "speed" prescribed readily by family doctors. They depressed the appetite center in the brain, which also interfered with the sleep center. They make you sleepless, but give you energy to burn. Minds on speed will run in creative circles, inventing all sorts of ambitious projects, but the impulse rarely produces anything concrete. When the effect wears off after a few weeks, takers need to increase the dosage to get the same effect.

Performers draw on superhuman amounts of adrenaline to enthrall their audiences, and stay awake hours after performing to come "down." Speed would have aggravated Elvis's naturally hyperactive metabolism and performer's lifestyle. He was soon also taking downers to sleep, the typical Hollywood doctor cocktail. The two medications create a manic/depressive roller coaster. Everything excessive that Elvis became had its roots in his impoverished youth, but was later enacted with the grandiose extravagance of a speed addict. The vampirish hours of a rock star made him into a man who reversed day and night, sleeping at dawn and rising to start the day at dusk. It was convenient for everyone around him, including women, to follow the same schedule, so Elvis enthusiastically converted them to the wonder pills too.

He was an overprotected mama's boy, a shy and sensitive soul ripe for loneliness, ostracizing, and bullying. He found identity in embracing his differences, in dressing like the black musicians who made Memphis's Beale Street a musical legend. Like many an outcast teenager, he took on a protective aggressive coloring. He hid his vulnerabilities behind the accoutrements of a fifties "hood," those black-leather-clad urban bad boys with the greaser hair, sideburns, and attitudes. He even dyed his hair and eyebrows black, covered his blond eyelashes in mascara. He ached to play football, but his over-protective mother forbid him to. The coach hated his long hair and wouldn't let him play without a buzzcut anyway. Years later, Elvis organized his Memphis Mafia into a football team. He was quarterback, of course.

An only child, he often gave the rare toys, a wagon or toy car, his family could ill afford to other children. As a wealthy and famous adult, he became famous for dispensing Cadillacs and other luxury cars by the dozen to friends and strangers, perhaps 280 in all. His impulses were always generous. Beneficiaries could be girls after only one date, poor workers on his one-time ranch, strangers, members of the Memphis Mafia. Jealousy swirled around Graceland when Elvis was on a buying jag: who would get the gravy? It wouldn't always be whoever most deserved the extra calories. His donations to charity were less quixotic and his generosity was inbred, not merely a speed-assisted profligacy. He arranged a liver transplant for one of his record producers, for instance.

Of course his music, the synthesis of white hillbilly and black blues music that got him attention, developed during his teen years on "lonely street," which was broader than Beale Street in Memphis, and included the "race music" on the radio and the gospel music in the church Gladys and Vernon attended.

When the Jaycees named him an outstanding young man of 1971, Elvis Presley reveled in the achievement because it was more than another performing benchmark. It was a testimony to character and personal worth. He was already outstandingly indentured to prescription medications by then, and Priscilla would leave him in a year. It was already the beginning of the end, but a proud moment. As he said in his acceptance speech, he'd fulfilled every dream he'd had as a child worshipping comic book heroes who would doff their impotent ordinariness, don a gaudy jumpsuit, and fly to everyone's rescue.

That was the problem, he had fulfilled every dream. Only the nightmares were left.

Get caught reading.

Jake Lloyd reading *ENDER'S GAME*.

A Message from the
Association of American Publishers